The Quiet Man

A Jefferson Winter thriller

JAMES CAROL

FABER & FABER

First published in 2017
by Faber & Faber Ltd
Bloomsbury House
74–77 Great Russell Street
London WC1B 3DA

Typeset by Faber & Faber Ltd
Printed and bound by CPI Group (UK) Ltd, Croydon CR0 4YY

A CIP record for this book
is available from the British Library

ISBN 978–0–571–32228–2

2 4 6 8 10 9 7 5 3 1

For Finn,
The more I get to know you,
the more you amaze me.
Love you now and always.

I

The countdown started three hundred and sixty-four days ago. Back then there had been all the time in the world. Now it felt as though it was about to run out, and fast. Because that was the thing with time. It was fluid and it lied. Nine and half hours from now August 4 would turn into August 5 and they'd be on the final stretch. Jefferson Winter was aware of the clock ticking, the seconds dripping away like sand flowing through an hourglass. Whenever he shut his eyes all he could see was the bright hot flash of the explosion.

He stepped into Arrivals and made a quick scan of the waiting crowd. The woman holding the sign with his name on looked just like a cop. It was her eyes. They were constantly on the move, searching for danger and taking everything in. She wasn't a cop, though. Not any more. Winter knew that for a fact. She recognised him in the same instant that he recognised her. It was easy to see why. He was average height, average weight, and had one of those faces that you wouldn't look at twice. Where he moved away from the average was his hair. He was only in his mid-thirties but it had already gone completely white. It turned when he was twenty. He used to dye it during his FBI days. Since quitting, he hadn't bothered. A lot of things fell by the wayside when he quit being a G-man. He walked over to where she was standing.

'You must be Laura Anderton,' he said.

'And you must be Jefferson Winter. Welcome to Vancouver.'

She held out her hand and waited for him to shake it. Her grip was firm and purposeful. It was the handshake of someone who was confident about where they fit in the grand scheme of things. Anderton was fifty-three, with big brown eyes and shoulder-length brunette hair. She was wearing jeans and a plain white blouse. Her ankle-length boots had a sensible heel. She must have been stunning in her younger days. She was still attractive now.

'Where, why, who,' he said.

'You say that like it means something.'

'It does. All we've got to do is answer one of those questions and we can save a life. If we know where the next murder is taking place then we can ambush the killer. If we know who the intended victim is we can protect them. Why is a little less obvious, but I'm confident that if we can work that out, the information will lead us to the killer or the next victim. Either one is a win.'

'Put like that, it sounds so simple,' Anderton said.

'I didn't say it would be easy. I'm just saying that that's what we need to do. Where, why, who. I'm telling you, it's a no-brainer.'

'Okay, here's another question for you. How? As in how do we find answers to those questions.'

Winter shrugged. 'I'm still working on that one.'

'Well, work harder.'

He followed Anderton to the exit, his suitcase trundling in his wake. The crowds were parting before her in a way that

2

was almost biblical. She didn't say a word. She didn't have to. Everyone just got the hell out of her way. She was five foot six and slim, so it wasn't as though she was physically imposing. And it wasn't like she was waving a gun around. A crowded airport, in the middle of the afternoon, that would definitely have got a reaction.

Outside, the sun was shining, the temperature in the mid-seventies. The day was about as perfect as it was possible to get. Winter checked his cell. There was no sign of the text he was waiting for. He put the phone away, found his sunglasses, then lit a cigarette. His last one had been in Detroit. Even without the four-hour delay that was too long.

The last couple of days it had been one thing after another. His original plan had been to fly here yesterday, but the Detroit case had dragged on. The arrest had gone bad, the killer ended up dead. Winter hadn't fired the shot, but he'd witnessed the whole thing, which meant jumping through a load of administrative hoops before he could leave. Then there had been that damn plane delay. Time was tight enough without having that to deal with.

Anderton started walking, Winter following close behind. The impression he had got from their email exchanges was that she was professional and businesslike, and maybe a little distant. So far he had seen nothing to contradict these impressions. In the near distance, a Boeing 777 decorated with Air Canada's livery lumbered into the sky, engines screaming as it fought against gravity, two hundred and fifty tons being thrust forward and upward at a hundred and fifty knots. The air stank of aviation fuel. According to the signs, they were heading away from the parking lots. Winter didn't bother asking why. Wherever Anderton was headed, she was walking as though it was where they were meant to be going.

She had first contacted him last year, back when she was still running the police investigation. At the time he'd been tied up with a case in Europe and hadn't been able to get away. He'd asked her to keep him in the loop, and she had. Most months he received an email updating him on the situation. Because of the nature of the case there was rarely anything new. That didn't matter, though. By the third email he'd concluded that the real reason for the updates was that she wanted the case to stay on his radar.

Not that it was about to fall off any time soon. This one had got him curious. It was the sort of puzzle he lived for. To start with, most murders happened without warning. They came completely out of the blue. The first you knew about it was when the call came through informing you that another body had been found. That hadn't happened here. The year-long gap between murders made these crimes unusual, but what made the series unique was the MO. Most serial killers wanted to be there at the moment of death. That was a big part of the thrill. They needed to see the lights go off in their victims' eyes. It gave them a massive ego boost. In that moment they were more powerful than God.

This killer hadn't been there at the end. In fact, he'd gone out of his way to make sure he wasn't. He'd gained access to each victim's house, overpowered them, and then bound them to a kitchen chair with duct tape. After attaching a homemade bomb to their chest and wiring it so that it would be triggered when the kitchen door opened, he had left. All three victims were female, killed when their husbands came home from work. Basically, he was using the husband as a murder weapon. Winter had come across killers who took a hands-off approach before, but never to this level.

'I guess this is where I'm supposed to ask if you had a good flight,' Anderton said. 'But since your plane was four hours late I don't think I'll bother.'

'There was a mechanical problem. One that needed to be fixed immediately.'

'I'd hope so.'

'You'd be surprised. Most aircraft have something wrong with them. If you insisted they were a hundred per cent operational a hundred per cent of the time they'd never fly anywhere, and that's not good for business. The reason they don't fall out of the sky is because there's so much redundancy built into the systems.'

'And you're okay with that?' Anderton said.

'So far, so good. I haven't been in a crash yet. And I fly a lot.'

'Yeah, well, I'd prefer to think that everything's in perfect working order.'

'Not going to happen.'

'Maybe so, but that won't stop me from telling myself that. This is one of those rare occasions where ignorance is most definitely bliss.'

A short while later they arrived at a restricted area. There were signs promising that very bad things would happen to anyone who parked there illegally. Anderton's SUV was next to a Vancouver PD cruiser. The SUV was a Mercedes, five years old and sparkling in the sunshine. Even the tyres were clean and gleaming. Anderton clearly loved her car. The card on the dash stating that she was on Vancouver PD business looked official enough. It made Winter wonder what else she'd kept from her cop days.

Anderton opened the trunk and heaved his case inside. It was a battered old Samsonite that he'd had forever and his whole life was in there. Since quitting the FBI, he'd been a person of no fixed abode. Home was whatever hotel suite he found himself booked into. Anderton slammed the trunk shut and got into the driver's seat. Winter climbed into the passenger side and buckled up. He checked his phone again. Still no sign of that text.

'Okay,' he said. 'Let's go talk to Nicholas Sobek. Since he's our client, it would be good to touch base. Plus there's the added bonus that he witnessed the first murder. Two birds, one stone.'

'I've got to warn you, he's a bit strange.'

'Define strange.'

Anderton looked as though she was going to answer, then shook her head slowly. 'It's probably best if you judge that one for yourself.'

2

Nicholas Sobek still lived in the house where his wife had been murdered, which could definitely be classed as strange. As far as Winter was concerned things didn't work that way. If the person you love is brutally murdered in the place you call home, you're going to get straight on the phone to a realtor. You're not going to spend another day there. You're not going to want to spend another minute there. So far, Sobek had spent one thousand and ninety-five days there, and counting. That added up to more than a million and a half minutes.

Strange thing number two: Sobek had only left his house twice during the past three years, both times to visit his wife's grave. On the anniversary of her death, he'd driven himself to Mountain View cemetery, arriving as the sun came up and leaving as it set.

The house was on Balsam Place, a tidy, spacious cul-de-sac in Kerrisdale. The neighbourhood was to the south-west of downtown Vancouver, prosperous and shiny, with wide streets and plenty of green. The homes weren't Hollywood A-lister massive, but nor were they shacks. Each one sat on its own large plot of land. The garages were large enough to accommodate two cars and the yards were kept tidy by groundkeeping companies.

Anderton stopped in front of the large gate and waited

for it to roll open. It was made from solid steel and looked relatively new. The ten-foot wall surrounding the property was topped with sharp pieces of metal and glass, and looked new too. Beyond the wall was a line of tall Douglas firs. All you could see of the house was the occasional glimpse of the roofline. The overall impression was that this was a fortress rather than a home.

Anderton drove onto the driveway and parked directly in front of the garage doors. The move was smoothly executed, like she'd done this a hundred times before. There was no hesitation. She just drove up to the garage like she owned the place. Then there was the way the gates had opened for her. Usually there would be a conversation with whoever was watching the security camera, a quick back and forth to establish whether you were friend or foe. Winter looked up at the house, then looked back at Anderton.

'What?' she asked.

'I'm just wondering how this works, that's all. Three years ago you were convinced this guy was the killer. Two years ago you were still trying to find a way to make the facts fit that scenario. Fast forward to now and you're best friends.'

'I wouldn't go that far.'

'You know what I mean.'

For a moment Anderton just sat staring up at the house. It was an impressive property. Five bedrooms at a guess, and a similar number of bathrooms. There would be a study for sure, and probably a gym, maybe even a home cinema. The architect had gone for an Art Deco look, bright white walls and elegant curves. There was no way this was built in the thirties, though. Or the twenties. Or the forties. Sometime during the nineties was a safer bet. If you wanted the world to know that you'd done good, this was the sort of place you would buy.

'Nicholas Sobek is as keen as I am to see his wife's murderer brought to justice,' she said.

Winter kept quiet and waited for her to fill the silence. There were things he knew about her and plenty he didn't know. He knew that since she retired she'd been working as a private investigator. And he knew that she only had the one client. He also knew that most retired cops had unfinished business, a case that haunted them to the grave.

'I don't like leaving a job half done,' she said eventually. 'The fact that the murderer is out there walking free kills me. But what gets me even more is the fact that in a little over twenty-four hours he's going to kill someone else. I'd do anything to stop that happening. Anything. Working for Sobek means that I get to stay in the game. I get to keep chasing him.' She nodded to the house. 'Sobek's got the means and he's definitely got the motivation. I've got the skill set he needs to pursue his goal. Like I said, we're both after the same thing here.'

'So, you're using him.'

'Only as much as he's using me.'

He waited for her to say something else. When it became clear that she was done, he said, 'Anything else I should know?'

She answered with a smile that hinted at a whole treasure trove of secrets. Maybe she was keeping something back, maybe she was just screwing with him. Not that it mattered. They got out of the car and followed the path around to

9

the front door. The grass in the front yard had been cut recently. Bright flowers filled the planters that lined the path. Winter checked his cell while they walked. Still no sign of that text. He became aware of Anderton looking at him over her shoulder.

'A watched cell phone never seems to beep,' he said.

'If you say so.'

There were two security scanners attached to the wall of the porch. Anderton pressed her eye against the top one, and her thumb against the bottom. Ten seconds passed, then the door clicked open and a disembodied voice said, 'I'm in the gym.' It took a second to locate the speaker. It was hidden in the roof of the porch. Whatever Sobek was doing, it sounded like hard work. Winter hated gyms. He worked on the theory that you were as fit as you needed to be for the lifestyle you were leading.

The entrance hall was two storeys high with exposed beams and an ornate chandelier that sparkled and threw off shards of light. The floor was pine, the staircase wide. Modern paintings hung in brushed metal frames on the walls. Anderton led the way to a corridor that took them behind the staircase. The door hidden in the shadows opened on to the basement stairs. There were two more scanners fixed to the wall here. Anderton went through the same song and dance she'd gone through at the front door. Eye against the top scanner, thumb against the bottom one. There was a quiet click as the lock released.

'How does Sobek know that I'm not forcing you to take me to him at gunpoint? Maybe I'm not even who I say I am.'

She answered with a look.

'I'm only half joking, by the way,' he added. 'I'm figuring that the security precautions don't end at the gate and the walls. Am I right?'

'Okay, you passed through a metal detector when you walked into the house, so unless your gun is made from polymer and doesn't contain any bullets, then we're good to go there. Also, your photograph was taken on the porch, and checked using facial-recognition software. That's why the door didn't open straight away. The photograph it was checked against came from me. I found an old one from your FBI days on the internet. You looked so young back then, almost wholesome. What happened?'

Winter smiled at that. 'I take it all these security measures weren't in place three years ago.'

'Correct. The Sobeks had a burglar alarm, but forgot to turn it on as often as they remembered. The wall and gate weren't here either. Back then, Sobek wanted everyone driving up this street to see the house. Image was very important to him. Take a look in the garage and you'll see what I mean. There's an Aston Martin Vantage and an S-Class Mercedes in there, both cars just gathering dust. He's also got a Cessna 206 that he hasn't flown since the murder. There's an airfield at Boundary Bay, twenty miles south of the city. That's where he keeps it. The maintenance is all up to date, but it never flies anywhere.'

'All this security, it's like locking the stable door after the horse has bolted.'

'Maybe so, but nobody's broken in during the last three years. On that basis you could argue that it's having the desired effect.'

They descended the stairs in single file, Anderton still leading the way. The stairway was the same width as the basement door, the roof low, which made it feel claustrophobic. They could have been descending into an old Cold War bomb shelter, or a dungeon. At the bottom, two corridors split off left and right. Anderton turned left. They passed another two doors, both closed, both made of brushed steel.

'Since the murder, this is where Sobek has been living,' Anderton said. 'He's got a bedroom, a kitchen and an office down here. He's even got a firing range.'

'You're kidding, right?'

Anderton shook her head. 'I'm totally serious. The person who owned the house before Sobek was a bowling fanatic. He had a lane built down here. When Sobek bought it, he had all the machinery ripped out and converted it into a firing lane.'

'Is he any good?'

'He shoots better than I do. I've seen him hit the bullseye six times out of six.'

'What's the deal with the rest of the house?'

'Everything up there is exactly how it was when his wife died. Sobek hasn't changed a thing. It's like some sort of shrine.' Anderton glanced over her shoulder. 'I told you he was strange.'

The corridor ended at a steel door that was identical to the ones they'd already passed. Anderton went straight in without knocking. The gym was fully kitted out, the equipment arranged neatly. There was a treadmill, an exercise bike, a cross-trainer and a multigym. A punching bag hung from a steel plate bolted to the ceiling. Martial arts weapons were displayed on a large board fixed to one wall.

Sobek was lying on the bench press, pumping iron. The amount he was lifting equated to an Anderton, maybe even one and a half Andertons. Each time he pushed up he let out a long, loud grunt. His arm muscles were bulging and the tendons in his neck were as taut as piano wires. He was in his mid-thirties with a full beard and piercing brown eyes. He did two more pushes then sat up and pulled his ponytail straight. It was straggly and shiny with sweat, and fell down to his shoulders. His face was red and he was taking deep, measured breaths.

He stripped off his T-shirt, grabbed a towel and started patting himself dry. He had good muscle definition on his arms and chest, and the full six pack. He hadn't gone overboard, though. Working out was clearly an obsession, but he was a long way from being a steroid-enhanced freak show. There was a small key on a chain around his neck. Both hands were wrapped up with white boxer's tape that had turned grey at the knuckles from where he'd been pummelling the punching bag. The T-shirt he put on was identical to the one he'd taken off. Plain and black. He dumped the towel on the back of a chair and walked over to Winter. For a moment, he just stood there staring.

'So,' he said. 'Do you think I murdered my wife?'

3

Sobek was still staring, waiting for an answer to his question. If this was an attempt at intimidation, it wasn't working. Winter had played this particular game with men a lot scarier than Sobek. While he was with the FBI he'd interviewed dozens of serial criminals. He'd come face-to-face with the worst of the worst. To survive those sorts of encounters you had to develop a thick skin. That said, he wasn't about to underestimate Sobek. He knew a predator when he saw one. Sobek stared for a couple of seconds more, then blinked. Winter took this as his cue.

'The police don't think you killed her,' he said. 'At the time of Alicia Kirchner's murder you were visiting your wife's grave. The same goes for last year when Lian Hammond was murdered. Witnesses place you in the cemetery on both occasions. They say you were there for the whole day, so, unless you paid them off, that's a fairly substantial alibi.'

'I do have alibis for Alicia and Lian's murders. However, I don't have one for Isabella's. There are plenty of theories flying around for how I might have done it. There's even a website: www.sobekkilledhiswife.com.'

'I've seen it. Do you know my favourite theory? You killed your wife, then the next year you hired a contract killer to kill Alicia. The reason the MO was the same was because you were able to supply the killer with the details.'

'And the following year, I was supposed to have paid him to kill Lian.'

'And this year you're going to pay him again to take someone else out.'

'Do you know how crazy that sounds?' Sobek asked.

'I've heard crazier.'

'I loved my wife. There's not a day goes by when I don't think about her. She's in my thoughts every minute of every hour.'

'Was that why you kept having affairs? One police report classed you as a serial philanderer. I prefer alley cat. That's closer to the mark, don't you think?'

'We had our problems, but we were working through them.'

'Was this before or after Isabella had her affair? That must have pissed you off. I mean, it's okay for you to screw around, but there's no way it would have been okay for her to do the same.'

Sobek didn't respond straight away. He took a long breath. It was easy to imagine him doing a slow count to ten. 'You still haven't answered my question. Do you think I killed my wife?'

Winter swept an imaginary dust speck from the multigym, then sat down. This was the cleanest gym he'd ever seen. He was looking up at Sobek now, but wasn't concerned about handing him the high ground. The fact that he didn't feel the need to keep hold of it was a power play in itself.

'The police spent a lot of time, energy and resources digging into your background,' he said. 'The picture that gets painted is of someone who was obsessed with making money and didn't care who they destroyed in pursuit of that goal. But let's face it, you're not going to earn a fortune trading stocks by playing nice. You screwed your customers, you screwed around, basically you screwed everyone you came into contact with. All that mattered was making a buck. If Gordon Gekko had been real he would have been first in line to shake your hand and welcome you to the club.'

'People can change.'

'In my experience they don't change that much.'

'And I'm telling you they can. When Isabella died I was forced to face up to some unpleasant truths about myself. But I faced up to them, and I sincerely believe that I'm a better person for having gone through that process.'

'That's good to hear, but I don't care about your past. All I care about is that you play straight with me. Can you do that?'

'Of course.'

Sobek was staring again. 'So, do you think that I murdered my wife?'

'No, I don't.'

He dipped his head slightly. 'Thank you for your honesty.'

'Okay, my turn. That key around your neck, what does it open?'

4

Sobek led them back up to the entrance hall and took the corridor on the opposite side of the staircase. The door at the far end had a large padlock attached to it. After all the high-tech security measures, it seemed oddly out of place, more a symbolic gesture than any sort of security precaution. You could jimmy it off with a crowbar in two seconds flat. A person who was halfway competent with a lock pick could crack it in five. Sobek took the key from around his neck and unlocked the padlock. He pushed the door open then stepped aside.

Winter and Anderton went inside. Sobek didn't. He was watching them from the doorway, his eyes following their every move. The blinds were drawn and the furniture made dim shapes in the gloom. Winter flicked on the light. By the looks of things, nothing had changed since the police moved out. There was evidence of the explosion wherever he looked. Chairs lay toppled on their sides. The walls, woodwork and floor tiles were all stained black. When he closed his eyes he could imagine the smell. The Fourth of July tainted by the stink of charred meat. The kitchen was coated with a thin layer of dust and fingerprint powder. The place where Isabella had fallen was marked with chalk that had grown faint over the years.

The table seated six but there were only five chairs. The one that Isabella had died on was missing. Four of the chairs lay scattered around the table. Two were lying on their sides and two had been spun away from the table, as though the occupants had got up and suddenly left. The fifth chair had been set up at the epicentre of the blast zone. Winter walked over and rested his hands on the back of it. For a moment he stood there gazing around the kitchen. He was aware of Sobek watching from the doorway. Anderton was watching as well. His eyes met hers.

'What's it going to feel like, being bound to this chair with a bomb taped to your chest?'

Anderton didn't respond straight away. If she was half the investigator he thought she was then this wouldn't be the first time she'd imagined herself in that chair. Working out what made the bad guys tick was only a part of the story. Understanding and empathising with the victim was the other part.

'It's going to be terrifying,' she said eventually. 'Totally and utterly terrifying.'

'And then some,' he agreed. 'Isabella was the first victim. She was thirty years old, fit and healthy. Her whole life was stretched out in front of her. She wouldn't have had a clue what was going on. Some guy had broken into her house, bound her to a chair, then just left.'

Anderton was still staring at the chair, imagining what it was like. 'When she heard Sobek come home she would have tried to warn him,' she said, 'but she couldn't do that because there was a strip of duct tape across her mouth. He opens the door, then boom.'

'Fast forward a year. This time the victim is Alicia Kirchner. The big difference is that she knows exactly what's happening. The story of Isabella Sobek's murder was all over the news. There was no way she would have missed it. Knowing what's going to happen cranks the fear level up another notch.'

Anderton was already ahead of him. 'Fast forward another year and the victim is Lian Hammond. Lian was Asian, which ups the ante. Up until this point he'd just been targeting Caucasians. She'd have felt safe. This just adds to the fear.'

'I've got to hand it to this guy, having the murders on the same day each year is a stroke of genius. The anticipation really helps to increase those fear levels. So who is he going to tape to the chair this year? Or to put it another way, what's he going to do to take this to the next level?'

'Maybe the next victim will be black,' Anderton suggested.

Winter shook his head. 'He's already shown that race isn't any sort of barrier.'

'What about a male? That way he'd be showing that gender isn't an issue. That would raise the stakes.'

'It would, but I don't think he's going down that road. As well as raising the stakes, that would significantly increase the risk factor. Generally speaking, men are stronger than women.'

'Careful with those generalisations. I reckon I could kick your ass.'

'Probably, but my point still stands. The way these crimes are presenting, this killer isn't physically imposing. He's going to be small build. Height somewhere in the region of five and a half feet. Certainly not much taller. This is someone with Small Man Syndrome. He controls his victims through coercion rather than force. That's why he's going to avoid targeting a male.'

Anderton opened her mouth to say something, then shut it again. Her brow furrowed then relaxed. Winter could almost see the thoughts cascading through her head.

'You think he's going to go after a kid,' she said.

'The thought's crossed my mind. Serial killers have their own hierarchy. Bombers are way down near the bottom. They're cowards. Only child killers rank lower. A bomber who kills kids would be the lowest of the low.'

'Lower than low,' Anderton agreed. 'Let's hope he doesn't go down that route.'

Winter moved around to the front of the chair and sat down. Sobek was still watching from the doorway. It was difficult to read his expression. If he was bothered, it didn't show. Equally, if he was curious then that didn't show either. There was a kind of blank indifference on his face, like he was cataloguing what was going on but didn't have an opinion one way or the other.

Winter shut his eyes, and the clock spun back. It was no longer him on the chair, it was Isabella. She was living through her final moments, each breath taking her closer to death, and there was nothing she could do to change that. This was more than imagination, it was a becoming. This was his gift. His curse. He took a deep breath and stepped into the zone.

*

The kitchen door closes and I'm alone. I listen to the killer's footsteps fading away into silence. The front door is too far away for me to hear it opening. The bomb is lighter than it looks, but it feels heavy. Some objects have extra mass because they're weighed down by their significance. This bomb is one such object. It's heavy enough to crush me. The weight of it pressing into my ribs suffocates me. I'm this killer's first, so I don't have a reference point to work from. Even so, I know exactly what this device is capable of, and the reason I know is because he told me. He would have laid everything out in a way that even my terrified brain would understand. All I can do now is wait for Nicholas to come home. I'm powerless to do anything else. This has all been explained to me as well.

When you're trapped between a rock and a hard place you're never stuck exactly in the middle. One side will always exert more pressure, and that's the side you'll feel compelled to move away from. Human beings are programmed to seek out the path of least resistance. This is true for death as it is for anything else. Nobody wants to die a slow, agonising death. And nobody wants to die a violent death, their bodies ripped to pieces by forces that have no respect for blood, bone, muscle and flesh. Why would anyone wish that upon themselves? No, what we're all looking for is a peaceful slide into the long goodnight.

Remember those poor souls who jumped from the Twin Towers? They faced an impossible choice. Either stay where you were and burn to death, or jump. Rocks and hard places. So why did they jump? They jumped because at that moment the fire was exerting more pressure. They had to get away. That was the only thing that mattered. And then they were tumbling head over heels, falling, falling, falling, plunging toward certain death, the ground getting closer and closer, and there wasn't a damn thing they could do about it.

And that's exactly what's happening here. Because I'm not

quite as powerless as I think. The killer would have told me all about mercury tilt switches. He would have explained how one wrong move would result in certain death.

I'm going to die. Nothing can stop that. But Nicholas doesn't have to. Even though the terror has forced my mind into melt-down, there's a strong likelihood that I'd managed to reach this conclusion. All I've got to do is rock the chair until it topples over. Do that and I can save Nicholas.

But I don't do that because I don't want to die. As long as I'm alive, there's a chance I'll be rescued. I don't know how that would work exactly, I just know that I can't give up yet. So long as there's a single breath left in my body I will fight. I've even set myself a deadline for that final breath. When I hear Nicholas, that's when I'll topple the chair. There's no point us both dying.

Except it doesn't work that way. I don't hear the front door opening, but I do hear him calling out my name. I'd shout out to warn him, but can't because my mouth is taped shut. This is the point where I should topple the chair. But I can't do that either. I'm still breathing. I'm still alive. I hear him moving around the house, calling out my name. And then he's in the corridor that leads to the kitchen, and I still haven't toppled the chair. And then he's standing outside the kitchen door, and I'm still sitting here. And then the handle starts to move and it's too late. The door opens and the explosion rips my chest apart. I'm dead before my body hits the expensive marble tiles.

5

The first thing Winter saw when he opened his eyes was Anderton watching him from four feet away. There was something that might have been concern in her gaze, but mostly what he saw was curiosity. He was starting to understand why Sobek had preserved this room. This was his sacred space. It was easy to imagine him sneaking up here in the middle of the night to commune with the ghost of his dead wife. He glanced over at the doorway. Sobek had gone.

'Liar, liar, pants on fire,' he whispered to himself.

'Who?' Anderton asked. 'The killer?'

He nodded. 'Bombs are fairly straightforward devices, right?'

'Correct. When you get down to it they're all pretty much identical. First, you need some sort of explosive material. Second, you need a detonator. Third, you need a switch to trigger the device. Everything else is just a variation on that theme.'

Winter stood up and looked down at the chair. He could imagine Isabella sitting here with a bomb taped to her chest, terrified and desperate, paralysed by her fear and indecision.

'The bomb is the killer's take on an old favourite,' he said. 'The pipe bomb. Where it differs is that he only used half a pipe. He cut it lengthways down the middle, fitted it inside a plastic sleeve and filled it with gunpowder and ball bearings.

The gunpowder came from fireworks. He waited for Canada Day to come around, then bought a job lot of rockets, as many as he could get away with without raising suspicions. Then he pulled them apart to cannibalise what he needed.'

Anderton walked over and stopped at his shoulder. 'Using half a pipe was ingenious. In most pipe bombs the casing turns to shrapnel. Red hot shards of metal are spread across the blast zone, killing or maiming everyone they come into contact with. But there's only one person here. Isabella. By using half a pipe he can direct the blast toward her.'

'The ball bearings weren't really necessary. The force of the blast alone was enough to destroy her heart. They were an insurance policy. His primary objective was to make sure that Isabella died. He wasn't taking any chances there.'

'The detonator is interesting.'

Winter glanced at Anderton, eyebrows raised. '"Interesting" is one word for it.'

'And what word would you use?'

He considered this for a second. 'No, "interesting" works for me.'

And it did. The police had found evidence that the killer had made his detonator from a Christmas-tree light bulb. He would have snipped the tip off, carefully so he wouldn't damage the filament. Then he would have filled the bulb with sulphur that he'd culled from crushing up match heads. These bulbs were designed to accept a one-volt charge, but he'd hooked his up to a nine-volt battery. When the bomb was triggered the filament overloaded and ignited the sulphur.

There was also evidence that he'd used a magnetic door

sensor to trigger the bomb, the same sort of sensor used in home alarm systems. The magnet had been superglued to the door, while the reed switch was glued to the frame. When Sobek opened the door, the switch closed and the circuit was completed. From that point on the explosion was inevitable. The device adhered to the laws of physics. Once the reaction had started nothing could stop it.

'What's the weak link?' Winter asked.

Anderton pointed to the chair. 'Isabella's the weak link.'

'Exactly. She's the chaotic element. Everything else is binary. The reed switch is either on or off. The detonator is either live or inert. And the explosives are either just sitting there or they're going boom.'

Anderton walked back over to the chair, deep in thought. 'The killer cannot afford for his victims to move. Not so much as a muscle. If they do then they might pull out the wire. If that happens then the bomb won't work.'

'So he tells them that the bomb is fitted with a mercury tilt switch. If they move, then it's going to go off.'

'But it isn't fitted with one. The crime-scene investigators confirmed that.'

'And that's his big lie. His victims don't know that, though. By now they'll be hanging on his every word. Whatever he says, they're going to believe.'

'Why not just fit the bomb with a tilt switch? They're easy enough to get hold of.'

'They are. But they're not as easy to get hold of as fairy lights and matches. Part of this guy's MO is that he wants to leave as small a footprint as possible. The beauty of his bomb is that he can get hold of the components without raising any suspicions whatsoever. Are you going to look twice at someone buying Christmas decorations in December? Or fireworks at the end of June? No, you're not. Superglue you can buy any time of the year, from any old hardware store. Same goes for the ball bearings and the wire and the nine-volt batteries and the lengths of steel pipe.'

'Okay, I get it. If he'd used a tilt switch then we might have been able to trace the sale.'

Winter caught that 'we'. She wasn't talking about the two of them. Once a cop, always a cop. 'That's not the only reason,' he said. 'I'd even go as far as saying it's not the main reason.'

'Because the main reason is that he doesn't want the bomb going off early.'

'That would spoil all his fun,' Winter agreed. 'It's imperative that the bomb is triggered by the husband.'

'Because that's another way for him to show that he's all-powerful.'

'That's how I read it. These murders are all about control and domination. We're back to Small Man Syndrome again. He's overcompensating for the inadequacies that plague his day-to-day existence. Remember, bombers are the lowest of the low.'

'Lower than low,' Anderton echoed. 'So we've established that he's lying to his victims. How does that help?'

Winter was thinking about the where, why and who of the situation again. This helped with the why, which was the hard road. If they worked out the why, then that would point them in the direction of the killer, but it wouldn't take them all the way to his door. Winter could think of one way to use the information, but he didn't know if Anderton would sanction the move.

Everyone had lines they wouldn't cross. Winter was still trying to establish where Anderton's lay. That sign on the dashboard of her Mercedes back at the airport indicated that there was hope for her. Then there was the fact that she'd been able to send him copies of everything gathered during the police investigations into the first three murders. Crime-scene photographs, autopsy reports, interview transcripts, witness statements. Information that was okay for the detective leading the investigation to have, but not so okay for a civilian, which was technically what Anderton now was.

'It doesn't *not* help us,' he said. 'At this stage we can't have too much information. Agreed?'

'Agreed.'

'Since Sobek's no longer here, I'm figuring he wasn't too impressed with me sitting on his chair.'

'His chair?'

'Who else is going to be coming up here day after day to sit here?'

'I'd never thought of it like that, but yeah, I can see how that might work. So what did you make of him?'

'Well, you're right about one thing. He's definitely strange.'

'And?'

Winter took a moment. 'And I'm wondering about his motivation. Before Isabella was murdered he was all about status symbols, and making sure people saw them. He had the cars, and the plane, and the house. Now, you could argue that Isabella was a part of his collection, too. A man like that is going to need the trophy wife on his arm, right? I've seen the

27

photographs of her and, speaking on behalf of red-blooded males everywhere, I'm telling you that she was stunning.'

Anderton nodded for him to go on.

'That's the reason he's obsessed with this. Somebody has stolen one of his things, and that's completely unacceptable. Think about it. He's got cars in his garage that he doesn't drive, a plane he never flies and a house he doesn't live in. Why do that? He does it because he's a collector and, like any collector, all that matters is owning the thing you covet.'

'And when you get hold of that thing, you're going to keep hold,' Anderton put in. 'The only way you're letting go is if it gets pried from your cold, dead hands.'

'We need to keep an eye on him. The last thing we need is for him to go vigilante on us.'

'Do you think that's likely?'

'I'm going to throw that question back. You've been dealing with him for the past three years. You know him as well as anyone. Do you think we should be concerned?'

Anderton didn't respond. She didn't need to. The answer was written all over her face. This was something she would have considered, and she would have reached the same conclusion. He checked his cell phone again, but the text still hadn't arrived. This would be a good moment for it to appear. The perfect moment. He gave it another couple of seconds but his phone stayed frustratingly silent.

'Still no sign of that text you're waiting for?' Anderton said.

'Still no sign. Okay, I've seen enough. What do you say we get the hell out of here?'

6

'Marilyn Monroe,' Winter said when they got back to the car.

'And what does she have to do with anything?'

'In the early hours of August 5, 1962, Marilyn Monroe was found dead in the bedroom of her house in Brentwood, California. If you believe the conspiracy theorists she was killed by the Kennedys. If you believe the LA County coroner she died of acute barbiturate poisoning. And if you believe Elton John then she was found in the nude.'

Anderton had the key in the ignition and was just about to turn it. She let go and the keyring rattled for a second before going quiet. 'Do you have any idea how many hours we spent trying to work out the significance of that date?'

'A few.'

'More than a few. We looked at that date in every conceivable way, then we looked at it in every inconceivable way. When we were done looking at it do you know what we concluded?'

'You concluded that it was arbitrary. I read your summation of the case.'

Anderton nodded. 'Exactly. It's arbitrary. The first murder was committed on August 5 three years ago. Why did the killer do that? Who knows? Maybe he just liked the way the planets were aligned. Anyway, a year passes and he gets the itch to kill again. August 5 is coming up and he's got good memories of what happened on that day last year, so he thinks what the hell and kills his second victim on the anniversary.'

She paused for a breath. Winter could sense her frustration. It was evident in every word, every syllable. He knew exactly where she was coming from. There was nothing more infuriating than a puzzle that refused to be solved.

'The unintended consequence was that he received a whole lot of attention that he wouldn't otherwise have had. Human beings like patterns. We're programmed to seek them out. So another year passes, and we're approaching August 5 again. Only this time things are different. The media has got a hold of this and they're winding the situation up. They're pouring fuel on the fire and the flames are climbing higher. There's a real sense of anticipation in the air. And our guy doesn't want to disappoint.'

'It's a good theory,' Winter said. 'The problem is that it relies on coincidence. He commits the first murder on the fifth because the planets are aligned, then the second murder a year later on some nostalgic whim.' He shook his head. 'We're dealing with a psychopath here and they're not the nostalgic type. They're pragmatic by nature. The bottom line: when it comes to serial killers, I'd prefer to steer clear of coincidence.'

'So what's your theory? Why the fifth?'

Winter shrugged. 'Right now, I've got no idea.'

'But you think it's significant?'

He nodded. 'If we can work out why this date is important, then we get an insight into who he is. The better we know him, the easier he's going to be to hunt down. The successful hunter isn't the one who chases the prey, it's the one who understands it well enough to be waiting at the correct watering hole. Where, why, who. This ties into the why. That's the road less travelled, but even the road less travelled will still get you to your destination.'

Anderton didn't say anything for a moment. 'Okay, you've turned me into a believer again. So how do you intend finding the answer?'

'The obvious place to start looking is in the files from the first three murders. Hopefully there's something in there that was missed. I made a start on the plane and my plan is to carry on looking tonight.'

'There's a lot of information there.'

She wasn't wrong. In the old days it would have taken up at least three boxes, one for each murder. These days you could fit everything onto a flash drive and still have enough space left over for more music than you could listen to in a lifetime.

'It's a big day tomorrow,' he said. 'I'm not anticipating getting much sleep.'

'I'd offer to help but I've been through everything a hundred times. Backwards, forwards and sideways. It's got to the point where I can't see the forest for the trees.'

'That's the reason I'm here. Fresh eyes and a fresh perspective.'

'And God knows we need it. Right now, everyone's just hanging around waiting for this guy to strike. The problem with that approach is that it means that someone else has got to die before this investigation can start moving again. I can't let that happen. Three women have already died. That's three too many, if you ask me.'

'That's why we need to hit this thing from as many

different angles as possible. In addition to going through the files, I want to talk to the other two husbands. That's my first priority. They might not have seen the killer, but they witnessed the murders. We're talking two degrees of separation here. On the basis of that, I need to speak to them.'

'Eric Kirchner still lives in Vancouver, so that shouldn't be a problem. David Hammond might be trickier. He moved to Montreal, where he's trying hard to forget that any of this ever happened.'

'Do you know where Kirchner lives?'

'Yeah, it's not far from your hotel. While we're down that way we can get you checked in and drop off your case.'

'Sounds like a plan.'

Anderton turned the key in the ignition and the engine burst to life. Before she could pull away, Winter's cell phone vibrated. He took it out and checked the screen. There was one new text. It was short and sweet, confirmation of a meeting that he'd been trying to sort out ever since he had an ETA for his flight landing in Vancouver.

Anderton waited for him to look up. 'Judging by your expression, I'm figuring that's the text you've been waiting for.'

He nodded.

'Good news or bad?'

'That depends on your perspective. If I said the name Charlotte Delaney, how would you respond?'

'As in Charlotte Delaney the crime reporter?'

'That's the one.'

'In that case I'd respond by telling you that the woman was a bottom-feeding, soulless, bloodsucking vampire. And that's being polite.'

32

'That's what I thought. So, from your perspective, I'd say that the news isn't so good.'

Anderton's eyes narrowed. 'What's going on, Winter? Why is Delaney sending you texts?'

'Remember what I said about hitting this thing from as many different angles as possible? Well, this is one of the different angles that I was talking about.'

7

Global BC's studio was in Burnaby, a city that was grafted on to the east side of Vancouver. The two cities had kept growing to the point where it was now difficult to see the join. The only indication that you'd moved from one to the other was the sign at the city limits. From Sobek's house it was a forty-minute drive, west to east. The fact that Anderton spent most of the journey trying to persuade Winter that he was selling his soul to the devil made for a long forty minutes.

The next right took them onto Enterprise Street, which was nothing more than an elongated, stretched-out business park. Large cubist buildings sat nestled amongst carefully designed areas of green and large parking lots. Global's building was a third of the way along. The black colour scheme, satellite dishes and aerials made it appear sinister, like this was a base for a shady government agency. Anderton pulled into the lot and found a space. She killed the engine.

'Last chance to back out,' she said.

'I know what I'm doing.'

She gave him a cynical look.

'I've used this tactic before,' he said. 'And got results. On that basis the end more than justifies the means.'

'So how does this work?'

'Serial killers follow the news religiously, so we use that fact to draw the killer out. Now, we've got two options. Either we attack him or we try to identify with him. The police and the media have been attacking him for the past three years, and all that's done is push him deeper into the shadows. So, instead of attacking him, we give him a sympathetic character to identify with. Me. Best-case scenario, he actually starts talking to us.'

'You really think that's going to happen?'

'At this stage all I can tell you is that it could happen. I once worked a case where I did a press interview saying that everyone had got the killer wrong. He was misunderstood, he'd had a crappy childhood, nobody loved him. Blah, blah, blah. Et cetera, et cetera. Two days later the police received a handwritten note. It was addressed to me. On the back was one sentence. *I am not EVIL*. There was a capital letter at the start, a period at the end, everything was spelled correctly and the sentence was grammatically correct, so straight away we knew that we were dealing with someone educated. We released the note to the media and three people came forward saying they recognised the handwriting. Turns out the killer was a radiologist with a college education.'

Anderton said nothing.

'At the moment this guy's had things his own way for too long,' Winter continued. 'Right now everyone's just hanging around waiting for him to make his move. That's what he's expecting to happen, because that's what happened last year. This is the ideal time to mount a pre-emptive strike.'

'I get all that. And if it was anyone else except Delaney, I'd say go for it. But you can't trust her, Winter. The woman's a rattlesnake.'

'It's got to be Delaney. Global's news programme is

watched by more people in Vancouver than any other, and Delaney is their go-to person for crime stories. This is about engaging with as large an audience as possible. There's no point going to one of those neighbourhood cable channels that's way up in the hundreds, because the only person who's going to be watching is the interviewer's mom. Maximum exposure, that's what we need here.'

'But this is Charlotte Delaney we're talking about.'

'I can handle Delaney.'

'Okay, my turn for a story. Delaney didn't like the way I handled the investigation into Isabella Sobek's murder. After Alicia Kirchner was murdered there were calls for me to step down, then, after Lian Hammond was murdered, the gloves really came off. Back at the start of my career, I worked under a guy who was taking kickbacks. I inadvertently couriered some of the money on a couple of occasions. In my defence, I was young and naive. I made a mistake, that's all. There was no intent to carry out a crime, and no financial gain on my part. Internal Affairs agreed that I was a victim of circumstance and no charges were ever brought against me.'

'I already know all this, Anderton. You don't need to justify yourself. You're one of the good guys. I get it.'

She showed him the hand. 'You need to know what Delaney is like, so shut up and listen. Anyway, she drags up the story, but puts a new spin on it. Basically, she made it look as though I was a co-conspirator. She also insinuated that I'd been having an affair with my boss, that I wasn't as innocent as I'd made out. Unfortunately, my old boss was long dead, so he wasn't around to deny the allegations. I, of course, denied everything, but it didn't make any difference. Trial by media is brutal. You're guilty until proven innocent, and there's no way you're going to find an impartial jury. When that shit sticks to you, it sticks forever.'

She stopped talking and stared out of the windshield. Winter knew where she'd disappeared to. She'd gone back in time to those dark days. Like so many businesses, police work was a results-orientated profession. From her superiors' point of view, she'd struck out three for three. Delaney's article was the final straw. They knew she was innocent, but her public image had been forever tainted. They couldn't have her heading up a major investigation. They offered early retirement and she accepted. What else could she do? By that point the writing was all over the wall.

'Here's another story for you,' he said. 'I once interviewed this kid in prison. He was nineteen but looked about twelve. He'd murdered his entire family. With a hammer and an electric drill. His dad, his mom, his little brother. The crime scene looked like a set from a horror movie. His first day in prison he murdered one of the other inmates. This guy had thought he was an easy mark. He was wrong. The kid managed to smash his head against the floor no less than a dozen times before the guards pulled him off. The other inmate was dead before he reached the infirmary, his skull cracked wide open. Witnesses said the kid was like a wild animal.'

'Okay, I get it. If you can handle that kid, you can handle Delaney.' She paused and took a breath. 'Do not underestimate her, Winter. Not for a second. Do you hear me?'

'Loud and clear. Do you want to wait here?'

Anderton looked at him as though he was crazy. 'No way. I'm coming with you.'

'Are you sure? I thought you wouldn't want to get within a hundred miles of Delaney.'

'You thought wrong. And anyway, until this thing's over we're partners. That means I've got your back. Always.'

'That's good to hear.'

'No, Winter, this is the point where you tell me that you've got my back.'

'Always,' he said.

'Are you planning on wearing that T-shirt?'

He glanced down and saw what she was getting at. TV was a visual medium. Appearances were everything. His Doors T-shirt just wasn't going to cut it. He'd have no problems connecting with rock fans, but there were whole sections of the population that this look just wouldn't work for.

'You've probably got a point.'

'No probably about it.'

Winter got out of the car and opened the trunk. The white cotton shirt buried right down at the bottom of his suitcase was for emergencies. Like now. He took his Doors T-shirt off, then pulled on the shirt and buttoned it up. The leather jacket helped to make him look a little less like a second-rate office worker.

'Last chance to back out,' Anderton said.

'Nope, I'm good. Okay, shall we do this?'

8

Anderton crossed the lot to the studio building like a woman on a mission. Her left hand kept bumping against her left hip. That was where she would have kept her gun during her cop days. They went inside and headed for the elevator. The reception area on the second floor dealt solely with traffic heading to and from the news studio. It was decorated in a way that was supposed to be cutting edge, but just looked jaded. There was lots of black. The floors, the desk, the furniture. Global's logo featured loud and proud on the wall behind the desk.

The assistant who met them was pretty, petite and eager to please. They did a round of quick introductions then she whisked them off to a small make-up room. Less than a minute later, Winter was sitting in a barber chair while the make-up woman dabbed on some foundation. She had just started fussing with his hair when Delaney appeared. She was as pretty and petite as the assistant, but at least ten years older. As far as Winter could tell she hadn't had plastic surgery. It wouldn't be long, though. Crow's feet had started to appear at the corners of her eyes, and her skin wasn't as elastic as it had once been. Her smile was radiant, ten thousand watts of full-on false charm. The navy pant suit was tight-fitting and flattering. She walked over to the chair with her arm outstretched.

'Good to meet you, Mr Winter.'

'Good to meet you, too.'

They shook. If anything her grip was too firm, like she was overcompensating. For once Winter didn't mind being called 'mister'. Anderton's warnings were still ringing inside his head. Establishing boundaries was imperative. She turned her smile on Anderton.

'It's good to see you, too, Laura.' She stopped talking. The smile somehow grew bigger and brighter. 'So, you're working as a private investigator these days. That must be exciting.'

Anderton was doing well to keep her cool. The only indication that she was rattled was the way her fingertips kept tapping against her invisible gun.

'It's good to see you, too, Charlotte. Always a pleasure.'

Delaney stared for a second longer before breaking eye contact and turning her attention back to Winter.

'Have you done any live television before?'

'Some.'

'Good. So you know the trick is to keep it as natural as possible. And feel free to talk. If I think you're going on too long I'll just jump in with another question. What I'm looking for is a portrait of the killer. I want to feel as though we're really getting under his skin.'

'No problem.'

'Fantastic.' She glanced at her watch. It was a Rolex, one from the upper end of the range. 'We'll be on in six minutes.'

She flashed a last quick smile for Winter, and one for Anderton, and then she was gone, leaving a trace of perfume in her wake.

'I don't know what you're worried about,' he said as the door swung closed. 'She's a pussycat.'

'No, Winter, she's a rattlesnake. Don't forget that.'

9

Winter was led across the studio to a large red sofa that had been set up in front of a green screen. Delaney was there already. A man wearing a headset was talking urgently to her, while a make-up woman was making some final tweaks to her hair. The small monitor on the floor showed what the people at home would see. It was surreal, like catching a glimpse of yourself in a parallel universe. Glance over his shoulder and all he saw was green. Glance at the monitor and there he was, sitting in a hi-tech news studio.

Winter picked up a water glass from the table and took a sip. A microphone had been clipped to his shirt and the wire scratched across his skin whenever he moved. As a general rule, he avoided journalists. That said, if he thought it would help move a case forward then he wouldn't hesitate about jumping into bed with one. It was like owning a pet tiger. The animal might appear tame, but at any moment it could turn around and chew your face off.

Delaney looked over. 'Thirty seconds,' she whispered. 'You okay?'

'I'm fine, thanks. What about you?'

She smiled at that. 'I'm good.'

Winter started a countdown inside his head. He'd been briefed by media consultants in the past, so knew the dos and don'ts. Avoid 'ums' and 'ahs' and uncomfortable silences, don't fidget, keep hand movements to a minimum. The man in the headset had moved over to the large autocue screen. He caught Delaney's attention and used his fingers to count down from three to one. Delaney switched on her smile and sought out the camera. There were no surprises in what she said next. It was being beamed onto the autocue in six-inch-high letters. When she spoke, her voice was two tones lower than it had been earlier. Deep, resonant, authoritative.

'This evening we're joined by ex-FBI profiler Jefferson Winter, one of Quantico's infamous mindhunters. During his eleven years with the bureau, he worked a number of high-profile cases. Now he's joined the hunt for the August 5 Bomber.' She turned from the camera and looked straight at him. 'Thank you for joining us this evening, Mr Winter.'

'My pleasure.'

'You've had a chance to review this case. What are your initial thoughts?'

'The first thing that strikes me is how intelligent this person is.'

The perfectly plucked eyebrows rose in surprise. 'Intelligent? Would you care to expand on that?'

'The police have been hunting this person for three years now and they still haven't caught him. To stay one step ahead like that requires discipline, planning and, yes, intelligence. This is not someone who dropped out of high school.'

'What else can you tell us?'

'People keep referring to him as a monster. They're wrong. He is not a monster.'

Delaney's smile gave way to a disbelieving chuckle. 'I'm

not sure our viewers would agree with that. So, if he's not a monster, what is he?'

'In a word: misunderstood. As a child, he would have been neglected. Nobody listened to him. Nobody noticed him. What must that have been like? Ignored by your parents and shunned by your peers? It must have been horrendous. That's no life for a child.'

'A lot of people have bad childhoods but they don't grow up to become serial killers.'

'I'm not speaking generally here, I'm talking about the man you refer to as the August 5 Bomber. And that's another thing. Why do people do that? Why do they need to apply labels? It turns him into a caricature. Which he's not. He's a living, breathing person. Let's not forget that. All of us deserve to have a voice, Ms Delaney. All of us deserve to be heard.'

Delaney's smile was back. 'That's a fairly controversial position you're taking. Then again, you're no stranger to controversy. When you were eleven your father was arrested by the FBI. He was one of America's most notorious serial killers. Over a twelve-year period he killed fifteen young women. He kidnapped them, then took them out into the woods and hunted them down with a rifle.'

'Was there an actual question in there? If there was, I missed it.'

'I spoke to one of your former FBI colleagues,' Delaney continued. 'He believes that your relationship with your father clouds your judgement. He said that you spent too much time trying to relate to the killers you were pursuing and that this could actually be counterproductive. He called you a fraud and a glory hunter.'

Winter shook his head and shrugged and threw his arms up, the three gestures coming together to underscore his growing annoyance. 'I'm still not hearing any questions. This is an interview, right? You ask the questions, I answer them. That's how it works, or have I got that wrong?'

'Are you a glory hunter?'

'No, I'm not.'

'You say that, yet here you are.'

'We're not here to talk about me. Next question.'

'What about being a fraud? How would you respond to that?'

'Next question.'

Delaney smiled, then softened her voice. 'Have you shared any of your ideas with the police?'

'Not yet. If they want to talk to me, all they've got to do is pick up the telephone. I'd be more than happy to share my findings.'

'I can't see that happening, though. You're working with Laura Anderton, aren't you?' Before Winter could respond, Delaney turned to face the camera. 'Regular viewers will remember that Ms Anderton led the police investigation into the three murders committed so far. She was removed from the case last September.'

Winter leant forward, pushing in toward Delaney's space. 'You're not a very nice person,' he said quietly. 'Has anyone ever told you that?'

'Excuse me?'

'You heard. So what happened? Did Daddy leave you when you were a little girl? Did Mommy shack up with someone who paid you maybe a little too much of the wrong

44

sort of attention? Because something must have happened. It takes time to grow a chip on your shoulder as big as the one you've got.'

The smile was still there, but it was starting to crack at the edges. 'With all due respect, this interview isn't about me.'

'Why not? You're happy enough to trash my name. And Laura Anderton's.' Winter shook his head sadly. 'You want to know something? She's ten times the person you'll ever be.'

'In your opinion.'

'In anyone's opinion.'

'There are a lot of people who would disagree with you.'

Winter smiled sweetly. 'Not as many as you might think. Laura Anderton was a homicide detective in this city for thirty years, and she was a damn good one. Believe me, working homicide is an unforgiving task. She deserves respect. I don't think that's too much to ask. What's more, I believe that anyone with a touch of decency would agree with me. Then again, you're just a journalist, so what do you know about decency?'

The headset guy gave a signal to wind things up. Winter reckoned he had about ten seconds. Maybe fifteen. 'This interview's over,' he said.

Before Delaney could respond he got up and walked over to the camera. The headset guy was giving the signal to cut. On the monitor, Delaney was motioning to keep filming. Winter stared the camera straight in the eye.

'Tomorrow evening one of you is going to find yourself sitting on a kitchen chair with a bomb strapped to your chest. This will be the single most terrifying thing that has ever happened to you. The bomber is going to tell you that it's

45

wired to explode if you move. This is a lie.'

He took another step forward. The red light on the camera was still lit. It just had to stay like that for another few seconds. The monitor was filled with a close-up of his face. His hair was wild. His green eyes were blazing. He could have been one of those fanatical Baptist preachers who traded in fire and brimstone and the comfort that came from giving yourself to Jesus Christ. His voice was calm and reassuring and totally at odds with the way he looked.

'You can save yourself,' he said. 'All you've got to do is tip the chair over and keep rolling until the wire comes out of the bomb. You're not going to want to do that, but it's the only way you're going to survive. Do that and you will live.'

Winter unclipped the microphone and pulled the wire out from his shirt. He unhooked the transmitter pack from the waistband of his jeans, then dropped it on the floor and headed for the studio door.

'Tell me you got all that!' Delaney yelled as he walked away. 'Please God, tell me you got it all!'

10

Anderton was waiting in the reception area, eyes glued to a television screen showing the broadcast and a cell phone glued to her ear. The focus had moved back to the main desk, where the two anchors were already discussing Winter's abrupt exit from the interview. She saw him and quickly wound up the call.

'I told you the woman was a rattlesnake,' she said.

'You did.' He nodded toward her phone. 'Anyone interesting?'

'Just Sobek. I was giving him an update.'

'And how is Mr Sobek?'

'Healthy and well. He sends his regards.'

'No, he didn't.'

She smiled. 'Okay, maybe I made that last part up. Come on, let's get out of here.'

They headed back downstairs to the main reception. This time they took the stairs. Winter needed to keep moving. There was just too much adrenaline burning through his body. The second he got outside he lit a cigarette. He took a drag and exhaled a long trail of smoke. The nicotine was cool and soothing. He could feel himself coming back down almost immediately. All psychosomatic. Nicotine was actually a stimulant. And a poison. He put on his sunglasses then started walking across the lot to the Mercedes. Anderton was beside him, giving him funny looks.

'Yeah, I know,' he said. 'It's a bad habit and I really should quit.'

'I didn't say a word.'

'You didn't have to.'

'Don't worry, I'm not going to get all preachy. I quit ten years ago. I know how hard it is. If you want to kill yourself that's your business.'

'I thought you weren't going to get all preachy.'

'Believe me, that wasn't preachy.' She paused. 'Okay, what the hell was that back there?'

Winter stopped walking and turned to face her. He could see his reflection in one of the nearby car windows. It was the face of an innocent man, someone completely transparent, someone who didn't do disingenuous.

'I don't know what you mean,' he said.

'Then let's see if I can put it another way.' Anderton hesitated as though she was struggling to find the right words. Winter could see what was happening. This was a common interview technique, one he'd used on plenty of occasions. Silence was uncomfortable. It gave time for the doubts to creep in. He waited for her to use her words.

'Do you really expect me to believe that the person who stared down the Driller Killer Kid is going to get his feathers ruffled by a journalist?'

'She was saying mean things about you, Anderton. Very mean things.'

'You were playing her, weren't you?'

'Like a violin.'

'Why?'

'Because I want this interview to be seen. Someone walks out of an interview, that's a great way to get it all over the internet. Maximum exposure. That's what we're looking for here.'

She nodded. 'We need to get this up on YouTube. How about calling it "FBI Guy Loses His Shit"?'

'Technically, I'm ex-FBI, and I didn't really lose my shit.'

'Yeah, but "Ex-FBI Guy Gets Mildly Upset in TV Interview" just doesn't have the same ring.'

Winter laughed. 'I guess.'

Anderton took out her phone and started punching the screen with her index finger. She looked up and saw Winter watching. 'I'm texting a friend. They'll upload the interview for us.' She finished texting and put her phone away. 'Thank you for defending my honour, by the way.'

'You're welcome. It's like you said earlier. We're partners, and partners cover each other's backs.'

Anderton started walking again and Winter followed, catching up within a couple of strides.

'We need to talk about the elephant in the room,' she said. 'You weren't completely honest with me earlier.'

'That's because I couldn't be.'

'Okay, let me ask you something. How certain are you that the killer isn't going to fit his next bomb with a tilt switch?'

'Ninety-nine per cent certain. And that's why I couldn't say anything.' He paused. 'Okay, let me ask you something. If I'd told you what I was planning to do, would you have sanctioned the move?'

'Yes.'

Winter shook his head. 'No you wouldn't. You were a cop

for thirty years. You took an oath to protect the public. Even one per cent of doubt is too much when there's a life at stake. Let's say for a second that I've called this wrong. What's going to happen? The next victim rolls the chair and ends up reduced to their constituent parts, and you've got a death on your conscience.'

Anderton said nothing.

'And that's what I'm talking about.'

'What about you? If you're wrong, that death is on your conscience.'

'Not going to happen. The psychology's on our side. Think about it. He could trigger the bomb a dozen different ways. He could have it wired up to a timer. Or he could be sat in a car, waiting for the husband to come home and trigger it using a cell phone. Or he could have it wired to a tilt switch just in case the victim tries to break free. Any one of those methods would produce the same result in that his victim would be just as dead.'

'Except this guy needs the bomb to be triggered by the husband.'

'That's what makes his heart sing. He needs that door to open, and the bomb to go off. In that order. Door then bomb. He wants the husband's hands soaked with the blood of his wife.'

Anderton stopped walking and waited for him to meet her eye. 'In future, if you get an idea in your head I want to hear about it. Even the crazy ones that probably won't come to anything. In fact, especially those. Are we clear on this?'

'Crystal.'

'In that case, I'll say no more on the subject.'

She was still staring. Her expression had changed from borderline pissed to puzzled.

'What?' he asked.

'During the first part of the interview you did a really good job building up that whole them-and-us dynamic, but then you undermined it all by warning the next victim.'

'Unfortunately, there wasn't much of an option. Where, why, who, remember? What I glimpsed back at Sobek's house was the why of the situation. That gave us the opportunity to save a life, which trumps everything else. When you get down to it, we do this to save lives, right?'

'Right. You know, I might resent every single breath that Delaney takes, but you couldn't have asked for a better person to go up against. She made it easy for you.'

That was worth a laugh. 'She did. The woman defines the concept of us and them. She lives to divide and conquer.'

They carried on walking to the car. Before getting in, Winter changed into a clean T-shirt, a Beatles one this time. It was a relief to get the shirt off, like learning to breathe again. The engine started smoothly with the first turn of the key.

'Okay let's go and see Kirchner,' he said. 'Where does he live?'

'Mount Pleasant.'

'ETA?'

'This time of day, I reckon we'll be there in twenty-five minutes.'

Eric Kirchner no longer lived in the house where his wife was killed. After the murder he hadn't spent so much as a single minute there. These days he rented a small apartment on East Seventh Avenue. The neighbourhood had once been seedy but was now on an upward trajectory, location and rising property prices driving the district's gentrification process. His apartment was in a rundown block that had so far resisted this. The developers would get here eventually, but not any time soon. There were much nicer properties to work with.

In the end it took thirty minutes to drive here, five more than Anderton's estimate. There had been a minor traffic collision and they'd had to make a detour. Not that it mattered. Kirchner wasn't home. Anderton knocked again just to be sure. Still no answer. She took out her cell, found Kirchner's number, then pressed the screen to connect the call.

'It's been a while since I spoke to him. Let's hope he hasn't changed numbers.'

Winter tilted his ear toward the phone so he could listen. Three rings, then it was answered. The person on the other end was male, but the voice was too muffled to make out what was being said. The conversation was short. Anderton hung up and put her phone away.

'Kirchner's on his way back from work. He should be here in about fifteen minutes.'

'He wasn't happy to hear from you, was he?'

'You could say that. He's doing everything he can to forget that any of this ever happened. And then he gets a call out of the blue and he's slammed right back into the past again.'

'Even if you hadn't called, it wouldn't have made any difference. It's the fifth tomorrow. His wife's murder is all he's going to be thinking about.'

'I guess so.'

'I vote we wait in the car. It's more comfortable.'

Winter headed for the stairs. Anderton gave it a second, then followed. The Mercedes was parked fifty yards from the entrance. They climbed in and got settled. The apartment was directly ahead. There was no way for Kirchner to sneak past without them noticing.

'All we need is some coffee and a bag of doughnuts and we could be on a stakeout,' Winter said. 'Talking of which, I'm starving. Once we're done here, I need to find food.'

'You know, I can't remember the last time I went on a stakeout. It's got to be years. Decades, even.' She stopped talking and shook her head. 'Jeez, where does the time go?'

'I know what you mean.'

Anderton laughed. 'No you don't. You're just a kid. The best years of your life are still ahead of you.'

'Come on, you're not that old, and I'm not that young.'

'I'm fifty-three. And believe me there are some days where I feel every one of those years.'

'Fifty is the new forty,' Winter said.

'And that's easy to say when you're in your still in your thirties.'

They fell into an easy silence, the seconds ticking by.

Winter was staring out the windshield at the apartment building. Waiting for Kirchner. Killing time. Just like a stakeout.

'You miss being a cop, don't you?'

'Every day. It's what I was born to do. I know how pathetic that sounds, but it's true. It was my whole life, and then it got taken away from me. That's why I'm here now, I guess. I just can't let it go.'

'And why should you?'

She turned to face Winter. 'I tried marriage once, but I didn't take to it. The man I married was one of the good ones, but in the end he just had enough. Too many long hours, too much dark stuff and crap to deal with. Being married to a cop is no bed of roses. If you're looking for a healthy relationship, it's not the way to go. As for having kids. Again, I liked the idea, but the reality was another matter. It just wouldn't have worked.' She sighed. 'And then you wake up one day and realise that what was once possible is now impossible and you've got to ask yourself, was it worth it? I sacrificed everything to be a cop, Winter.'

'And was it worth it?'

'Once upon a time I believed it was. Now, I'm not so sure.'

Anderton went back to staring out of the windshield and Winter checked his watch. If Kirchner was running to schedule then they still had another ten minutes to wait.

'Charles Lindbergh,' he said.

'Has this got something to do with August 5, by any chance?'

'Not this time.'

54

'Okay, I'll bite. What's Lindbergh got to do with anything?'

'Lindbergh's baby son was kidnapped on March 1, 1932. The body of the boy was found a couple of months later close to the Lindberghs' house in New Jersey. The kidnappers screwed up and accidentally killed the kid, then dumped the body. Then they pretended that he was still alive so they could collect the ransom.'

Anderton frowned. 'You're going to have to help me out. How's a kidnapping that happened almost a hundred years ago even remotely relevant to what's going on here?'

'It's relevant because this was the greatest unsolved crime of the twentieth century.'

Anderton's frown deepened. 'The way I remember it, the police caught the kidnapper.'

'But did they get the right person?'

'You don't think they did?'

Winter shook his head. 'Bruno Richard Hauptmann was convicted of the abduction and murder of Charles Lindbergh Junior on February 13, 1935. He was executed in the electric chair at Trenton State Prison in New Jersey on April 3, 1936. His final words before the switch was thrown were *Ich bin absolut unschuldig an den Verbrechen, die man mir zur Last legt*. I am absolutely innocent of the crime with which I am burdened.'

'Need I remind you that prisons are full of innocent men?'

'And need I remind you that miscarriages of justice do occasionally happen?'

'Fair point, but I still don't see how this ties in with our case.'

'Charles Lindbergh was one of the most influential figures

of his generation. He was also a control freak. From the word go, he was right in there, dictating the direction the investigation should take. If he'd kept out of it and let the police and the FBI do their jobs, I'm confident the kidnappers would have been caught.'

'And you think that Sobek is in danger of doing the same thing.'

Winter nodded. 'If you lose control of an investigation, it's almost impossible to get it back. We're the investigators here. At best, Sobek is a back-seat driver. He's entitled to an opinion, but we're equally entitled to ignore it. We needed that established from the word go. That's why I gave him a hard time earlier.'

Anderton took a moment to process this. 'You know,' she said eventually, 'I have no trouble imagining Sobek killing someone. That's why I put so much time and effort into chasing him at the start. The guy looked guilty, and he was a good fit, too. I don't need to tell you that most murders are carried out by someone known to the victim.'

'You don't need to justify yourself.'

'I'm not. I'm just stating facts.'

Winter looked out of the windshield again. There was a man walking toward the apartment building. For a moment he thought it might be Kirchner, but the guy just kept going, past the entrance and on down the street. He had only seen a handful of people since they got back to the car. It was a quiet neighbourhood. A good place to come if you were looking to hide away from the world.

'So what do you think?' Anderton pressed. 'Is Sobek capable of murder?'

'If we applied the Hare Psychopathy Checklist he'd probably score somewhere in the mid-thirties.'

'Which would make him a psychopath.'

'But a score that high doesn't necessarily mean you're a killer.'

'You're talking about good psychopaths, right?' Anderton said.

Winter nodded. 'For want of a better term. The thing you've got to remember is that you get CEOs and politicians and movie stars who'd score just as high, and most of them haven't killed anyone.'

'So you think Sobek's a good psychopath?'

'Until the bodies start turning up, then yes, that's what I think.'

Anderton turned and gazed out of the windshield. Lots of waiting and boredom and time to kill. Just like a stakeout. Winter wished they had coffee. And doughnuts. Particularly the doughnuts. He could feel his blood sugar level starting to dip. Anderton looked at him.

'Okay, getting back to the Lindbergh kidnapping. Earlier you referred to the kidnappers in the plural, yet the authorities seemed happy to pin the whole thing on Hauptmann. You clearly don't agree with the lone-wolf theory, so what's your take?'

'Maybe I don't have one.'

'Based on the fact that you can quote dates and places, I'm figuring that you do.' Anderton checked her watch. 'We've got five minutes until Kirchner arrives, so let's hear it.'

'Okay, from his arrest all the way through to his death, Hauptmann claimed to be innocent. His wife, Anna

Hauptmann, lived to be ninety-five, and she claimed that he was innocent right up until her death, too. The thing is, Hauptmann was definitely guilty of something. The kidnapping required a specially constructed ladder, and Hauptmann was a carpenter who just so happened to have drawings of ladders in his notebooks. Also, he once worked for the timber merchant where the wood for the ladder came from. Also, the ransom notes were written by a semiliterate German immigrant and, lo and behold, Hauptmann was a semiliterate German immigrant.'

'So what you're saying is that the police put together a case that was built on circumstantial evidence.'

'*Mostly* based on circumstantial evidence. What's harder to explain away is the fact that he owned a keg of nails that came from the same batch as the nails used to build the ladder. Oh, and he had a third of the ransom money hidden in his garage. Despite claiming that he was just "looking after" the money, his standard of living took a dramatic upswing after the ransom was paid. Then we get to the single most damning piece of evidence. Rail sixteen of the ladder was made from one of the floorboards in his attic.'

Anderton was nodding. 'Okay, Hauptmann was clearly involved, but it doesn't necessarily follow that he was guilty of the murder, or that he was even involved in the actual kidnapping.'

'Exactly. If Hauptmann had received a fair trial then he would have got off on the grounds of reasonable doubt. But he was never going to get a fair trial. The Lindbergh kidnapping was the crime of the century. Every single detail had been hashed and rehashed a thousand times in the press.

Everyone had an opinion, which made finding an impartial jury an impossibility. Then there's the fact that the public was baying for blood. This was a crime that needed to be solved, and Hauptmann looked good for it.'

'So who did it?'

'Unfortunately, we'll never know since the main players are long dead.'

'But,' Anderton prompted.

'But we do know two things for a fact. Firstly, kidnapping was big business in the 1930s. Secondly, Hauptmann had criminal records in both the US and Germany. Is it possible that he was part of a shady group of German immigrants who got together to carry out the kidnapping? Yes, it is. In fact, I'd argue it was more than possible. After all, Lindbergh was one of the richest men of his generation, which made him the perfect mark. And, if this was a gang kidnapping, it would also explain why Hauptmann chose to go to the electric chair rather than give up his fellow gang members.'

Anderton was nodding again. 'If they'd threatened his wife, then I could see how that might work.'

Two minutes later a Ford Focus turned into the street and pulled into a space close to the apartment block. The car was at least a decade old, dated and dirty. Streaks of rust were visible on the side panels and fenders. The man who got out walked with a stoop, like the weight of the world had crushed him into submission.

'Eric Kirchner?' Winter said.

'Got it in one.'

12

The sound of their car doors banging shut startled Kirchner. His head jerked up and his body tensed as though he was getting ready to bolt.

'Mr Kirchner,' Anderton called out.

Kirchner stopped and turned. When he saw Anderton he visibly relaxed. Not all the way, but he no longer looked as though he was about to make a run for it. They walked over to where he was standing. According to the police files he was only thirty-four. Up close he looked like he was pushing fifty. His suit was cheap and worn. The cut of the collar dated it. Anderton handled the introductions. Kirchner's handshake was soft and boneless.

'I don't understand,' he said. 'I saw on the news that you weren't involved in the investigation any more.'

'I'm no longer involved in the police investigation, but I'm still investigating the murders. I believe that the person who killed your wife needs to be caught and brought to justice.'

Kirchner just stood there looking lost and unconvinced.

'Would you mind if we talked in your apartment?' she added.

'Sure, whatever.'

Kirchner led the way inside. The building was as neglected and forgotten as he was. It was as though the world had given up on the both of them. He let them into his third-floor apartment and they went through to the living room.

'Please, make yourself at home.'

Kirchner motioned toward the threadbare sofa. None of the furniture matched. It was a safe bet that everything had been bought from a thrift store, chosen for a purpose rather than how it looked. Financial considerations had been top of the list, aesthetic concerns at the bottom. Landlord chic. Winter had lived in enough rental properties to know what he was seeing. There were no personal touches whatsoever, not even a picture of Alicia. That in itself wasn't a huge surprise. Grief was intensely personal. Some people built shrines, others did their best to forget. Sobek belonged to the first group, Kirchner the second.

Except forgetting wasn't an option, not when there were reminders everywhere. Whenever Kirchner came back to his rundown apartment, he'd remember. Whenever he looked in the mirror and saw the haunted look in his eyes, he'd remember. And, at this time of the year, there would be even more reminders. The murders would be all over the TV news, all over the papers. Then there would be the well-meaning words and sympathetic glances from his friends and family and work colleagues. It didn't matter how much he wanted to escape, it was impossible.

'Can I get you anything to drink?' Kirchner asked.

Anderton waved him away with a 'Not for me, thanks.'

'A glass of milk,' Winter said. 'And a peanut butter and jelly sandwich, please.'

Kirchner gave him a disbelieving look. 'Sure. And what about you?' he asked Anderton. 'Can I get you anything to eat?'

Anderton waved him away with another 'Not for me.' She waited until he'd left the room before turning to Winter.

'Seriously? A peanut butter sandwich?'

'PB and J,' he corrected.

'Is that really appropriate?'

'Probably not, but it is necessary. The last time I ate was on the plane, and that was hours ago. My blood sugar level is about to nosedive. Believe me, you don't want to see the fall-out from that one.'

'Whatever you say.'

'If it's okay with you, I'll handle the questions.'

'Fine with me. You know what you're looking for.'

Kirchner came back in and handed Winter a plate with a sandwich on. It disappeared in half a dozen bites, chased down with some milk. The bread was a day past its best, but he was too hungry to care. Kirchner was on the armchair opposite the sofa. He was perched right on the edge like he was getting ready to run.

'I've got a couple of questions,' Winter said.

'And who exactly are you?'

'My name's Jefferson Winter. I used to work for the FBI. I'm consulting on this case.'

'I was interviewed at the time of my wife's murder. You know that, right? I told the police everything I know.'

There was a slight hesitation before he said 'murder'. Two years had gone by, but in every way that mattered no time had passed. Murder had a way of freezing the victims' loved ones in the past.

'I want to try a cognitive interview. Do you know what they are?'

Kirchner shook his head. 'No.'

'In that case I'll walk you through it,' Winter said. 'In a moment I'm going to ask you to shut your eyes. Then you're going to go back to the evening of Alicia's murder and describe what you see, hear and smell. That's how a cognitive interview differs from a normal interview. Basically, you're reliving the memory through your senses. The advantage of this approach is that it increases your level of recall.'

'"Reliving the memory",' Kirchner echoed. 'I'm not sure I want to do that.'

'I understand your reluctance, but it'll really help us out.'

'And how exactly will digging up the past help? Will it bring Alicia back?' Kirchner shook his head. 'I don't think so.'

'You're right, Mr Kirchner, nothing will bring her back. However, her killer is still out there, and if we don't catch him, then tomorrow evening someone is going to come home from work and open their kitchen door, and they're going to step into a nightmare that's identical to the one that you live through every single day.' Winter paused. 'Let me ask you something. What would you give to change the past?'

'Everything,' Kirchner said quietly. There was no hesitation. This was clearly a question he'd asked himself a thousand times, probably in the dead of night when the hours felt the loneliest, and the bed too big.

'Unfortunately that's not going to happen. But you can influence the future. That's what I'm offering here. An opportunity to make it so this nightmare doesn't happen to anyone else.'

Kirchner didn't say anything for a while. He was looking more troubled than ever. 'All right. What do you want me to do?'

'Close your eyes.'

Kirchner closed his eyes.

'If something comes into your head, I want to hear about it. I don't care how crazy it is. In fact, the crazier the better. What's important is that you don't censor your thoughts.'

'I think I can do that.'

'Good.' Winter's voice had dropped to a notch above a whisper. Like a hypnotist, he'd slowed his delivery, stretching out the syllables. 'I want you to imagine you're lying on a sun lounger on a beautiful beach. You can feel the sun, warm on your skin, and you can hear the waves rolling in, the water ebbing and flowing. Take a moment to lose yourself in the scene. Can you hear the gulls crying and calling? Can you taste the salt on your lips and tongue?'

Kirchner nodded.

'Good. Now count slowly from ten to zero. With each passing number you're going to sink deeper into the sun lounger.'

Over the next thirty seconds Kirchner noticeably relaxed. His breathing slowed and deepened. The lines on his face smoothed away, making him look younger again.

'Let's go back to the evening of the murder. You're in your car, driving home from work. Maybe you've got music playing, or maybe you prefer silence.'

'The radio's on,' Kirchner whispered in a dreamlike voice.

'You pull up outside the house. Do you park in your usual parking space?'

Kirchner nodded.

'You kill the engine and get out of the car. What's the weather like?'

'The sun's shining. I've got my tie off and my shirt sleeves rolled up. It's too hot for a jacket.'

'What happens next?'

'I go into the house. I know Alicia's home because her bag is in the closet. I hang up my coat and call out her name, but she doesn't answer. I try again. This time I shout up the stairs in case she's in the bedroom. There's still no answer. I'm figuring that she must be in the kitchen.'

His voice hitched and his face creased up with misery. Winter jumped in before he lost him. 'Okay, I want you to stay in the hallway for a minute. What can you see?'

'All the doors are closed.'

'Is that unusual?'

'No. We keep our cat confined to the kitchen while we're at work because he keeps throwing up hairballs everywhere. Except he's somehow got out. He's at the top of the stairs.'

'Describe him.'

'He's a black and grey tabby. A big one.'

'What's his name?'

'Mouse. It seemed appropriate when he was a kitten. Because he was so small. He wouldn't stop growing, though.'

'What happens next?'

'Mouse comes down the stairs and walks over to me. I pick him up, give him a scratch and tell him off for being out of the kitchen.'

'How are you feeling?'

'Puzzled. Mouse shouldn't be out here. Alicia must have accidentally locked him out of the kitchen. It wouldn't be the first time.'

'But this time feels different. Something's not quite right about the picture. What?'

A small shake of the head. 'I don't know.'

'Take a look around. Does anything seem different or out of place?'

Another small shake of the head. 'I don't think so.'

'What can you smell?'

Kirchner's face creased into a frown.

'What is it?' Winter asked gently.

'I can't smell anything.'

'And that's unusual?'

He nodded. 'Alicia gets back from work before me, so she cooks dinner during the week. I cook at the weekend.'

'I want you to walk over to the kitchen door.'

As soon as Winter said this, Kirchner's breathing sped up and he started to shift around in his chair.

'Put your hand on the door handle. Does the door open toward you?'

'No. Away from me.'

'So you push it open. What happens next?'

Kirchner's eyes suddenly sprang open. 'You know what happens next,' he hissed.

'I know what I think happened. That's not the same.'

'What happened was that I opened the door and killed my wife.'

'That's the censored version. What I want to know is what actually happened. I need the details. What did you see? What did you smell?'

'Why would you want to know something like that?'

'Because it's my job to get into the heads of the people who

66

carry out these crimes. I catch them by understanding them.'

Kirchner didn't look convinced. He looked like he wanted Winter to get the hell out of his apartment, like he wanted him to get the hell out of his life. It was understandable. The scar tissue covering his wounds was thin, and here was Winter scratching it off.

'Mr Kirchner,' Anderton said. 'We know this is hard, but if you could help us out here.'

'Why? It's not like you're real detectives.'

Anderton flinched, the criticism hitting her where she was most sensitive.

'Let me ask you something,' Winter said. 'How many times a day do you relive Alicia's murder?'

Kirchner said nothing. The guy was a mess. There were signs that he'd been self-medicating. Alcohol for definite, but possibly prescription meds, too. Red veins snaked through the whites of his eyes and his skin had a graveyard sheen. His hair was wild from where he'd been running his hands through it. There was a slight tremor in his hand. Maybe it was all the questions, but more likely it was because it was fast approaching Happy Hour.

'The moment of Alicia's death plagues your entire existence,' Winter said. 'Even when you're not consciously thinking about it, those memories are bubbling away just below the surface. They inform every second of your day-to-day existence. And when you do remember, it's brutal. When it comes to emotional responses, the brain doesn't make any distinction between what's memory and what's actually happening. Every time you remember, it's like you're reliving the whole thing all over again.'

67

'You don't know what you're talking about.'

'That's the thing, Mr Kirchner, I know exactly what I'm talking about. Look, all I'm asking is that you share one of those action replays with me. Maybe it won't help. Then again, maybe it will. If there's even an outside chance of it doing some good then that's got to be worth a little discomfort on your part, right? Particularly since you're going to be crucifying yourself with the memory anyhow.'

Kirchner took a deep breath while he wrestled with his decision. It was one thing to sit in an empty movie theatre while your memories played on an endless loop on the big screen. It was another thing entirely to fling the doors open and invite the whole world to come and watch. When he finally spoke, his voice was flatlining. It was emotionless, uninflected, dead.

'I opened the door and it was like being kicked by a horse. I fell backwards and somehow ended up on the floor, slipping and sliding and trying to scramble away. My brain had switched off and I was just reacting. I got to my feet and my ears were ringing. I knew something bad had happened, but couldn't work out what. Slowly I worked it out, though. There had been some sort of explosion. And then I remembered that Alicia was in the kitchen. I stumbled back to the door and went in. The smell of the explosion was overpowering. I could see the kitchen chair lying on its side. And I could see there was someone on it. I ran over. It was Alicia. I tried to wake her up, but couldn't. I kept trying and trying, but she just wouldn't wake up. That's what happened.'

'Thank you,' Winter said.

Kirchner just glared, tears streaming down his face. 'Get out of here,' he said.

13

Frankie's was a sports bar down by the river. The walls were decorated with Canucks memorabilia. Hockey sticks, helmets, shirts signed by the team members. The big screen was tuned to a soccer game that nobody was watching. The table Winter ended up at was close enough to the bar that he could watch what was going on, but far enough away that he wouldn't be disturbed. He usually avoided sports bars on principle, but Frankie's was half empty this evening, and it was only a short walk from his hotel, and it had a decent enough whisky selection. That last one was the clincher.

David Hammond had turned out to be a complete bust. The cell number Anderton had for him still worked, but he hadn't wanted anything to do with the investigation. Montreal was 3,000 miles away. He was using geographic distance to create emotional distance. His wife was dead and buried and he wanted to move on. Anderton had pushed hard, but it hadn't done any good. It wasn't the end of the world. Winter had already got most of what he was looking for from Kirchner.

He sipped some whisky, then took out his cell and navigated to his emails. Anderton's were in a separate folder. He scrolled through them until he reached the ones that had attachments. She'd sent the case files through at the start of their correspondence. Bait to get him hooked, and then she'd reeled him in.

Winter downloaded the autopsy report on Isabella Sobek and began to read. Isabella. That was another indicator that Sobek had viewed her as a possession rather than a person. A name like that just cried out to be shortened. Bella. Izzy. Isa. Take your pick. You got to know someone, and you got close to them, and those little terms of endearment slipped in. But that hadn't happened here. As far as Sobek was concerned she was Isabella. For now and for always. Winter couldn't see him shortening it. He couldn't even imagine him calling her darling or sweetheart or honey. That would somehow diminish her. It would somehow lessen the value of the possession. Winter had seen the photographs. If he'd been married to her she would have been a Bella. No doubt about it.

He skimmed through the autopsy report, taking in details. When you got down to it, every death could be attributed to one of two causes. Your lungs stopped pumping air, or your heart stopped pumping blood. If either one happened then death was an absolute certainty. Everything else was just a variation on those two themes. Sometimes, as was the case here, the themes merged. According to the medical examiner, the explosion had shocked Isabella's heart to a standstill and ruptured her aorta. Then the ball bearings had slammed into her chest, ripping through her lungs and rendering them useless. The same thing had happened with Alicia Kirchner and Lian Hammond. The blast killed them, the shrapnel made sure they stayed dead.

You could argue that the ball bearings weren't necessary. And so far they hadn't been. In all three murders the explosion alone had been enough to get the job done. The problem with using fireworks was that it would be difficult to know how big the blast would be. That was the unknown quantity in the equation. The killer would have carried out tests, so he would have had a rough idea of what to expect, but there would still have been some doubt. Was the blast going to be big enough? Would it do what it needed to do? The ball bearings were his insurance policy. If by some miracle the victim survived the explosion, then the shrapnel would finish them off.

Where, why, who. Winter was wondering about the why again. The road less travelled. When dealing with serial killers, the actual murders usually happened for one of two reasons: necessity or gratification. The problem was that neither explanation seemed to fit. Necessity would cover a scenario where the killer raped his victim and was worried about being identified, or a scenario where his fantasies had pushed him into going too far. Winter couldn't see how that would work here. Which left gratification. Except that didn't work either. This killer didn't get their hands dirty. Nor did he need to look into the eyes of his victims as he took their lives.

It wasn't unusual for serial killers to hang around at the scene of the crime. They got off on the confusion and pandemonium. The sense of superiority that this gave them was intoxicating. Anderton had known this. That's why she'd had cameras and eyes on the crowds who'd gathered outside the murder houses. Nobody had stood out, though.

Another possibility was that the killer had been hanging around outside his victims' homes prior to the explosion.

That would fit with him taking a hands-off approach. Except that didn't sit comfortably, either. The murders had all happened in residential areas between the hours of six and eight in the evening. People would have been home from work by then. Someone would have seen something.

Again, Anderton had been diligent. The neighbourhoods had been canvassed, but nobody had seen anyone acting suspiciously. Winter took witness statements with a pinch of salt. They could be useful, but sometimes they created more problems than solutions. People placed too much importance on them and that could lead to a wild goose chase. Memory was fluid and easily corrupted. The drapes in your childhood bedroom weren't blue, they were in fact red. You'd actually had the chicken dish when you last went out for a meal, not the beef.

In this case Winter would be happy to accept an eyewitness statement as gospel. If the killer had been hanging around in a car, waiting for the bang, someone would have seen him and said something. Even if they hadn't been able to give a halfway decent description of the killer or the car, they would at least have been able to confirm that he'd been there.

But that hadn't happened at any of the crime scenes. On that basis Winter was happy to accept that the killer hadn't been outside the victims' houses when the bombs went off, which meant that gratification was off the table, too. If you took gratification and necessity out of the equation all you were left with was a large question-sized hole. Serial killers didn't do anything without a good reason. The risks were too great to have your actions controlled by whims. Winter decided to park this one for now. He'd let his subconscious play around with it, see what it came up with. Sometimes hitting things straight on just led to that hole growing bigger.

Winter finished his whisky and put the glass back on the mat. The sensible thing would be to head back to the hotel and carry on working through the files there. Then again, that first whisky had gone down a little too easily. There was a mirror on the wall behind the bar. Light shone through the bottles lined up on the shelves and reflected back, sparkles of colour, like amber jewels. Faces were reflected there too. Laughing faces. Serious faces. Smiling faces. Sad faces.

A curious face.

Winter stood up and went over to the bar. The same guy who'd served him earlier served him again. He was in his late fifties with small eyes set in a fleshy face. He had the look of a hardened drinker, someone who should avoid bar work. Winter saw liver failure in his future. He knew what that one looked like because that's what killed his mom.

The barkeep poured in silence, one eye on the big screen. He was the only person watching the game. Winter carried his drink back to his table and got settled. He put it down and squared the mat, making sure it was absolutely parallel with the table edge, whisky sloshing gently against the sides of the glass. The curious guy was at a table close to the bar, one where he could watch the reflections in the mirror without being obvious. He was shielded by two rowdy kids who were competing to see who could drink the most. It was good cover. Anybody looking in that direction would hone in on the kids.

Winter didn't think he was here when he arrived, but couldn't be certain. The timing was crucial. If this guy had

73

been here, then he was just being paranoid. He hadn't planned on coming here for a drink. This bar had ticked enough boxes to tempt him inside, but he could easily have kept on walking to the next one. And if this guy was watching him, how did he get here first? That would require the ability to see into the future, or a time machine, and Winter wasn't buying either of those explanations.

On the other hand, if he'd come in after him then that raised a whole host of new questions. Winter picked up his glass and took a sip. His gaze skirted across the mirror, and kept going, stopping at the big screen. For a short while he watched a bunch of grown men chase a ball around a perfectly manicured acre of grass, and thought about what this all meant.

He glanced at the mirror again. The curious guy had positioned himself so the angles were conducive with catching his reflection, but that meant the angles also worked in reverse. At the moment the guy had his head down, eyes fixed on his phone, thumb swiping from bottom to top as though he was reading something. Maybe he was, maybe he wasn't. That didn't matter though. He was exercising his right to be invisible, and the cell phone was as good a prop as any. Who was going to look twice at someone playing with their cell? Every single day you were going to see a hundred people doing that exact same thing.

Winter took out his own cell and unlocked it. He found Anderton's number and typed a quick text.

In Frankie's. Down by the river. Being watched.

Her reply arrived ten seconds later.

What? Who?!?

White male, early 30s, five five, slight build. Unremarkable. Surveillance savvy.

The killer?

Interview aired two hours ago. Do the math.

Calling Freeman. Stay where you are. Be there soon.

Before Winter could respond, another text appeared.

DON'T DO ANYTHING!!!

His response was short and sweet:

14

Certainties only become absolute after the fact. Up until that point there is always something waiting to crop up and prove the theory wrong. Winter had a pretty good idea what was happening here, but there was still that sliver of doubt. The curious guy was nursing a beer, eyes occasionally straying toward the big screen so that he had an excuse to look in the mirror. Winter was doing the same. An occasional glance at the big screen, his eyes tracing an arc that meant his gaze passed over the mirror. The fact that the guy was still here supported two possible theories. What happened in the next ten minutes would decide which one was correct.

The first thing that happened was that Anderton turned up. Winter noticed her in the doorway and waved her over. She'd changed outfit since he saw her last. She was still wearing jeans but these were new on, clean and pressed. Her blouse had been swapped for a grey T-shirt with a picture of the New York skyline on the front. Her sneakers were newer and a lot less battered than his. Her hair was wet, from either the shower or a bath. Winter was betting on her being a shower person. Pragmatists preferred showers, dreamers preferred baths. The curious guy was playing it cool. He hadn't reacted at all, just carried on watching the game.

The second thing happened twenty seconds later. By the time Anderton had got halfway across the room, the door opened again and Freeman entered. Freeman was Anderton's successor, and as such the buck now stopped with him. The fact he was here without a SWAT team, or body armour, or a gun, meant that theory number one had just become an absolute certainty.

Winter stood up again and waved to him. For a moment Freeman looked confused, as though he wasn't sure how to respond. Should he wave? Should he acknowledge him? In the end, he didn't do either, he just kept walking across the room and stopped at the table. He was in his late forties, handsome, with a solid chin and good facial symmetry. This was a face made for TV. His superiors would have been looking for someone they could present to the media. It made sense. This investigation had come under a good deal of criticism, so they would be searching for ways to win back some support. According to Anderton, Freeman was an idiot, but her opinion was understandably biased. At the very least he'd probably turn out to be halfway competent. Unfortunately, halfway competent didn't cut it. You wanted your best people on something like this. Looking at Freeman, Winter wasn't convinced. He'd met enough politicians over the years to know one when he saw one. He nodded to the table where the curious guy was sitting.

'There's your killer.'

Freeman didn't look over. He just stared at Winter and said nothing.

'He's a white male,' Winter went on. 'Which puts him in the right racial demographic. He's in the right age group, and the right sort of build. And he just so happens to have turned up here after I was on TV. I say we get the handcuffs out and arrest him. What do you think?'

'I think we should all sit down so we can discuss this in a civilised manner.'

'Yes, we should,' Anderton said.

Nobody moved. It was like a Mexican stand-off, albeit without the guns and the inherent sense of danger. Winter sat down first. Then Freeman. Anderton gave it a couple of seconds then joined them.

'You're using Winter as bait,' she said.

'No, he's using himself as bait. Isn't that right?'

The question was aimed in Winter's direction. Winter kept his mouth shut.

'The purpose of the interview was to draw the killer out,' Freeman went on. 'You're looking for him to contact you.'

'Me or you guys, it doesn't matter who. If we can establish a direct line of communication then that would be massive step forward. Even one letter or email would give us a wealth of new information to work with.'

'Let us be clear about something, there is no "us".'

Winter smiled. 'My mistake. By "us" I meant "me".'

Freeman didn't return the smile. His mouth and eyes were tight, his expression severe. 'Okay, I'll admit it. On the off chance that the killer might contact you, I made the decision to have you followed.'

Anderton said, 'And at what point were you planning on informing us about this?'

'I wasn't.'

'And that doesn't cause you any sort of crisis of conscience? You're using a member of the public to lure out a serial killer who's already brutally murdered three people.'

'A member of the public who also happens to have been trained as an FBI agent. Not only that, he's an expert on serial killers. Let's not forget that.' Freeman shrugged. 'Put yourself in my shoes. What would you have done?'

'I would have at least had the decency to inform him that that's what I was doing.'

'No you wouldn't. And the reason you wouldn't is the same as mine. This sort of trap works better if the bait doesn't know they're being watched. They're less likely to give the game away. You know that as well as I do, Laura.'

'It's not ethical, Peter.'

Freeman raised his eyebrows. 'Do you really want to get into an ethics debate?'

'You should have told us what you were doing.'

'Like the way you told me that you were bringing in an expert on serial killers.'

'That's not the same. Not even close.'

'Isn't it? You've never been much of a team player, Laura. All that matters is that you get your man, isn't that right? My guess is that you've got this fantasy where you catch the killer and end up looking like a hero.'

'All I care about is that he's brought to justice. I don't care who makes the actual arrest.'

'That's very noble of you. It's also bullshit.'

Anderton said nothing.

'The thing is, I do care. The department needs a win. Bringing this killer down would be a major victory for us.'

Winter cleared his throat. Both Anderton and Freeman turned to look at him. 'It's like watching a brother and sister going at each other. All you do is bicker and fight, but deep down you love each other really.' He paused and smiled. 'Okay, I think we're all agreed that the important thing is stopping this guy from blowing people up. Yes?'

There were reluctant nods from both Anderton and Freeman.

'Well, the best way to achieve that is if we work together.'

'You're talking about sharing information?' Freeman said.

'That's correct. It's like they say, two heads are better than one. Although in this case, you've got the heads of the whole of the Vancouver PD's homicide division, while we've got just mine and Anderton's. Group them all together and that's a hell of a lot more than two heads, though. If we put our minds to it we could move mountains.'

'You're serious, aren't you?'

'As a heart attack. There will be things we discover that you miss and vice versa. You claim you want to catch this guy. I'd argue that the best way to achieve this is by pooling our resources.'

Freeman considered this. 'Okay. But there are limits to how far we can go. Due to the nature of the investigation, there will obviously be some information I can't share.'

'I understand. We'll be happy to take whatever we can get.'

'And I'm not so naive as to believe that you'll share everything you've got.'

'Of course you're not. And I wouldn't insult your intelligence by suggesting otherwise. What I can promise is that we will pass on whatever we can. One more thing. I need you to call off your watcher. I spotted him, which means that the killer would have spotted him as well.'

'But you're a member of the public. I wouldn't be able to

live with myself if anything happened to you.'

Anderton laughed. 'Seriously?'

'Okay, I won't have you tailed. But you've got to promise me that if you get even a sniff of this guy you contact me.'

Winter crossed his heart. 'Hope to die,' he said.

'Let's hope it doesn't come to that.'

'It won't. This guy prefers a hands-off approach, which means he won't want to get too close. The only place he might make a move on me is at my hotel. And before you say anything, I don't need anyone watching my hotel. I can handle him if he comes for me there.'

Freeman didn't look convinced.

'So, is there anything you'd like to share?' Winter asked.

'Not at the moment. What about you?'

'Not at the moment.'

Freeman stood up and straightened his jacket. 'Laura's got my cell number, should you need to contact me.'

He started walking toward the door. The curious guy joined him at the entrance and they went out together. Winter watched the door close, then turned to Anderton.

'So, what do you think?' he asked.

'What I think is that I need a drink.'

'I know somewhere we can go. It's not far.'

'What's wrong with this place?'

Winter looked at the big screen and the tired-looking sports memorabilia and the miserable barman, and saw the bar for the depressing dive that it was. He got up and grabbed his jacket from the back of the chair.

'Come on, let's get the hell out of here.'

15

The Shangri La was one of the most exclusive hotels in Vancouver, which also made it one of the most expensive. Winter felt no guilt about staying here. Sobek could afford to pay for an airplane he never flew, cars that he never drove, and a luxury house that he didn't live in. He was throwing money away hand over fist. On that basis Winter was more than happy to have some thrown in his direction.

Anderton was walking around the suite, picking things up, putting them down, exercising her right to be curious. She had a tumbler of vodka and Coke in her hand. Winter was drinking a twenty-one-year-old Springbank, courtesy of Sobek. Last time he checked, this was retailing for four hundred bucks a bottle. And that was the second reason he'd wanted to get out of Frankie's. Blended whisky was fine as a means of getting alcohol into your bloodstream, but a single malt was an experience. Mozart's 'Jupiter' Symphony was playing quietly in the background, the music providing a pleasant counterpoint to the buzz he was getting from the Springbank.

Anderton stopped by a large map of Vancouver that was fixed to one wall. There were six photographs next to the map, three a side. Isabella Sobek. Alicia Kirchner. Lian Hammond. The pictures on the left had been taken during happier days. There were smiles and laughter and no indication that they were living on borrowed time. The pictures on the right had been taken at the crime scenes and showed their brutalised bodies. The three murder sites were marked on the map with red crosses. Anderton picked up a Sharpie and drew a red circle that enclosed them. The circle more or less matched the one that Winter had already drawn in his mind.

'This is his hunting ground,' she said. 'He's operating inside his comfort zone.'

'It's also where he lives,' Winter added. 'More than any other place that comfort comes from the place you call home.'

'Do you have any idea how many people live in that area?'

Winter shook his head.

'Almost a hundred thousand.'

'So we go door to door.'

'Do you have any idea how many houses are in that area?'

'I didn't say it would be easy.'

Anderton walked over to the window and looked out. It was almost nine and the sun had more or less disappeared. The horizon was glowing orange, the city lights coming on.

'You know, this suite's bigger than my whole apartment,' she said.

Winter laughed. 'Stop exaggerating.'

'I wish I was. My place has two bedrooms, although one of them is more like a closet, and the living room is the size of your bathroom. I bought it twenty-eight years ago, before I was married. Back then it was all I could afford. I could buy a bigger place now, but what's the point? Mine does everything I need it to. It's got somewhere for sleeping, somewhere for working, and somewhere I can fix meals. I guess I've never been much of a homebody.'

'Me, either. I tried it once but it never really took. I had a house in Virginia when I was working at Quantico. Correction, I've still got a house in Virginia.'

'But you don't live there?'

'I haven't been back in years. I should sell it. I don't know why I haven't.'

'Sobek's got a house that he doesn't really live in, too.'

'Yes, but at least my kitchen doesn't look like Beirut on a bad day. And why the comparison?'

'Just thinking about good psychopaths again. So how high do you score on the Hare Psychopathy Checklist?'

Winter smiled and said nothing.

'Higher or lower than Sobek?'

'What is this? The Guantanamo Bay admission test?'

'No, Winter, it's a conversation. So, have you ever been married?'

'You're kidding, right? Seriously, who'd have me?'

Anderton looked him up and down. 'A shave and a haircut, and some new clothes, and you'd look almost presentable. We might have to smooth off some of your sharper edges, though. For a start, we'd need to do something about your pedantic streak. That could get annoying real fast.' Anderton laughed briefly, then turned serious. 'Freeman doesn't play nice. He'll smile to your face, then stab you in the back. He's not going to give up information easily.'

'I don't expect him to, but every little helps, right? What's important is that we've opened up a line of communication with the one person who theoretically knows everything about the investigation. We're talking the mother lode. And, anyway, he's not our only potential source of information within the department, is he?'

'What's that supposed to mean?'

'No need to get so defensive. It's just a question. It's what people do when they're having a conversation.'

Anderton stared and said nothing.

'Up until you were pushed out, you were the Vancouver PD's lead investigator. You clearly made some enemies, otherwise Freeman wouldn't be doing your job. But I'm betting you made plenty of friends, too. Friends you still keep in contact with. Friends you chat about the weather with, and last night's game, and, I don't know, any relevant developments in the investigation, perhaps.'

More staring. More silence. Anderton took a sip of her drink then walked over to the sofa and sat down. Winter sat in the armchair. For a while they said nothing, the music washing over them. This was the last symphony Mozart composed, and it was arguably his finest. It contained so many emotions. Hope, despair and everything in between. It was the human condition set to music. Each new hearing was a unique experience.

'I'd never have taken you for a classical music fan,' Anderton said. 'Rock music, yes, but not classical.'

'My mom was a piano teacher. Mozart was her favourite composer. When she was pregnant she used to put headphones on her bump so she could play his music to me.'

Anderton laughed. 'People actually do that?'

'You'd better believe it.'

'You said that your mom *was* a piano teacher. She's not retired, is she?'

Winter shook his head. 'No, she died.'

'I'm sorry.'

'Why? It's not your fault.'

'No, it's not, but that's what people say in these situations. So, did your mom teach you to play?'

The question sparked a memory, a good one from the days before their lives were ripped apart. Winter was sat at the piano in the practice room, his mom squashed up against him on the stool, their hips pushed hard together. His mom would play a phrase and he would play it back in a higher octave. Part of the game was that his eyes were closed. Whenever he peeked she'd tell him off. 'You don't need your eyes, Jefferson. Learn to listen. Feel the notes.' She'd be smiling as she said it, though. There was always a lot of laughter during those lessons. In her later years she never laughed. Albert Winter did plenty of unforgiveable things, but stealing his wife's laughter was right up near the top of the list. There were times like now when Mozart reminded Winter of his mom. The despair, the hope and everything in between.

'Yeah, she taught me to play,' he said.

'Are you any good?'

'I'm okay.'

'Which means you're a damn sight better than okay. You're an overachiever, Winter, someone who has to be the best at everything they do.'

It was his turn to stare and keep quiet. He picked up his tumbler and took a sip. The third movement had just started. Where the second movement was sombre, this was playful. For a moment he was almost able to forget why he was in Vancouver.

'Okay,' he said. 'Let's play I'll show you mine, you show me yours.'

'As much as I'm flattered, I should remind you that I'm almost twenty years older than you.'

'That wasn't a pass.'

'Good to hear.' Anderton smiled and reached for her glass. 'So how does this work?'

'You've been working on this case for three years. In that time there will be things that must have struck a discordant note with you. Things that just didn't fit.'

She nodded. 'The victimology is the big one for me. There's nothing that ties them together. They have different colour hair, different colour eyes. Isabella and Alicia are Caucasian. Lian is Asian. Their ages range from twenty-eight to thirty-two, but that on its own doesn't really help. There are plenty of people living in our target zone who fall within that age range.'

'There's got to be something that links them, though. This killer is highly organised. Something about the victims must have resonated with him.'

'But what?'

'Maybe he saw them in his everyday life. Maybe he worked in a store they frequented, or he was a delivery man. Hell, maybe he's their dentist.'

'He's definitely not their dentist.' Anderton cracked a small smile. 'I'm not a rookie, Winter. Believe me, we dug as deep into their lives as we could get, but there were no points of intersection.'

'Not even between two of them?'

'Not even.'

'I find that hard to believe. In any given day you're going to have dozens upon dozens of interactions. Most of those will be so small that they barely register. Like a thank you for the kid at the store who bagged your groceries, or a quick shared look with the person sitting opposite you on the bus, or asking that guy who just stepped into the elevator what floor they want. But if one of those people happens to be a serial killer, and you happen to be their type, then you can bet your ass that it's going to register with them.'

'And I agree with everything you just said, but my previous statement still stands: as of right now we have yet to come up with an intersection point. Okay, your turn. What's bugging you?'

'The fact that this guy doesn't profile like a bomber. He devotes a lot of care and attention to building his bombs. They're a real labour of love. Which is exactly what you'd expect to see. But that's where it ends. A big part of the game for a bomber is the bang. This guy doesn't seem bothered by that, though. It's like sex without the orgasm. He's done the wining and dining, and the foreplay, he's even got naked and sweaty, then he pulls out before the big payoff. It doesn't make sense.'

'Yeah, that's been on my mind, too. So why go to the trouble of building a bomb if you're not going to watch it explode?' Anderton fell quiet for a second. 'It's like he doesn't care what happens. He plants his bomb and that's where it ends for him.'

'Like I said, it doesn't make sense.'

'No, it doesn't.

'Okay, your turn,' Winter said.

'What about the lack of escalation? I'd expect to see the

ante being upped significantly with each kill, but that hasn't happened. We're on the countdown to murder number four. The buzz won't be anywhere near as intense as it was for Isabella Sobek's murder. He's going to be gaining in confidence as he gets more practised, and he's going to be getting dulled to the experience. So why aren't we seeing this reflected in the murders?'

'It's like he's got himself locked into a groove that he's happy to stay in.'

'But serial killers don't operate like that,' Anderton said.

'No, they don't.'

'So what's going on?'

Winter shook his head. 'It's a good question.'

'Well, when you get a good answer, feel free to share. Okay, your turn.'

'The cat feels like a missed opportunity.'

'The one the Kirchners owned? What was it called again? Mouse?'

'Yeah, that's the one. Anyway, Mouse was locked in the kitchen because he kept throwing up hairballs, so the killer would have seen him when he arrived. Now we know this guy's a sadist. He's looking to terrorise his victims. And we know that people love their pets.'

'So why not leave Mouse in the kitchen with the victim?' Anderton said. 'Why let him out?'

'Exactly. Imagine you're taped to the chair and the cat is wandering around, blissfully unaware of what's going on. Maybe it rubs up against your legs looking to be fed. Maybe it jumps up onto your lap wanting to be stroked. Whatever it's doing, you're going to be aware of it.'

'And you're going to be aware of the fact that you're power-less to do anything to save it,' Anderton put in. 'Because that's this guy's main weapon. He disempowers his victims. Leaving the cat with them would be another way for him to underline the fact that he's in control. Okay, here's another thought, why not just kill the cat? He could even have made Alicia watch.'

'Like I said, it's a missed opportunity.'

They drifted into another silence, Mozart playing gently in the background. Full dark had fallen and the moon sat big and fat in the night sky. Up here on the fifteenth floor they could see the lights of West Vancouver stretching into the distance. In the foreground, the water of the harbour stole the darkness and held on to it.

Anderton finished her drink and stood up. 'I'm going to go.'

Winter nodded to her empty glass. 'Sure I can't tempt you to another? Sobek's paying.'

'You can tempt me, but I'll have to say no. It's a big day tomorrow. I really should try to get some sleep. You as well.'

'Not going to happen. I get the feeling tonight's going to be one of those nights where the insomnia wins.'

After showing Anderton out, he locked the door and made sure the limiter was in place. It was unlikely the killer would come after him here, though. This one was a shy boy. A move like that just didn't fit with what they knew. Winter went back into the main part of the suite, topped up his tumbler and sat down on the sofa. He picked up his laptop and found a recording of Mozart's Requiem. Everything that Mozart ever composed was stored on his hard drive. That said, he was always on the lookout for new recordings. His aim was to find the defining versions of each piece. New recordings were appearing all the time, so this was a work in progress, one that would keep him going to his dying day.

The orchestra started up and Winter stretched back on the sofa. This was the last piece Mozart ever wrote, one that he never got around to finishing. All sorts of legends and stories had grown up around it, which gave it an added air of mystique. The music was dark and oppressive, as though death was stalking the space between the notes. It seemed to suit the mood. There were just too many uncertainties right now. Was the killer going to strike tomorrow? If so, where? Everyone was living on borrowed time, but for one person in the city time was running out quicker than they could possibly imagine. Perhaps they'd seen the interview. Perhaps they'd be able to save themselves. Winter hoped so. When he closed his eyes all he saw was the sand running through the hourglass faster than ever.

In a little over two hours' time August 4 would become August 5. Neil Armstrong had been born on August 5, 1930, and gone on to great things. His one small step would be talked about for as long as mankind was writing history.

And last year on August 5 Lian Hammond had died.

And on August 5 the year before that Alicia Kirchner had died.

And the year before that it had been Isabella Sobek's turn to get taped to the chair.

The date had to be significant. It couldn't be random. Winter navigated to the folder containing the emails from Anderton, and scrolled down until he found the attachments relating to Isabella. He opened the transcript of Anderton's first interview with Sobek and began to read. He could hear Sobek's arrogance in the printed words. He could sense the perceived superiority. Some people considered psychopaths to be the next stage in human evolution. Who knows, maybe they were. And if that turned out to be the case, world watch out. Winter picked up his tumbler and took a sip, then carried on reading, searching for the significance of that date. It was going to be a long night.

16

Winter woke up on the sofa with a crick in his neck, a banging in his head, and no answer to the question of why August 5 was so important. His laptop was on the table, but he couldn't remember putting it there. The last time he'd checked his watch it was after two. There was a quarter-inch of whisky left in the tumbler.

The banging started up again and it took a moment to work out that this wasn't the start of a hangover. He stood up, scrubbed at his face to work the sleep away, then went to answer the door. Before opening it, he checked the spy hole. Just in case. The woman standing beside the room-service trolley looked too awake for this time of the day. According to his watch it wasn't even six yet.

Winter yawned, then stood to one side so she could push the trolley in. She parked it by the sofa, then left quickly. Thankfully, she didn't say anything. He walked over to the trolley and checked it out. There was a bit of everything. Pastries, fruit, cereal. Bacon and pancakes. Lots of coffee. He hadn't been sure what he'd feel like, and Sobek was paying, so he'd used the scattergun approach when ordering. Right now, though, he didn't feel much like eating anything. He poured a coffee, loaded it with sugar and called that a good start.

It looked like it was going to be another beautiful day. The sun was on the rise and the water of the harbour was glowing orange. The birds had the cloudless sky all to themselves. He drank some coffee and checked his cell. The world he'd woken up to was as close to the one he'd fallen asleep on as to make no real difference. Nothing happening on the case. Nothing out of the ordinary happening anywhere.

He finished his coffee and hit the shower, blasting it hot then cold until he felt human again. He dressed quickly. Clean jeans because yesterday's were a bit stale, and a clean T-shirt because he wasn't a complete slob. Frank Zappa was staring out from the front of the T-shirt, wild eyed and crazy as a loon. The long hair reminded him of Sobek's. He still wasn't hungry but forced himself to eat. There was no telling how long it would be before he got the chance to eat again.

A cab was waiting at the Shangri La's entrance. The driver looked half asleep and was giving off a vibe like he'd rather be anywhere but here. This wasn't a problem. If he'd been looking for conversation it wouldn't have ended well. Winter knew how and where to hide the bodies. The driver asked him where he wanted to go. Winter told him. The driver's surprise lasted all of two seconds. He shrugged a 'whatever' then pulled away from the hotel.

Winter spent the first part of the journey checking to make sure they weren't being tailed. Freeman had promised to back off, but Winter had been around long enough to know that words meant only as much as you wanted them to mean. This time of day, the streets were practically empty. If anyone had been following they would have stood out straight away.

Fifteen minutes later the cab stopped outside the tall iron

gates that marked the main entrance of Mountain View Cemetery. An Aston Martin Vantage was parked a little further up the street. It was a fine-looking vehicle. Sleek, grey and stylish. The cemetery was a 106-acre swathe of green that sat slap bang in the middle of Vancouver. As the name suggested, there was a great view of the mountains to the north. The location was a developer's dream. They'd kill to get their hands on a site like this. The sign on the gate stated that the cemetery opened at seven. According to Winter's watch it was five before. According to his eyes, the gates were wide open. It didn't matter where you were in the world, money talked.

Winter told the driver to keep the meter running and got out. He closed the door and walked over to the gates. The area was deserted. Anyone with any sense was still in bed. He glanced back at the cab. The driver was already tugging his baseball cap over his eyes and settling down for a nap. Winter had printed off a map of the cemetery in the Shangri La's business centre. Isabella Sobek's grave was marked with a red cross.

He lit a cigarette and started walking. He was almost down to the butt by the time he reached the grave site. It was a picturesque spot in the shade of an alder tree. Rows of headstones spread out in all directions. They'd been positioned with military precision, order imposed on the chaos and uncertainty that inevitably followed every death. Winter took one last drag on his cigarette, stubbed it out, then pushed the butt into his cigarette pack. He'd find a trash can later.

Nicholas Sobek was already here. He would have arrived as the sun came up, and he'd be here until it went down again.

That's what had happened for the last two years. Why should this year be any different? He was sitting on a fold-up camping chair at the foot of his wife's grave, gazing toward the mountains. The sun was still working at warming up the day and he was wearing a leather jacket. His long hair had been washed and brushed through and hung down loose to his collar. It looked as though he'd trimmed his beard.

Isabella's grave was marked with a five-foot high white marble angel. The pedestal was engraved with her dates. She'd been born in March 1982, which made her a Pisces, and she'd been murdered on August 5 three years ago, which meant that she'd only lived to be thirty. The epitaph read: A THOUSAND YEARS BEGINS AND ENDS WITH YOU. The words sounded impressive and heartfelt, but what did they actually mean? That was the thing with death, the big gestures always seemed to ring hollow. There was an empty camp chair next to Sobek's. Winter sat down and crossed his legs, then gazed toward the north where the mountains were rising up from the land, huge and humbling.

'I was wondering when you'd turn up,' Sobek said.

17

'On this day in 1966, the Beatles released *Revolver* in the UK,' Winter said.

'And four years earlier in 1962, Nelson Mandela was arrested,' Sobek replied.

'And three years ago you killed your wife.'

Sobek stopped staring at the mountains and turned to face Winter. 'I thought we established that I didn't do it.'

'No, we established that you didn't murder her. That's not the same thing. You killed Isabella when you opened the kitchen door. That's a fact. There's no doubt whatsoever. You killed your wife.'

Sobek locked eyes with Winter. 'Do you have any idea what it feels like to kill someone you love? Do you have any idea how much guilt that entails?'

'I can imagine.'

'No you can't. There's no reference point for something like this. Either you've passed through the hurricane, or you haven't.'

'Believe me, I know what it's like to pass through the hurricane.'

'I don't think so.'

'I guess we'll have to agree to differ, then.'

'Anderton tells me you spoke to Eric Kirchner yesterday, and that you tried to speak to David Hammond. Is that why you're here? You want me to describe what it felt like to kill Isabella?'

'Actually, I was hoping you'd tell me how you two met.'

That stopped him in his tracks. 'And how will that help to catch her killer?'

'Something about the victims resonated with this guy. He didn't choose them at random. Because Isabella was his first, that resonance would have been stronger with her than it was with the other two victims. She was the catalyst for turning fantasy into reality. If we can work out how she appeared on his radar, then we can catch him. The more I know about Isabella, the more chance there is of that happening.'

Sobek picked up a flask and nodded a question. Winter nodded an answer. The coffee was strong and bitter. No sugar, but he drank it anyway. The smell of coffee wafted between them for a second before being picked up by the breeze and blown away to nothing.

'Isabella applied for a job at my company. I was looking for a new PA. I still remember the moment I first saw her. The door opened and there she was, the most beautiful woman I'd ever set eyes on. Have you ever wanted someone so much that it feels like your heart is being cut from your chest?'

Winter shook his head. 'I can't say I have.'

'Well, up until that point, neither had I. But that's what it felt like.'

'Did she get the job?'

'Of course she did. It took a month before she would agree to have dinner with me. Eight months later we were married. And two years after that she was dead.'

Winter drank some coffee and went back over what Sobek

had just said. It sounded plausible, but it didn't sound like the whole truth. He thought about Isabella being a possession, something for Sobek to own.

'When you hired Isabella she was seeing someone, wasn't she?'

'She was,' Sobek replied carefully.

'Which would have made her all the more attractive. After all, it's the forbidden fruit that tastes sweetest. So how did you get the boyfriend out of the equation? You couldn't just leave things alone and hope that they'd split up. That's too passive. And you wouldn't have been happy having an affair because you needed the world to see that you owned her. And you couldn't just buy the boyfriend off because he might have told Isabella, and then she wouldn't have wanted anything to do with you. My guess is you framed him.'

'Watch what you're saying. This is my wife you're talking about.'

'What's interesting about that statement is that you haven't refuted what I said.'

Sobek stared and said nothing.

'If you see something you want, you've got to have it, right? Whatever it takes. Planes, cars, houses. Women. So how did you frame him? If I were in your position, I'd make it look as though he was having an affair, and then I'd arrange it so that Isabella found out.'

'You're wrong.'

Winter noted the slight tightening of his jaw. It was the tiniest of tells, but a tell nonetheless.

'There was a white van parked near the entrance to the cemetery. I'm assuming that it has something to do with you.

How many people have you hired to watch the cemetery?'

Sobek's jaw tightened again. Tiny twitches of the muscles. He ran a hand through his hair, pushing it away from his face. 'I don't know what you're talking about.'

'Serial killers like to visit their victims' graves,' Winter said. 'It gives them an opportunity to relive the crimes. The anniversary of the murder is the optimal time for these visits because emotions are that much higher. That's why you're here, isn't it? This has nothing to do with honouring the memory of your wife, and everything to do with drawing the killer out. Seeing you at the gravesite would really give those memories an extra charge.' He paused a moment, then added, 'Yesterday we agreed to play straight with one another. It's time to fess up.'

For a moment Sobek said nothing. This silence was different, though. It was a pause for breath rather than an evasion. He sipped some coffee and looked at the stone angel guarding his wife's grave. 'There are private investigators watching all of the cemetery entrances. I've also got investigators watching the cemeteries where Alicia Kirchner and Lian Hammond are buried.'

'And what happens if the killer turns up?'

Sobek smiled. 'If that happens I'll do my civic duty and make a citizen's arrest, and then I'll hand him over to the police.'

'What happens if he resists arrest?'

'Then I will match his resistance with whatever force I deem necessary.'

'And whose face do you see when you're using the punching bag in your gym?'

'I can control my emotions.'

'Of that I have no doubt. What I would question is how much you might want to control them.'

Sobek said nothing.

'You know,' Winter went on, 'the most helpful thing you could do right now is keep out of the way and let everyone do their jobs. The last thing this investigation needs is a vigilante running amok.'

'That sounds like good advice,' Sobek replied sarcastically. 'I'll take it on advisement.'

Winter placed his cup on the ground and stood up to leave. 'Thanks for the coffee.'

'I'm expecting regular updates throughout the course of the day.'

'I'm sure that Anderton will be happy to provide them for you.'

Winter walked away without looking back. His phone buzzed when he was in sight of the main gates. He took it out. The ten voicemails from Anderton covered the time he'd been with Sobek. The grave must have been in a dead spot. Literally and figuratively. Winter played the first message. The signal kept breaking up but he was able to hear enough.

Another bomb . . .

A kid . . . ten years old . . .

Call me now.

He found Anderton's number and connected the call.

Then he started running.

18

There were four news trucks already on Spencer Avenue, technicians and reporters buzzing around them. The largest was black with Global BC's logo on the sides. Charlotte Delaney was standing beside it, giving orders, arms jerking to emphasise whatever point she was making. She was smaller than Winter remembered, as though being away from the studio had somehow shrunk her.

Barriers blocked off the road on the other side of the news trucks, and beyond that police vehicles were parked nose to tail. Cruisers, vans, SUVs. The house was twenty yards further on. It was cosy looking, with crimson cladding and a tidy tree-lined front yard. Two bedrooms, probably. Certainly no more. According to Anderton, this was where Myra Hooper had lived with her ten-year-old son, Cody. It was Cody who detonated the bomb. Myra and her husband were separated.

There were ten cops in uniform on the far side of the barrier, and eight plainclothes detectives. Freeman would already be in the house. He'd want a ringside seat. For now there was only a handful of people watching, neighbours for the most part, curiosity getting the better of them. As the news spread, the crowd would grow.

Winter settled up with the cab driver, gave him a healthy tip for breaking the speed limit, then got out. He wasted no time getting into Anderton's Mercedes. Delaney's attention was focussed on what was happening on the other side of the barriers, but she could turn around at any moment. The last thing he wanted was to talk to her. It was early days. Information would be scarce and she'd be looking for anything she could get hold of to pad out the story. For a moment he gazed out of the windshield, hypnotised by the scene. Like ants in an ant farm, he thought, everyone scurrying around and keeping busy.

'We didn't save her,' he said, breaking the silence.

'You can't blame yourself for what happened.'

'I don't. Did I build the bomb? Did I tape it to anyone's chest?'

'Yeah, well, I do feel guilty. I can't help feeling that I could have done more. It's like this guy's been getting the better of me for the past three years.'

'Maybe so, but you need to park that guilt. It isn't helping.'

'I guess. At least you were wrong about the next victim being a kid.'

'And for once I have no problem with being wrong.'

'So what happened? Did he fit the bomb with a trip switch?'

Winter shook his head. 'I'm certain there was no trip switch. The killer used Cody as leverage. Eight words is all it would have taken. *Do what I say or the boy dies.* The bond between a mother and her child is sacred. It's the strongest there is. Put in that situation, most mothers would sacrifice themselves without a second thought. There is a bright side, though.'

'There is?'

'This investigation has just turned hot again. That means

a whole load of new information will come to light. Information that we didn't have yesterday. To start with, he decided to strike in the morning this year. Then there's the fact that he used Cody to trigger the bomb rather than the husband. So why change his MO?'

'He used Cody because Myra and her husband were separated.'

'Okay, but why not target someone who is married?'

Anderton shrugged. 'Good question.'

Winter watched the cops milling around outside the crime scene for a moment. 'We need to get into the house. That's where we'll find answers.'

'And how do we do that?'

'We could march up to the front door and demand to be let in. You've got thirty years of experience as a homicide cop under your belt, and I've been around the block a few times. They'll welcome us in with open arms.'

Anderton almost smiled. 'I don't think that Freeman will see it like that.'

Winter looked at the house, and then over toward the news trucks. Delaney was as animated as ever. It was like she'd been mainlining caffeine.

'I've got an idea. Follow my lead.'

He got out of the car and walked over to the Global BC news truck. Anderton was right behind him. Delaney noticed them when they were ten yards away. She waved a cameraman in behind her and came over to meet them.

'Mr Winter, it's so good to see you again.' She glanced at Anderton. 'Laura.'

'Charlotte,' Anderton replied.

'No hard feelings about the interview, then?' Winter said.

'Of course not,' Delaney replied. 'It was a good interview. I haven't had that much fun in a long time.'

'How would you like an exclusive?'

'I'm listening.'

'First we need to talk. Off the record. That means the camera is switched off and pointing away from me.'

Delaney smiled then turned and spoke to the cameraman. He lowered his camera and took a step back. The reporters and technicians hovering around the other trucks were starting to pay attention. They were looking and pointing and speculating.

'We're now off the record,' she said.

'We spent last night going over the evidence again, and we noticed something that was missed. Something that points us toward the killer.'

'What?'

'Not so fast. We need to talk to Freeman and tell him what we've found. Then we'll be back to talk to you.'

'It would save time if you talked to me now.'

'Nice try.'

'I've got to ask, why are you doing this?'

'I thought that would be self-explanatory. Freeman will try to claim the credit for himself. I don't want that to happen.'

The explanation seemed to resonate with Delaney. She smirked like they were in this together. They weren't.

'I think the best place for the interview would be over there by the barrier,' Winter said. 'Having the house and all those cops in the background would provide a suitably dramatic background, don't you think?'

'I agree. And I'm still thinking that we should do the interview right now.'

'Of course you are.'

'Come on, you can't leave me hanging like this. At least give me a hint of what you've got.'

'We'll be back in five minutes. Be ready.'

Without another word, Winter headed for the barriers, Anderton at his side. 'Okay, the next part is down to you,' he whispered. 'This is the tough bit. We need to get through the front door of the house.'

'Easy. All we do is act like we're meant to be there.'

They ducked around the barrier, but only managed four steps before being challenged. The uniformed cop doing the challenging looked like a high-school student.

'You shouldn't be here,' he called out. He started walking on an intercept course, stopping when he was a couple of yards away. Anderton kept going and stopped directly in front of him. She was pushing right up into his personal space, holding her ground. The kid took a step back. 'What's your name?' she demanded.

'Didn't you hear what I said? You shouldn't be back here.'

'What's your name?'

'Matthews,' the kid stuttered.

'Officer Matthews, we're here on Detective Inspector Freeman's request. Now, we can go back to our car and call to tell him that you wouldn't let us through, but I can't see that one playing out too well. I take it you've heard his little speech about being part of the problem or part of the solution. How do you think he's going to react to someone who's adding to his problems?'

Winter almost felt sorry for the kid. His cheeks had gone pink and he didn't know where to look. Before he could say anything, Anderton put her fingers in her mouth and let out a long sharp whistle that made everyone in a twenty-yard radius stop and look.

'Jefferies!' she yelled out. 'Come here!'

A detective who'd been standing near the CSI truck started toward them. He was a good-looking black guy in a neat grey suit. Age-wise he was somewhere north of forty. Even at a distance Winter could sense the been-there-done-it vibe. Jefferies stopped in front of Anderton. His smile was wide, warm and genuine. He had neat, white, even teeth.

'You just can't keep away, can you?'

'I missed your ugly face too much.'

The smile disappeared, the eyes narrowed. 'With all due respect, shouldn't you be on the other side of the barrier?'

'Actually, I'm hoping you can help with that. I was just telling Constable Matthews here that we've got some information for Freeman. Urgent, time-sensitive information.'

'I don't know, Anderton. As you can imagine, he's pretty busy right now.'

'We met with him last night. He wanted to hear from us if we had anything to share. We've got something to share.'

Jefferies widened his gaze to include Winter. 'You're that guy who did the interview.'

'Guilty as charged.'

'The clip's had more than fifty thousand views on YouTube. "FBI Guy Loses His Shit", it's called. I tell you, it made me smile. So, this is what you do, then? Chase serial killers?'

'It's what I do.'

'Well, this is my first, and all I can say is that it's a whole new ball game. Give me a domestic homicide any day, or a drive-by shooting. At least there's a motive you can understand. Wife cheats, husband shoots her dead. Dealer cheats someone he shouldn't and winds up dead. That's where the story ends.' Jefferies turned back to Anderton. 'Here's an idea. Why not tell me what you've got and I'll pass the information on to Freeman.'

'So you can take all the credit? I think I'll pass. Look, all we need is five minutes.' When Jefferies didn't respond she added, 'Come on, if this wasn't important I wouldn't be asking.'

Jefferies went quiet for a second, then nodded. 'Okay, let's do this before I change my mind.'

He turned and started walking. Winter and Anderton fell in line behind him. Matthews was standing off to one side, out of his depth and happy to let the grownups make the big decisions. Jefferies made them wait at the kerb while he went inside the house to find Freeman. Winter kept getting strange looks from the people milling around outside the house. These were different from the looks he usually got. It made him wonder who else had seen the interview. He was beginning to wonder who *hadn't* seen it.

This was another reason he avoided talking to the media. Unwanted attention made him uncomfortable. Why did people chase fame? It made no sense. He could see Delaney getting organised on the public side of the barrier. The woman was a moth who would bash herself up against the limelight until her dying breath. Why? What was missing from her life? He just didn't get it.

It was another four minutes before Freeman and Jefferies appeared. Freeman was dressed from head to toe in a white forensic suit. He removed his face mask and let it dangle around his neck, then he pulled down the hood and walked over. Even though his hair was ruffled from the hood he would still have looked great on TV.

'You have one minute,' he said.

'I need to see the crime scene,' Winter told him.

'Goodbye.' Freeman turned to leave.

'Let me take a look. There's going to be something there that your people will miss. I guarantee it.'

Freeman turned back. There was anger in his face, impatience in his stance. 'Are you saying that my people are incompetent?'

'No, what I'm saying is that this is my specialty. You guys have got no experience of dealing with serial killers. I do. What's more, I'm happy to be used and abused. In fact, I welcome it. Anything to catch this guy.'

'Read my lips: it's not going to happen.'

Winter motioned to where Delaney was waiting by the barrier. 'I've promised Ms Delaney an interview. She's expecting an exclusive on how we've managed to uncover some new information that's going to lead you guys straight to the killer's door. That's why she's standing there salivating like one of Pavlov's dogs.'

'Except that hasn't happened, has it? There is no miracle breakthrough.'

'Which is why I'm going to talk about the way you're screwing up this investigation. You saw what happened to

Anderton. It wasn't pretty. Now put yourself in her shoes.'

'Is that supposed to be a threat?'

'There's no supposing about it.'

'I want you to leave. If you don't go voluntarily, I'll have you escorted.'

'Not going to happen. Delaney is desperate to fill up airtime, and I know how to give good media.' Winter paused and waited for Freeman to meet his eye. 'The thing is, so do you.'

Freeman stared over at Delaney while he worked through his options. Nobody liked to be forced into a corner, particularly when they were supposed to be in charge. He took a deep breath and forced out a sigh. His face was tight and he looked more pissed than ever.

'Okay, you can see the crime scene, but Jefferies will be babysitting you the whole time.' He turned to Jefferies. 'Do you understand? Don't let him out of your sight. Not for a second.'

'Yes, sir.'

He turned to Anderton. 'You don't get to go anywhere near the house. Do you understand?'

'That's fine with me, Peter.'

He stared for a second longer, then turned back to Winter. 'Anything you discover, you share. Do you understand?'

'That goes without saying.'

Freeman stomped off toward the house, pulling the hood and the mask back into place as he walked. Winter watched him go, considering the possible repercussions, then deciding he didn't care. All that mattered was that he'd just got his hands on that elusive Golden Ticket.

19

The Tyvek suit was too big and rustled whenever Winter moved. His breath was hot and moist from being bounced back by the mask. Jefferies was dressed the same and looked just as uncomfortable. Winter followed him up the path to the house and stopped at the front door. There was no evidence of a break-in, which was consistent with the earlier murders. According to one of Anderton's contacts, the current theory was that the killer had knocked on the door sometime yesterday evening, and the victim had opened it and let them in. This wasn't so far-fetched, not if the victims had known the killer. If that was the case then it was good news. The point where their lives had intersected hadn't been found yet, but it would.

Even if the victim hadn't known the killer, the theory might still hold. The key case was Ted Bundy. He hadn't charmed his way into his victims' homes, but he had charmed them into the back of his van by faking a broken arm. The point was that serial killers could be incredibly persuasive. This killer was profiling as being on the small side of average, so he wouldn't be physically intimidating. It wouldn't be too difficult for him to come up with a plausible sob story. And maybe he didn't need one. Maybe he posed as a delivery driver or a pollster, or maybe he wore a cop uniform. Because the terrifying truth was that most people were more than happy to open their door to a complete stranger.

Except that couldn't have happened here. The problem was Cody. It was possible that the killer had waited for him to go to bed before making his move. Possible, but unlikely. Again, the later and darker it got, the more suspicious you were going to be. The bomb had detonated at twenty after seven this morning. Working back, the most likely scenario was that the killer had got here in the early hours. The chronology didn't work. No one opened the door to a stranger in the middle of the night, not without thoroughly vetting their credentials to make sure they were who they claimed to be. Which meant that he had *not* got in through the front door.

'How did he get in?' Winter asked Jefferies. 'The back door or a window?'

'The back door.'

'Let's go.'

Jefferies led the way to the rear of the property. The backyard was small and tidy. There was a trampoline and a free-standing basketball hoop. Like any ten-year-old, Cody would have energy to burn. Planters were arranged neatly on the decking and there was a barbecue under a green tarpaulin cover. The garden table had space for four. Winter could hear the ghost echo of summer laughter hanging in the air.

The killer had made a small circular hole above the door handle with a glass cutter, then reached through, unlocked the door and let himself in. A CSI was dusting the door for prints. It was patient, careful work. Time always stretched out in crime scenes, everyone taking it slow, the worry of destroying evidence hanging constantly at your shoulder. They walked past the forensics specialist and went into the kitchen. Unlike the earlier scenes, it was still intact. Winter looked at Jefferies.

'I'm not seeing any devastation.'

'He did it in the bedroom this time.'

'Which is yet another change to his MO.'

'You make that sound like a good thing.'

'Not a good thing, the best. By understanding the reasons he changed MO we get an insight into his original intentions. By understanding those, we get to know him better.'

Jefferies was shaking his head, unimpressed. 'That all sounds unnecessarily complicated. Like I say, give me a drive-by shooting any day.'

'You're loving this really,' Winter said. 'Go on, admit it.'

'You think?'

Evidence of Myra and Cody's last evening together lay scattered throughout the kitchen. The wine glass with the red stain in the bottom, the tablet charging at one of the wall sockets. The backpack on the table, zipped up and ready for morning. All four dining chairs were upright and pushed neatly into their spaces.

The refrigerator was a place for hoarding memories. Photographs were held in place with magnets. Cody was in all of them. He appeared to be a happy kid. Dark hair, brown eyes, a goofy grin. Looks could be deceptive, but not this time. Sometimes what you saw was what you got. There were a couple of pictures with Mom, the resemblance immediately apparent. Same eyes, same turn to the mouth when they smiled. There were no pictures of Dad. Winter reached out with a gloved hand, his fingertips brushing down over the photographs. Then he closed his eyes and stepped into the zone.

*

The night has the magic to turn the mundane into something re-markable. The moonlight is the catalyst. It has carved the trampoline and basketball hoop into shining grey sculptures. The lawn is a grey lake, the fence and trees rising around it like mountains. The world I now inhabit is a world of unlimited potential. I walk carefully and quietly to the back door, aware of every breath, every heartbeat, every footfall. The neighbouring houses are as silent as this one. I cut a hole in the glass and use the sucker cup to lift it away. In my mind I can see it crashing to the ground and shattering into pieces. I can see the lights coming on. I can hear the sirens.

I lay the circle of glass carefully on the ground and let myself in. The air holds the memory of the last meal that was eaten here. The silence holds the promise of everything that's yet to come. I pull the kitchen door open and walk through the darkness to the hall. For a moment I stand at the bottom of the stairs, listening. Nobody is moving around upstairs. Mother and son are fast asleep. I go up to the second floor and make my way along the landing. Do I go to the boy's room first? Probably. I'd need to assure myself that he's not going to be a problem. I take a peek inside. He's fast asleep.

I back out of the room, closing the door gently, then walk along the landing to the mother's room. For what feels like the longest time I just stand there watching her sleep, imagining the possibilities.

So much potential.

She comes awake in an instant, eyes wide, her scream caught in my gloved hand. She's struggling and the fear makes her strong.

'Do what I say or the boy dies.'

This is spoken in a sharp whisper. She goes still immediately. There's hatred burning in her eyes, but she's hanging on my every word, waiting for the next order.

20

Winter stood in the doorway of Myra Hooper's bedroom, momentarily transfixed by the devastation. Two CSIs were working the scene as painstakingly as their colleague downstairs. It only took a moment to turn a home into a death house. One squeeze of the trigger, or a single thrust of the knife. Or, as was the case here, a Christmas-tree light bulb overloading and exploding. Yesterday Myra and Cody's existence had been travelling on a familiar track of school, work and mealtimes, the familiar routines that define so many lives. Today that train had been well and truly derailed. Nothing would ever be the same again.

Winter took a breath and his nose filled with the stink of Myra's death. The Fourth of July tainted by the smell of charred meat. There was an earthy undertone there too. Piss and shit. The stench of death. He walked over to the bed and looked down at Myra's ruined body. Pieces of the bomb were still taped to her chest. Tape to bind her ankles together, tape to bind her hands. A strip across her mouth to stop her screams and shouts escaping. Her chest was a bloody shredded mess. It had been ripped apart when the bomb went off and the red-hot ball bearings had slammed into her. Like buckshot at point-blank range. Her hair and skin were burnt. Clothes and bed linen, too. After the explosion, Cody had rushed in here. He'd used a quilt to stop the fire getting hold, starving it of the oxygen it craved. His quick thinking meant that there was a crime scene to investigate. Unfortunately, no amount of quick thinking had been enough to save his mom.

'Any thoughts?' Jefferies asked.

'Nothing yet.'

'Okay, let me explain how this sharing thing works. We give you access to the crime scene and you tell us who this guy is. And what his Social Insurance Number is. And his address. And, most importantly, how we catch him.'

That was worth a laugh. 'If only it was that easy.'

'Freeman's going to give me the third degree. You need to give me something to work with here.'

'And I will. As soon as I've got anything you'll be the first to know.'

Winter walked out of the room, closing the door behind him. Then he shut his eyes and imagined that he was a ten-year-old boy who was just about to kill his mom.

*

The first thing I see when I wake up is the bedside clock. I have to look twice because there must be a mistake. Usually Mom has got me up before now. I head downstairs, wiping the sleep from my eyes and wondering where she is. Maybe I call out for her. Then again, maybe I'm still too sleepy for that.

There's no sign of her in the kitchen. Usually she has breakfast ready by now. I call out, but she's not answering. I head to the living room, but she's not there either. I go back upstairs. I'm wide awake now, and starting to worry. What if she died during the night? She's not old, but young people can have heart attacks.

Or maybe she's run away. Maybe that's it. Or maybe she's been kidnapped or something.

I call out again as I run up the stairs. By the time I get to her bedroom I'm shouting at the top of my lungs, yelling out for her over and over like I'm four again. I pull down on the handle. The door opens an inch, then the explosion slams it back into the frame.

21

Winter opened his eyes, then opened the bedroom door. Jefferies was standing on the other side, watching. Beyond him, Myra was lying still and lifeless.

'Why has he moved upstairs?' Winter asked.

'This one I do know the answer to. He was worried that he'd wake the kid if he tried to take his mom downstairs.'

'So, it comes down to risk management?'

'That's how I see it,' Jefferies said. 'The killer breaks in, overpowers mom and gags her. The kid's room is at the other end of the landing. So long as he's quiet, he could pull this off without waking him.'

A quick nod. 'Yeah, that works.'

Winter retraced his route to the back door, only this time he was thinking about how Myra and Cody had lived rather than how Myra died. He stopped in the living room and looked around. Like the other rooms, it was cosy and comfortable. The sofa was well worn and the wall-mounted TV had a games console wired into it. The controller was lying discarded on the floor next to a bright yellow beanbag.

Collages of holiday photographs were displayed in two large frames behind the sofa. Photographs taken on tropical beaches, photographs on mountains, a photograph with a volcano in the background, evidence of a family who'd liked to travel and have fun together. Scott Hooper wasn't in any of the pictures. Maybe he'd taken these, but more likely they'd been censored in light of the separation. The framed photograph near the door had been professionally shot. Myra and Cody were looking at each other and laughing. They looked so happy together. There was a band of brighter paint around the frame. Clearly there had been a larger picture here at some point in the recent past. One that had Scott Hooper in as well?

Winter stopped at the kitchen door and pushed it closed. Then he pulled it open and imagined the blast tearing a heart apart. Jefferies was standing close by, looking impatient.

'And?' he asked.

Winter shook his head. 'I've got nothing.'

'How did I know you were going to say that?'

'I'm not holding back.'

'I'd expect you to say that, too.'

'It's the truth. Right now, I'm suffering from information overload. It's making it difficult to see things clearly. I feel like there's something staring me straight in the face but I just can't see it.'

'Bullshit.'

'Believe what you want.' Winter paused. 'Why did he change his MO? Why did he choose to strike in the morning rather than the evening? Why the bedroom rather than the kitchen? Why risk breaking into the house? Those are the questions that need to be answered. That's how you're going to catch this guy.'

Jefferies smiled then nodded his head like everything had suddenly become obvious. 'Okay, I see how this works. This is the point where you get hit by a sudden moment of inspiration and tell me who did it. Just like Columbo, right?'

'If only.'

Winter walked into the kitchen. He still couldn't shake the feeling that he was missing something. The problem was that the harder he chased it, the more elusive it became.

'Still waiting for that Columbo moment,' Jefferies said at his shoulder.

'Tell you what. Give me your card and I'll call you as soon as I've got anything worth sharing.'

Jefferies pulled a card from his wallet and handed it over. His face broke into a broad grin. 'I'm getting a real sense of déjà vu here. They always promise to ring, but they never do.'

'This is a two-way street, Jefferies. If you get anything worth sharing, you contact us.'

The grin turned to a laugh. 'And why is it that there are always strings attached?'

22

Delaney was still waiting at the barrier when Winter got outside. She caught him looking and waved. He held up a finger to indicate that he'd only be a minute. Not that the interview was ever going to happen. He'd just used her as a stick to beat Freeman with. Anderton was on the sidewalk, lost in thought. Winter walked over and joined her in staring at the house.

'What are you doing?'

'I'm getting a new perspective. With the first three murders I was always inside the house. I hardly spent any time outside.' She waved her arm in a loose arc that went from left to right and took in half a dozen houses. 'I look over there and what I see is a row of houses that appear more or less the same. Except they're not the same. One of them is now a murder house. So what made Myra Hooper and her son so special? What made them stand out?'

'In other words, how did they appear on the killer's radar?'

She nodded. 'We've already established that this killer is highly organised. He didn't just walk along this street and think to himself, you know what, that looks like a nice house, there are probably some nice people living there, I think I'll go and knock on the door and turn their lives into a nightmare.'

'He knows his victims' routines,' Winter said. 'With the

first three murders he knew that they got home before their husbands. He also knew that there would be enough time to set up the bombs and get out of there.'

'That much I've already worked out. Tell me something new.'

'Okay, how about this? The fact that he knows their routines is one of the reasons he changed his MO.'

'I'm listening.'

'Because it's summer break, Cody was at a kids' club while his mom was at work. She picked him up on the way back, so they arrived home together. But the killer needed it to be staggered. He needed Cody out of the way so he could get everything organised. That's why he broke into the house in the middle of the night. Cody would have been fast asleep and blissfully unaware of what was happening. When he woke up the next morning he went around the house looking for her. He opened her bedroom door and that's when the bomb went off.'

Anderton shook her head in frustration. 'What's going on Winter? It's like he's taken his MO and just ripped the whole thing up.'

'What if Cody *was* the target?'

'So why not follow through?' She paused for a second, then answered her own question. 'Because of your interview with Delaney. Assuming Myra had seen it, she would have tried to topple the chair. But, like we discussed earlier, she couldn't do that if he was using Cody for leverage.'

'That's how I see it, but we're getting away from the point. How did he know their routine?'

'Because he was watching them.'

'Except we know from the previous murders that he wasn't. No one saw him hanging around outside the houses. That's the one part of his MO that won't be changing any time soon. This guy lives in the shadows. He doesn't want to be seen.'

'Cameras?'

'That's the obvious solution. He sets up a camera to cover the front of the house, and removes it when he arrives to carry out the actual murder. Or maybe he does his surveillance a week or two before. After all, he's just trying to get a rough idea of his victims' day-to-day routines and that won't change much from week to week. Leaving a gap would make it harder for a witness to connect him to a crime. You might remember someone suspicious hanging around your street the day before a murder. But two weeks? Or a month?'

'And it would also explain why we didn't find any evidence of camera surveillance.'

Winter turned full circle, wondering where you could hide a camera. The trees that bordered the left-hand side of the property were the best bet, but the angles weren't brilliant. He crossed the street. The front yards on this side stopped at a line of tall fir trees that looked as though they'd been here since the houses were built. He walked to the right, glancing back every couple of steps to make sure he could still see the front of Myra's house. He stopped when he lost sight of it. Anderton was doing the same, but in the opposite direction.

It took longer to walk back. Every tree needed to be checked. It was slow, careful work. Winter could see Anderton up ahead, mirroring what he was doing, checking the trees along her stretch. Ten minutes later he was starting to think this was pointless. If the killer had carried out his surveillance some time back in July then it was unlikely that they'd find anything. He glanced over and saw Anderton move in to get a closer look at something. Her body language changed in an instant. She was alert and poised, ready to jump for joy. Before she could call him he was already moving, covering the distance in less than ten seconds.

'Take a look,' she said.

She was pointing to a spot on the trunk about six feet up from the base. A ragged patch of the tree's smooth bark had been stripped away from the trunk. It was roughly the size of a cigarette pack, maybe a little bigger. A couple of the nearby branches looked as though they'd been snapped off. There was an unobstructed view all the way to the front door of Myra's house. Anderton pointed to the ground.

'And this,' she added.

There was a partial footprint in the dirt. Judging by the size, it had been made by an average sized woman, or a male who was below average height.

'I'm thinking he might be getting lazy,' she said. 'There was nothing like this at the other crime scenes.' She looked at the bare patch on the trunk again. 'If he used superglue, it would have taken seconds to position the camera. Then all he had to do was snap those branches away to clear a sightline. Maybe he pretended to be a jogger. He stops to catch his breath, checks the coast is clear, then sticks the camera to the tree and carries on his merry way.'

'And if he did use superglue that would explain the bald patch on the trunk. It must have come away when he removed the camera.'

'Also, superglue would tie in with the MO. That's what he used to attach the door sensors. Forensic evidence would be able to confirm if that was used here.'

Winter found the business card Jefferies had given him and punched the number into his phone. The detective answered on the third ring with a curt, 'Yeah, what is it?'

'I'm missing you, Jefferies.'

'Winter?'

'And you said I'd never call.'

'You've got something?'

'Maybe. We're across the street.'

'I'll be right there.'

'I'm counting the seconds.'

They were perfectly placed to see Jefferies launch himself from the front door. He stopped for a second, searching for them, then jogged over, undressing as he went. The hood went down first, then the mask. By the time he reached Winter he was pulling off the latex gloves and scrunching them into a ball.

'What have you got?'

Anderton fielded the question. This was her show. While they talked, Winter went back over what he'd seen inside the house, searching for that elusive something and hoping that it wasn't an elusive nothing. He closed his eyes but all he kept seeing was Myra's bedroom door opening, then the bright flash of the explosion. The picture in his head changed and he was now looking at Sobek's kitchen door. Again, it opened an inch and the picture in his head disappeared in a nuclear flash. One door opens, another closes. The phrase jammed in his head, the rhythm of the words creating a melody that, in turn, became an annoying earworm that wouldn't leave him alone. One door opens, another closes. One door opens, another closes. He was back outside Myra's bedroom, pushing the door open. And now he was back outside Sobek's kitchen, pushing the door open. And now he was standing with Eric Kirchner and he was about to push the door open. And now he was downstairs at Myra Hooper's house, pulling the kitchen door open.

He felt his breath catch and his heart accelerate and tried not to get too excited. Very occasionally you got a flash of insight that changed everything, a moment of total clarity where the only thing you knew for certain was that things would never be the same again. Anderton and Jefferies had stopped talking. He had no idea how long they'd been staring at him.

'What's going on?' Anderton asked. 'You've got a strange look on your face.'

'Who's your go-to guy for bombs?' he asked.

'Why?'

'Because I need to see him. Now.'

23

Anderton's go-to guy turned out to be a go-to gal. Heather Barnfield had been a bomb disposal expert for the British Army until she retired ten years ago. Her husband was originally from Canada and they'd decided to relocate here to while away their twilight years. Their house was on the banks of Harrison Lake. It was only an hour and a half from Vancouver but it might as well have been a different planet. The lake was surrounded by trees and mountains and plenty of fresh air. The water reflected the sky, shimmering and shining and perfect. Boats were skimming across the surface, sails blustering. The only sounds came from the birds and the breeze.

Anderton had spent most of the journey on her cell, calling in favours and mining for information. She'd managed to establish that Myra Hooper was thirty-one and had lived in Vancouver for most of her life. There was a three-year gap while she was at college in California, and six months spent travelling in Europe, but they were the only occasions she'd spent any real time away from the city. For the last three years she'd worked as a buyer for a firm that imported coffee. She'd been living apart from her husband for six months, but neither party had filed for divorce. Add in the fact that she was still using her married name and that got Winter wondering about a possible reconciliation. Cody was at elementary school, and by all accounts doing well. His grades were good and he'd never been in any real trouble. He liked sports and was on the school's soccer and basketball teams.

They parked next to a battered old pickup that must have had a couple of hundred thousand miles on the clock. Barnfield was waiting on the porch with a steaming mug of coffee in her hands. Her grey hair was tied up in a bun and she was wearing gold-rimmed spectacles. She could have been a librarian. Then again, looks could be deceptive. There was evidence of her previous occupation in the way that she carried herself. Her movements were economical and precise, and her brown eyes didn't miss a thing.

She waved and called out a 'hello'. Her accent was more working class than ruling class. Winter liked it, though. He'd always been a sucker for a British accent. She came down the porch steps to meet them, limping slightly, a Labrador at her heel. He looked more closely and noticed that her left leg was missing. Her jeans hid most of the prosthetic limb, but the sandals couldn't hide the fact that her feet didn't match. One was flesh and blood, the other titanium and latex. Judging by the way she moved, the limb had been amputated below the knee.

Barnfield caught him staring. 'It's not what you think. Shortly after we moved here I had a cycling accident. My advice, if you're going to pick a fight with a car make sure you're driving a lorry.' She laughed. 'It's ironic, really. I spend three decades working with bombs without losing so much as a fingernail and then something like that happens.'

'Not that it's slowed her down any,' Anderton put in. 'Last year Heather ran the Vancouver marathon. How much did you raise again?'

'Almost five thousand dollars. But that's by the by. The real achievement was that I got a better time than Dale. I still haven't let him forget that one.'

'And where is Dale?'

Barnfield pointed to a boat out in the middle of the lake. It was painted blue and didn't seem to be going anywhere any time soon.

'That's him out there. He tells me that he's fishing, but he never catches anything. I think it's just an excuse to get away from me.' She turned back to Winter and held her hand out. 'Heather Barnfield. You must be Jefferson Winter.'

They shook hands.

'So, can I get you a coffee? Tea, perhaps?'

'Coffee for me. Two sugars, please.'

'What about you, Laura? Anything?'

'A coffee would be good, thank you.'

Barnfield went up the stairs to the porch, one hand on the railing to keep the weight off her injured leg. There were two chairs on the porch, both pointed toward the water, a small table between. The view was spectacular. If Winter ever decided to settle down, this was the sort of place he would gravitate toward. He'd only been here for five minutes but he could already feel his thoughts and heartbeat quietening down. He accompanied her into the neat, orderly kitchen. Everything was squared away, every surface shone. The Labrador followed them in and headed straight for its bed in the corner.

The only nod to Barnfield's previous occupation was a framed photograph on one of the walls. She was standing in the middle of a group of soldiers, everyone dressed in battle fatigues. The fierce light and the sand-blown environment indicated that this had been taken a long way from Canada.

Given her age, Iraq or Afghanistan seemed most likely. She was a head shorter than her colleagues, and the only woman, but there was no question of her not belonging. She came over to where he was standing and handed him a coffee.

'Afghanistan, November 2001,' she said. 'Interesting times. It was just after 9/11 and everyone was still waiting for the dust to settle. Two of the men in that photograph are dead now, killed by IEDs. Whenever I start feeling sorry for myself this reminds me that there are worse things to lose than a leg.'

'I've got a few questions,' he said.

'And there was me thinking that this was a social call.' Barnfield smiled briefly, then turned businesslike. 'So, your bomber's struck again. He's a bit early this year.'

'He is. You were involved with the police investigation into the first three murders, right?'

Barnfield nodded. 'That's right. And I'm expecting to be called in to help with this one, too. That's who I thought was calling when Laura phoned earlier. The latest murder is all over the news.'

Winter hesitated for a second, aware that Anderton was watching. He'd run his theory by her in the car on the way here. She'd thought it was a good one. At least, she'd thought it was worth driving all the way out here to check it out, which amounted to much the same thing.

'The design of these bombs is fairly unique,' he said carefully.

'There's no "fairly" about it. They're completely unique. You work in law enforcement so you know all about fingerprints. Everyone's are different. With bombers, the design of the device is like their fingerprint. They all have materials they prefer to use, techniques they prefer to employ. Put two bombs side by side and I'd be able to tell you if they'd been built by the same person.'

'I'm figuring that a lot of thought goes into the design.'

'You have no idea. Bomb makers take an inordinate amount of pride in what they do. It's sick, when you think about it. A bomb has one purpose. To kill and maim. That's the only reason you build one.'

'What if there was another reason? What if it was designed to save lives?'

Barnfield frowned. 'I guess that the IRA would occasionally issue warnings so the area around the bomb could be cleared. But even then the bombs were designed to kill.' She shook her head. 'A bomb that saves lives, I just don't see it.'

'This bomber uses a pipe that's been cut down the middle in his design. By doing that the blast is deflected toward the victim. It all comes down to physics. Something that has forward momentum, whether that's a river or a waveform or the blast wave from an explosion, will always seek out the path of least resistance.'

'That's what's happened here. The blast is directed toward the victims. Ultimately, that's what kills them.'

'And because of the half-pipe, the ball bearings would have been directed toward the victim, too. Usually they would be spread over the blast zone.'

'That's correct.'

'And usually with pipe bombs, the pipe gets turned to shrapnel, which increases the killing power of the device. But that hasn't happened here. Again, it all comes down to taking the path of least resistance. The pipe doesn't get blown apart because it was cut in half. It doesn't enclose the explosion.'

'There is only one person being targeted here. The whole design of these bombs is informed by that.'

'Not the whole design. Bombs explode outwards, the blast wave growing uniformly until something gets in the way. But the blast wave from this bomb has been channelled toward the victim. And that's the perfect explanation. Firstly, because it's true, and secondly, because it plays into our prejudices. It's easy to believe in a crazed bomber who's hell bent on causing death and mayhem. Okay, let me ask you something. Let's say you were the bomber and you wanted to protect the person who opened the door and triggered the device, what changes would you make to this design?'

Barnfield thought this over for a second. A slow, sly grin spread across her face. 'Well, I'll be damned. I wouldn't change a thing. So why would he want to do that? Why not kill them as well?'

'That's the million-dollar question.'

'Judging by the fact you've driven all the way out here, you clearly believe this is significant.'

'This changes everything. Up until now, everyone has been focussing on the dead, but what if they're just collateral damage? What if he was actually targeting the people who triggered the bomb? What if this is all about the living?'

'And why do that?'

Winter shrugged and shook his head. 'At this stage, I'm not sure. The first thing I needed was confirmation that this theory was feasible. Which you've just given me.'

'It's definitely feasible. I've got to ask, though. How on earth did you reach this conclusion?'

'Because of the doors,' Anderton said.

'I'm not sure I follow.'

'At the first three scenes the doors all opened into the kitchen. The force of the blast pushed them back against the frame, creating a barrier between the person who'd opened the door and the blast.'

'They said on the news that the latest victim died in her bedroom. Based on that and what you've just said, I'm guessing that the kitchen door at the latest scene opened outwards?'

Anderton nodded. 'That's correct. The living-room door opened the same way, but the bedroom door didn't. If he'd done his thing in the kitchen, the force of the blast would have slammed the door into the person opening it, possibly injuring them. This guy doesn't want them hurt. Not even a little bit.'

Barnfield was shaking her head again. This time her smile didn't quite reach her eyes. Winter couldn't work out if she was feeling disgust, admiration or disbelief. Perhaps it was a combination of all three.

'I spent thirty years disarming bombs, everyone's from the IRA's to the Taliban's. You think you've seen everything, then something like this comes along.' Another shake of the head. 'A bomb designed to protect lives. Wait until I tell Dale about this.'

'I need to call Freeman,' Anderton said. 'He should know about this. Heather, thanks for your help.'

'My pleasure. And when you speak to Freeman tell him that I'm expecting to hear from him.'

Without another word, Anderton headed outside to the porch to make her call.

24

Barnfield sat down at the kitchen table and waved Winter into the seat opposite. The dog stirred and got up and started sniffing around his legs. He leant down and scratched it behind the ears. Judging by the way its tail kept bashing the floor, the gesture seemed to be appreciated.

'You don't mind dogs, then?' Barnfield said.

'I'm fine with them. I always wanted one as a kid, but my father wouldn't let me.'

'I'd always wanted one, too, but that was impossible while I was in the army. We got Zeus when we moved here. He's a good boy.'

On hearing his name, Zeus walked over to Barnfield, tail wagging. She fussed him for a bit, talking to him like he was a baby.

'Do you miss it?' he asked her.

'The army?' She shook her head. 'Not really. I guess there are days where I get nostalgic, but it doesn't last long. On the whole I much prefer life here. Nobody's trying to blow me up. What about you? Do you miss the FBI?'

'Not in the slightest.' He nodded toward the Afghanistan photograph. 'You belonged in the army. That much is obvious. I never belonged in the FBI. I was always the odd one out. I loved the work and I was good at it. It was the people and the politics that I had a problem with.'

'You don't play nicely with the other children?'

'I can play nice, but it gets to the point where I just want to poke their eyes out with a sharp stick.'

Barnfield laughed. 'I think that's true of every job.'

'I prefer the way I work now. I deal with people in short bursts. By the time I'm ready to start sharpening the sticks, I've already moved on.'

Barnfield glanced out the window and Winter followed her gaze. Anderton was talking on her cell, smiling and happy and more animated than he'd ever seen her. She had good news to share and was enjoying every minute. She moved to the left and momentarily disappeared from sight. Without her in the picture, the view looked like a painting. Water, mountains and that immaculate sky.

'It was wrong what they did to Laura,' Barnfield said. 'She gave everything to that investigation. I don't think anyone could have done a better job.'

'She's one of the good ones,' Winter agreed. 'But that's politics for you. It's not about competence, it's all about whether or not your face fits.'

'What's Freeman like? I haven't met him yet.'

'Let's just say that his face fits and leave it at that.'

Winter picked up his mug and took a sip. It was a damn sight more palatable than Sobek's coffee. Good-quality beans, just the right amount of sugar, and it hadn't been stewing in a flask. It was almost as perfect as the view.

'What sort of person would you need to be to build a bomb like this?' he asked.

Barnfield didn't answer straight away. She drank some coffee then put her cup down on the table. 'Interesting question. The first thing you'd need is patience, but that goes without saying. I take it you've heard the phrase "measure twice, cut once"? Well, that's doubly true when you're building bombs. Make a mistake and you'll wind up dead. Those are the stakes. But that's not what you want to know, is it?'

Winter shook his head.

'I'm not sure how to answer your question,' Barnfield said.

'If it helps, try imagining yourself as the bomber.'

'Okay, I'll give it a go.' She hesitated a moment while she thought this through. Her eyes were searching the corner of the room without really seeing anything. 'First, I'd need to establish what the bomb was for. In this case we have a rather unique situation. I want to kill someone, however, I want to make sure that a person who's only a few yards away is unharmed. The amount of explosives would be crucial. Too much and I'll end up blowing the door out, which could injure them. Too little and the person the bomb is attached to might live. At some point I'll have to carry out experiments to see how little I can get away with.' She stopped talking and looked at him.

'What is it?'

'That's your first big difference. Usually you wouldn't be too concerned with limiting the size of the explosion. Generally speaking, when it comes to IEDs, the bigger the bang the better. The people who build them are after the shock factor.'

'Good. What else can you tell me?'

'The bomber doesn't have a military background.'

'Why do you say that?'

'Because the design of this bomb requires a degree of lateral thinking, and that's not something you see much of in the military. You want soldiers to follow orders. When they start thinking for themselves, that's when the problems start. Also, he's not a professional bomb maker. If he was, I would have recognised the design. Something this distinctive would have been flagged up. What we're dealing with here is a talented amateur.'

'Okay, let's talk about the bomb. How does a talented amateur go about making something like this?'

'Like everything else these days, your start point is the internet. That's where you'll find everything you need. The internet has a lot going for it, but it also has a dark side. Anyone can get access to this information. The Taliban, Islamic State, some poor brainwashed kid in Iraq or Paris or wherever who decides they want to make their mark on history.'

'Is there anything about the design of this bomb that jumps out at you?'

'The fact that he uses fireworks. It's easy enough to build a detonator, but getting hold of explosives is much harder. You can't just walk into a shop and buy some Semtex. Using ammonium nitrate is one possibility, but there are a limited number of places you can buy fertiliser from. If you start buying in bulk then you might be remembered. Then there's the problem of getting the recipe right. It's not as easy to make a fertiliser bomb as you might think.'

'But fireworks are easy enough to get hold of.'

'They are. And you know that they're going to explode. To stretch the analogy, the recipe has already been cooked. That's what makes it the ideal solution. Experimenting with how much explosives you'd need is easy too. All you've got to do is wait for Canada Day to come around and you can make as much noise as you need and nobody will bat an eye. Okay, time to turn the question back on you. What sort of person do you think would build a bomb like this?'

Winter reached for his coffee and took another sip. 'It's like you said, this person is patient, which means that they're not going to be young. Let's face it, how many teenagers have you met who are happy to wait for tomorrow to come around? Generally speaking, serial killers tend to get started in their late twenties and thirties, and most of them are male.'

'What? You don't get female serial killers?'

'You do, but it's rare. Aileen Wuornos springs to mind. She killed seven men in Florida. Beverly Allitt is another one. She's from your part of the world.'

'Okay, what else can you tell me?' Barnfield asked.

'Aside from Lian Hammond, all his victims have been white, which means that he's most likely white. Serial killers tend to stick to their own racial group. He's also going to be below average height. Anderton found a footprint at the latest crime scene to support that, but even if she hadn't, the MO and choice of victims is indicative of that. And you're looking at someone who's socially adept. If you met this guy he'd probably come across as charming. This is someone who's brazen enough to walk right up to a front door in a middle-income neighbourhood and ask to be let in.'

'Or a higher-income area, as was the case with Nicholas Sobek.'

'Exactly,' Winter said. 'Also, this person is unlikely to be a blue-collar worker. I can't imagine him as a mechanic or a factory worker. This guy doesn't like getting his hands dirty. Figuratively or literally. As for what he does, I wouldn't rule out one of the creative fields.'

'Like an artist?'

'No. I'm thinking technically creative, like an architect or a software designer. He's going to be drawn to a profession that requires both logic and a creative flair.'

'So you're looking for a white male in his late twenties to early thirties, who's below average height and works as an architect or a software designer.'

'That's the bones of the profile,' Winter said.

'And you get all this from looking at the crime scenes.'

'The crime scene is important, but it's only a part of the story. The other part is examining the pre- and post-offence behaviour. Ultimately, I want to work out the why. What actually drives the behaviour?'

'Fascinating.'

'Well, it keeps me out of trouble.'

The door clattered open and Anderton came back in. Zeus was up and padding over to her in a heartbeat, demanding attention. She gave him the half-hearted pat of someone who'd never owned a dog. Zeus humphed his disapproval then flopped back down onto his bed and got comfortable again.

'Freeman says well done,' she said.

'I can feel the warm glow starting at my toes and spreading through my entire body.'

'He's also offered us a seat at the table.'

'Meaning?'

'Meaning that he would like to meet with us.'

'Well, that's progress, I guess,' Winter said. 'We must have impressed him.'

'Or he wants to keep us where he can see what we're up to.

Remember the old saying: Keep your friends close and your enemies closer.'

'So cynical.'

'No, just realistic.'

Anderton turned and smiled at Barnfield. 'Heather, thanks again for your help. Next time you're in the city, give me a call and we can go grab a coffee.'

'Or something stronger, perhaps?'

Anderton laughed. 'Yeah, that would work for me.'

They headed outside. Zeus brought up the rear, his tail circling around and around like a helicopter's rotor blades. Winter could see Dale's boat out in the middle of the lake. It was hard not to feel envious. The reality was that he'd probably be bored of fishing within five minutes, but the fantasy worked just fine. A world of peace and serenity rather than one defined by mayhem, destruction and murder was not without its appeal. There was another round of handshakes, then they climbed into Anderton's Mercedes and headed back west, granite and stone eventually being replaced by the tall steel and glass mountains that defined Vancouver. The sky was the same, though. Wide and clear and impossibly blue.

25

Anderton kept her foot down the whole way, shaving almost fifteen minutes off the return journey. By the time they hit the city limits it was noon. She hadn't said much since leaving Harrison Lake. Neither had Winter. Sometimes you needed quiet. Space to think. Winter was wondering about Freeman's agenda. Because there had to be one. When you were dealing with a political creature like Freeman there was always going to be an agenda.

The Vancouver PD's headquarters was based in an ugly utilitarian building on Cambie Street, right out on the edge of Mount Pleasant. It was constructed from brick and glass and ferocious right angles, and would never be beautiful no matter what was done to it. A five-minute walk east would take you to Eric Kirchner's depressing little one-bed apartment. Five minutes north and you'd be at the Shangri La.

Anderton pulled into a parking slot and killed the engine. She got out and they went inside. They passed through security quickly and headed for the elevator bank. The investigation was being run from an office up on the sixth floor. Anderton led the way like she'd been here a million times before.

'Is it weird being back?' Winter asked her.

'A little,' she admitted. 'You know, I've probably spent more of my waking hours in this building than anywhere else on the planet.' She shook her head and snorted to herself. 'I've never really thought about it like that up until now. That is so depressing.'

She hesitated at the incident room door, then pushed it open. The desks all faced a row of evidence boards that had been erected at the front of the room. There were only four detectives manning them. Three were on the telephone, one was on his computer. All four were animated and hard at work, which was understandable. A case that had been cold for the last three hundred and sixty-three days had just turned red hot. The clock was ticking. Forty-eight was the number in everyone's heads. If they didn't get this guy in the next forty-eight hours then it would be another three hundred and sixty-three days until he struck again.

Freeman was at the side of the room, giving one of his detectives a hard time. The detective seemed to be taking it all in his stride, like this sort of thing happened every day. And maybe it did. Freeman's management style was one of the reasons that Winter worked for himself. The only thing worse than being told what to do was being told what to do by a person you had zero respect for. They walked over. Freeman held up a finger to indicate that he'd be with them in a second, then went back to busting balls.

Inactivity had always made Winter edgy. Whenever he got bored his brain started looking for mischief. It had been the same when he was a kid. He'd always be reading or playing computer games or practising piano, anything to keep the boredom at bay. 'I'm going to take a look at the evidence boards,' he whispered to Anderton. 'Call me when Freeman's done.'

'Sure.'

He walked toward the row of boards at the front, aware that he was being watched. One of the first things he'd learned in the FBI was what it meant to be a necessary evil. The Behavioral Analysis Unit were called in to consult because when it came to profiling they were the best. The flipside was that there was always going to be someone on the investigation who viewed their presence as an affront to their competence. This time it was the person leading the investigation who viewed him as a necessary evil. Judging by the looks he was getting, he had a pretty good idea of what was being said behind his back. Not that it mattered. Having a serial killer for a father meant that he'd had to develop a thick skin. Being a Fed had toughened it up.

Winter started with the board at the far left and worked his way right. There were multiple pictures of the victims, both alive and dead. These were the attention grabbers, particularly the ones shot post-mortem. This time he was more concerned with the pictures of Cody and the husbands. There were plenty of them, too. They were the real targets. So, what had the killer seen in them? What had made him sit up and take notice? They'd been given a glimpse into how this guy thought. Now they had to work out what to do with that information.

The map on the middle board covered the same part of Vancouver as the map on the wall of his hotel suite. The difference was that Freeman had used red pins instead of inked crosses, and there were four rather than three. The newest pin marked Spencer Avenue, where Myra and Cody Hooper had lived. Once again it was within the circle that

Anderton had drawn on his map. A hundred thousand people lived in that area. Was the killer one of them? It seemed likely. Four times out of four he'd chosen to hunt here. This was an area he clearly felt comfortable in. These were streets he would have been intimately familiar with. If he didn't live there now, he'd lived there at some point in the past.

The board at the far right had three photographs, all pinned up that day. Myra Hooper was alive in the top one. This was a vacation photo taken in New York. She was standing outside the Majestic Theatre on Broadway. In the background was a partial glimpse of a *Phantom of the Opera* poster. She was happy and relaxed, totally oblivious of what the future held. The next photograph was from the crime scene. Myra was lying on her bed, her body destroyed by the blast. The third and final photograph was of Cody, the one from the refrigerator. He was staring at the camera and grinning his goofy grin. The background was too blurry to work out where it had been taken.

A low whistle carried through the room. Winter turned and saw Anderton gesturing to him. He walked quickly back past the boards, removing some photographs of each of the husbands as he went. Freeman and Anderton were talking footprints when he got there. The CSIs had concluded that the one found across the street from Myra's house had come from a man's shoe. The size was well below average, so the person who'd made it was probably well below average height. The depth of the impression pointed toward someone who was below average weight.

Anderton was nodding and making noises like this was

the first time she'd heard this information. It was too early to say whether the footprint had been made by the killer, but it was looking hopeful. The clincher would be finding traces of superglue on the tree trunk. Samples were being fast-tracked through the lab, but these things took time.

Winter cleared a space on a nearby desk, shuffled the photographs, then laid them down in three rows of three. The distribution of faces was completely random, which was what he had been aiming for. The first row started with Eric Kirchner in the top left corner and was completed with two pictures of Nicholas Sobek, one with a beard, one without. The second row began and ended with David Hammond. The third ended with Kirchner. Winter nodded toward the photographs.

'There's your killer.'

26

Freeman gave Winter a puzzled look, silence stretching between them. The incident room was filled with the noise of constant speculation, but it seemed to be happening a long way away.

'From the very start there's been a huge question mark hanging over the victimology,' Winter said. 'Well, that question mark has just been erased. The thing that connects the victims is the husbands. So, with that in mind, take another look at the photographs and tell me what you see. And I'm talking broad strokes rather than fine details.'

Freeman took a look, then said, 'They've all got black hair and brown eyes. And they're all in their thirties.'

'Exactly. And that description is going to apply to the killer. You're looking for someone with black hair and brown eyes who's in their thirties. Also, he was married at some point. I guarantee it.'

Freeman was shaking his head. 'That's sounds like one hell of a leap.'

'No it's not. Organised serial killers spend an inordinate amount of time selecting their victims. The victim is the foundation of the fantasy. It's the centre of everything. The process of choosing is not informed by whim, and that's why I've had a problem with this case right from the very beginning. The randomness of the victims makes no sense. Choosing Isabella,

Alicia and Lian just doesn't work. There are no physical similarities. They come from different age groups, two are Caucasian, one is Asian. If this was a disorganised killer then I could see how this might work. But this isn't a disorganised killer.'

'Winter's right,' Anderton put in. 'We've finally found a link.'

'Okay, but what about Myra Hooper's son? He's not in his mid-thirties. Nor is he married to the victim.'

'The latest murder is an anomaly,' Winter said. 'And that's something we should be thanking the gods who look down on murder detectives for. We're already a mile further down the road than we were yesterday. If we can answer the questions that this new murder poses then that road is going to take us all the way to his front door.'

'Is that something else you guarantee?'

'Yes, it is.'

'Okay, let's say you're right. How does this help?'

'It helps because it gives us an insight into how the killer is thinking. What are the husbands doing here? They're killing their wives. So the question becomes: why does the killer want his wife dead?'

'Maybe she cheated on him,' Anderton suggested. 'Or maybe she just got fed up and left him. Being married to a serial killer is not a recipe for long-lasting happiness.'

'You'd be surprised. My parents were married for thirteen years. They only got divorced after my father's arrest. Believe it or not, there were plenty of happy days before then. My mom wasn't stupid, she was just invested in making the marriage work. In that sense she wasn't any different from a lot of wives. That said, I agree that something must have gone wrong with the killer's marriage.'

'Could that have triggered the first murder?'

'That's what I'm thinking.' Winter turned to Freeman. 'Do you believe there are situations where lying is appropriate?'

'Excuse me?'

'It's a simple enough question. Is it ever okay to lie?'

'Do you really think I'm going to admit to something like that.'

'If it helps, I'll rephrase the question. Do you think that it's okay to lie if it serves the greater good?'

Freeman said nothing. He glanced over his right shoulder, then the left, like he was looking for hidden cameras.

Winter patted his Zappa T-shirt. 'It's okay, I'm not wearing a wire.'

'If you have something to say, then say it, but can we please dispense with the bullshit and the dramatics.'

Winter turned the picture of Sobek with a beard face down, taking it out of the equation. There were now eight faces staring up from the desk. All with black hair and brown eyes. All in their mid-thirties. All clean shaven.

'Do you have a sketch artist?'

'I said no dramatics.'

'I'm not being dramatic. It's a legitimate question.'

'No, we don't employ a sketch artist. These days we use software to create photo composites.'

'Who's the best person you've got?'

'That'll be Geneva Tarantini,' Anderton said.

Freeman gave her a pointed look. 'Tarantini would be my first choice.'

148

'Well, since you're both in agreement, Tarantini it is.' Winter picked up the eight front-facing photographs from the desk, tapped them into a neat pile, then handed them to Freeman. 'She needs to create a single facial composite from the pictures of the three husbands. Once she's done that, you're going to give the picture to the media and tell them that there was an eyewitness who saw someone acting suspiciously near Myra Hooper's house.'

'Which would be a lie.'

'A white lie,' Winter said. 'A lie to serve the greater good. The killer's confidence is built on two ideals. Firstly, he believes that he's calling the shots. Secondly, there's precedence. Not only has he got away with this three times in the past, but you guys haven't even got close to him. So what happens if he thinks that you're closing in? What happens if he thinks you're sniffing at his heels?'

'Those sound like rhetorical questions.'

Winter smiled. 'What happens is that the doubts start to creep in. And where there's doubt, there are mistakes. We'd like to believe that serial killers are caught as a result of our brilliant detective work, but that's another lie, one we tell ourselves because our egos need to be fed. The truth is that most serial killers are caught because they make mistakes.'

Freeman didn't say anything for a moment. He was staring at the evidence boards, eyes moving slowly from left to right, taking in the desolation. Winter's gaze tracked the same arc. They lingered when they reached the last board.

'You need to start thinking proactively rather than reactively,' Winter said. 'If you don't, then next year you'll be adding another board, and the year after that you'll be adding another, and so on until they circle the room. Serial killers don't just quit. They keep going until they're forced to stop, either because they get caught or they die. This guy is in his thirties, which means he's got plenty of years ahead of him.'

'Okay, I can see the upside. What's the downside?'

The question wasn't a complete surprise. It was a politician's question, and Freeman was a politician first and a cop second. He wasn't going to stop until he was sitting in the big chair.

'There isn't one,' Winter said.

'There's always a downside. What happens if the media discovers that we've been using them?'

'They'll get over it. It might take time, but they'll forgive you in the end.'

'Easy for you to say. You don't have to live with them.'

'Look, I can't force you to do this. This is your call. That said, if you'd brought me in to consult on the case, this is what I'd be advising you to do. *Strongly* advising. Opportunities like this don't present themselves very often, so when they do, you grab them with both hands. You'd be crazy not to.' Winter gave it a moment to make sure he had Freeman's complete and undivided attention. 'I've seen strategies like this one work. It's a good plan.'

Freeman was staring at the boards again, weighing the pros and cons. He breathed out a long sigh. Decision made.

'Adams,' he called out.

A detective at one of the nearby desks looked over. 'Yes, sir?'

'Get hold of Geneva Tarantini. Tell her it's urgent.'

27

Twenty minutes later Winter and Anderton were sitting in a booth at the Lollipop Diner. Even though it was the tail end of the lunchtime rush the place was still busy. Ninety per cent of the clientele were cops. Anderton had used the five-minute walk from headquarters to call Sobek and give him another update.

The diner was decorated like it was the 1950s. White was the dominant colour, pastel pinks and blues providing some contrast. A Betty Boop mural had been painted on one wall, and a giant plastic ice cream and hot dog had been fixed to another. The juke box was just for show, but the music was authentically fifties. Jerry Lee Lewis had been playing when they arrived. Little Richard was playing now. Great tunes from the early days of rock 'n' roll.

A waitress came over and took their order. There was a pad in the pocket of her apron and a pencil wedged into her ponytail. She gave the impression that she was counting the minutes until her shift ended. They both ordered burgers. Winter had coffee, Anderton a Coke. The waitress took their menus and hustled back over to the counter. Anderton was staring across the table.

'What?' Winter asked.

'Hypothetically speaking, what would have happened if Freeman hadn't agreed to your idea?'

'Then I would have stolen the photographs, used my laptop to create a composite and leaked it to the media. Hypothetically speaking, of course.'

Anderton laughed. 'Yeah, that's what I figured.'

The waitress returned with their drinks, then hustled away again. Winter tipped some sugar into his coffee and took a sip. It was nowhere near as good as Barnfield's, but it contained caffeine and right now that's all he cared about. Those 6 a.m. starts were a killer. He glanced toward the grill, wondering if their burgers were cooking yet.

'So, where are we at?' he asked.

'Where we're at is that we now have three murders that make some kind of sense, and one that doesn't. Which means we're considerably further forward than we were yesterday. Keep going at this rate and we'll have this whole thing wrapped up by the end of the afternoon and we can all go home.'

'I admire your optimism.'

'There are no problems,' she said in a mock-serious Buddha voice. 'Only challenges and solutions.'

That was worth a smile. 'So the challenge here is understanding the reasons behind the latest murder. That's the anomaly.' Winter thought this over for a second. 'We've ruled out the idea that this is a copycat, right?'

Anderton nodded. 'The lab has confirmed that the detonator was once again made from a Christmas-tree bulb. We've always held that detail back from the press so we could sift out the crazies.'

There was that *we* again. Once a cop. 'And we've established workable theories for the killer moving the action to the bedroom, and for him striking in the morning instead of the evening.'

'Yes to the first part,' Anderton said. 'Maybe to the second. You theorised that Myra had to arrive home before Cody because the killer needed time to set things up. But what if that wasn't the only reason? This year the murders have had more publicity than ever. If the killer is doing this for attention, then it's working. However, the downside of all that attention is that it increases the level of expectation, which in turn increases the risk. In other words he's become a victim of his own success. If I was married, I'd be on full alert. I'd be giving strangers a wide berth, and there's no way I'd answer the door without having the security chain in place. And I can guarantee that I wouldn't be alone there.'

'It might also go some way to explaining why he's moved from targeting married couples to targeting a mother and son.'

'It might. Myra Hooper probably thought she was safe. Why shouldn't she have? Up until now the killer has gone after married couples.'

Winter thought this over for a second. It was a good theory, one that led to even more theories. 'Okay, here's another idea. What if this is a bluff? What if Myra and Cody are a diversion? What if it's actually business as usual?'

'You think he's going to strike again this evening?'

'It's possible. He left that footprint near the Hooper house. You said yourself that nothing like that had happened at the other crime scenes. If his plan is to strike twice then he's going to be spreading himself thin, which would explain that mistake. Carrying out surveillance on two victims means twice the work. There's nothing so far to suggest that he's got a partner, so that means he's having to do it all by himself.'

'So he starts cutting corners.' Anderton nodded to herself and found her cell. 'I'm calling Freeman. He needs to get that photo composite out to the media sooner rather than later. If you're right then the killer is feeling the pressure. Which means that we need to pile on more.'

While Anderton made the call, Winter glanced over at the grill again. The cook was constructing two burgers. He probably built a thousand every shift, so there was no guarantee that these were destined for their table. Chuck Berry's 'Johnny B. Goode' was currently playing. When Winter closed his eyes, he could see himself behind the wheel of a big old Cadillac, cruising across town to Lover's Lane, his best girl in the passenger seat beside him.

'Freeman's going to get things moving along.'

Anderton's voice broke into the fantasy, pulling Winter back into a world where he was chasing down a killer who got his kicks from taping bombs to his victims' chests. Life in the fifties had never seemed so appealing, or so far away.

'Has he got the composite yet?' Winter asked.

'Not yet. It shouldn't be much longer, though. He said he'd send it through as soon as he gets it.'

'And you believe that.'

Anderton snorted a laugh. 'No. Which is why I'll keep hassling him until he does send it.'

The waitress appeared with their food. Up close, it smelled even better than it had when it was cooking on the grill. Winter picked up his burger and took a bite. It seemed like forever since he had last eaten. Anderton went to say something and he showed her the hand. He took another bite, then put the burger down on his plate.

'You're hungry then?' Anderton said.

'Like you wouldn't believe.'

Before she could say anything else the diner door opened and a man entered. He stood in the doorway for a second, head moving from side to side, looking for someone. He noticed Anderton a split second after she noticed him. They shared a smile and he came over. There was an empty space next to Winter, and an equally empty one next to Anderton. His head did a quick side-to-side, then he sat down next to Winter.

'Let me introduce you to Dr Death,' Anderton said.

'The name's Datt,' he said. 'Jack Datt. Laura really needs to work on her stand-up routine.'

'Jefferson Winter. It's good to meet you.'

Datt twisted around and they shook hands. His skin was soft and newly scrubbed. His fingernails were clipped and clean. At a distance he could have been in his mid-forties. Up close, you could add ten years onto that estimate. He was a handsome guy who was wearing well. The years had clearly been low-mileage ones. Unlike Winter, Datt dyed his hair.

'Datt's the city's chief medical examiner,' Anderton said. 'He carried out the autopsies on the first three victims.'

'Working on anything in particular at the moment?' Winter asked.

Datt smiled. 'It's been a busy morning.'

'And I suppose you just happened to be passing by?'

The smile widened. 'Something like that.'

'My guess is that you've already carried out the autopsy on Myra Hooper.'

'You guess right.'

'That was quick.'

'We try to be efficient. The fact that the murders happen on the same day each year helps. We don't normally get advanced warning. I was able to schedule things accordingly.'

'So what's the lowdown?' Anderton asked.

Datt laughed and turned to Winter. *'What's the lowdown? Don't you just love it when she talks like a cop?'* The laugh stopped as quickly as it had started. His face turned serious. 'The cause of death was massive internal trauma caused by the explosion. The same as the three previous victims. This time one of the venae cavae was ruptured. Free histamine levels indicate that she was fully conscious when the explosion happened. Again, it was the same story with the other three victims.'

'Was there anything different this time?'

Datt shook his head.

'So, no signs that Myra struggled or fought back.'

Another shake of the head. 'There were no defensive wounds. Which is consistent with the other three victims.'

Anderton turned to Winter. 'It also supports your theory that the killer was using Cody to coerce Myra.'

'"Do what I say or the boy dies,"' Winter said.

'Exactly.'

Anderton turned back to Datt. 'Is there anything else you can tell us?'

'Unfortunately, no.'

'Have you spoken to Freeman yet?' Anderton asked.

'Not yet. I was just on my way to meet him.' Datt stood up. 'Look, I should get going.'

'Thanks, Jack. I really appreciate you doing this.'

'Any time.'

Datt did a quick round of handshakes then walked away. He glanced back at the door, eyes searching for Anderton, then he was gone. Winter waited until the door closed before speaking.

'There's nothing Datt told us that couldn't have been said just as efficiently over the phone.'

'Your point?'

'I'm just saying, that's all.'

'No, you weren't just saying. You were inferring. There's a difference.'

'I think he likes you.'

'I know he likes me. The problem is that he's married.'

'Happily?'

'Happily enough. I've met his wife a couple of times. She's really nice.'

'Damn.'

'Damn indeed.'

Winter took another bite of his burger, drank some coffee, ate some fries. Anderton checked her cell to see if the photo composite had come through. It hadn't. She tried Freeman's phone but couldn't get an answer. Either he was busy or he was ducking her calls. The latter was more likely. Freeman would want to exercise his right to be the alpha in the relationship. She tapped her cell on the tabletop. Once, twice, three times. Plastic connected with plastic to make a sound that was as annoying as a dripping faucet.

'I'd really like to see that photograph,' she said. 'Would

you say that I've given Freeman ample opportunity to send it through?'

'Probably not. However, I'm sensing that you're not after the truthful answer here, so I'm going to say yes.'

Anderton started swiping and jabbing at the screen of her cell phone.

'Who are you calling?'

'Geneva Tarantini.'

'Will she give the picture to you?'

'Of course she will. She got promoted last year. Guess who recommended her?'

Winter laughed. 'This was your plan all along. That's why you suggested her.'

'No, I suggested her because she's the best person for the job. The fact that she'll give us a copy of the picture is purely coincidental.' Anderton jabbed at her phone one last time then brought it up to her ear.

28

Anderton's cell beeped twice as they were driving through Renfrew. She checked to see who it was, one eye on the screen, one eye on the road. Her sudden smile indicated good news.

'Geneva Tarantini?' Winter asked.

'She's sent through an attachment containing the composite.' She tossed the phone over. 'Open it.'

It only took ten seconds to download the attachment. Tarantini had done a good job. There were glimpses of all three husbands, but look again and it was like seeing a completely different person. Did the killer look anything like this? Not that it mattered if he didn't. Photo composites were a vague approximation of a vague witness's vaguest memory. Most of them looked nothing like the person they were supposed to look like. Then there was the fact that the purpose of this one had nothing to do with identification and everything to do with unsettling the killer.

Anderton turned into King Street and pulled up at the kerb. She killed the engine and held out her hand. Winter handed her the phone and she spent almost a full minute studying the composite. He could sense her excitement. It would be so easy for her to convince herself that she was looking at an actual picture of the killer. She had been chasing this guy for the past three years and at last she'd caught his scent. There was still a long way to go, but there was a sense that things were finally moving in the right direction. Winter could feel it. He was sure that Anderton could, too.

Scott Hooper's apartment block was ten yards further on along the sidewalk. It had been constructed in the fifties or sixties from concrete, steel and glass. The neighbourhood was a determinedly middle-income one. The vehicles parked on the street were relatively new and the buildings were all in a good state of repair. They walked over to the entrance foyer side by side and took the stairs to the second floor. Hooper's apartment was the first one they came to. Anderton knocked and stepped back. Winter heard a door opening somewhere inside. He could hear footsteps coming closer. The door swung open.

It took one second for recognition to kick in, and another second for Hooper to react. His hand curled into a fist and he took a step forward. Before Winter could work out what was going on, Hooper punched him in the face. The pain was immediate and all consuming. His left cheekbone felt as though it had been shattered and his sinuses were on fire. He couldn't see for shit because his eyes were watering so much.

Hooper brought his hand back to punch again, and Winter brought his arm up to block the blow, already knowing it was too late. Some people were built for combat. He wasn't one of them. His brain worked fast enough to process what was happening, but his reactions let him down every time. He shut his eyes and braced himself, waiting for a whole world of pain to come crashing down. This was the punch that would have him down on the canvas, the one that would put him out for the count.

It didn't happen.

Winter was suddenly aware of a whole flurry of movement going on around him. He opened his eyes. Anderton had a hold of Hooper. His arms were behind his back and his face was pressed hard up against a wall.

'Get off of me!' he yelled.

'Mr Hooper, I need you to calm down.'

Anderton was talking calmly, like this sort of thing happened all the time. Winter was betting it had been a while since she'd pulled a move like this. Even so, she still had it. Some things you never forgot. A noise from the hallway caught his attention. A scared face was buried in the shadows on the other side of the doorway, eyes shining in the gloom.

'It's okay, Cody,' Winter called out. 'There's just been a small misunderstanding here. Everything's fine.'

'Stay away from my son,' Hooper hissed. 'Do you hear me? Keep away. You've done enough damage.'

Anderton pulled on his arm and he let out a yelp.

'Hey, you're hurting me.'

'Mr Hooper, you need to calm down. If you can do that, I'll let go.'

'But he said that Myra would live.'

All the fight suddenly went out of him. His body went slack as his muscles lost tension and strength. One second he was ready to take on the world, the next he was beat. Anderton held on for a second longer, then let go and stepped back. Hooper sagged against the wall. There were tears in his eyes. Cody came up behind his father and grabbed hold of his arm. In that moment he looked much younger than ten. Winter rubbed at the spot on his cheek where he'd been punched. It was swollen and tender and hurt like hell. There would be a bruise there for sure, but at least nothing seemed broken.

'Mr Hooper,' he said, 'I understand that you need to blame someone for your wife's death, but I'm not that person.'

'You said that she'd live.'

'No, all I did was offer a strategy that would have worked if the killer had stuck to his original MO.'

Winter was being purposefully vague. He couldn't say that Myra died because the killer had targeted a mother and son. And the reason was Cody. Technically speaking, Cody had killed his mom. He'd opened the bedroom door and triggered the bomb. It didn't matter what was said to him, it didn't matter how often he was told that none of this was his fault, he'd be blaming himself for what had happened for the rest of his life. The bottom line here was that things could always get worse. What happened this morning was devastating for him, but how much more devastating would it be if he discovered that he really was the reason his mom was dead?

'What does any of that actually mean?' Hooper asked.

'It means that no matter what I or anyone else said or did yesterday, your wife would still be dead today.'

Hooper opened his mouth to say something, then closed it again. Thoughts came, thoughts went, and he said, 'She shouldn't have died. It's not fair.'

'No, she shouldn't have. And you're right, it isn't fair.'

'Mr Hooper, do you mind if we come in?' Anderton asked.

'Who are you, anyway?'

'We're investigating the murders.'

'But you're not from the police. I've already spoken to them. You know it's illegal to impersonate a cop, don't you?'

'We never said we were cops. I headed up the police investigation into the first three murders. I'm retired now and working as a private investigator. My client has asked me to look into the murders.'

'Who's your client? And why does he care?'

'Look, Mr Hooper, we just need five minutes. That's all. If that helps us track the killer down then it has to be a good thing, right? I'm assuming you want to see him caught.'

'Of course I do.'

'In which case, let's go through to the living room so we can talk.'

29

Like Eric Kirchner's place over in Mount Pleasant, Scott Hooper's apartment had been decorated by the landlord. The only real difference was that the furniture had been bought new instead of secondhand. That said, there were clearly limits to how deep the landlord's pockets were. The cabinets and tables and bookcase were all self-assembly rather than purpose-built by craftsmen, the walls were the same shade of white as the ceiling, and the drapes were single ply rather than lined.

Everything about the living room seemed temporary. The TV was on a cabinet in the corner of the room rather than fixed to the wall. One shelf of the bookcase was taken up with a small stereo that had piles of CDs lined up on either side. Aside from a small framed vacation photograph of the Hoopers, the rest of the shelves were empty. The sofa might have been made from cheap leather, but it was comfortable enough. Winter was at one end, Anderton the other, like bookends. Hooper lowered himself into the room's only armchair. Cody had pulled a bright red beanbag over to his father's chair and was sitting cross-legged on it.

Hooper was in his early thirties but moving like he was eighty. Grief could do that. It sucked at your soul, and would keep sucking until there was nothing left. That's what had happened here. Winter knew the signs. The same thing had happened to his mom. Hooper was still wearing his work clothes. Cheap suit pants, a crumpled white shirt, no tie. Wherever he'd been, whatever he'd been doing, the news had come through that his wife was dead, and life as he knew it had come screeching to a very sudden and definite halt.

'You were looking at getting back together with your wife,' Winter said.

Hooper glanced down. 'Cody, can you go through to your room while I talk to these people?'

Cody shook his head. 'I want to stay.'

'We won't be long. You can play on my laptop.'

'I don't want to play on your laptop. I want to stay here with you.'

Hooper looked like he was going to push it. At the last second he backed down. Whatever fight he'd once possessed was long gone. 'Okay, but you need to keep quiet.'

Cody settled back into the beanbag.

'So were you looking at reconciling with your wife?' Winter asked.

Hooper didn't respond. His attention had been captured by the small framed photograph on the bookcase. The three of them were on a beach. They looked like any other happy, smiling family. Hooper was staring at it, a million miles away and drifting further with every passing second. He wiped his eyes. 'Do you have any idea how difficult this is?'

'Honestly?' Winter shook his head. 'I can't even begin to imagine what you're going through. The fact that you're sat there able to string a sentence together is nothing short of a miracle.'

'I love her.' Hooper realised what he'd said and corrected

himself. '*Loved* her. The only person I've ever loved more is Cody.'

'I know that, but for this to work you need to answer our questions. And you need to be honest, otherwise there's no point us being here.'

'I know.' Hooper took a deep breath and let out a long heart-weary sigh. 'We'd been together for twelve years, ever since we met at college in California. After we graduated, Myra wanted to move back here because she missed her family. I came with her. A year later we were married. The year after that we had Cody.'

'Why did you split up?' Anderton asked.

Hooper shrugged and shook his head. 'For no reason and every reason.'

'That's a bit vague. Were you or your wife having an affair? Was that it?'

'No one was having an affair,' Hooper snapped.

'I'm sorry, but these questions need to be asked.'

'No one was having an affair,' he repeated quietly. 'After twelve years, we'd started falling out of love. It happens. When you're dealing with all the day-to-day crap it's too easy to forget why you fell in love in the first place. We were arguing about nothing, just trying to score points against each other. Myra decided we needed a time-out. That's what she called it. A time-out. She couldn't bring herself to call it a separation. That was Myra, though, she was always good with words. She was an English major at college.'

'You were thinking about getting back together, weren't you?'

Hooper nodded. 'We were seeing a marriage counsellor,

166

and seemed to be making progress. Myra wanted to take things slowly, so that's what we were doing. We were getting there. A couple of weeks ago we went on a date together. I'm not going to lie and tell you things were like they'd been at the beginning, because they weren't, but it was a good night.'

Hooper paused as though he was going to say something else, then burst into tears. For a while, he just sat there, tears streaming down his face. He was holding on to Cody's shoulder like it was the only thing keeping him tethered to the world. The kid was weeping too. This was the hidden side of murder, the bit you didn't see splashed all over the front pages. The misery that followed in its wake was as long as it was deep.

'Back in a second,' Winter whispered to Anderton.

He stood up and went out into the hall. The bathroom was behind the second door he tried. Four toilet rolls were piled up on top of the cistern. Winter grabbed two and went back through to the living room. He handed one to Cody, the other to Hooper. Eyes were wiped dry, noses blown.

'We need to ask Cody some questions,' Winter said. 'Is that okay?'

'Is that really necessary?' Hooper said. 'He's already been questioned today.'

'This is important. If it wasn't, I wouldn't be asking.'

Hooper glanced at Cody. 'Is that okay, buddy?'

Cody nodded reluctantly. He looked nervous and scared. The way he was sitting, nestled into the beanbag, he could have been a baby bird. Winter understood where he was coming from. He'd been a year older than Cody when his world came crashing down, but he could still remember every last detail. The days following his father's arrest had been filled with confusion and misinformation. Up had become down and down had become up. It was like he hadn't known anything any more. Winter got off the sofa and sat cross-legged on the floor. He was still a whole head taller than Cody, but at least they were closer to the same level. When he spoke, he did so quietly, gently. No sharp syllables, no sudden movements.

'I'm not going to lie to you, Cody, this is going to be tough. You're going to feel like you don't want to talk to me, so I'm going to need you to be brave here. Now, I'm going to make a promise. I promise that I'm going to track down the person who did this to your mom, but to do that I need your help. When it feels like you can't answer any more questions, I want you to remember that. Can you do that for me?'

Cody's head went down and up. It moved only a fraction of an inch, but that was enough. When dealing with traumatised witnesses you grabbed everything you could get. Winter took a moment to consider the best way to approach this. The kid had been questioned in detail about what had happened this morning. There was nothing to be gained from rehashing all that again. Nothing but a whole lot of pain.

'Your bedroom window looks out over the street,' Winter said. 'Have you seen anyone you don't know hanging around out there during the last couple of weeks?'

Cody shook his head. 'No,' he whispered.

'What about when you were outside? Have you ever had the feeling that someone's been following or watching you?'

Another shake of the head. 'No.'

A worried expression clouded Hooper's face. 'Do you think the killer was watching him?'

'It's possible.'

Anderton passed her cell to Winter. The photo composite filled the screen. He handed the phone to Cody.

'We think this is the man who killed your mom. Take a good look. Have you ever seen him?'

Cody looked at the screen. The hand holding the phone started shaking.

'Have you seen this man?' Winter repeated in his gentlest voice. 'It's really important that you tell us if you have.'

Cody was still staring at the cell-phone screen, his hand shaking worse than ever. He glanced up at his father.

'It's okay, buddy. You're not in any trouble.'

'I might have,' Cody said quietly. 'He didn't look exactly like this, though.'

'When?' Winter asked.

'A couple of days ago. I was having a picnic at the park with Mom. He'd lost his dog and was asking people if they'd seen it. He had a picture of it on his phone.'

'How tall was he?'

'He was smaller than my dad.'

'How much smaller?'

'A lot.'

'Can you remember what he said?'

Cody paused. One second became two, became five. Winter was tempted to jump in with another question but kept quiet.

'He said that his dog had been missing for a week and then he asked if I liked dogs,' Cody said quietly. 'I told him that I wanted one, but Mom and Dad wouldn't let me. He tried to persuade Mom to get one, but he was joking. Mom thought it was funny.'

'Did he seem friendly?'

'He was real friendly. And he seemed real sad that he'd lost his dog. I felt sorry for him.'

'Did he say anything else?'

'He asked me what my favourite MLS team was. It was probably because I had my ball with me. I told him the Whitecaps. He wanted to know what position I play. I said in midfield.'

'Anything else?'

Cody shook his head.

'Look at the picture again,' Anderton said. 'You mentioned that the man you saw looked different. How did he look different?'

'I don't know. His hair was shorter maybe.'

'Anything else?'

Another shake of the head. 'I don't even know if it was the same person. Maybe it wasn't.' Cody looked at the phone again then handed it back. 'I don't think it was him.'

Winter passed the phone back to Anderton. 'We need to get Tarantini over here as soon as possible.'

'Yeah, that's what I'm thinking.' She turned to Cody. 'We're going to get someone to come and see you. Would you be able to tell them how the man you saw was different from this man, so they can make a picture of him.'

Cody nodded.

'What park were you having the picnic in?'

'Alexandra Park.'

'Can you remember where you were sitting?'

'Near the bandstand.'

There was a knock on the front door and Hooper went to answer. He came back with Jefferies and one of the detectives Winter had seen in the incident room, a stern-looking thirtysomething woman. Jefferies was holding a computer printout of the photo composite.

'I suppose you just happened to be passing,' he said.

'Something like that,' Anderton replied.

'Do you have anything you feel like sharing?'

'Only that Cody recognised the man in the picture. You'll need to get Geneva Tarantini over here to speak to him.'

'And how exactly did you get hold of the composite?'

Anderton just smiled.

'I think we can take things from here.'

'Of that I have no doubt. I have every faith in you, Detective Jefferies.'

Anderton stood up to leave and Winter followed suit. She thanked Hooper for his time, then they headed for the door.

30

Anderton was on her cell the second the apartment door closed. The conversation lasted just long enough for them to get outside to the sidewalk. Fast, punchy questions, lots of affirmatives, plenty of head nodding even though there was no way for the person on the other end to read her body language. She killed the call.

'It's like I thought. Freeman is having the photo composite shown to the husbands.'

'Will your VPD contacts let us know if it rings any bells?'

'Of course.'

She tapped the phone against her palm a couple of times then made another call. There was no answer this time. She didn't leave a message, just hung up and started working her phone screen, thumb swiping, finger jabbing. One final jab, then she put the phone away.

'Sobek?' Winter asked.

Anderton nodded. 'He's not answering so I've texted him. If the composite sparks anything with him, I want to know about it sooner rather than later.'

'It's probably going to be later. Like after the sun sets.'

She gave him a quizzical look.

'He's at the cemetery,' Winter added. 'Isabella's grave is in a spot where there's no cell coverage.'

'You say that like it's a fact.'

'I was there this morning.'

Anderton fired off another look.

'It was all very friendly and civilised. He even offered to share his coffee.' Winter paused. 'You know, Sobek could have headed straight to the cemetery after being at the Hooper house. The times work.'

'He didn't do it, Winter.'

'But wouldn't it be so convenient if he had?'

'Yes, it would. Unfortunately, life is never that simple, or that neat.'

'How far to Alexandra Park?'

'This time of day, it'll take us twenty minutes to get there. It's right on the water, not far from your hotel.'

Traffic was light and they made good time. Anderton found a parking space near the park entrance and they got out. Winter lit a cigarette and took a drag. It was the hottest part of the day and the sun was beating down. Not that he was going to start complaining about the heat. As far as he was concerned, sunshine trumped rain any day. He found his sunglasses and put them on. Anderton was already wearing hers.

The park was small. On one side, the water stretched all the way to the horizon. On the other, skyscrapers reached up to touch the impossibly blue sky, and beyond them, the mountains were there to keep things in perspective. However impressive those skyscrapers might be, they had nothing on the mountains. Ten thousand years after the last building had crumbled those mountains would still be standing.

At first glance the bandstand looked as though it had been built a century ago. It was newer than that, though. This one had probably been built to replace the original. It was octagonal and resembled a pagoda. It would have looked great on a postcard. Any angle would have worked. The water as a backdrop, or the buildings and mountains. The brown paint helped it to blend in with the trees.

Winter walked over to the steps and sat down. Anderton sat down beside him. For a while he sat there smoking his cigarette and taking in the view. It was good to have a moment to slow down and take stock. Most investigative work progressed so slowly it was like wading through treacle. That wasn't the case here. Things were moving fast, and that was great. The downside was that something important might be missed. When you were acting in haste it was all too easy to skip over a vital clue.

'How's your face?' Anderton asked, breaking the silence.

'Sore. Hooper's got a hell of a right hook.'

Anderton snorted and shook her head. 'I could hit harder.'

'Easy for you to say. You weren't the one being hit.' Winter took a drag on his cigarette. 'Why did you become a cop?'

'Because I hate injustice. Always have done. When I was at school, if I saw someone being bullied, I had to get involved.'

'Even if it ended up with you getting your ass kicked?'

Anderton laughed. 'Yeah, that happened a couple of times. Nobody likes having their fun spoiled. Especially bullies. It didn't stop me, though. As soon as I was able to I joined the police. So, what about you? How did you end up in the FBI?'

'That's one of those questions that doesn't have a straightforward answer.'

'Of course it doesn't. But something happened to push you in that direction.'

An image of his mom jumped into his head. She was sitting in their cheap little landlord-decorated apartment weeping silently to herself. She was so drunk she didn't even know he was there. This might have been an actual memory. At the same time it could have been an amalgamation of memories, like the photo composite. Coming home from school to find his mom drunk and weeping was not a one-off event. The apartment could have been a composite of memories, too. There had been a whole string of those, each one as bad as the last, all of them blending together to create a depressing whole.

'After my father was arrested all I wanted was answers,' he said. 'How could he have done what he'd done? How could I not have known he was a killer?' He hesitated, then added, 'And why did my mom have to suffer so much? She didn't deserve it. Before the arrest she was so full of life. Afterwards she was just a shadow. It was like my father had reached into her chest and torn her heart out.'

'I can't even begin to imagine what it was like.'

'No, you can't. No one can. Even Scott and Cody Hooper would struggle to understand because it's just too personal. Every situation is completely unique. Theirs, mine, everyone's. I'm fortunate, though. I survived. Not everyone can say that.'

'How are you getting on with finding those answers?'

Winter laughed and shook his head. 'Still working on it.'

'Some questions just don't want to be answered. You realise that, don't you?'

'It doesn't mean we shouldn't try.'

'Talking of questions, do you think Cody saw the killer?'

Winter took another drag. 'What I think is that eyewitnesses are hugely unreliable at the best of times. When it comes down to it I'll take hard forensic evidence over the testimony of someone who thinks they *might* have seen someone. In this case we've got a double whammy in that the photo composite is a complete fabrication.'

'But,' Anderton prompted.

'But the man with the lost dog was real. And something about him resonated with Cody. At the moment the kid is in survival mode, which means that his medulla oblongata is working overtime. That part of the brain doesn't work by committee. If it sees danger then the klaxons start howling and the warning lights flash, and you'd best pay attention or you're going to end up getting eaten by the sabre-tooth tiger.'

'Except we don't have sabre-tooth tigers any more.'

Winter smiled. 'No, we don't.'

'Also, that part of the brain might be shouting danger, but it doesn't call the shots. Did you see what happened? Cody started off thinking the dog guy was the killer, then the logical part of his brain kicked in and he talked himself out of it.'

'I noticed that, too.'

'Okay, let's assume that the dog guy is the killer. Where does that lead us?'

Winter took a last pull on his cigarette, then crushed it out and swept it to the edge of the step, out of the way. There was a trash can near the entrance to the park. He'd dispose of it later. Anderton was staring off into the middle distance, thinking hard. Winter glanced around. It was a busy little park, a great place to come and people-watch. There were moms with strollers and moms trailing toddlers. There were

176

joggers and a couple of teenagers walking hand-in-hand. And there was a woman walking a dog.

It was easy to imagine Cody and his mom sat on a blanket eating their picnic. Easy to imagine the guy from the composite walking over and giving them some sob story about how he'd lost his dog. Maybe his hair was shorter than in the composite picture. He definitely would have looked different. Maybe a lot different, maybe only a little. It was easy to imagine him taking his cell out and showing the picture of his dog to Cody and his mom. Easy to imagine him charming them. Because that was the thing. Some serial killers could be so charming. You want to think that they're loners, that you'd spot them straight away, but it just didn't work that way. The most dangerous ones were the chameleons, and that's what they were dealing with here, someone who could hide in plain sight without raising suspicions. Winter took a moment to go over what Cody had told them, looking for anything that stood out. The thing he kept coming back to was the cell-phone picture of the dog.

'Why didn't the dog guy have a flyer?' He put the question out there, then glanced at Anderton, looking for a reaction.

'Okay, I'm listening.'

'According to Cody, he claimed his dog had been missing for a week. If that happens you hit your computer and find the cutest picture you've got and make a flyer. You have LOST DOG in bold capital letters at the top. Then you have a paragraph or two saying where it got lost and how much it's going to be missed. Then you have details of the reward. And right down at the bottom you're going to have your telephone number, maybe a whole row of numbers all neatly snipped so they're easy to tear off. Once you've done all that you're going to print it out and canvas the neighbourhood where the dog went missing. You'll stick the flyers to streetlamps near your favourite park, and on noticeboards, and hand them out to strangers.'

'But this guy didn't do that. All he had was a picture on his cell.'

'Exactly. Dog owners can be pretty obsessive. If their pride and joy goes missing they're going to move heaven and hell to get it back.'

'The fact that the dog guy didn't have a flyer doesn't prove that this is the killer. It's not even close to being conclusive.'

'No, it's not. But you've got to admit, it is a bit strange.'

Anderton did a quick scan of the park, her gaze tracing a one-hundred-and-eighty-degree arc that moved from left to right, taking in people, taking in the sights.

'Okay, let's say the dog guy is the killer. How did he track them here? He couldn't have followed them from the house. That would be too risky.'

'Agreed.'

'So how did he know they'd be here?' She paused. 'Okay, we still haven't answered the question of how he chooses his victims. Maybe this is how he does it. Maybe he hangs around parks just waiting for the right person to come along, then gives them a sob story about his lost dog.'

'Then what? He follows them home so he can find out where they live.' Winter shook his head. 'That's as risky as following them from their homes. Also, Cody said the picnic at the park was a week ago. This guy likes to take things slow and careful. He's going to want to spend more than a week surveilling them. Remember, there's a year between the murders. That's a lot of time for planning.'

'So how did he do it? How did he know that they'd be having a picnic here?'

Winter smiled. 'That is so the right question, Anderton. How did he know? Because this guy is omniscient, right? He knows everything. He's like some sort of god. Except nobody has those sort of powers. I mean, who's got the power to see into other people's lives like that? To know what they're up to and what they're planning on doing, and when they're planning on doing it? That's just so not going to happen, is it?'

Anderton laughed. 'Okay, okay, I get it. You think he's been watching her Facebook account.'

She took out her cell phone and Winter scooted closer so he could watch. Myra Hooper wasn't a particularly common name so it only took thirty seconds to find her profile. She was the third Myra Hooper on the list. Anderton clicked to open the profile. Myra had used a photograph of Cody for her profile picture. Dark hair, dark eyes and that goofy grin. Winter thought of him looking lost and alone on the beanbag and wondered if he'd ever grin like that again. The answer was no. Sure, he would smile again, and he would laugh and joke and have a good time, and there would even be days when he didn't think about his mom, but he would never grin like this again. There was an innocence there that had been lost forever. Out of all the things that had happened here today, that was what got to Winter most. It was always the little things.

Myra had eight hundred and fifty-three friends and her relationship status was set to *It's complicated*. Her privacy settings were on the lowest level, which meant that they could access her timeline without friending her. Which meant that the killer would have been able to access it as well. The murder had only happened this morning but there were already twenty condolence messages, all of them saying much the same thing. *RIP. You're going to be missed. Thinking of you.* The outpouring of love was understandable but it wasn't going to bring her back.

Myra had last posted a status update at 11.23 the previous evening. *Looking forward to camping with Cody at the weekend. Hope it doesn't rain LOL. Last time we went the tent leaked and we ended up drowned. Where's Noah's Ark when you need it!!!* That was another thing with murder. It came slamming out of the blue and the clocks just stopped. That book you were reading would never be finished, that film you wanted to see would never be watched, and that camping trip you were planning on taking with your ten-year-old son was never going to happen. For Winter, it was a gig that never got seen. His mom had bought tickets for a U2 concert. Winter had never been to a rock concert before and U2 were one of his favourite bands. He was beyond excited. This was going to be the best day of his life. His father was arrested the day before the concert. By the time he remembered about the tickets, the gig had been and gone.

Anderton scrolled down. Myra was a Facebook addict. Every aspect of her life was on there for the whole world to see, described with words and photographs. The tears and joy, the heartbreak and celebrations. At 7.23 on the evening of July 27 she'd written a brief post about how she and Cody were going on a picnic to Alexandra Park the next day.

Anderton sighed and looked over at him. 'It's almost too easy.'

'Yes, it is.'

'I don't get it,' she said. 'Do people not realise that this stuff actually goes public?'

'Oversharing is currently at epidemic proportions. And what's really worrying is that it's only going to get worse.'

'Talking of which, do we pass this on to Freeman? At the moment I feel like we're doing all the work and getting none of the credit.'

'Agreed, but we should still pass it on. He's got the re-sources of the whole of the Vancouver Police Department at his disposal. On that basis I'd give him the ball and let him run with it. If he finds anything, then your winged monkeys will tell us, right?'

'They will.'

'In which case it's a win/win.'

'So why doesn't it feel like one?'

While Anderton made the call, Winter went over things in his head, wondering what their next move should be. As always, there were just too many questions and nowhere near enough answers. There was one question that kept niggling away and just wouldn't let go. Anderton finished her call and put her cell away. She turned around and caught him staring.

'Why are you looking at me like that?'

'Just thinking.'

'Well, can you think without making your eyes spin? It's creeping me out.'

Winter did his best to look serious. 'Better?'

'Not really. So, what are you thinking about?'

'Escaping. Or, to be more precise, escapology.'

'Okay,' she said, drawing the syllables out. 'Would you care to expand on that?'

'A couple of months before he died, Harry Houdini spent ninety-one minutes in a coffin that had been lowered into the pool at the Shelton Hotel in New York. In doing so he smashed the previous record by thirty-one minutes. This is widely regarded as being his greatest feat. Considering some of the things he got up to, that's saying something.'

'And when exactly did this take place? Or should I take a wild stab in the dark?'

'Go on, give it your best shot.'

'August 5.'

'August 5, 1926, to be exact.' Winter jumped to his feet. 'Come on, let's go see if we can work out why today is so important to the killer.'

31

Granville Square was a thirty-storey high-rise in Downtown. The top floor had been commandeered to provide air-traffic control for the seaplanes using the harbour. The building was four hundred and sixty-five feet tall, making this the highest air-traffic control centre in the world. The *Vancouver Sun* had called this building home since 1997. The journalist who met them at reception was old school. Estimating her age was tricky. She looked about seventy, but might only have been fifty. Her skin had a waxy yellow sheen to it and she spoke like she smoked two packs a day. She was tall and thin and wearing a bright red dress that matched her bright red lipstick. Her spectacles were dangling from a chain around her neck.

'Jefferson Winter meet Rebecca Byrne,' Anderton said. 'Rebecca Byrne meet Jefferson Winter.'

They traded handshakes and welcome smiles.

'I saw you on TV last night,' Byrne said. 'It was good to see Delaney taken down a peg or two.'

'I take it you're not a fan.'

'You could say that. The TV people look down on the radio people, and the radio people look down on us poor lowly print hounds. And I'm fine with that. But Delaney is in a league of her own. The woman is a major pain in the ass. She sits up there in her ivory tower and thinks her shit smells better than everyone else's.'

'Rebecca heads up the crime desk,' Anderton said. 'She's been here since forever. If she ever leaves then this whole building is going to come crashing down. At least that's how the legend goes.'

Byrne's cackling laughter was as dry as old sand. 'It's good to see you again, too, Laura. How's the PI business?'

'It has its moments.'

'And how is our Mr Sobek?'

Anderton cracked a smile. 'He has his moments.'

'I've got to admit, your call got me curious.'

'Which is why you've come to meet us personally rather than sending one of your minions.'

'Curiosity kind of goes with the territory. So why do you want to see our back issues? Has this got anything to do with the August 5 Bomber, perchance?'

Anderton nodded. 'Winter thinks the date is significant.'

'If memory serves, you didn't.'

'He's coming at this with fresh eyes. He might see something I missed.'

'And that's what I've always liked about you, Laura. You've always had an open mind. You should never have been kicked off the investigation, you know.'

'I'm not going to disagree with that.'

'So, do you think Freeman's going to catch this guy?'

Anderton laughed, then turned to look at Winter. 'You saw what she did there, right? She softens me up with a compliment, then slides her question in there real smooth, hoping I slip up and answer.'

'Yeah, I saw.'

She turned back to Byrne. 'There's no way I'm going to an-

swer that, Rebecca. I can see the headline now. DISGRACED
COP RIPS INTO HER SUCCESSOR.'

Byrne shrugged and looked sheepish. She wasn't really
owning the emotion. 'You can't blame a girl for trying. And
anyway, I'd come up with a better headline.'

'Just so we're clear, unless I clearly state otherwise,
everything I say to you from now until the end of time is off
the record. That goes for Winter, too.'

'And just so we're clear, if this fishing expedition nets anything I expect to be informed before my esteemed peers.'

'That goes without saying.'

'Actually, it does need to be said. Which is why I said it.'

'So, where are the back issues kept?'

'This way.'

Byrne led them down a corridor that could have been in
any office building, anywhere in the world. The walls were
white, the brown carpet hardwearing and cheap, the
striplights too bright. A door opened and a hassled-looking
guy came hurrying out, a blast of noise and chaos following
in his wake. Before the door swung shut Winter caught a
glimpse of the newsroom. The messy desks were laid out in
neat rows and people were working the phones hard. In a lot
of respects it wasn't much different from the incident room.

The back issues were kept in a room at the end of the corridor. Byrne pushed the door open and switched on the light.
It was twelve feet by twelve, bigger than a broom closet but
not by much. The volumes holding the back issues were lined
up neatly on the shelves. The large table positioned under the
striplight in the middle of the room had a computer terminal
sitting on top, and two chairs slotted underneath.

Byrne followed his gaze to the table. 'The more recent editions are digitised, but anything before 1998 you'll need to look up the old-fashioned way.'

'You still keep hard copies of the current editions, though.'

'That's because at heart we're still a news*paper*. Technology is all well and good, but you need to be careful not to lose your soul.'

'Amen to that.'

'Okay, I'm going to leave you to it. Remember, though, if you find anything, I want to know about it.'

32

Winter stood for a moment staring at the shelves. The newspaper had been founded in 1912. The early years were each represented by a single volume. By 1962 two volumes were needed, and from 1971, three. In 2006 it was back to two volumes again. He could feel the weight of all those millions upon millions of words pressing in on him. So much history. So much despair and tragedy. Some joy, but not a whole lot. This was a newspaper, after all.

So, where to start?

Anderton was staring, too, and no doubt wondering much the same thing. She walked over and reached up to the newer volumes on the top shelf. These looked a lot less ragged than those on the bottom shelf. The year of each volume was etched on the spine in gold. *The Vancouver Sun* was etched there, too, also in gold. The volume she was aiming for was from four years ago, the year before the murders began, which made sense. Then again, just because something made sense, it didn't necessarily make it the right thing to do.

'Hold up a second,' Winter said. 'We need to get clever or we'll be here all night. I take it you've already had someone go through these.'

'Of course.'

'And they did exactly what you're about to do? They started four years ago and worked from there, checking the headlines for the days around August 5 to see if anything jumped out?'

Anderton nodded. 'That's right.'

Winter glanced at the volumes of back issues lined up on the shelves, searching for inspiration, searching for ideas. 'What's the first difference between then and now?'

'The fact that we've established the killer is targeting the husbands rather than the wives.'

'Exactly. The dynamic has completely changed. We need to bear that in mind when we're looking through the back issues.'

Anderton reached up to the shelf again.

'Wait,' Winter said.

Her hand froze in midair and she turned to face him.

'We need to try a different approach,' he went on. 'Like Einstein once said, insanity is doing the same thing over and over again and expecting different results. The reason that became a maxim is because it's true. It's the curse of large bureaucratic organisations like the Vancouver Police Department. The two of us might be lacking in manpower, but no one will ever accuse us of being a large bureaucratic organisation. I say that we embrace our flexibility.'

'Okay, so what constitutes a different approach?'

Winter pressed a finger against his lips to shut her up, then closed his eyes. He could sense her frustration. She was champing at the bit, anxious to get going, and he kept pulling her up. He took a couple of deep breaths and tried to clear his mind. Then he thought about Nicholas Sobek and David Hammond and Eric Kirchner, looking for the things that connected and separated them. He thought about the photo composite and the way that the three faces had been blended together to create a brand-new face. One that was similar but different. Black hair, brown eyes, early thirties. The age worked with how the killer was profiling. The hair colour and brown eyes could be taken as read. Without realising it, the killer had told them what he looked like. But what was motivating the crimes? That was the key question here. Winter opened his eyes.

'Yesterday we were chasing a sadistic killer who got his kicks from making his victims suffer through a nightmare that's almost impossible to comprehend. What must their last moments have been like? Sitting there waiting for the door to open and knowing that they were going to die? Any rational person would look at that situation and conclude that this guy was a complete sadist. So we fast forward to today and it's like we've woken up on a brave new world. The whole landscape has changed and nothing is as we remember it. For starters, he isn't a sadist.'

Anderton's face creased with disbelief. 'How can you say that? The guy's a complete psycho.'

'I agree that he's a psychopath, but it doesn't necessarily follow that he's a sadist. Not all psychopaths are cold-blooded killers. Some are, some aren't. Psychopaths are wired differently, they think differently. It's not uncommon for the actual murder to be a secondary consideration. Sometimes it has nothing to do with the fantasy whatsoever. A good example is your first-time rapist. Once he's played out his fantasy he realises that he's got a witness that needs to be disposed of, so he disposes of them. The point is that the murder was never really a part of the fantasy. He's just tying up loose ends.'

'So, what are you saying? That our guy's pathologically pragmatic?'

'That's exactly what I'm saying. These murders serve a purpose. The question we should be asking ourselves is what that purpose is.'

'So what purpose do they serve?'

Without another word, Winter shut his eyes and imagined he was the person from the photo composite. Then he stepped into the zone.

*

It's been a long day and I've just got home, weary after spending the day at the office. I push open the kitchen door and the bomb goes off. To start with I'm confused and disoriented, but that eventually gives way to a kind of numb realisation. At some point I'll work out that there has been an explosion. Slowly, I'll start piecing things together, but to do that effectively I need more information, and that information is on the other side of the kitchen door. So, I open it again. This time there's no explosion, but I do get hit with a second wave of confusion when I see my wife lying on the floor taped to a chair. I rush over to help her, only there's no point. She's already dead. Confusion slowly gives way to understanding, and that understanding trails nothing but guilt in its wake. In no time that guilt becomes all-consuming, smothering me until I can't see or hear anything else.

*

Winter opened his eyes and caught Anderton staring.

'Where do you go to?' she asked.

'Do you really want to know?'

She thought this over for a second then shook her head. 'Not really.'

'If the husbands are a projection of the killer, who do the wives represent?'

'Maybe he's married. That would be the obvious answer.'

'So, what happened to his wife?'

'Well, she didn't die in an explosion. I looked into every explosion that's happened in the city over the last twenty years. There were six of them. Nine people died in total. No women. Therefore, no wife.'

'So the way the wives die is symbolic. It doesn't matter how they die, what's important is that they're killed by their husbands.'

'Except that doesn't work either. This doesn't link to any unsolved homicide. That's another angle I looked at.'

'But what if it wasn't a homicide? What if the death was accidental and the killer was somehow responsible? A traffic accident, for example. Maybe he crashed his car and his wife died as a result.'

Anderton looked over at the volumes of back issues. 'So, we search for accidents involving husbands and wives. And we start by looking four years ago.'

Which again made sense, thought Winter. Because something must have triggered the murders, and that something could well have happened exactly four years ago today. With trigger events, something happened to instigate a new event. Hence the name. You pull the trigger, the gun goes bang. It was cause and effect. For every action there was an equal and opposite reaction, just like Newton worked out three centuries earlier. Anniversaries were common trigger events, and maybe that's what had happened here. Maybe the killer's wife had been killed in an accident. A year later, the anniversary getting closer, he snapped and killed Isabella Sobek.

It all made sense.

But.

'What about Cody?' Winter asked.

Anderton was moving toward the shelves again, ready to pluck one down. She stopped walking and turned to face him. 'What about him?'

'Where does he fit into all of this? The fact that the killer talked to him means that he's significant. If he wasn't, then why take that risk? Where's the upside? But he did talk to him. And before talking to him he stalked him on Facebook. He was specifically targeted.'

'We're only assuming that the dog guy is the killer. As far as that goes, all we've got is circumstantial evidence.'

'But if you put all that circumstantial evidence together it starts to look somewhat more substantial. We don't have to prove any of this in court, remember? That's Freeman's job. All we've got to do is convince ourselves. And right now, I'm a believer. The dog guy's the killer.'

Anderton didn't say anything for a second. Winter could almost see the cogs turning inside her head. 'If you're right then this is a major anomaly. On the one hand we've got three husbands who killed their wives. On the other we've got a ten-year-old kid who killed his mom.'

It was Winter's turn to fall quiet, his turn for the cogs to start whirring. It was hard to shake the feeling that something obvious was being missed. He pulled out a chair and sat down. For almost a minute he didn't say a word. He was trying to see Cody the way that the killer had seen him. Trying to focus on the wood when there were just too many trees.

'Is Cody an anomaly?' he asked. 'He's got black hair and brown eyes. That's two things he has in common with the husbands straight away.'

'Yes, but he's more than twenty years younger.'

'And maybe that's the whole point. Right now we're working on the theory that the husbands represent the killer. But what if Cody is representative of him as well? Only a version that's twenty years younger.'

Anderton opened her mouth but nothing came out. It slowly shut and a thoughtful expression came over her face. Winter wouldn't blame her if she thought the idea was crazy. Then again, if there was one thing he'd learned it was that crazy came with the territory. The benchmark case was Richard Chase, the Vampire Killer. Chase broke into houses in Sacramento and checked the bathroom soap. His decision to kill was based on whether the bottom was gooey. If it wasn't then he would move on to another house. He also drank his victims' blood because he believed that his own was turning to dust. This was the world that Winter inhabited. When you're dealing with this level of crazy, anything goes.

'Cody's ten,' Anderton said, 'and the husbands were all in their early thirties when the murders happened. That means we're looking at the years 1995 through to 1997.'

'If we get nothing there then we start looking at the years either side.'

'Sounds like a plan.'

They walked over to the bookshelves. The years they were interested in were three-volume years. August was covered by the middle one. Anderton pulled down the books and Winter carried them to the table. For the whole of its history the *Vancouver Sun* had been a broadsheet, which made the volumes heavy and unwieldly. They sat down opposite each other and went to work. Anderton took 1995, Winter took 1996.

Because they were interested in what happened on August 5, Winter went straight to August 6. Daily newspapers were always twenty-four hours out of date. The lead for August 6, 1996 was a story about a factory closing down with the loss of two hundred jobs. Losing your job was a top-five trigger event, but Winter couldn't see how this particular factory closure might fit with this case. He flipped to the next page. He was interested in any stories involving women who were in the twenty-four to fifty-four age group. Statistically speaking, that's where you were most likely to find a mom with a ten-year-old kid.

He reached the sports pages without finding anything. Just to be thorough, he went through the edition for August 7. If it was a light news day they might well have used something that hadn't made the cut the previous day. Anderton had moved on to August 7, too. Winter went from cover to cover but nothing jumped out. The book made a solid thump when he closed it. He pushed it to one side and reached for the 1997 volume. Anderton finished with hers a couple of minutes later. She closed it with a bang then went over to the shelves for the 1994 volume.

An hour later they'd covered the whole of the nineties and the tail end of the eighties. Nothing had jumped out. They'd even gone back to the volumes from 1995 through to 1997 and looked at August 8 and August 9, just in case. Still nothing. They leant back in their seats and locked eyes across the table. The only noise was the hum of the air conditioner.

'Face it, Winter, the date might be arbitrary.'

He shook his head slowly. 'It has to mean something.'

'Just because you want something to be true, it doesn't mean that it is.' She stopped talking and grinned to herself. 'You know, that sounds like the sort of bullshit line you'd come out with.'

'Very funny.'

'Look, don't feel bad. It was a good idea.' She stopped talking again. This time she was thinking rather than grinning. 'If it makes you feel better, I can call one of my contacts. If she died in a traffic accident then it might not have been a big enough story to make the paper.'

'If someone had died, it would have been in there, even if it was just a paragraph or two.'

Anderton put her hands up. 'Hey, I'm just trying to make you feel better.'

'I appreciate it, but don't bother. I know how this works. Some ideas pan out, most don't.'

'So cynical for one so young. What happened?'

Winter laughed wryly. 'You want to know what happened? Life happened.'

33

By seven that evening Winter was back in his hotel suite at the Shangri La. The TV was on, the sound muted. It was tuned to Global BC's news channel. Charlotte Delaney was on the screen. Her lips were moving, but he couldn't hear a word she was saying, which wasn't necessarily a bad thing. He poured a generous measure of Springbank and settled down on the sofa. Mozart's Piano Concerto Number 23 was playing on the room's sound system. For a while he just sat there with his eyes closed, listening to the music and sipping from his glass. Mozart and a good single malt. Life didn't get much better. This was his salvation. When the darkness threatened to overwhelm him this was where he came.

He could feel the frustrations creeping in, which was nothing new. Most detective work seemed to involve two sideways steps for every one forward. They'd made progress today, but the killer was still out there. The bottom line: they had thirty-six hours to catch him before the trail went cold. If that happened it would be another year before it turned hot again.

The first movement of the concerto was frenetic and playful, and made Winter itch to play. He didn't play anywhere near as often as he should these days. His lifestyle didn't allow for it. Guitars were portable, pianos weren't. There was a baby grand at his house in Virginia. It was a beautiful instrument. The keys were weighted just right and the tone was incredible. He hadn't been back there since the execution. At some point during the long drive home from California's San Quentin prison he'd made the decision to leave the FBI. He'd quit the next day, just packed up his desk, then gone home and packed a suitcase. He'd headed to the airport with no real plan of where he was going or what he might do when he got there. And here he was, still travelling, and still not sure where he might end up next.

The second movement started playing. It was slow and melancholic and as heartrending as anything that Mozart had ever written. The piece reminded him of his mom, but from the days after the arrest rather than the days when she still knew how to smile. After the arrest things had been unbearable for her, yet she'd hung on in there. Winter had often wondered why she hadn't killed herself.

Her funeral was the loneliest thing he'd ever witnessed. He was the only mourner, and that more than anything else brought home what his father had done to them. An instrumental version of 'Abide With Me' was playing through the crappy stereo system when Winter arrived at the chapel. He had traced the music to the source and pulled the plug. This had earned him a strange look from the priest, but he didn't care. His mother had loved music. There was no way he was subjecting her to this. He hadn't been able to save her, but at least he could spare her this final indignity.

He could still picture the coffin sitting at the front of the crematorium's tiny chapel, the sunlight laid across the wood, pink and green and golden, tinted by the cheap stained glass. A priest had gone through the motions, reciting his lines like a bored actor, his performance wooden and lacking any real emotion. And then her body had been consigned to the flames. As soon as the coffin was out of sight, Winter had walked away, the sound of his footsteps following in his wake and echoing in his ears. He hadn't looked back. There was no point. Whoever or whatever was in that coffin, it wasn't his mother.

The second movement drifted to a gentle close and he opened his eyes. He drained his glass and poured another inch. Myra Hooper's murder was still dominating the news. Right now, it was the only story in town. Winter checked his watch. Twenty-three after seven. So far, so good. The killer hadn't struck again. Not yet, at any rate. The two-hour window between six and eight was the danger zone. If they lasted through the next thirty-seven minutes they should be okay. 'Should' being the operative word. If they'd learned anything from today it was that they couldn't take anything for granted. Winter felt like he should be doing something, but what? Anderton had felt the same thing, too. In the end they'd decided to call it a day. The best thing they could do was get some rest so they could hit the ground running tomorrow.

The picture on the TV changed and Charlotte Delaney was back. She looked intense. Whatever she was saying, the future of mankind depended on it. The camera cut away and did a slow scan of the area. Winter recognised Spencer Avenue from this morning. There was still a major police presence, but the energy had changed. Earlier, everything had been charged by the newness of the situation. A little under twelve hours on and everyone was starting to get jaded. It was like everything had been dialled down a couple of notches. Cops were still milling around but without the same sense of urgency. The CSI truck didn't look as though it had moved. The area around the tree where Anderton found the footprint had been cordoned off with crime-scene tape.

Even though it was getting late there was a bigger crowd than earlier. That was to be expected. As soon as the news of a murder got out, people gravitated toward the crime scene. What were they hoping to see? The blood? The body? Because if that was the case then they were going to be sorely disappointed. Those were the first things to get hidden away. Crime-scene tents weren't just there to protect the evidence. It was the same mindset that encouraged people to try to see into the back of ambulances. Even though they were flying past, siren blaring, lights flashing, you still tried to peer through the dark glass to catch a glimpse of whoever was inside.

Winter still couldn't shake the feeling that they were close to a breakthrough, and that Cody was somehow the key. Assuming he was the only one who'd been approached by the killer, what made him so special? Why single him out? An updated version of the photo composite had been created from his description, but none of the husbands had recognised this new face. Sobek included. Freeman had sent someone to the cemetery to talk to him. The fact that nobody had recognised the face in the composite was far from conclusive. Eyewitnesses were unreliable at the best of times, and, in the case of Sobek, three years had passed since Isabella was murdered. Most people struggled to remember what they'd eaten for breakfast, never mind something that happened three years ago.

The third movement came to a satisfying close and for a

while Winter sat there in silence. It was an hour until sunset and the suite was slowly getting darker. The light from the TV flickered faintly around the room and painted ghostly abstract images on the wall. He took another sip of whisky and put the tumbler down. Was Sobek still at the cemetery or had he gone home? Winter decided that he'd still be there. He'd hang on in there until the bitter end, until the last trace of light had drained from the day.

An idea suddenly occurred to him and he chased it around for a while. The more he chased, the more he thought that he might be on to something. One of the big problems with this case was the lack of escalation. Serial killers were like drug addicts in that they were always chasing the perfect high. As the series progressed they took more and more risks in a futile attempt to attain that. The fact that the reality always fell short of the fantasy didn't put them off. If anything, it spurred them on.

When you looked at these murders, though, there was no escalation. The way Isabella Sobek was killed was the same as Alicia Kirchner, and her murder was the same as Lian Hammond's. There were differences with Myra Hooper's murder, but no real escalation. The way that all four women had been murdered was efficient and businesslike. There was no emotion. It was as though the killer was following a script. The impression being given here was that the murders were a means to an end. Which now made sense, because that's exactly what they were. A means to an end. The killer's real targets were the husbands.

And Cody.

The fact that the killer had talked to him marked a definite escalation. But there had to be some sort of payoff, otherwise what was the point? Serial killers had been known to join the crowds at crime scenes. Standing there knowing that they were responsible for all the chaos gave them a thrill. The fact that nobody knew who they were just made it more intense. Anderton had checked the crowds gathered at the earlier murder scenes to see if anyone stood out. No one had. Freeman would no doubt be doing the same thing with the latest scene, but Winter wasn't holding his breath.

Funerals sometimes drew killers out, and for the same reasons. It helped to intensify the memories. Anderton had been on the ball there, too. She'd filmed the mourners at the funerals, but nobody had stood out. Freeman would record those at Myra Hooper's funeral. Again, Winter had no great expectations.

At the moment it was as though the killer had set up the murders and that's where his involvement ended. This seemed like a lot of hassle for very little return. He'd be following the news. That much went without saying. But would that be enough to justify the time, effort and risk?

There was something missing from the picture. But what? What was actually going on here? Winter picked up his tumbler and sank back into the sofa. The glass was cold against his lips and the whisky burned his throat. He thought about Nicholas Sobek imprisoned in the basement of his luxury house. Then he thought about Eric Kirchner, broken and alone in his cheap landlord-decorated apartment. Then he thought about David Hammond three thousand miles away on the other side of the country. And Cody, nestled into his beanbag, lost and guilt-ridden and missing his mom.

With any murder the spotlight always fell on the victim. That's where the real action was. But what about the secondary victims? The ones who fell between the cracks? The Nicholas Sobeks and Eric Kirchners and David Hammonds and Cody Hoopers? Usually they were forgotten about, but not this time. This killer didn't care about the dead women, but he did care about their husbands. And Cody. They were the ones who resonated with him. Those were the ones who made his heart sing.

The killer had chosen his targets carefully, and he'd arranged it so they had killed someone they loved. And then he'd just walked away and hadn't looked back? That wasn't going to happen. Newton's Third Law came into play again. This guy had caused something to happen, and now that it had happened he would be curious to see what the reaction was. Winter was curious too, and he was nowhere near as invested.

So what had the killer seen when he glanced back over his shoulder?

It was a good question. This time Winter knew where to start looking for the answer. He called down to the front desk and asked the receptionist to call a cab. Then he drained his tumbler, grabbed his leather jacket and headed for the door.

34

A cab was waiting at the kerb when Winter got outside. He climbed into the back and gave the driver Eric Kirchner's address on East Seventh Avenue. Traffic was light and it only took ten minutes to get there. The driver pulled over to the sidewalk opposite the apartment and Winter got out. He watched the cab pull away before walking over to the entranceway of a nearby building and merging with the shadows gathering there. Then he lit a cigarette.

The sky was turning to orange and getting darker, the temperature dropping as night closed in. Eric Kirchner's apartment was on the third floor of the building directly opposite. The second window on the right was his living room. The drapes were drawn, the lights on, and the thin material was glowing like a Chinese lantern. Kirchner had probably closed them after they'd left earlier. Drapes didn't just keep the dark at bay, they also created a barrier that separated you from the rest of the world. It defined your safe place. Today was the anniversary of Alicia's murder. If there was ever a day when Kirchner wanted to keep the world at arm's length, this was it.

Winter took a long drag on his cigarette, the tip glowing hot and orange. Maybe the killer had walked along this street. Maybe he'd stood in this doorway and watched for a while. He could have done that easily enough without raising much suspicion. In the time Winter had been here ten cars had passed by and a couple of pedestrians, and no one had given him a second glance. And why should they? He was just a guy smoking a cigarette. Probably just waiting for someone. Nothing suspicious here, move on. And he wasn't even trying to be inconspicuous. If he had been, he would have had his cell out. Cell phones were perfect urban camouflage. Winter looked over at the apartment building and half expected Kirchner's face to appear at one of the windows. Had the killer harboured those same expectations? If so, had he been disappointed when it hadn't come to pass? And what had he done to curb that disappointment?

At some point watching wouldn't have been enough. He'd want to get closer. Like he'd done with Cody. Winter finished his cigarette and crossed the street. There was no lock on the apartment building door so he was able to walk straight in. He passed the line of mailboxes and headed for the stairs. So far he'd seen a total of zero security cameras. He climbed the stairs to the third floor and walked along the corridor to Kirchner's apartment. Still no cameras.

He knocked on the door. No answer, so he knocked again, harder this time. Still no answer. He tried a third time, really putting his weight into it. This was a full-on cop knock. Kirchner should be rushing to answer. Winter reckoned that he should be hearing hurried footsteps in the hall, and the rattle and thump as the lock was hastily undone. The door should be opening about now, and Kirchner should be standing there dazed and confused and looking like he was wondering who'd died.

But that wasn't happening, which was a concern. The

fact that the lights were on indicated that he was home. The fact that his beat-up heap of a car was parked outside reinforced this. Winter went through possible scenarios in his head. Worst case: Kirchner was in there with a belt wrapped around his neck, one end attached to a door handle. Or lying in a warm bath with his veins sliced open from elbow to wrist, the water turning pink. Or staring at the revolver on his lap, psyching himself up.

Because August 5 wasn't just a special date in the killer's calendar, it was special to Kirchner as well. Trigger points didn't just precede murders, they preceded all sorts of crazy irrational behaviour. It was a statistical truth that there were more suicides at Christmas than at any other time of the year. Why? Because Christmas was all about family and memories and having a good time. And if those memories were bad ones, and if the relationships had broken down, then things were going to get emotionally charged, and that's when suicide might start to seem like a good idea. The anniversary of a loved one's death would be high on that list too, particularly if the loved one had died violently and unexpectedly.

Winter knocked one last time, loud and insistent. Nobody came running to answer. His lock picks were wound up in a leather wrap in the inside pocket of his jacket. They were made from tungsten carbide and, in most instances, as good as a key. The lock was a standard Yale. No big deal. He might have come last in the self-defence classes at Quantico, but he'd aced lock-picking.

The tension wrench went in first. Winter laid it against the pins, moved it slightly to the left, then bounced it a couple of times to get a feel for how much pressure was required. Then he inserted the pick all the way to the back of the lock and slowly pulled it forward, disengaging the pins one by one. The last one released and he removed the pick. A quick twist of the tension wrench and the door was open. By his reckoning, he'd broken the ten-second barrier. He took one last look along the corridor then slipped quietly into the apartment.

35

The bathroom door was open but the bathtub was empty. No sign of steam rising from it. No water turning pink. Kirchner wasn't in the bedroom either. There was no belt attached to the handle. No body straining against the leather. Winter found him lying on the living-room sofa, eyes shut, not moving. His first thought was pills. Sleeping tablets or painkillers, or maybe antidepressants. But there were no empty pill bottles or bubble packs lying around. The only items on the table were a laptop, a large bottle of cheap vodka and a tall highball glass. Depending on your perspective, the glass was either half full or half empty.

Winter walked over to the sofa to check for a pulse. Before he got there Kirchner let out a loud snore and shifted to get comfortable. Winter froze. Any moment now Kirchner's eyes were going to spring open and the shouting would start. This was the sort of apartment block where people kept to themselves, the sort of place where shouted arguments were no doubt a common occurrence. It was unlikely that anyone would call the cops, but they might. Spending the night in a cell was not his idea of a good time.

Kirchner let out another snore and shuffled around on the sofa again. Winter stood very still and tried not to breathe. Kirchner moved one last time before settling down. His chest rose and fell, rose and fell. Winter counted six more breaths before deciding it was safe to move.

He walked over to the table and picked up the vodka bottle. If this had been opened today then Kirchner had drunk almost a pint and a half. If that turned out to be the case then he'd be out cold until morning. Winter put the bottle back down and tapped the laptop's trackpad. The screen flared to life and Alicia Kirchner's Facebook page appeared. There had been a flurry of new remembrance posts over the last couple of days. Not so many as last year and nowhere near the number there had been on the year of the murder. That was how it worked. With each passing year fewer and fewer people would remember, until no one did.

Winter clicked through the tabs. Kirchner had been surfing suicide websites. Sites that outlined the dos and don'ts, chat forums where depressed people could go to talk each other into killing themselves. When you got down to it the same questions were being asked over and over again. How did you make it quick and painless? How did you make sure you got it right? Most people didn't want to suffer. Nor did they want to wake up the next day and find that they'd screwed up. Judging by some of the material that Kirchner had been looking at it was probably just as well that he had passed out.

An old armchair was positioned next to the sofa. The chair was a faded blue, the sofa a dull red. Winter sat down in the armchair and thought about where he might hide a camera. The living room was an obvious first choice, since this was where Kirchner would spend most of his waking hours when he was at home. The TV tucked away in the corner was the room's focal point. It was a standalone unit rather than wall-mounted. The screen was maybe twenty inches, small by modern standards. Both the sofa and the armchair were angled toward it. The sofa had prime position, which indicated that this was where Kirchner preferred to sit. The fact that he was currently crashed out on it backed up this theory.

Winter walked over to the TV and hunkered down in front of it. From here he could see everything that was happening in the room. If you were looking to hide a camera this would be your start point. He checked the TV first, then the cabinet, then the walls and the ceiling surrounding it. Nothing. Next he moved clockwise around the room, checking everywhere he could think of. When he reached the door he walked back to the TV and went counterclockwise. Still nothing.

The bedroom was next. Assuming that passing out on the sofa wasn't a regular occurrence, this was where Kirchner would spend most of his time when he was at home. Eight hours a night. Maybe more, maybe less. It depended on his sleep pattern. The room smelled stale and the laundry basket was overflowing. The quilt was wrapped into a ball that had been discarded in the middle of the bed. The bed linen was crumpled and hadn't been washed in a while.

Winter perched on the edge of the bed and took a look around, wondering where he'd put a camera. Then he went searching. Five minutes later he admitted defeat. He tried the bathroom next, then the kitchen. Nothing and nothing. The kitchen was a health inspector's worst nightmare. It was a miracle that Kirchner hadn't poisoned himself. Winter felt sorry for him. He hadn't asked for any of this. He'd clearly given up on life. In that respect, Kirchner reminded Winter of his mom. She'd given up, too.

Kirchner was still alive when Winter got back to the living room. World War Three could have kicked off and he wouldn't have woken up. He moved Kirchner's feet to clear a space, then sat down. This didn't make sense. What was the killer hoping to gain by targeting Kirchner? As far as Winter could see he was getting nothing out of the deal. Zip, nada, zilch. But he had to be getting something. You didn't go to this amount of trouble without there being some sort of reward.

Winter tapped the trackpad and Alicia's Facebook page appeared on the screen. Another message of condolence had come in while he'd been going through the apartment, this one from one of Alicia's girlfriends. *Remembering the fun times. Miss you babes xxx.* The laptop was in easy reach of the sofa, a lifeline to the world that Kirchner was in danger of leaving behind for good.

It suddenly occurred to Winter that the TV wasn't the only focal point in the room. What about the laptop? He looked at the TV, then looked back at the laptop. It was a definite possibility. He checked Kirchner one last time to make sure that he was still breathing. He was lying on his side. If he threw up then at least he wouldn't choke to death.

Winter closed the laptop, then tucked it under his arm and headed for the door.

36

The sun was all the way down by the time Winter got outside, streetlamps burning the length of East Seventh Avenue. He dug Jefferies's business card from his back pocket and made the call. The detective answered on the fifth ring with a 'Yeah, who is it?' He sounded bright and alert, like he was cruising on adrenaline. Winter could relate.

'And you said I wouldn't call.'

'Winter?'

'You were expecting someone else? I've got to tell you, Jefferies, I'm hurting here. I thought I was the only one.'

'Whatever this is about, make it quick. I'm up to my eyes here.'

'Just wondering if there were any developments.'

'Nope. What about you? Got anything to share?'

'Not right now.'

'And how did I know you were going to say that.' Jefferies paused a second. 'Okay, now we've taken care of the preliminaries, how about you tell me why you're really calling?'

'I'm at Eric Kirchner's apartment. His lights are on, but he's not answering the door.'

'And why, pray tell, are you at Kirchner's apartment?'

'You're kind of missing the point here, Jefferies. Today is the anniversary of his wife's murder. When we saw him this afternoon he seemed depressed.'

'Yeah, I get all that. My question still stands, though. What are you doing at his apartment in the middle of the night?'

'It's not the middle of the night.'

Jefferies said nothing.

'I had a couple of follow-up questions,' Winter went on. 'He wasn't answering his phone, so I made a house call. His apartment's not far from my hotel. It's no big deal.'

Jefferies was still saying nothing.

'You have a duty to serve and protect. Right now, I'm just a concerned citizen who's worried about one of his fellow men. So are you going to send someone around to check on him or not?'

'Yeah, I'll send someone around.'

'Thank you.'

'I'd love to know what you're doing there.'

'It's no big deal.'

'You keep saying that.'

'Because it's true.'

'Well, when it ceases to be true, you give me a call, okay?'

The line went dead. Winter called a cab firm and asked to be picked up a couple of blocks from Kirchner's apartment. The police arrived before the cab. He'd figured that might happen. The systems used for dispatching the cars was the same. Whatever car was closest when the call came in got the job. The police cruiser that pulled up near the entrance to the apartment block was an old Crown Victoria. It was white and decorated with the Vancouver PD's livery. The roof bar lights were off, the siren silent. This was just a routine house call.

Two cops got out and banged their doors shut. The driver walked around the hood of the vehicle and stepped up onto the sidewalk. For a moment he stood there looking both ways along the street. His buddy was doing the same. Clearly they'd been told to be on the lookout for someone. A white male, no doubt. Five-feet nine, mid-thirties, white hair, green eyes. Winter pressed a little deeper into the shadows. They weren't looking too hard, which was just as well. If they had been, they probably would have spotted him. The driver said something and his buddy responded with a shake of the head. The exchange was perfunctory and easy to interpret. *You see him? Nope. Okay, let's go then.* They headed for Kirchner's apartment block and a second later they'd disappeared from sight.

A couple of minutes later his cab came along the street. Winter flagged it down, climbed into the back, then gave the driver directions to Nicholas Sobek's house in Kerrisdale. It was nine-thirty by the time he arrived.

Unlike the neighbouring houses, Sobek's was dark and silent. It reminded Winter of a haunted mansion, and to some extent that's exactly what it was. The house was haunted by Isabella's ghost. There were no lights on inside, no lights outside. That didn't mean Sobek wasn't at home. If he was here he'd be hidden away down in the basement. Down there it didn't matter whether it was night or day. Down there it didn't matter what anyone was doing out in the big bad world. The sun had set forty minutes ago. It didn't take forty minutes to drive here from the cemetery.

Winter walked up to the big steel gate and pressed the button on the intercom panel. Then he waited. Thirty seconds passed without any response. He stepped forward and pressed it again. This time his thumb stayed there for a good ten seconds. Still no response. There was no point trying a third time. Sobek was paranoid about security. The second the buzzer was pressed, all hell would have broken loose in the basement. Sirens, klaxons, warning lights and God only knew what else. There were two possibilities. Either he wasn't at home or he'd put a noose around his neck and jumped off of the balcony. Given that Sobek didn't strike him as suicidal, Winter was veering toward the former.

He went back over to the intercom and studied it more closely. There was no numeric keypad, so no opportunity to beat the system by punching in potential security codes. There was a button you pressed to speak, a microphone to talk into, and a small sensor for a remote gate key. There were only two ways to get through these gates. Either someone inside the house let you in or you had the remote key. He glanced up. Even if he could climb the wall it wouldn't have done any good because he would have ended up cut to pieces on the glass.

Winter crossed the street. Then he waited some more. Five minutes later a vehicle turned into the cul-de-sac. Judging by the low throaty roar, this was a high-spec performance car. Winter turned toward the sound and saw the unmistakeable profile of an Aston Martin Vantage. It was too dark to make out the driver's face, but it was a safe bet that it was Sobek.

The Vantage pulled up to the big iron gate. No one got out to use the intercom. No windows buzzed down. The big steel gate started to slide open, the motor straining to move all that metal. Before it had got even a quarter of the way along its track, the exterior lights suddenly slammed on, the bright halogens blasting the darkness away and illuminating the front of the property.

The car rolled forward onto the driveway and Winter crossed the street, making sure he kept out of the rear-view mirror, heading for the pillar that had the intercom attached to it. He pressed up against the wall to make himself smaller. The stone still retained some of the heat of the day. Every five seconds he would steal a glance to check on Sobek's progress. It was like watching a time-lapse video. Sobek was three-quarters of the way along the driveway. Now he'd stopped in front of the double garage. Now the doors were halfway up. Now they were fully up. Now the car had disappeared inside.

Winter waited until the gate had slid almost all the way closed before moving. The gap was down to a couple of feet, just wide enough to admit him, but shrinking with each passing second. He slipped through and started walking up the driveway. Behind him, the gate ground to a halt and the motor died. The sudden silence was eerie and unsettling. There was no point in attempting a stealth approach. That game was over. The exterior lights were so bright it was like the middle of the day. Whatever he did, Sobek would spot him.

A car door slammed shut in the depths of the garage. Five seconds later Sobek stepped out, blinking in the brightness. He was looking straight at Winter, following his progress as he walked toward him. His black hair was tied back into a ponytail and his gaze was as intense as ever. Winter stopped in front of him.

'Good day?' he asked.

'I've had better.'

'I take it the killer didn't turn up at the cemetery?'

'Nor at any of the other graves.' He nodded toward the

laptop. 'You've brought your computer. Is there something you want me to see.'

'It's not mine. It's Eric Kirchner's.'

Sobek raised a questioning eyebrow. Winter waited for the question to be verbalised, but it didn't happen.

'Let's talk inside,' Sobek said.

37

Sobek led the way along the path that bordered the front of the house. The bright halogens made the flowers in the planters look washed out. The grass looked artificial. They stopped at the front door. Sobek pressed his eye against the top scanner, his thumb against the bottom. Ten seconds passed, long enough for the metal detector to do its thing. The door clicked open.

'It's okay,' Winter said. 'I don't have a gun.'

'Should I be worried if you did?'

'That depends on whether you're a good guy or a bad guy.'

'I didn't murder my wife.'

'That doesn't necessarily make you one of the good guys.'

Sobek went inside. He hit a switch and the chandelier came on. Winter followed him through the impressive entrance hall, heading for the corridor that went behind the staircase. Sobek stopped at the basement door. He pressed his eye against the top scanner, his thumb against the bottom. The quiet click as the lock released was like a sigh. They descended the stairs in single file and turned right at the bottom. The door Sobek stopped at was made from the same brushed steel as all the other doors down here. It was heavy and unwelcoming. He opened it and they went inside.

Anderton had mentioned there was an office down here, and Winter figured that that's what he was looking at. There was a desk, a chair, a telephone and a computer, but that's where the similarity ended. The things you would usually expect to find were missing, all those little touches that helped to mark your territory. There was no ego wall, no bookcase, no filing cabinet, no sentimental ornaments. There were photographs, only there was nothing sentimental about them. At least, not in the traditional sense. They were displayed on three of the walls, one for each of the first three victims. Pictures from the crime scene and pictures from the autopsy. A morbid gallery of death and desolation.

The photographs relating to Isabella's murder had pride of place. These were on the wall directly opposite the desk. Whenever Sobek looked up this would be the first thing he saw. In one of the autopsy photographs Isabella's ribcage had been cracked open and her organs were exposed, wet and glistening under the bright surgical lights. In another the top of her skull had been removed, exposing her brain. The crime-scene photographs weren't much better. It made Winter wonder again where Sobek's head was at. Who the hell would want to see their wife looking like this?

Some of the crime-scene photographs were familiar because Anderton had sent through the same ones. And some were familiar because they'd been on the evidence boards in the incident room. And some he'd never seen before. It made him wonder how Sobek had got hold of them. At the same time he wasn't surprised. Motivation and money made a potent combination.

Alicia Kirchner's photographs were on the wall to the right, Lian Hammond's on the wall to the left. More crime-scene and autopsy pictures. More death and desolation. The fourth wall was blank. Presumably this had now been earmarked for the pictures from Myra Hooper's murder. Winter held out the laptop and waited for Sobek to take it.

'I'm figuring that either you or one of your private army of PIs knows a computer expert. I need them to take a look at this.'

'What exactly should they be looking for?'

'Evidence that the webcam has been accessed remotely.'

'You think the killer has been using it to watch Kirchner?'

'It's possible.'

Sobek didn't say anything for a moment. Winter was wondering how long it would take for him to catch up with what was happening here. In the end it took less than five seconds.

'Do you think he's been watching me?'

'If it turns out that he's been watching Kirchner, then he's probably been watching you, too. David Hammond as well.'

'Why?'

'First we need to work out if he has been accessing the webcam, then we can look at answering that.'

'If you've got some ideas, I want to hear them.'

'And you will. As soon as there's anything worth sharing I'll share it with Anderton, and then she'll share it with you.'

'I'm not the enemy here.'

'No you're not, but you do have a vested interest. Let's face it, you're not exactly an impartial observer.'

'All I want is for the bastard who killed my wife to be brought to justice.'

'And when you shut your eyes at night how exactly does that particular dream play out?'

'I just want to see him behind bars.'

'Do you? So you don't dream about putting a gun to his

head and pulling the trigger? Or driving a knife into his gut and keeping going until it pierces his heart?'

'I'm not going to lie, those thoughts have crossed my mind. But if you spoke to Eric Kirchner or David Hammond they'd tell you the exact same thing. Unfortunately, the reality of the situation is that I'd never get close enough to do anything like that. Right now, the best I can hope for is that the killer gets caught and the arrest goes bad.' He stopped talking and stared Winter in the eye. 'You know, if that was to happen, I'd be happy to pay a bonus.'

Winter said nothing.

'You were working a case in Detroit recently,' Sobek went on. 'That arrest went bad. And it's not as if this is the first time that something like this has happened on a case you were involved in. Statistically speaking, your strike rate seems to be above average.'

'There's no great conspiracy. The people I'm hunting know they've reached the end of the line. All they've got to look forward to is life imprisonment or a cell on death row. Faced with that prospect they go looking for a way out. Wouldn't you?'

'I'm betting that you don't lose much sleep, though. In fact, I doubt you lose any.'

'No, I don't. All that matters is that they've been stopped. Whether they're dead or in prison, it makes no difference.'

'So you don't even get a little bit of pleasure out of seeing them die?'

They locked eyes. Nobody spoke. It was Winter who eventually broke the silence.

'How big a bonus are we talking about here?'

'Name your price.'

'You couldn't afford me.'

'You think?'

'Two million bucks. And just so we're clear here, this is non-negotiable. If anything goes wrong, it's my ass that ends up in prison.'

For a moment Sobek just stood there with a calculated look on his face, like he was giving the proposal some serious thought. Then he grinned. 'If only it was that easy.'

'If only. Look, the last thing I need right now is you going vigilante. Even if you're going vigilante by proxy. Do you understand?'

The grin turned into a smile.

'I'm figuring that you're a bottom-line sort of guy,' Winter went on. 'So I'm going to lay out the bottom line for you. I can catch this guy, but if you get in my way that's going to make a tough job that much harder. And just so there's no misunderstanding, once he has been caught, he's going to go to trial, and then he's going to prison for the rest of his life. Do you understand?'

'I can live with that. Prisons are dangerous places. They're filled with thieves and murderers. You've got to wonder how long he'd survive in an environment like that.'

'And if he did end up stabbed in the shower, I wouldn't have a problem with that. Just so long as you had nothing to do with it.'

'It's good to know that we're on the same page.'

'Sobek, we're not even close to being on the same page.' Winter nodded to the desk, where Kirchner's laptop was lying. 'So, do you know anyone who could take a look at that?'

'Yes, I know someone.'

Sobek walked around the desk and sat down in the chair. He pulled the telephone toward him. While he made the call, Winter walked over to the wall that contained Isabella's pictures. Hidden away amongst all the devastation was a seven-by-five photograph that stood out because it had nothing to do with death and everything to do with life. It had been taken someplace hot. Isabella was standing next to a palm tree wearing a bikini with a loose wrap over the top. She looked happy and beautiful and full of life. Winter took it down and carried it over to the desk. Sobek was winding up his call. He dropped the receiver back into the cradle and rocked back on his chair.

'Someone will be around to look at the computer.'

'Tonight?'

'They're not in the city so it might take them a couple of hours to get here.'

'Get them to look at your computers as well.'

Winter placed the seven-by-five photograph on the desk and slid it over. Sobek picked it up and studied it. Even though he must have seen this photograph a thousand times, he was looking at it like this was the first. There was a wistful expression on his face, as though he was back in the moment. Chances were he'd taken the picture. That's where he was now. He was standing there with a camera in his hand, hoping to capture the perfect moment. Because that was the hope you harboured whenever you took a photograph. For every hundred taken, only one would have that extra something. Maybe the light was just right, or you somehow managed to catch the subject in a way that was interesting, a way that made you want to look at that picture again and again. It didn't happen very often but when it did it was like capturing a piece of magic. That's what had happened here. Sobek had captured a little piece of magic.

'Tell me about this photograph.'

'Why?'

Winter pointed to the wall that contained Isabella's pictures and Sobek followed his finger. The wistful expression had gone, replaced by something harder. The only photographs left there were the death ones. There was no cohesion to the narrative. Pictures of Isabella lying in the kitchen fought for space with pictures of her body after it had been brutalised by the ME's tools.

'That is not your wife.' Winter tapped the desk, bringing his attention back to the photograph in his hand. 'This is your wife.'

Sobek took another look at the photo. 'This was from our honeymoon in Antigua. Isabella had always wanted to go there. We were on our way back from the beach and it was just before sunset. I asked her to hold up for a second and took a quick picture on my cell. Just before I took it, she whispered that she loved me. It's my favourite picture of her.'

'Thank you for sharing that. Call me when your guy's had a look at the laptop.'

Winter headed for the door. He glanced back over his shoulder before opening it. Sobek was staring at the photograph, deep in thought. In that moment, he was just another victim, someone who'd lost someone dear to him. In a lot of respects he wasn't any different from Eric Kirchner or Scott Hooper. Sobek had said that he'd managed to escape from the hurricane. Looking at him sitting there, Winter wasn't so sure. There were some things that were impossible to move on from.

38

It was after eleven before Winter got back to the Shangri La. Even though he was exhausted, he wasn't ready to sleep. He poured a glass of Springbank, found the remote and settled down on the sofa. For a while he killed time surfing the channels. He was looking for a distraction, but kept coming back to the news. Myra Hooper's murder was still the only story in town. In another forty-seven minutes August 5 would become August 6. The countdown clock inside his head was ticking louder than ever.

The screen changed from a reality show where everyone was trying to out-humiliate each other to a film where all the actors had bad eighties haircuts and bad eighties clothes and really bad dialogue. Winter punched in the number for the news and the screen flickered and changed. To start with he thought he'd got the wrong channel. The picture was grainy and low-resolution, like it had been shot on a cheap cell phone. It had the feel of a film that would feature on *America's Funniest Home Videos*. But this wasn't the wrong channel. The Global logo was in the corner of the screen and the newsfeed was running along the bottom.

Winter turned up the volume then leant forward on the sofa. There was a bunch of kids on the screen. College students, by the looks of things. It was dark and they were drunk and overexcited, their attention fixed on something that was happening in the near distance. At this range, in this light, it was difficult to work out what they were staring at. He willed the camera operator to zoom in closer, and a second later that's exactly what happened.

The object everyone was focussed on was a stuffed toy bear. It was as large as a small baby, with brown fur and a happy smile. Three fireworks were attached to its body. For added authenticity they were held in place with duct tape. The fuses had been twisted together to create one single fuse. Someone moved in from stage left. The face was pixelated and the clothes were gender neutral, making it difficult to tell if they were male or female. A prank like this, male seemed more likely. They were holding a lit taper, which inferred a minimal amount of common sense and a passing acquaintance with firework safety. They touched the taper to the fuse then ran like hell, which suggested that self-preservation had been considered, albeit fleetingly.

The laughter stopped and everything fell silent. Winter couldn't see the other students, but he could sense their presence. They'd be pushing forward as close as they dared, eyes fixed to the toy bear. The fuse flared and burned, getting shorter and shorter, then it split into three, the flames chasing closer to the fireworks. All three went off at more or less the same instant, creating a series of bangs that sounded like rapid gunfire. The bear jumped three feet in the air before landing in a heap and bouncing to a stop. It was lit up white, blue, red and green. Unlike the killer, these kids hadn't bothered to separate the gunpowder from the flash powder.

The cheering and laughter had started up immediately

after the bangs, and was getting louder and more frenzied as the mob mentality kicked in. The last firework burned out and the kid with the camera ran over to get a closer look. The bear had been completely destroyed. Its head was hanging off and the stuffing had been blown out of it. The fur was smouldering and burning, the flames getting bigger. The picture cut back to the news studio. The anchor was describing how police had been called to break up a student party near the university. She actually called it an execution party. The whole thing had been organised via social media. Apparently a similar thing had happened last year.

Winter had seen enough. He switched off the TV and picked up his tumbler. This was just a case of dumb college kids acting like dumb college kids. There was no real harm intended. They were just out looking for fun. It had no doubt seemed like a good idea at the time. Drink some beers, have a few laughs, cause a little mayhem. As far as they were concerned it was all a big joke. This had nothing to do with reality. If they were to come face to face with that it wouldn't end well. Put them in a crime scene or an autopsy lab and they'd last two seconds before puking or passing out. His cell phone rang. He picked it up, checked the caller ID, then connected the call.

'People are going to talk, Jefferies. You know how gossip spreads around police stations.'

'I just thought you'd like to know that Eric Kirchner is alive and well. His sister lives in the city. She's gone over to his apartment to make sure he stays that way.'

'That's good to hear.'

'Now here's an interesting thing, and maybe it's something

you can help with. Kirchner is claiming that someone broke into his apartment and stole his laptop. He's pretty pissed, and understandably so. I don't suppose you know anything about this?'

'Maybe he misplaced it.'

'Or how about this? Maybe someone broke into his apartment and stole it.'

'What else was taken?'

'Nothing else was taken.'

'Mmm,' said Winter. 'Someone goes to the trouble of breaking into his apartment but all they take is the computer. Doesn't that strike you as strange?'

'That depends on their motivation.'

'You know, when I was interviewing Kirchner, it occurred to me that he might have a drink problem. Maybe that's what's going on here. Maybe he got drunk and misplaced it.'

'We've been all through his apartment and couldn't find it. As you know, it's not that big. There really aren't that many places where he could have *misplaced* it.'

'Looks like you've got a mystery on your hands.'

'It certainly looks that way.'

'Did you hear back from the lab about superglue being used on that tree?'

'We did. It's bad news, I'm afraid. No trace of superglue or any other solvents was found. And it gets worse. We matched the shoe print to the owner of the house opposite Myra Hooper's. He was able to fill us in on what happened. Someone had stapled a lost cat poster to the tree. When he pulled it down, a chunk of bark came with it.'

'Don't you just hate it when an idea doesn't pan out?'

'We've got a first-rate IT department. They'd love to take a look at Kirchner's laptop.'

'And what would they be hoping to find?'

'You tell me.'

'Nothing springs to mind.'

'You know, they'd be really pissed if they discovered that an amateur had been poking around in it and that evidence had been destroyed.'

'I could understand that.'

'So if I came over there I wouldn't find the laptop.'

'No, you wouldn't. And I can state that categorically.'

'Okay, let's say that hypothetically the computer did somehow come into your possession, and let's say, hypothetically speaking, that you found something on there. If that was to happen I would expect you to let me know exactly what was found.'

'Hypothetically speaking, I wouldn't have a problem with that. No problem whatsoever.'

'Call me.'

'Missing you already.'

39

Winter was dreaming of Marilyn when his cell rang. She was emerging slowly from a giant cake, singing 'Happy Birthday, Mr President' in a breathy whisper. The sequins of her dress were glinting in the bright stage lights. People were laughing and cheering. It was impossible to tell if they were laughing at her or with her. That was the tragedy of Marilyn. It could have gone either way.

The phone rang again and a rush of adrenaline burst through his body. His eyes sprang open. It was dark outside, which meant that it was still the middle of the night. Nobody called at this hour with good news, not unless they were in a different time zone and had got the math wrong. He grabbed his cell from the coffee table and connected the call. According to the screen it was twenty-three minutes after two. Whoever it was, they were calling from a phone that his cell didn't recognise. For a brief second he wondered if the killer had somehow got hold of his number. Weirder things had been known to happen.

'Who is this?'

'Sobek. You said to call when my guy had looked at Kirchner's laptop. Well, he's looked at it.'

'And?'

'He found a rat.'

'I take it we're talking in acronyms here. You mean a Remote Access Trojan, right?

'That's correct. The killer is able to access the webcam whenever the computer is switched on. It's set up so the camera light is disabled. Kirchner wouldn't have known he was being watched.'

'Is there any way to trace the RAT back to the killer?'

'Let me ask.'

'Your computer guy's still there?'

'He is.'

'Put him on.'

There was a quick muffled conversation, then a new voice came on the line.

'How can I help?'

The voice sounded too bright and efficient for this time of the day. Winter was picturing a guy wearing the most expensive suit he could afford, a mid-level white-collar worker with aspirations. A realtor or an accountant or maybe an office manager. What he wasn't picturing was your standard-issue computer geek.

'I want to know if it's possible to trace where the RAT came from.'

'Not really. This guy's hidden his tracks well. He's routed and rerouted through multiple servers. Given enough time and computer power you might be able to find him, but it wouldn't be easy.'

'He must have known Kirchner's IP address.'

'He targeted Kirchner's laptop specifically, so, yes, that's my conclusion.'

'How difficult would it be to get hold of that?'

'Assuming that Kirchner is as negligent with his security as ninety-nine point nine per cent of the population then it wouldn't be too difficult.'

'How would you do it?'

The line went quiet. 'Do we know where he lives?'

'We do.'

'In that case I'd go in through his Wi-Fi router. I'd park as close to where he lives as I could, then I'd compare signal strengths so I could make an educated guess as to which router was his. Once I'd done that I'd launch a brute force attack to break the password.'

'How long would this take?'

'It could take a while. Am I worried about being seen?'

'Yes.'

'In that case, I'd lock my laptop in the trunk, leave the car parked at the kerb and come back later. You don't need to be sitting in the car while the program's running.'

'What about Sobek's computers? Any RATs on them?'

'No, his computers are clean. There was evidence that someone had tried to infiltrate his systems. Fortunately, he belongs to the point one per cent who take security seriously.'

'When did this happen? Kirchner's RAT, I mean.'

'Three months after his wife was murdered.'

'Was any attempt made to infiltrate his computer before the murder?'

'No. Only afterwards.'

Winter went quiet while he thought things through. The victims had not been chosen at random, they'd been targeted, which meant that the killer needed to carry out surveillance. Two facts came into play here. Fact number one: this guy took a hands-off approach. In hindsight, sneaking around outside Myra Hooper's house, planting cameras, just wasn't his style. Fact number two: the killer had accessed the web-cam on Kirchner's laptop and that established a behaviour. If he was using webcams to watch the victims post-offence, then it made sense that this was how he'd be watching them *pre*-offence.

'Are you still there?' the computer guy asked.

'I'm still here. Can you put Sobek back on?'

The line went quiet and there was a muffled conversation that was the complete reverse of the last one. The computer guy would be holding his hand over the mouthpiece and telling Sobek that he was wanted.

'What?' Sobek asked.

'Did Isabella own a laptop?'

'Of course she did.'

'And do you still have it?' Before Sobek could answer, Winter added, 'Dumb question. Of course you do. Get your computer guy to take a look at it. I want to know if the killer managed to get a RAT in there. Call me as soon as you've got anything.'

Winter hung up and tapped the phone against his leg. The tune going around inside his head was annoying, and of his own invention. It seemed to blend everything that was bad about pop and dance music. The tempo was 120 beats per minute and the tune was annoyingly repetitive. It could have been a hit. Sobek called back six minutes later.

'He got into Isabella's laptop.'

40

Anderton answered on the fourth ring with a sleepy, 'This better be good, Winter. It's the middle of the goddamn night.'

'I've had a breakthrough.'

There was a rustle of covers and a gentle grunt. It was easy to imagine her sitting suddenly bolt upright in bed, alert and completely awake. 'Okay, I'm listening.'

'This is one of those things that's best done in person.'

A sigh. 'Fine. I can be at the Shangri La in twenty minutes. I just need to throw some clothes on.'

'You don't need to go anywhere. I'm standing outside your apartment block.'

'Seriously?'

'Seriously.'

'Do you have any idea how creepy this is?'

From where Winter was standing in the middle of the street he had a good view of Anderton's apartment block. One of the windows on the second floor suddenly lit up. A second later the drapes parted and a face appeared. He gave Anderton a little *toodle-oo* wave. She didn't wave back.

Winter hung up and hurried over to the entrance. The door was buzzing when he got there. He went inside and took the stairs two at a time. Anderton was waiting in the doorway of her apartment. She'd thrown on a baggy Canucks T-shirt and some jeans. Her hair was pulled back into a quick ponytail. The look suited her. It seemed to smooth off some of her sharper edges. She headed back inside without a word. The implication was clear. *Follow me.* Winter walked into the narrow hallway and pushed the door closed behind him. Anderton was already at the other end of the hall. She disappeared through a door on the right. The hallway was short, so it didn't take long to catch up.

The living room was as neat and tidy as her SUV, which was no great surprise. Anderton lived to impose order on a world that was fast turning to shit. All the books were lined up neatly on the bookshelf, the remote controls were in a pile next to the DVD player, and the cushions were plumped and arranged on the furniture like a magazine photoshoot was about to take place.

'Take a seat,' she said.

'I'm not sure I want to. I don't want to mess anything up.'

'Very funny. So how did you know where I live?'

'Sobek told me.'

'So, what? You're BFFs now?'

Winter smiled. 'I wouldn't go that far. Let's just say that we've put our differences aside and found a place where mutual co-operation, although tenuous, is obtainable.'

Anderton let loose with a small chuckle. 'Yeah, that's pretty much the same place that I've got to. Okay, start talking. What's got you so excited?'

'The killer has been watching Kirchner. He planted a Remote Access Trojan on his laptop and is using that to hack into his webcam.'

Anderton took a moment to process this. If she was excited by the news, it didn't show. She was chasing the implications inside her head, seeing where they might lead. Her expression was pensive and thoughtful, her gaze fixed on one of the wall pictures, a print of a poppy on a large canvas.

'And how exactly did you reach this conclusion? Or to put it another way, how did you get access to Kirchner's laptop?'

'I broke into his apartment and found him passed out drunk. Given the state he was in, I figured that he wouldn't be needing his laptop for the foreseeable future, so I stole it. Sobek had one of his people take a look at it and they found the RAT.'

Anderton shook her head. She was trying to look serious but the hint of a smile was tugging at the corners of her mouth. 'I'm going to be honest with you, Winter. Right now, I'm not sure whether you should be praised for your initiative or arrested.' She fell silent again. 'What about Sobek and David Hammond? Have their computers been infiltrated?'

'Sobek's haven't, but not through want of trying.'

'Because he's so paranoid about security?'

'Exactly. Isabella's laptop had been, but that would have happened before the paranoia kicked in. As for Hammond, I don't know. I'm considering letting Jefferies run with that one.'

'That's very generous of you.'

Winter responded with a shrug.

'Winter?'

'Okay, okay. Jefferies suspects that I stole the laptop. I'm figuring it wouldn't do any harm to throw him a bone.'

'You do know that stealing is a crime?'

'And you've never broken the rules, Anderton?'

'Maybe once or twice,' she admitted. 'But only when the end justified the means.'

'And in this case the end justifies the means.'

'Are we thinking that the killer is some sort of computer genius?'

Winter shook his head. 'He would need to be comfortable with computers, but he wouldn't necessarily need to be an expert. The malware is readily available online. The people who download it are mainly teenage boys, and men who want to spy on their wives and girlfriends. These programs are simple enough for a kid to use, which means that our guy isn't going to have too much trouble using it.'

'Okay, now that we have a direct connection with the killer, how do we use that to our advantage?' She went quiet, considering the question. 'I need coffee. What about you?'

'Always.'

Anderton got up and headed for the hall. Her office door was open so Winter was able to get a good look as they passed it. If you compared the size of the room against the footprint of the apartment, then this had to be the main bedroom, which meant that she was using the spare one for sleeping in. Her map of the city covered more or less the same area as the map in his suite. She'd marked off the target area with a red circle. Red crosses for the murder sites, and a brand-new cross where Myra Hooper had died. The photographs were arranged in three distinct groups, one for each of the first three victims. Winter had seen most of these before. Some of them were on the wall of his suite. All of them were in Sobek's office. There were no pictures of Myra Hooper. It was too early for Anderton to have got hold of those yet.

The kitchen was as spotless as the living room. Anderton filled the kettle and put it on to boil. She didn't say anything, just used the time to chase her thoughts. She finished pouring and handed Winter a mug. He sugared it and took a sip.

'The killer's at his most vulnerable when he accesses the webcam,' she said. 'There must be some way of working backwards to find his computer. If we find that then we can work out where he is.'

'Sobek's guy doesn't think that would work, but it's worth getting a second opinion. When you speak to Jefferies ask him to get his computer people to look into that.'

'We could use the webcam to contact the killer directly,' Anderton suggested. 'But what do we say to him?'

'Before we answer that we need to work out what's motivating him. If he's hacking into the webcams before the murders then the reason is fairly obvious. He's gathering intel on his victims. The more information he's got, the smoother things are going to go. But why would he want to watch the husbands afterwards? I'm figuring that he must be interested in their reactions. That's his payback.'

Anderton made no response to that. Winter gave her another few seconds, but she still had nothing to add. He took another sip of coffee, then shut his eyes and imagined the killer sitting in a darkened room.

*

Everything is quiet and still and I'm all alone. Except I'm not alone because I have Eric Kirchner for company. He's on my computer screen. I watch him pour out a large glass of neat vodka, watch him take a long swig. His face screws up, but he doesn't stop drinking. He keeps going until his glass is empty. He's a shadow of the person he once was. And I'm the reason for that. This empty shell is my creation.

*

Winter opened his eyes.

'Cause and effect,' he said. 'It's not money that makes the world go round, it's Newton's Third Law. That's what's going on here.'

Anderton gave him a puzzled look. 'I'm not really following.'

'Earlier I was watching TV and it seemed that every other programme was a reality show. They all follow the exact same format. A group of people are put in a high-pressure situation and the viewers at home get to watch. The killer is doing pretty much the same thing. In this case the husbands kill their wives. That's your high-pressure situation. The big difference is that there's only one viewer watching at home.'

'So, what? The purpose of all this is entertainment?'

Winter shook his head. 'That's where the analogy falls down. He's not doing this for fun. This is serious business. And I doubt he's sharing with the viewers at home. This is very much for his own benefit. All of us are voyeurs to one degree or another. That's why reality shows are so popular.' He paused. 'The early reality shows were billed as social experiments, because back then they needed to be justified. Except they weren't experiments. Not even close. They were mob events. In that respect they had more in common with the gladiator battles in ancient Rome than any form of legitimate science. This, however, *is* like a sociological experiment. Basically he's caused something to happen and, like the good scientist he is, he's sat out there somewhere observing and recording the results.'

'Okay,' Anderton said, 'back to my original question. What do we say to him?'

'At this stage we don't say anything.'

'We don't?'

'First we need to get his attention. We need him to understand that he's no longer calling the shots. And we do that by making it so that he can't watch. Believe me, that'll make him sit up and take notice.'

Anderton shook her head. 'That won't work. If we disable the RAT then we won't be able to communicate with him.'

'Who said anything about disabling it?' Winter walked over to the refrigerator. A pad of sticky notes was fixed to the door with a magnet. He took the pad down, peeled off the top sheet and held it up. 'If you want to stop someone spying on you with a webcam, this will work every time. Stick it over the lens and your privacy is guaranteed. When we want to talk to him, all we've got to do is take it off.'

'Yeah, that'll work.' Anderton found her cell phone and switched it on.

'Who are you calling at this time?' Winter asked.

'Freeman. He needs to know about the RAT.' She paused, smiled. 'If I'm awake I don't see why he shouldn't be. After all, technically this is his case.'

41

Winter woke up with a stiff neck and warm sunlight on his face. The drapes didn't quite meet in the middle and the light was flooding in. All that brightness was making his eyes ache. Anderton's sofa was smaller than the one in his suite, and nowhere near as comfortable. It was better than sleeping on the floor, but not by much. He sat up and stretched and scrubbed the sleep from his eyes. Anderton was already up and about. He could hear her getting busy in the kitchen. Whatever she was up to in there, it sure smelled good.

He pulled on his jeans, then went through to join her. She was over at the stove, a frying pan in one hand, a spatula in the other, an apron to protect her clothes from fat splashes. The omelette looked impressive. Mushrooms, onions, peppers, the works. There was something almost maternal about the way she was looking at him. He half expected her to check behind his ears for dirt.

'You look like crap,' she said.

'I'll be fine after a coffee and a cigarette.'

'The coffee I can help with, but if you want a cigarette you need to go outside.'

She poured a coffee and handed him the mug. Winter sat down at the table and took a sip.

'This is great coffee.'

'Glad you approve. You want something to eat?'

'Does the pope shit in the woods?'

She laughed at that, then dished the omelette out on to two plates, half each, equal portions all around. She put one of the plates in front of Winter then sat down opposite him.

'This is amazing,' he said between mouthfuls. 'Oh, and thanks for the use of your sofa.'

'You're welcome.'

'What time is it, anyway?'

'Eight-thirty.'

'It's later than I thought.'

'You were snoring when I woke up, so I left you to it. I figured you needed your beauty sleep.'

'Yeah, it was a busy night.'

'Busy but productive.'

'Any news from Freeman?' Winter asked.

'Freeman's dodging my calls. No great surprise there.'

'What about your winged monkeys? Anything from them?'

'Not yet. I'm hoping to hear something soon, though.'

Winter finished eating then went outside for a cigarette. Anderton was in her office when he got back. She gave him another quick once-over, starting at his head and working down to his toes.

'I've got to say, I'm not seeing any improvement.'

'Thanks.'

The fold-up chair leaning against the wall didn't look as though it had been moved in a while. Winter set it up at the side of the desk and sat down. He glanced at the map, then the photographs. Then he looked at Anderton.

'Some people believe that dreams are a way for the subconscious mind to communicate with the conscious mind.'

Anderton leant back in her chair and made a big deal of giving him her full attention. 'I take it you're going somewhere with this.'

'Last night I dreamt of Marilyn Monroe. She was coming out of a giant cake, singing "Happy Birthday" to President Kennedy.'

'Is this about August 5 again?'

Winter nodded.

'Okay, so your subconscious was trying to communicate something through this dream. Any idea what?'

'I think it was trying to tell me to simplify things. Everything about the dream was blown out of proportion. For a start, Marilyn never climbed out of a giant cake, she just stood on a stage under a spotlight and sang the song. And everything in my dream was in bright Technicolor. The only footage that exists is black and white. This got me thinking. Sometimes a birthday is just a birthday. It's no big deal really. Same goes for death. It's just one of those things that happen. So far we've been focussed on the trigger event being a big deal. What if it wasn't? What if the killer's mom just passed away? I want the names of all the women who died in the city on August 5. I don't care how they died. In fact, the less spectacular the better.'

'We already looked at that.'

'But you only went back fifteen years. Let's assume that Cody represents the killer as a boy and Myra represents his mom. Cody's ten, Myra's thirty-three. That means the killer's mom died twenty-three years ago. So that's where we need to start looking. Do you have a contact at the records office?'

'You could say that.'

The response was purposefully vague. Before Winter could push for an explanation, Anderton's cell phone rang. She glanced at the display, then grinned to herself.

'It's one of my contacts.'

The call lasted less than thirty seconds, just long enough for the caller to pass on whatever information they needed to pass on. It was easy to imagine her contact skulking around the corridors at headquarters, looking for somewhere they wouldn't be overheard. She was still grinning when she hung up.

'Good news?' Winter asked.

'There was a RAT on David Hammond's computer. And there was one on Cody Hooper's laptop, too.'

'All we've got to do now is work out what the killer sees when he's watching them.'

'Easier said than done.'

'That's why they pay us the big bucks, Anderton. What time does the records office open?'

Anderton glanced at her watch. 'About five minutes ago.'

'In that case, let's hustle.'

42

Anderton's contact gave the impression that he'd been working at the records office since the beginning of time. He had to be well into his sixties, maybe even pushing seventy. He was wearing a flamboyant paisley-print vest under his jacket and a bright red bow tie. His impressive moustache had curled waxed tips. He was grossly overweight, but all those extra pounds seemed to suit him. His name was Alan Smith, which was a disappointment. There was something Dickensian about him. His name should have reflected this.

His office was small but tidy. And dark. The view from the window was blocked by the neighbouring building, which also affected how much light got in. Judging by the lack of space, the two chairs in front of the desk had been brought in especially for this meeting. There was a coffee in front of each chair. White for Anderton, black for Winter. They sat down and Smith got settled in the chair on the other side of the desk.

'It's good to see you again, Uncle Alan.'

'Always a pleasure, my dear. By the way, you need to phone your mother. I was having lunch with her last week and she was complaining that you never call.'

'I spoke to her last night.'

Smith raised an eyebrow, calling her on the lie.

'Okay, okay, I'll phone her tonight.'

Winter was battling to keep a straight face. His own family might have been the textbook definition of dysfunctional but he knew how the theory worked. Everyone had their place in the hierarchy. It didn't matter how old you got, those positions were set in stone. He'd just witnessed a fifty-three-year-old woman being reduced to a child again.

'You said on the telephone that you need help with the August 5 Bomber case.'

'That's right. We've had some new information and we think it could shed light on why the date is significant.'

'Well, anything I can do.'

Anderton gestured toward Winter, indicating that this was his show.

'We're going to need a list of all the women who died in the city on August 5, 1992. Ages as well.'

'No problem. You'll have to bear with me a second, though.'

Smith pulled the keyboard closer and went to work. In the end it took a couple of minutes to get the information and print it out. He handed the printout to Anderton.

'Thanks. May I borrow a pen, please?'

Smith took a pen from the desk drawer and passed it over. Anderton laid the printout on the desk and Winter crowded in to get a better look. There were seven names on it. The killer's mother would have been older than fourteen but younger than forty-five when she gave birth. Working on the assumption that the killer was the same age as Cody when his mom died, they could eliminate anyone younger than twenty-four and older than fifty-five.

That left one name. Anderton's brown eyes were shining

with hope but her mouth was shut tight. She wasn't saying a word in case she jinxed things. Winter had a good idea of what she was feeling because he was feeling it as well. Smith, too. He'd rolled his chair as near to the edge of the desk as his gut would allow and was leaning in to get closer to the action.

'The third name on the list,' said Winter. 'Catriona McDonald. Does she have any children?'

Smith ran a search. Even before he spoke, it was clear that the news wasn't good. His shoulders sagged and he looked like someone had stolen his candy. 'No,' he said.

'This could still work,' Anderton said. 'Try Julia Macey. Number five on the list. She would have been forty-eight when she gave birth, which is old to have a child but not outside the realms of possibility.'

Smith did another search. 'She had two daughters. Both were in their thirties when she died.'

'Not Julia Macey, then.'

'It's not over yet,' Winter said. 'Remember, we're working on the fact that Myra is thirty-three and Cody is ten. The killer and his mom might have been slightly older.'

'Or younger,' Anderton put in. 'Uncle Alan, can you run searches for 1991 and 1993, please?'

'Certainly.'

Smith clicked with the mouse and pecked at the keyboard with his fat fingers. He hit enter with another flourish then walked across to the printer. There were two printouts this time. One for each year. Eight names on one, six on the other. Anderton beat Winter to the pen. When she was finished they were left with two names for 1991. She passed the printouts back to Smith and he started searching the birth register.

No one was talking because no one needed to. By now they all knew their respective roles. Smith finished searching and sat up a little straighter.

'They both had one son. Esme Brown's was fourteen when she died. Gemma Wood's was ten.'

'Gemma's son was the same age as Cody, so let's start with her. How did she die?'

'It says here that she had a cerebrovascular accident.'

'Thirty is way too young to be having a stroke. Was she married?'

Smith did another search. 'Yes, she was. To Nathaniel Wood.'

'Run another search. See if he's still alive. If he is, we're going to want to speak to him.'

The small office had gone very still and quiet. Winter and Anderton were both staring across the desk at Smith. He hit the enter key. There was no flourish this time. He'd picked up on how serious this was and reeled in his eccentricities. A couple of seconds later the results pinged up onto the screen and his eyes widened.

'Nathaniel Wood died on April 21, 1991. He was thirty-five. The cause of death was internal bleeding.'

'Which was a little over three months before his wife,' Anderton said.

'It was,' Winter agreed. 'And if they'd been old I wouldn't have a problem with them dying so close together. That sort of thing happens. You get two people who have spent their whole life together and are so devoted to each other that they can't bear to be apart. When one of them dies the other just fades away.'

'But Gemma Wood was only thirty.'

'Exactly. And Nathaniel was only thirty-five. They're in completely the wrong age group for something like that to happen.'

Winter jumped to his feet and headed for the door. Anderton was on her feet as well.

'Where are we going?' she asked.

'The *Vancouver Sun*'s offices.'

He stopped so suddenly that she almost ran into him. He turned back to Smith.

'By the way, what's the son called?'

It only took a couple of clicks for Smith to backtrack to the relevant page.

'His name is William Wood.'

43

'Two visits in two days, Laura. I'm honoured.'

Rebecca Byrne strode through the reception area with her arm outstretched and a grin on her face. She shook hands with both of them. Anderton first, then Winter. Today's dress was as red as yesterday's but a different design. If anything her lipstick was a shade brighter. It contrasted starkly against her pale, waxy skin. That two-pack-a-day voice was exactly the same, though.

'So you want to see our back issues again. Anything you feel like sharing?'

'Not at this precise moment,' Anderton said.

'But you're making progress?'

'I think so.'

'You think? Either you are or you're not.'

'Okay, we've made some progress.'

'But you're not prepared to enlighten me.'

'Not at this stage, no.'

'Can I ask why?'

'You can ask.'

'But you're not going to tell.'

Anderton smiled briefly. 'We're trying to find a way to draw the killer out. The last thing we want is to drive him any deeper underground.'

Byrne opened her mouth to speak. She hesitated as

something occurred to her. There was a tiny smear of red on one of her front teeth.

'Do you know who the killer is?' she asked carefully.

'No, we don't,' Winter said.

She turned her head to the right and met his eye. 'You're close to identifying him, though.'

'We have a possible lead, that's all. There's still a lot of work to be done.'

'That wasn't a no.'

'Rebecca,' Anderton said, and the journalist's eyes snapped back to her. 'Stop digging. As soon as we have anything worth sharing, we'll share.'

'If you could get something to me before today's deadline that would be really helpful.'

'Stop digging.'

Byrne smiled. 'Shall we?'

They followed the same route as the day before. The newsroom door was closed, but Winter could still hear the bustle and the raised voices. He could sense the chaotic energy that was being generated back there. Byrne stopped outside the door of the archive room. She pushed it open then stepped aside.

'I'll be expecting your call, Laura.'

'You can count on it.'

They went inside and walked over to the shelves. April was in the first of 1991's three volumes. He pulled the book down and carried it across to the table. Nathaniel Wood had died on April 21, so the logical place to start looking was April 22.

'A car crash would cause internal injuries,' Anderton said.

'Another possibility is that he committed suicide by jumping from a skyscraper.'

'Or maybe he was a parachutist and his lines got tangled.'

'So we know the sort of thing we're looking for?'

'We do.'

Anderton crowded in closer. She was smelling fresh, like she'd managed to get a shower this morning. Winter was suddenly conscious of the fact that he hadn't had one since yesterday. He flipped the book open and started turning the pages. Days and weeks flashed by, random headlines jumping out. Melodrama in a large bold typeface.

The lead story for April 22 centred on a nursing shortage at Vancouver General. Other than there being a delay in getting treatment, Winter couldn't see how this might be linked to Nathaniel Wood dying from internal injuries. That was a stretch, though, a real clutch for a straw. All hospitals operated a triage system. It didn't matter if you were on the frontline of a war zone, or in a small country hospital, or a large urban facility like Vancouver General, that was the way it worked. If someone was brought in presenting life-threatening injuries they'd get bumped to the top of the list. Staff would be found to deal with the emergency.

The story continued on page three and took up most of the space above the fold. The rest of the page was taken up with a political story, so that was a bust. Page two was a bust as well. Winter turned to the next page. The second he saw the headline his mind lit up with a whole host of possibilities. Anderton inhaled a sharp breath and exhaled a whistle. She glanced at him, looking for confirmation that her eyes weren't playing tricks. He was looking at her, searching for the same thing. The left-hand quarter of page five had been given over to the story. The headline read: MOTHER AND SON IN MIRACLE ESCAPE FROM PLANE CRASH.

Winter scanned the story. The crash had happened on April 21, a Sunday. The plane was a small single-prop Cessna. It had been flying for forty minutes when it developed engine trouble. The pilot had sent out a Mayday then tried to perform an emergency landing on a highway. Witnesses told how the plane had come in steep and hard and tipped over. The pilot had died instantly. The mother and son had been airlifted to Vancouver General. At the time of the newspaper's deadline no names had been released.

The crash had happened in the late afternoon, which was reflected in the way the story was presented. It felt as though it had been thrown together from sketchy information, like whoever wrote it was pushing a hard-and-fast deadline. This was backed up by the fact that it was buried away on page five. Newspapers operated a triage system too. If a big story came in just before the deadline then that edition would be rearranged accordingly. A plane crash was always going to trump a story about a nursing shortage. It had drama and excitement and a strong human interest angle. Unfortunately, it wasn't quite big enough for the presses to be halted. For that to happen they would have needed more deaths. If the plane had ploughed into a crowded building or taken out a coachload of tourists, that would have done it. But that hadn't happened.

'What do you think?' Winter asked.

'I think that an air crash would cause internal injuries.'

'Me, too.'

He flipped through the pages and stopped when he got to April 23. The story had made it to the front page, which supported the theory that the deadline had been too tight the day before. There was a new angle, too. The headline read: AIR CRASH MOTHER IN COMA. There was a photograph of the wrecked Cessna lying on the edge of a long, lonely, straight stretch of highway. The wings had sheared clean off and the plane had come to rest lying on its side.

'We've got names,' said Anderton.

She was pointing to the first paragraph. Winter followed her finger. Nathaniel Wood had been named as the pilot and Gemma had been named as the mom. She'd suffered serious head injuries in the crash and been placed in a medically induced coma. William was named in the second paragraph. He'd been in the back seat of the plane when it went down. His right wrist had been fractured and he had some scrapes and bruises, but those were his only injuries. The reporter had called it a lucky escape. Winter wasn't buying. William had gotten off lightly because the grownups had taken the best seats, while he'd been relegated to the back. This combined with the fact that his bones were softer and more flexible had led to him being able to walk away from the crash when his parents hadn't. Luck had nothing to do with it.

Winter sped through the rest of the article, picking out the salient details. According to eyewitness reports, Nathaniel Wood had almost pulled off the emergency landing. Unfortunately, 'almost' wasn't good enough. He'd hit the highway hard and, at first, seemed to be in control. The impact must have weakened the left wheel strut because a couple of seconds later it gave way and the plane rolled. He fetched the next volume from the shelves and went straight to August 5. Nothing there, so he went to August 6. Gemma Wood's death merited two paragraphs buried on page nine.

Anderton pushed back from the table. She was beaming. Moments like this were rare. You needed to appreciate and savour every single second. It would be a crime not to. Winter had been chasing this guy for a couple of days and he was feeling pretty damn pleased with himself. Anderton had been chasing him for three years, so you could take that feeling and multiply it by a hundred.

'William Wood's our guy, isn't he?' she said.

'He's got to be. The fact that his mother died on August 5 can't be a coincidence. The way I see it, with Cody and Myra, he was reliving the whole thing. I'm figuring that he somehow blames himself for his mother's death. That's why he had Cody trigger the bomb.'

'It sounds as though you're talking about survivor's guilt.'

'That's exactly what I'm talking about. Guilt can be one hell of a motivator.'

Anderton let out a long sigh. She was still smiling, though. 'I can't believe I've finally found him.'

'Well, you better believe it.' Winter held up his hand with the palm facing toward her. She looked at it, then looked at him.

'Come on, Anderton. Give me some skin. You know you want to.'

She hesitated a second longer then high fived him. The sound reverberated around the small room.

Winter grinned. 'Yeah, that's what I'm talking about.'

44

The incident room was buzzing when they got there. Anderton had phoned ahead and every person who could be spared was working to find whatever they could about William Wood. Identifying the killer was one of those pivotal moments when everything changed. There was before and there was after, and now that they'd reached this moment it was impossible to go back. Even if they wanted to, they couldn't. Time moved in one direction, and that was resolutely forward.

What had William Wood been up to for the last twenty-four years? That was the big question. Twenty-four years was a huge chunk of time. It was almost a quarter of a century. Winter had Googled the name on the way here. The only hit he got with a Vancouver connection was for a twenty-year-old college kid who liked alternative rock and *Jackass*-style humour. He tried Bill Wood next, in case he'd shortened his name. Then Will Wood. Neither variation came up with anything worth pursuing.

Freeman was at the front of the room, marshalling his troops and acting important. They walked over and waited their turn. The evidence board behind Freeman had been cleared of photographs. WILLIAM WOOD was written at the top in large, neat capitals. Freeman dismissed the detective he was talking to and turned to Anderton.

'I want to be there when you arrest this guy,' she said.

'Good to see you, too.'

'I'm serious.'

'I thought you said you weren't bothered about that.'

'I changed my mind.'

Freeman sighed. 'Don't you think you're jumping the gun here? It's a little early to be talking about arrests.'

'No it's not. Knowing the killer's name is as good as having him in custody. I know that and you know that.'

'I've got to admire your optimism, Laura.'

'Please don't patronise me, Peter.'

The words had barbs but the delivery was as pleasant as if they'd been talking about the weather. If they'd been shouting, everyone in the room would be looking at them. As it was, Winter was the only person paying them any attention.

Freeman glanced at Winter, then looked back at Anderton. 'I can assure you that was never my intention.'

'I should be there.'

'No, you shouldn't. Arrests can be highly volatile situations, not to mention dangerous. Given that you're a member of the public, it would be irresponsible of me to put you in harm's way.'

'Bullshit. I've got ten years on you, Peter. Do you have any idea how many arrests I've been involved with? And guess what? I'm still standing.'

'Even so, the answer is still no.'

Anderton stared for a second, then changed tack. 'How far have you got with investigating William Wood?'

'We're making progress.'

'What sort of progress?'

Freeman said nothing.

'This is the point where I'm going to remind you that you wouldn't be making any progress at all if it wasn't for us.'

'That's not the way I see it. We would have got to William Wood.'

'But would you have got there by next August 5? Or the August 5 after that? In other words, how many more people were going to have to die?'

'Despite what you might believe, we're not completely incompetent.'

'You think I don't know that? Last year, most of the people in this room were working for me. I know exactly what they're capable of.' She paused, the silence stretching and warping. 'The fact that we've come up with William Wood's name proves that we have something useful to add to this investigation.'

'And I thank you for your contribution.'

'I don't want your thanks, I just want you to keep us in the loop. Share what you discover. What have you got to lose? Best-case scenario, we might just come up with something that helps you nail this guy sooner rather than later.'

Winter was watching from the sideline. They were fast approaching that point where they'd start going back and forth over the same old ground. It was that sort of argument. The tone was still pleasant enough, though, both of them talking like they were discussing the sunshine and the rain.

He wandered over to a nearby evidence board and made out like he was suddenly fascinated by something posted there. For a while he studied the photographs on the boards and read the notes, slowly working clockwise around the room. Most of the photographs he'd seen before, and the notes didn't really add anything to his understanding of the case. He tuned out Anderton and Freeman and tuned in to what was happening in the rest of the room. Random snippets of conversation filtered through the noise. Some were one-sided because the detective doing the talking was on the telephone. Others were reciprocal, information being swapped, ideas and theories being aired.

They were chasing William Wood through time, and starting to make progress. From what Winter could gather they'd covered his teenage years and were now trying to find out what he'd been up to in adulthood. Chase that one hard enough and it would eventually lead them to where he was today. At least, that was the theory. William had gone into care after his mom died, first to an orphanage then to a foster family. Nathaniel's parents were both dead. Gemma's mother was suffering from early-onset Alzheimer's, so going to live there wasn't an option. There were no other living relatives, which was why he'd ended up in the care system, fostered by a couple named Gifford.

Winter tuned back in to what was happening with Anderton and Freeman. Anderton was still going for it but seemed to be running out of steam. He walked over to where they were standing.

'You know,' he said to Freeman. 'Co-operation is a two-way street. We could have kept William Wood's name to ourselves, but we didn't. And the reason we didn't was because we realised that more ground would be covered if we shared. You've got the resources of the whole of the Vancouver PD at your disposal. We don't.'

'It's good that you recognise that.'

'Just stating facts. Okay, here's a question for you to mull over. The next time we get a breakthrough, do you think we're going to be in a hurry to share? And if that breakthrough leads to the killer's door, how is that going to reflect on you?' He locked eyes with Freeman, waited for him to look away first, then turned to Anderton. 'Time to get out of here. Places to go, people to see.'

He started walking to the door. Anderton caught up within a couple of strides.

'Nice performance,' he whispered to her.

'Thank you,' she whispered back. 'So, did you get anything?'

'Yeah, I got another name.'

45

They didn't say anything else until they reached the car. Every person they passed was either an enemy or a spy. Cops and civilians alike. Once you'd slipped into that cloak-and-dagger mindset it was hard to get out of it again. Winter climbed in and fastened his seatbelt. Anderton climbed into the driver's seat and fastened hers. She turned to face him.

'You said you had another name.'

'William Gifford. After his parents died, William went into foster care. He was never adopted, but my guess is that he started using his foster family's surname. We know he didn't go back to using the name Wood.'

'Because there were no photographs of him on the boards in the investigation room.'

'Exactly. Checking passport and driver's licence records would have been the first port of call. Most people have one or both. If William had been using his birth surname they would have had his photograph already, and it would have been displayed on the empty board at the front of the room.'

'It would have had pride of place,' Anderton agreed. 'Applying the same logic, we can assume that he's no longer using the name William Gifford.'

'Not necessarily.'

'How come?'

'Because the fact he was fostered is brand-new information. People were still trying to work out what to do with it. No doubt they've gone looking for photographs, but they wouldn't have heard back yet. That's something you can check with your contacts. If he is calling himself William Gifford, we'll want a copy of his picture as soon as it arrives.'

Anderton took out her cell and made the call. She hung up without speaking, then fired off a quick text. Whichever contact she'd hit for the information, they must have been somewhere they couldn't talk, or their phone was switched off, or they didn't have a signal. Whatever the reason, it would mean waiting a little longer.

'Okay,' she said. 'Assuming the killer is calling himself William Gifford, our first port of call has to be Google.'

Winter took out his cell and navigated to the web browser. Anderton was a couple of seconds ahead and acting like this was a race. He typed *william gifford vancouver* into the box and hit search.

'I've got one possibility,' Anderton said. There was a brief pause, then, 'Scrub that. If that's him in the profile picture, then he's got to be at least seventy.'

Winter was looking at the same Facebook picture. The face staring back was too old, and black. There was no way this was their guy. Wrong racial group, wrong age group.

'You try Bill,' he suggested. 'I'll try Will.'

Anderton was off and running, swiping and typing, and determined to cross the finish line first. Winter's search was a bust. The closest he got was a link to the Facebook page for the same black guy as before.

'I might have something.'

Anderton was holding her cell up. Winter looked over, expecting to see the familiar graphics for a social networking site, but that wasn't what he was looking at. The site she'd navigated to had BILLY GIFFORD PHOTOGRAPHY in the title box. He ran a new search. Two seconds later he was looking at the same page.

'What do you think?' she asked.

Winter was thinking plenty. Modern photography was one of those professions that required both logic and a creative flair. A lot of the work was done on computers, and you had to know all about shutter speeds and f-stops and lighting and all sorts of technical details. But that was meaningless if you didn't have an eye for a picture. Logic and creativity. One was useless without the other.

The other reason he wasn't saying anything was because he didn't want to jinx things. The logical part of his brain knew that this was ridiculous. It didn't matter what he said or didn't say, or what he did or didn't do, the outcome had already been decided and there was nothing he could do to influence that. However, the creative part of his brain had a different take on things and right now that part was shouting loudest. So he was keeping his mouth shut just in case this guy turned out to be black, or as old as Methuselah, or was living in a different Vancouver altogether.

Winter clicked through to the contact page. There was no address, but there was a landline number with a Vancouver code. He went to the 'About Me' page, hoping for a photograph of Gifford. A self-portrait of him holding a camera would do. Even if the face was obscured, they'd still be able to ascertain his race and get a rough idea of his age. But there wasn't even that. The only picture was a cute baby one. It was the sort of shot that would melt a new mom's heart and have her reaching for the telephone to book a session.

Gifford's biography was light on specifics. There were no clues as to how old he was, no indication of how long he'd been in business for, and no mention of when or from where he'd graduated. There was nothing to say that he had actually been to college, nor that he'd taken any photographic courses. It was possible that he'd dropped out of high school. Maybe he had a natural ability and had decided to cash in on it. There was only one paragraph. In short, he loved taking photographs and was looking forward to helping create 'memories that would last a lifetime'. Near the end of the blurb, he mentioned that he would travel to his clients. 'To make them feel more comfortable' was the reason he gave. More likely he couldn't afford to run a studio.

Winter navigated to the gallery page next. The order in which the sections were laid out gave a good indication of where Gifford's business priorities lay. At the top was a link for families and children. That was his bread-and-butter work. Next were weddings, which would have been lucrative but not so regular. Beneath that was a link for corporate photography. At the bottom was a link for miscellaneous. Winter clicked on 'Families and Children', then opened the first photograph in a new window. This would be the starting point for any prospective customer. This was what Gifford had chosen to lure them in.

The two little girls in the photograph were around three and five. There were enough similarities to conclude that they were sisters. Gifford had gone for a head-and-shoulders shot. The older girl had a silver butterfly in her hair and was cuddling her sister protectively. Both of them were looking to the right and focussing on something just out of shot. There were no cheesy smiles, no fake laughter. Gifford had caught the girls in a moment where they were absolutely fascinated by whatever they were looking at. It was a good photograph, cute without being cloying. There was plenty of evidence that Gifford had talent, and plenty of evidence that he had the technical know-how to make the most of that talent.

'So what are you thinking?' Anderton asked again.

'I'm thinking that this is worth pursuing,' Winter said carefully. 'What are you thinking?'

'I'm thinking that I'd concur with that,' she replied just as carefully.

'There's a landline number on the contact page.'

'Then let's run a reverse phone lookup, see if we can find an address. You get the number and I'll pull up the Yellow Pages website.'

It took Anderton less than ten seconds to access the site on her phone. Winter reeled off the number and she typed it into her cell phone.

'Here we go,' she said. 'I've got an address for Argyle Street, in Fraserview. It's residential rather than industrial, so presumably Gifford is running his business from home.'

'Is it in our target area?'

'It's pretty much slap bang in the middle.'

'Let's go, then.'

Anderton leant forward and pushed the key into the ignition. She went to turn it, but stopped at the last second. She leant back in the driver's seat.

'What's the matter?' Winter asked. 'I thought you'd be anxious to get over there.'

'I am.'

'So what's the problem?'

'Is this our guy?'

'It's possible.'

'How possible?'

'At this stage, I'd say fifty-fifty.'

'No higher?'

'Would it matter if it was?'

'If it's higher, then really we should be leaving this to Freeman. If it's lower then it's no better than a hunch and there's nothing stopping us investigating it on our own. In fact, it would be the right thing to do. After all, we don't want to waste police time with hunches, do we?'

'No, we wouldn't want to do that.'

Anderton sighed. 'This whole situation pisses me off. Freeman is such an asshole. We've done good, solid work here, but does he want to acknowledge that? No, he doesn't. Not even a little bit.'

'Okay, I'm going to throw your question back at you. Do you think this is our guy?'

Anderton smiled. 'Honestly? I'd say it's about thirty-seventy. You know, it might even be as low as twenty-eighty.'

'Which is as good as saying that this is just a hunch, right?'

'Exactly.'

'So, what are we waiting for?'

46

At some point one of Freeman's people was going to connect the dots. It might have already happened, in which case Winter reckoned they had about a thirty-minute head start. It would take that long for Freeman to arrange a raid. He'd need to get a team together, and brief them, and then they'd have to hustle over to Argyle Street. The curse of the large organisation was its lack of flexibility. The advantage of being a self-contained two-person unit was that they could make decisions and act immediately. Anderton was feeling the urgency, too. She had her foot down and was driving as fast as the traffic conditions allowed.

Winter spent the whole journey going through the gallery pictures. The photograph of the two sisters wasn't a one-off. Gifford had a great eye. He seemed to have a knack for capturing those moments that another photographer might have missed. The pictures were so natural, the emotions totally genuine. Even when the photograph had clearly been staged, nothing looked forced.

He clicked through to the miscellaneous section. These pictures were in a different league altogether. They could have been hanging in a gallery and selling for a small fortune. If Winter had had a place to call home, he would have been happy to put these on his walls. This was what made Gifford's heart sing. The pictures were arty and surreal. Vague impressions rather than actual images. It was almost impossible to tell what the original subject had been, but that didn't matter because the subject matter was just a springboard for Gifford's imagination.

One photograph in particular caught Winter's eye. It was a manic swirl of reds, pinks and whites. Maybe once these had been lights on a highway caught in time-lapse. That was before Gifford had manipulated the image into something else entirely. The more Winter studied the image, the more unsettled he became. There was violence and death in this picture. Danger and mayhem. The next picture was different but the same. This time the swirls were coloured blue, purple and black. The overall effect was to cool down the violence and calm the mania. Considered together, the two images were like yin and yang.

Why would someone this talented choose to make a living taking baby photographs? Granted, it might not be through choice. Talent alone wasn't enough to guarantee fame and fortune. That said, Winter reckoned that Gifford could have done better for himself. Which begged the question of why he would be happy to exist in the shadows. The second thing that had occurred to him as he was looking at the red-swirl photograph was that fifty-fifty has just gone up to sixty-forty.

Winter had just moved on to the corporate photographs when Anderton announced they were almost there. He glanced up from his cell phone and saw that they were passing through a middle-income neighbourhood. The houses were bigger than the one Myra Hooper had shared with Cody, but way smaller than Sobek's place over in Kerrisdale.

He went back to his phone and swiped through the corporate pictures. Compared to some of the other photographs on the site these were fairly pedestrian. Then again, how much artistry could you bring to a head-and-shoulders shot of a CEO? He was swiping quickly, not really paying much attention to the faces flying past. Something spiked at his subconscious and he swiped back a picture. Whatever it was that had caught his attention it had nothing to do with the woman staring out from his phone. He swiped from left to right and a new face appeared on the screen. His heart thumped uncomfortably against his ribcage then settled again. Anderton must have sensed something. She looked over from the driver's seat.

'What?' she asked.

He held his cell up and she glanced at the screen. Just for a second, but a second was all that was needed. The hair was shorter, the beard was gone, but there was no mistaking who this was.

'That's Sobek,' she said.

'Which means we now have a direct link between Gifford and the crimes. There's no way that this is some fluky cosmic coincidence. When you hear quacking, there's going to be a duck in the vicinity.'

'I should call Freeman.'

'Yes you should, but you're not going to, so let's not waste time going down that route.' Possible scenarios were rushing through Winter's head at the speed of electricity, neurons sparking and firing and lighting up bright. 'This is a game-changer. We could be about to go head-to-head with a serial killer. I'd rather not do that unarmed. Given

Canada's stringent weapons laws, this is a bit of a long shot, but have you got a gun stashed in the trunk? Two would be better. That way you could have one, too.'

'No guns, but look under your seat.'

Winter leant forward and felt around beneath his seat. His fingertips touched tape, then something plastic. He gave the mystery object a tug and it came away with a sticky tearing sound. It turned out to be a standard police-issue taser. Anderton glanced over.

'For emergencies,' she said.

'I don't suppose you've got another one tucked away under your seat?'

'Sorry. And just so we're clear, that's mine.'

Thirty seconds later Anderton turned into a quiet, narrow lane and pulled over to the kerb. The house they wanted was thirty yards further on. It was a tidy-looking property with a small fenced yard out back. Three bedrooms, maybe four at a push, but the fourth would be tiny. The clapboard was painted dark brown, making the house appear gloomy and dark. It was almost as if it was trying not to be seen.

Anderton held out a hand and Winter reluctantly handed her the taser. They got out and walked along the narrow strip of sidewalk toward the house. Most of the neighbouring properties appeared empty, the residents no doubt at work. They passed an elderly woman who was tending the flower beds in her front yard. She wished them a cheery good morning as they passed by, then pretended to go back to her gardening. Winter could sense her eyes following them all the way to Gifford's front door.

The house appeared to be as empty as those around it.

There were no lights on, but given that it was daytime that didn't necessarily mean anything. The empty parking slot in front of the house was more telling. Gifford advertised that he travelled to his clients, so it was a safe bet that he owned a vehicle. There was no driveway or garage, so the front of the house would be the logical place to keep it. If he was at home.

Anderton knocked and they waited. The day was still and quiet. There was no breeze to carry the sound or stir the trees. Today's weather was as perfect as yesterday's, the sun burning bright and hot against a hazy blue sky. As the day progressed, the haze would melt away and the mercury would rise. Way off in the distance, an airliner was coming in to land at the airport. Anderton knocked again, half-heartedly, like she was going through the motions. She'd clearly reached the same conclusion about no one being home.

There were two locks on the door. A Yale and a five-lever mortice. The Yale didn't pose much of a problem, but the deadbolt was a challenge. In the end it took Winter almost a minute and a half to pick them both. Anderton had positioned herself so the old woman wouldn't see what they were up to. She seemed to be absorbed in her gardening, but Winter still had the impression that she was watching them. He pushed the door open. Before he could say anything, Anderton had the taser out and was already stepping inside.

47

The hall walls were white and completely bare. There were no photographs, no paintings, no mirrors. No personal touches whatsoever. Nothing that said 'this is where I live'. The space was cold and unwelcoming. Given Gifford's profession, Winter would have expected to see a photograph or two. He took a closer look at the nearest wall. There were patches where the paintwork was brighter. He ran his fingertips over the wall, felt the way the texture of the plaster changed. There had been picture hooks here once upon a time. Quite a few, by the looks of things. After they were removed, the holes had been plastered over and smoothed out and the affected areas repainted.

Out of habit Winter sniffed the air. No dead bodies. No smell at all, really. Which was almost as unusual as the lack of pictures. Most houses held the aroma of the last meal prepared there. Which meant that it had been a while since the kitchen had seen any cooking. Which made him wonder how long Gifford had been gone for. The old woman a couple of doors down would be able to answer that. She'd know everything that was happening around here.

The first door led to the living room. Like the hall, the walls were white and completely bare. There had been pictures here as well once upon a time, dozens of them. All of the hooks had been removed, the marks plastered and painted over. The TV had a layer of dust on the screen and didn't look as though it had been used for a while. There were no cushions on the sofa and the bookcase was empty. The room had the temporary feel of Eric Kirchner's apartment. Where it differed was that this furniture hadn't been picked up cheap in a thrift store. Someone had gone to the trouble of co-ordinating this room. The drapes were a shade of pink that complemented the red sofa, and the furniture styles blended to create a pleasing whole.

'This is weird,' Anderton said. 'So does he live here or not?'

'I know what you mean.'

The next room gave an answer to Anderton's question. It was half the size of the living room. At some point in time it might have been a study or a dining room. It was filled with Gifford's photography gear. His lighting gear was stored neatly against the back wall. There were lights on tripods, umbrellas, diffusers and a small A-frame stepladder. A tall rack of steel shelves held everything else he might need. It was arranged methodically, a section for each item. Cameras, lenses, filters. The bags on the bottom shelf were grouped according to size. The largest on the left, the smallest on the right.

The window had a heavy wooden shutter that blocked all the light. A desk had been positioned beneath it. There was a computer tower underneath the desk and a large high-resolution monitor on top. Winter sat down and glanced over his shoulder. Anderton was busy examining the shelves, looking but not touching. He hit the on button and the computer buzzed and clicked through the first part of the booting procedure before grinding to a halt with a password popup in the middle of the screen. He hunted around for an adhesive note containing a scribbled password reminder. It was a long shot and it didn't pay off. He tried the underside of the desk. Nothing stuck there, either.

For a moment he sat wondering what the password might be. The problem was that he'd only just made Gifford's acquaintance. He typed in his name. No space, the 'I's in Billy and Gifford substituted with ones, the 'O' substituted with a zero. An incorrect password warning flashed up on the screen. He tried again, this time using William instead of Billy. Ones for the 'I's, a four for the 'A'. Still no joy. He didn't try a third time. They might only get three strikes. Having the hard drive wipe itself wouldn't help anyone.

'This is probably a job for the police's department's IT geniuses,' Anderton said at his shoulder. 'Don't worry, though, if they find anything, we'll know about it.'

Winter rolled back from the desk and spun around to face her. 'Yeah, but there's nothing to beat seeing things first hand.'

The next door led to the kitchen. Like the hall and the living room the marks made by the picture hooks had been painted over, and there was no sense that Gifford actually lived here. Winter felt like he'd stepped into a show house. What was actually in here was almost as interesting as what wasn't. There was a kettle and a toaster, but aside from that the work surfaces were clear. There was no microwave, no knife nest, no scales, no recipe books, no clutter anywhere. The sink was clear of dishes and gleaming. The stove was gleaming, too. The water in the kettle was cold, but it had been used at some point in time. The crumb tray in the toaster was clean, but there were a few stray crumbs, which indicated that this had been used at some point as well.

The first cupboard he opened was empty. The second had a single cup, bowl and plate, all lined up neatly on the lowest shelf. The third was filled with pots of Cup Noodles. The cutlery drawer contained one fork, one knife and one spoon. The drawer next to it contained a pile of dish towels, all white, all neatly folded. All the other drawers were empty. There wasn't even a pair of scissors.

'You've got to see this,' Anderton called out.

She was over by the refrigerator. Both doors were open and she was peering into it. There was a dozen packets of ham on the middle shelf, all sealed and all within their sell-by date. The bottom shelf held four large tubs of margarine. No juice or milk in the door, no salad stuff in the drawer. She pulled open the top drawer of the freezer section. It was filled with loaves of bread.

'The other two drawers are exactly the same.'

'It looks like Gifford is existing on a diet of toast, ham sandwiches and instant noodles.'

'Which is just plain weird.'

'It's also pragmatic. The less time he spends cooking, the more time he's got to pursue his other interests.'

'Like stalking his victims and watching the husbands,' Anderton suggested.

'Yeah, exactly like that.'

The window overlooked the small backyard. One third was decking and the remaining two-thirds was covered with an overgrown lawn. High fences shielded the yard from the neighbours. There was nothing on the decking. No chairs, no table, no barbecue, no planters. They left the kitchen and went upstairs. There were four doors leading off the landing, all closed. The first bedroom had empty closets, empty drawers and no linen on the bed. Ditto for the second.

The main bedroom was behind the third door. There was evidence that Gifford had been here at some point. The quilt was dumped in the middle of the bed and the pillows had been left at an angle. The top drawer of the bureau held his underwear. Boxer shorts folded neatly on the left, socks balled neatly on the right. All the other drawers were empty. His clothes were in the closet. Plain white button-down shirts hanging to the left, tan chinos hanging to the right. The shoe rack at the bottom of the closet held two pairs of brown loafers. The leather was shining.

Anderton appeared at his shoulder. 'Looks like he's as pragmatic with his clothes as he is with his eating habits.'

'It certainly looks that way.'

'Why?'

'Because every life contains a finite amount of hours and minutes. Say you sleep eight hours a night, then that's one third of your life taken up right there. So what are you going to do with the other two-thirds? If we asked Gifford that question he'd tell us that he wasn't going to waste it deciding what to wear or eat.'

'That's pretty extreme.'

'So is strapping a homemade bomb to someone's chest.'

The fourth door opened on to the bathroom. There was a single towel on the rail and one toothbrush in the holder. This room told them as little as the preceding ones. Which, in its own strange way was telling. Anderton turned to face him.

'Okay, so what have we learned?' She mulled the question over for a second. 'We know that he's single. And judging by this place, that's his default setting.'

'And what else?'

She shook her head and shrugged. 'Other than the fact that he prefers chinos to jeans, not much.'

'So, where's Gifford?'

48

'Gifford could be anywhere,' Anderton replied.

Winter shook his head. 'I'm not talking about where he is in space and time. We'll get to that one in a minute. I'm talking about where he is in this house. Someone's personality gets stamped on to the place they live. Even if they only use it as a flophouse you'd expect to see something more than what we're seeing here. So where is he?'

'There was evidence of him in the room he was using as an office.'

'But not much. That was nothing more than a glorified storeroom.'

'What about the computer?' Anderton asked. 'There's got to be something on there. We know that he stalks his victims online, and that he's been watching the husbands. Maybe he's one of those loners who spends all his time online.'

'There's probably going to be something on there, but not the good stuff.'

Anderton frowned. 'How do you work that out?'

'Because he left in a hurry, and he has no intention of coming back,' Winter said. 'If there had been anything important on the computer he would have taken it with him. Did you see the size of the screen? And it was a high-resolution model, too. That computer was primarily for work.'

'So he has another computer for stalking his victims and

watching the husbands. And that will probably be a laptop, because everyone has laptops these days. Which is portable. All he had to do was grab it on his way out the door.' Anderton frowned. 'And how can you be so sure that he's not coming back?'

'You're kidding, right? Did you see the state of his bed?'

'I saw that it hadn't been made,' Anderton replied 'I wouldn't say that it was in a state, though. My bed looks the same most of the time.'

'No, it doesn't. I've seen your car, and your apartment. Your bed gets made every morning without fail. The sheet gets pulled tight, the quilt gets straightened, the pillows plumped. I'd hazard that Gifford does the same.'

'Okay, but my point still stands. Just because his bed is a little messy, it doesn't mean that he's not coming back. You can't make that leap.'

'I can, and for that exact reason. Did you see how neatly the packets of ham were lined up in the refrigerator? The noodle pots were the same. Chicken and mushroom on the left, beef and tomato in the middle, curry on the right. Then there's the fact that he left in a hurry.'

Anderton fired off a sceptical look. 'And what are you basing that on?'

'I'm basing it on the fact that he didn't take any underwear with him. Your other clothes can be worn for a few days without too much of a problem, but not underwear. That starts to get a bit grim. There were five pairs of boxer shorts, five pairs of socks, five shirts and five pairs of tan chinos. There was also one of each item in the laundry basket. Presumably he's wearing some now, which implies that he's on a weekly wash cycle. Something got Gifford spooked and he left in a hurry.'

'Eric Kirchner's laptop?'

'That's my guess. It was switched on when I arrived at his apartment. Maybe Gifford had tuned in to watch The Eric Kirchner Show and saw me instead. He'd know who I was from the interview with Delaney. If he thought we were closing in, that would be enough to make him run.'

'Which leads us to the question of where he is in time and space. Any ideas?'

Winter shrugged and shook his head. 'Okay, let's try a slightly different approach. If you were still in charge of the investigation, what would your next move be?'

'I'd run Gifford's name and see if he had a connection to any other properties. I'd also be checking hotels and guest-houses.'

'All of which is labour-intensive.'

'So we need to call Freeman. He's got the manpower to chase down any paper trails. We don't.'

'You're right. But I'd hold off on calling him for a moment.'

'Why?'

'Because we're here now. We should dig deeper. It's about playing to our respective strengths. Freeman's strength is manpower. Ours is the experience we've got investigating crime scenes. As soon as you call Freeman he's going to tell you to get the hell out. How can we investigate the crime scene if we're standing out on the sidewalk?'

'Okay, I'll hold off on calling him.'

'You know, I don't think this house was always so bare. There are marks on the walls made by picture hooks. Lots of them. Someone filled in the holes and painted over them, and I'm betting that someone was Gifford. Also, don't you think that the house is a little big for one person living on their own?'

'So, what? You think he might have lived here with someone?' She mulled this over, then nodded to herself. 'I guess it's possible that he had a wife or a girlfriend. The old woman we passed who was working in her garden would be able to confirm that.'

Winter nodded. 'She'll know, for sure.'

'So we should go talk to her.'

'Not quite yet.'

Before Anderton could say anything else Winter walked out of the bathroom and headed downstairs. She stopped him as he was coming out of Gifford's office carrying the small stepladder.

'Should I ask?'

'We can walk and talk,' he said.

She stood aside to let him through and they went back toward the stairs.

'Hypothetically speaking, let's say Gifford was in a relationship, and the relationship went south. His wife-slash-girlfriend moves out, taking her stuff with her. Except she doesn't take everything because you never do. There's always going to be something left behind. So what does Gifford do with that stuff? He can dump it in the trash or donate it to Goodwill, which doesn't really help us because it means it's lost forever. Option number two, he can put it in the garage, but that doesn't work here because there is no garage.'

'Or he could store it in the attic,' Anderton said.

'Bingo.'

The attic hatch was halfway along the second-floor landing. Winter stopped beneath it and unfolded the ladder. It was made from aluminium and four feet high. Plenty big enough for shooting pictures over a crowd. He climbed up to the second step from the top and pushed against the hatch. It was hinged on one edge and opened like a trap door. Anderton grabbed the ladder to steady it and he moved up to the top step, still pushing. The hatch passed the vertical point, then gravity took over and it clattered all the way open. A retractable ladder was attached to one side. Winter gave it a tug and it tipped up on its hinge and started to telescope open. He climbed back down to the ground, pulling the ladder with him. It opened with a rattle and a clank.

He found his brass Zippo in the front pocket of his jeans. It was battered, scratched and ancient, but still worked as well as the day it was made. He climbed the ladder into the darkness and sparked the lighter to life. The breath caught in his lungs and he let out a low whistle.

'Is everything okay?' Anderton called out from below.

'I think we've just found Gifford,' Winter called back. He looked down from the hatch and locked eyes. 'And I'm not talking about where he's disappeared to. This is where he exists in this house. Come on up. You've got to see this.'

49

There was a light switch near the hatch entrance. Winter hit it and the darkness disappeared. He clicked the Zippo closed and shoved it back into his pocket. Someone had spent time and money converting the attic into a useable space. Sheetrock had been screwed into the rafters to create two new walls. Chipboard had been screwed into the ceiling joists to create a floor. Two striplights had been fixed to the apex of the roof to create light. The floor space matched the footprint of the house, making this the largest room in it.

The ladder clattered and Anderton came through the hatch. She stopped with her body half in and half out. Her gaze started at one end of the attic and kept going until she got to the other end. She didn't say a word. There was a wondrous expression on her face, like she'd just stepped into an Egyptian tomb that had lain undisturbed and undiscovered for the last five millennia. Winter knew where she was coming from. There wasn't much you could say to something like this. He held out his hand to help her. She took it and climbed the last three steps.

Most attics were black holes for junk. Not this one. There were no boxes and no junk. Whatever had happened to the wife-slash-girlfriend's stuff, it hadn't ended up here. At one end of the attic a work bench stretched the width of the house. At the other end was an actor's make-up table. There might not have been any pictures in the rest of the house, but there were plenty up here. The walls were covered with ten-by-eight prints. They'd been arranged in pairs and held in place with staples, one in each corner, the long sides of the staples running exactly parallel with the tops and bottoms of the photographs.

Winter moved in closer to get a better look. Eric Kirchner was on the left side of the pair that had caught his eye. His face was all screwed up and he was crying. Fat tears ran down both cheeks. It was an intensely personal moment that had been captured without his knowledge or permission. The picture had originated from a webcam. It had been cropped and manipulated and enhanced. Quality-wise it was nowhere near as good as the pictures on Gifford's website, but it was still excellent work. Gifford's talent lay in his ability to capture those unique moments. That was his trademark, and that's what was evident here.

Winter had never seen the man in the right-hand photograph before, but it had to be Gifford. He slightly resembled the photo composite. At the same time he looked nothing like it. There were tears on Gifford's cheeks too. His expression was almost identical to Kirchner's. Winter moved to the next pair of photographs. Again, they'd been set out with Kirchner on the left and Gifford on the right. There were no tears but Kirchner's face was still masked with misery. Gifford was trying to copy the expression.

David Hammond was in the next pair of pictures. He might have run to the other side of the country to escape the past, but the past wasn't quite done with him. That was the beauty of the internet. You could reach out and touch anyone, anywhere in the world. There were no borders or limits to how far you could reach. It didn't matter how far someone ran, or how hard, you could still find them. Hammond was desperately trying to hold back his grief. This was one of the hardest things he'd ever done. This was the face of someone who missed their wife every single day. Every single minute. This was the face of someone who would never forget.

And there was Gifford in the next photograph, doing his damnedest to copy the expression.

Anderton was moving along the wall, her gaze flitting from one pair of photographs to the next. She glanced over her shoulder and met his eye. 'I've seen some things in my time, Winter, but this is something else. This is about as weird as anything I've come across.'

'No argument there.'

Anderton moved across to the opposite wall and started examining the pictures that had been stapled to it. Winter carried on examining those on his side, moving slowly along the wall from left to right.

'Take a look at this,' she called over.

He walked across to where she was standing. This grouping of photographs was different. To start with, they hadn't been separated into pairs. There were a hundred of them in total, arranged in a ten-by-ten formation. Gifford and the husbands weren't in these. Instead, there was a woman that Winter had never seen before. These ones had also been taken without the woman's knowledge or permission.

'Gifford's wife-slash-girlfriend?' Anderton suggested.

'That would be my guess.' Winter pointed to a picture on the left side of the arrangement. 'This one was taken downstairs in the living room. I recognise the sofa.'

'What's the chance that she's still alive?'

Winter glanced at the pictures again. 'I'd say it's pretty unlikely.'

'What do you make of these?'

Anderton was pointing to a three-by-three grid of photographs. Some of the pictures had been taken at weddings, while others had been taken during the house calls Gifford had made to create those everlasting memories. The picture of Cody belonged to this latter group. He was ginning his goofy grin, oblivious to the fact that the person behind the camera would end up murdering his mom. The pictures of David Hammond and Eric Kirchner had been taken at weddings, cropped from crowd shots to isolate their faces. Sobek was there as well. Gifford had cropped the head-and-shoulders shot from the website so that his face filled the entire frame. Winter didn't know the people in the other five photos, but they were still familiar. Three of them could have been related to Sobek. The other two could have been Cody's brothers.

'This is how Gifford chooses his victims,' Winter said. 'He gets called in to do a job and if he sees someone who meets his criteria their picture goes up here. Sobek he saw at his office, Kirchner and Hammond were wedding guests, Cody ended up here because his mom wanted a nice photograph to remember him by. One of the pictures from this session was on the wall of their living room.'

'Approaching him in the park was a huge risk. What if Cody had recognised him?'

'Judging by what I'm seeing here, I'd say the picture was

taken a couple of years ago. Do you remember everyone you met two years ago?'

'Even so.'

'We also need to take into account the fact that he's got away with this three times already.'

'You think that he's getting overconfident?'

'They always do.'

Anderton looked at the grid of pictures again. 'The five faces we don't recognise must be possible victims for the future. He's spotted them while he's been working, decided that they tick the boxes, and so they've ended up on this wall.'

Winter nodded. 'Exactly. He's working on a year-long cycle. For the moment the latest murder will be meeting his needs but somewhere along the line he's going to start thinking about next August 5. When that happens he's got options.'

'How long do you think he stalks his victims for?'

'You're looking at months rather than weeks, maybe as many as six or seven. Gifford likes to move slowly and carefully. By the time he arrives on his victim's doorstep with a bomb he's going to know them as well as they know themselves. That's the beauty of watching them on a webcam. He gets to see his victims with their masks off.'

Anderton was nodding to herself. 'This is the intersection point that I've been looking for. It's like you said, he wasn't planning on stopping any time soon.' She paused. 'These people actually let Gifford into their lives. The really scary thing is that none of them had a clue what sort of monster he was.'

Winter turned his attention back to the photos of

Gifford's wife-slash-girlfriend. He honed in on one of the pictures on the bottom row. The woman's eyes were red from crying and she was trying to pull herself together. Her face wasn't distorted from an overload of emotion, so he was able to get a better idea of what she actually looked like. She was in her late twenties. Black shoulder-length hair, brown eyes. She had the sort of face that you wouldn't look at twice. Back at high school, she would have been one of the last girls to get asked to the prom. That said, she would definitely have got a date.

He glanced over at Anderton. She'd moved further along the wall and was completely absorbed by what she was seeing. Winter grabbed the photograph, folded it in two and stuffed it into the back pocket of his jeans. A second later, she turned to face him. There was no suspicion in the look, just wide-eyed curiosity. She stared for a second longer then shook her head and returned her attention to the photographs.

Winter took one last look at the pictures of Gifford's wife-slash-girlfriend then walked across to the workbench. A tool board was attached to the gable wall. All the tools were neatly arranged and within easy reach. There was a pair of magnifying glasses for the fiddly work and a bench-mounted clamp to hold things still. There was enough evidence scattered across the surface to put Gifford away for life. Anderton coughed at his shoulder. A pair of latex gloves was dangling between her thumb and forefinger. He took them and put them on. Anderton was already wearing hers.

Dozens of fireworks were piled up on the left side of the bench. The packaging was bright and garish and they had names like Krakatoa and Dragon's Breath. The fireworks had been bought over the counter and, in most respects, were no different from the fireworks that were sold in their millions every Fourth of July. But these fireworks weren't about fun and celebrations. They were about death, destruction, carnage and suffering. There were two sealed plastic tubs next to them. One for the gunpowder, one for the coloured flash powder.

A little further along was a box of matches and a small plastic tub that held the Christmas-tree light bulbs. A second tub contained three finished detonators. Winter picked one up. The glass part of the bulb had been wrapped with insulating tape to contain the sulphur scrapings from the match heads. The two wires coming out of it had a quarter-inch of exposed copper at each end. It felt so light and harmless, but it wasn't. Touch the exposed wires to the terminals of a nine volt battery and it would flare to life. So simple, yet potentially deadly. Winter put the detonator back into the tub and moved along to the end of the bench. There was a finished bomb here. He picked it up and Anderton took a sharp intake of breath.

'Should you be doing that?'

'Relax. They only become dangerous when you add electricity. We could play catch with it and we wouldn't be in any real danger.'

'I'd rather we didn't.'

Winter walked beneath the closest striplight so he could study the bomb more closely. It wasn't as big as he'd imagined, or as heavy. It was three inches long and had a diameter of about an inch. The size wasn't a complete surprise. Look how big bullets were, and there was no question how lethal they could be. Despite everything, he couldn't help being impressed. The killer had a problem and he'd thought long and hard about it, and this was the solution he'd come up with. There was an elegance to the design that was hard to deny. It was pragmatic and simple. And deadly. And that's the point where Winter stopped being impressed. At the end of the day this device had been designed and built with one purpose in mind. He held the bomb out to Anderton.

'Do you want to take a look?'

She held up her hands and stepped back. 'I'm good, thanks.'

'It's perfectly safe.'

'So you keep saying.' She took out her phone. 'We're now up to one hundred per cent. Gifford's our guy. No doubt about it. Freeman needs to know about this.'

'You'll get no argument from me on that score.'

Winter put the bomb back where he'd found it, then walked the length of the attic to the make-up table. The mirror was two feet square and surrounded by lit bulbs on three sides. The chair was upholstered with padded black vinyl and comfortable to sit in. There was nothing on the surface of the table. No brushes or make-up. No nail varnish or eyeliner pencils. No lotions or potions. A small ball of adhesive putty was stuck to the edge of the mirror frame. Anderton's footsteps came up behind him. A second later her face appeared in the glass.

'How's Freeman?' he asked her reflection.

'He's not answering. I've left a voicemail.'

'So, have you worked out what this make-up table's for?'

'It's so he can practise his facial expressions. He watches

the husbands on their webcams and when he sees an expression that appeals to him he freezes the frame and manipulates it until the picture is as good as he can get it. Then he prints it onto a sheet of photographic paper.' She pointed to the small ball of putty. 'Then he uses that to attach the photograph to the edge of the mirror and starts practising. And when he's mastered the expression he takes a self-portrait and the two pictures go up on the wall, side by side.'

'But why do that? What's he actually trying to achieve?'

'Good question.'

Winter jumped to his feet and made his way back along the sloped sheetrock wall to the workbench. He was going more slowly this time, his gaze moving from one pair of photographs to the next. Anderton was a step behind, doing the same. They stopped halfway along and turned to face each other.

'Why are there no smiles and laughter?' Winter asked her.

50

'And what about the thoughtful expressions?' Anderton asked. 'Or the curious ones? Or the puzzled and perplexed ones? Gifford seems obsessed with the negative emotions. The despair, grief, guilt and devastation. That's what seems to fascinate him. But why?'

It was another good question. Winter turned his head and looked at the workbench, his eyes travelling from left to right. The detonators, the explosives, the finished bombs. How much time and effort had Gifford put into the design? How much time had he spent building them? When it came to their favourite pastimes, serial killers didn't do anything by halves. Nor did they do anything unless there was a damn good reason. Winter turned his attention back to the make-up table. It was easy to imagine Gifford sitting there for hours on end, experimenting with different expressions, wearing each one like a mask. What was he trying to achieve?

'What are you thinking?' Anderton asked him.

'I'm not sure.'

'Well, here's an idea: Try thinking out loud. Maybe that'll help you to get your thoughts straight.'

'Okay, we know that the actual murders are a means to an end. Isabella, Alicia, Lian and Myra were collateral damage. Gifford was actually targeting the husbands. Question: what purpose do the murders serve? What is the end game here?'

Winter paused. 'It's like Gifford wants to get as close as he can to the grief and despair. He does that by studying the effect that the murders have on the husbands. The murders are instigating events. They're catalysts.'

He looked back along the photographs, his gaze moving down the wall they were standing next to and returning along the opposite one.

'Sobek's not here,' he said. 'It's just Eric Kirchner and David Hammond.'

'That's because the security on his computer was so much better.'

Winter went quiet again, thinking things over. If you threw the pieces in the air where would they land and what sort of picture would they make? In other words, what did the chaos look like?

'The first murder in any series often tells you more than all the other murders put together,' he said.

'So what can we learn from Isabella Sobek's murder?'

'That's not quite the right question. Remember, the murders are a means to an end. This is about Nicholas Sobek. So, the question we should be asking is what did Gifford see when he met him? It must have been something fairly monumental because Isabella was his first.'

'So we start by looking at the point where their lives intersected. That would have been when Gifford was called in to take photographs of the staff at Sobek's company.'

Winter nodded. 'Those sort of photoshoots are done in the workplace. An office or conference room is commandeered. The workers file in one at a time, have their picture taken, then file out again. Everything is over in thirty seconds. Back then, Sobek was the big cheese. Time was money. He would have wanted things over and done with as quickly as possible. If everyone else was doing it in thirty seconds he'd want to do it in twenty.'

'And since time was money he wouldn't have been involved with organising the shoot. That would have been left to one of his underlings. Which means that the only time the two of them had any sort of interaction was when the photograph was being shot.'

'So the question becomes: what did Gifford see during those twenty seconds? In other words, what were his first impressions?' Winter looked at Anderton. 'What were your first impressions?'

'I thought he was a murderer. And you?'

'I thought he was a psychopath.' Winter went to say something else, but the words never made it out. He shut his mouth then went back over what he'd just said. 'Maybe that's it. The thing that they have in common is that they're both psychopaths. On some level that must have registered with Gifford. The difference is that Sobek is functioning at a much higher level. He's rich and successful and has his own business. You could argue that society has accepted him for what he is. He's mastered the art of blending in.'

'And Gifford hasn't?'

Winter shook his head. 'No, he hasn't. Gifford is an outsider. Look what he does for a living. He's a photographer. He spends his whole life on the outside looking in.'

'So, what? He does all this because he needs acceptance?' It was Anderton's turn to shake her head. It was going from side to side in a way that made it clear that she wasn't buying.

'That sounds a little too much like pop psychology for my liking.'

'It's not that straightforward. Psychopaths don't need validation in the same way most people do. It means nothing to them.' Winter stopped talking. The pair of photographs at eye level showed David Hammond and Gifford with their heads in their hands. They looked as though the world was about to end. 'One characteristic that defines Gifford is his pragmatism. He eats ham sandwiches and instant noodles because it's quick and easy and he doesn't have to waste time thinking about cooking. He wears chinos and button-down shirts for much the same reason.'

'And he kills because he wants to provoke a particular reaction,' Anderton put in.

'It's all about being pragmatic,' Winter agreed. 'The same goes for fitting in. If he can find a way to swim with the flow then that's got to make his life easier.'

'All well and good, but why the fascination with negative emotions?'

'Because psychopaths don't possess empathy. Most people have a full palette of emotions to work with. Psychopaths don't. If Gifford is going to fit in then he needs both the negative and positive emotions.'

'And the problem with the negative emotions is that they are much harder to fake. It's easy to conjure up a smile, but much harder to produce tears.'

'Exactly.'

Anderton moved a little further along the wall, looking at the photographs she passed. The pair that she stopped at showed Hammond and Gifford both in tears.

'How is he able to cry on demand?' she asked. 'I mean, thinking about a favourite pet that died when he was a kid isn't going to work. You need empathy to do that and, as we've already established, Gifford doesn't possess any.'

'He could try holding his eyes open until they start to water. Failing that, cutting an onion in half would provide the desired effect. Or he could try jamming a knife into his leg. That would work.'

Anderton gave him the look. It was part *Did I hear right?* and part *What the hell planet are you from?* 'You're joking, right?'

'Only half joking. Remember, the key word here is pragmatism.'

'Is there anything else we can learn from the first murder?'

Winter thought this over for a second.

'You're frowning,' said Anderton. 'What is it?'

'I was thinking about Sobek sitting all by himself over at Mountain View Cemetery yesterday. I'm figuring that Isabella's funeral was a circus. A high-profile murder like that is going to attract plenty of media attention.'

'Yeah, it was a circus all right.'

'So, someone wandering around with a camera, pretending to be a press photographer wouldn't have stood out.'

'You think Gifford was at Isabella's funeral?'

'I wouldn't rule it out. Since the very start, the lack of escalation has bugged me. We now know that the reason we didn't see any is because we were focussed on the wives. When you look at the husbands, that's when you start to see signs of escalation. It was three months before Gifford attempted to infiltrate Sobek's computer. That feels like an afterthought rather than a part of the original plan. He killed Isabella, and for a while that would have been enough to sustain him. But it wouldn't have sustained him forever. So he starts looking for ways to take this to the next level and that's when he comes up with the idea of hijacking Sobek's webcam.'

Winter stopped talking and Anderton nodded for him to continue.

'Serial offenders start small and build up. There's always going to be a progression because enough is never enough. So a serial killer will start by killing and torturing small animals before moving on to cats and dogs, and finally people. Similarly, with serial rapists there's often a history of minor offences before they progress to attacking women. Stealing underwear, exposing themselves, voyeuristic behaviour, that sort of thing.'

'How does this relate to Gifford? You think he started off by killing the neighbourhood pets?'

Winter shook his head. 'No, I don't. Not this time. Gifford is driven by curiosity rather than sadism, so he would start with something that feeds that particular desire.'

'Such as?'

'What if he started out by hanging about at funerals watching the mourners? Nobody's going to look twice at a guy in a black suit at funeral. Everyone's just going to assume that he knew the deceased. So Gifford gets a ringside seat to witness the grief first hand. Afterwards he would have spent hours going over what he'd seen, replaying those emotions like there's a film show going on in his head.'

'But at some point that won't be enough,' Anderton said. 'Somewhere along the line he'll want something more permanent to look back on.'

Winter nodded. 'Right. Wearing a black suit won't raise any eyebrows, but if he starts waving a camera around, that would. Then one day he attends a high-profile funeral. Maybe it's a murder victim. Or maybe it's someone famous. Whoever it is, there are cameras around, and the thing is, nobody is looking twice at the people who are operating them, which gets Gifford wondering. So he starts thinking about how he can create a similar scenario.'

'And Isabella Sobek ends up dead,' said Anderton.

'So he turns up at her funeral and takes some pictures, and nobody looks twice at him. For a while that's enough. But enough is never enough. There's always going to be a way to push the envelope further.'

'So he decides to use Sobek's webcam to spy on him. He's already got the malware because he used it on Isabella's laptop, and he knows it's a great way to watch because he spent hours and hours watching her in the run-up to the first murder. All he needs to do is install it on Sobek's computer.'

'Which is where the idea falls down. The problem being that Sobek's security is too efficient. So what does he do? He starts hunting around for another victim. After all, the idea is a good one.'

'And there's your escalation,' Anderton said.

'The good news is that he's still escalating. Look at the latest murder. He actually approached Cody Hooper in person. Next he'll be looking to approach his targets after the murders. At some point he's going to overplay his hand.'

'Well, let's hope he overplays it sooner rather than later. I don't want to wait another year before we catch him.'

They stopped talking and for a while stood there staring

at each other. The silence was uncomfortable. It was a silence that demanded to be filled.

'It's a nice theory,' Anderton said eventually. 'But you realise that's all it is. A theory. There's no proof that this is what actually happened.'

'But you've got to admit that it's a compelling one.'

Anderton didn't say anything for a second. 'If I was still running this investigation, I'd task someone with digging a little deeper into this. It's possible that Gifford got noticed at one of the funerals. Maybe someone reported him to the police. I'd be interested to know if he was in the system.'

'You'll run this by Freeman, then?'

'No, Jefferies might be better for this. He's more likely to take it seriously.'

'I like Jefferies.'

Anderton's eyes narrowed. 'Good to know. But I've got to say, that one came a little out of left field.'

'I was just thinking, that's all. One thought led to another and I started wondering about how far back the two of you went.'

'Why not say what's really on your mind?'

'Jefferies is your number-one winged monkey, isn't he? He's the head of the troop? The top banana?'

Anderton cracked a small smile. Her brown eyes were shining and there was guilt writ large all over her face. 'I couldn't possibly comment on something like that.'

'I thought we were partners, Anderton. Aren't partners supposed to share everything?'

'Not everything. There's such a thing as oversharing.'

A sudden loud banging from downstairs made them both

turn toward the hatch. Winter counted four bangs in total, each one as impatient as the last. The banging was followed by muted shouting. They were too far away to make out the actual words, but Winter recognised the tone. The bemused expression on Anderton's face indicated that she did, too.

'Looks like we've got company,' he said.

'Yeah, we should let them in.'

Winter climbed down the ladder and headed along the landing to the stairs. He'd almost reached the bottom when the front door suddenly exploded open. The cop standing there was dressed in full battle gear and holding a large steel battering ram. He moved aside and two more cops stepped in to take his place. One had a semiautomatic gun pushed hard into his shoulder and aimed at Winter's chest. The other was aiming at Anderton. Winter's guy was screaming for them to get down on their knees and put their hands behind their heads. Winter didn't move. So long as they didn't make any sudden movements they'd probably be okay. He reckoned that they were due another couple of shouted warnings before the shooting started. Anderton was clearly thinking along the same lines. She hadn't dropped to her knees either.

It took a couple of seconds for recognition to kick in. There was just too much adrenaline and testosterone flying around. Anderton's guy got there first. The muzzle of his gun wavered briefly then he dropped the weapon to his side. He gestured to his buddy, who kept his gun aimed at Winter for a few seconds longer before lowering it. Winter moved to the side, looking for a way out, but the doorway was blocked by the cops.

'Freeman!' he yelled out. 'Tell your people to stand down. Gifford isn't home.'

51

Argyle Street was busier than it had ever been. Police cruisers were parked across both ends of the street to block access, and there were more cars parked at the sidewalk opposite Gifford's house. Winter had counted twelve people in total. The advance guard had helmets, vests, semiautomatics, the works. The rest were in their detective clothes, and the compulsory Kevlar vest. The old woman from further along the street had stopped working and set up a lawn chair in the shady part at the front of her house so she could watch.

Winter and Anderton had moved to the sidewalk while the police searched the house. Anderton was on her cell, talking to Rebecca Byrne and making her promise not to release William Gifford's name until after an arrest had been made. She hung up and put her phone away. A short while later Freeman and Jefferies came out of the house and walked over. Winter and Anderton were standing on the kerbside, facing the building. Freeman and Jefferies were backed up to the lawn as though they were daring them to come closer. The posturing was unnecessary. Winter had already seen everything he needed to. Freeman looked seriously pissed. This was his big moment and he'd been beaten to the punch. It was hard to feel sympathetic.

'So I guess you just happened to pick this address out of

thin air,' Freeman said. 'Out of all the homes in the city you somehow ended up in this one.'

'Something like that,' Anderton replied.

'Don't be cute, Laura. Right now, I'm searching hard for a good reason not to arrest you.'

'Then let me help you out, Peter. How will it look if it gets out that we discovered where Gifford lived before you did? There's only two of us. How many people have you got working on this? That's not going to play out well in the media, is it? You want to talk about incompetence, there's your definition right there.'

Freeman's face was turning red. He was managing to hold on to his temper, but only just. 'You must have had an idea of what you were walking into.'

'Not at first.'

'But at some point it became evident that William Gifford was the killer.'

'It did. And that was the point when I called your cell phone. If you don't believe me check your voicemail.'

'And that's when you should have got the hell out of the house.'

'Since we were already inside it made sense to get as much information as possible. I figured that you'd want to be fully apprised of the situation. Both myself and Winter are experienced investigators, so I couldn't see how this would cause a problem.'

'I'm sure you couldn't.'

Anderton glanced at her watch. 'I'm not busy for the next five minutes. Maybe I can apprise you now. Does that work for you?'

'That would be the least you could do.'

'Before you get into that,' said Winter. 'I've got a quick question.'

Freeman turned and glared. Winter took this as his cue to ask away.

'Have you got a copy of Gifford's passport photograph yet? Or his driver's licence picture?'

'You're joking, right?'

'No.'

Freeman shook his head. 'Unbelievable,' he muttered to himself.

'If you do get hold of it, we'd like to see it.'

Winter turned and started walking down the street in the direction of the old woman's house. He'd only taken four steps when he heard footsteps behind him on the sidewalk. Two steps later Jefferies was alongside him.

'I'm assuming that you've been tasked with keeping an eye on me,' Winter said. He was talking in a low voice and staring straight ahead.

'My orders are to watch you like a hawk.' Jefferies was staring straight ahead too, and talking in a tone of voice that was every bit as low.

'I know that you're working with Anderton,' Winter whispered.

Jefferies hesitated for a moment. There were a whole load of trust issues at play here. The question at the forefront of his mind was clearly, 'Friend or foe?'

'It's a reciprocal arrangement,' he said eventually. 'Anderton is one of the best detectives I know, and this case is one of the most challenging I've ever seen. We need her on this.

If you ask me, she should never have been cut loose. And for such a bullshit reason, too. It was like everyone lost their senses for a moment. By the time they got them back it was too late.'

'We need a copy of Gifford's picture.'

'No, what you need to do is get Anderton to check her cell phone more regularly. I've already sent his passport photo through.'

They stopped in front of the old woman's house. She was still in her lawn chair. Her focus had changed, though. Instead of watching what was happening further along the street, her attention was now fixed on Winter and Jefferies.

'Are you coming, or waiting here?' Winter asked.

Jefferies looked over his shoulder. Anderton and Freeman were talking. At a casual glance it appeared that they were being civilised enough, but look a little closer and it was a different story. Freeman was just about keeping his rage in check, while Anderton looked like she might actually be enjoying herself.

'Like I said, my orders are to watch you like a hawk, so I guess I'm tagging along.'

'I'm handling the questions.'

'Fine by me.'

52

Winter walked along the path then cut across the lawn to where the old woman had set up camp. She had her hand on her forehead to shield her eyes from the sun and was tracking their progress. They stopped in front of her. There were ridges and wrinkles etched into her ancient face. The backs of her bony hands were covered with liver spots. She had to be at least ninety. Her dress was faded from too many turns through the washing machine, but her sunhat looked new. It was made from straw and had a bright yellow ribbon tied around it. Her wedding ring was so dirty and scratched it appeared black rather than gold. She tilted her head and looked up at Winter. Her eyes were bright. Eyes that didn't miss a trick. There was a small table next to her chair. A jug of iced tea was set on top of it. Her glass was half full and there was a yellow straw sticking out of it.

'So, did he kill his wife?' she asked.

'What makes you say that?' Winter asked back.

She let out a burst of laughter that sounded more like a witch's cackle. 'Because it's the quiet ones you have to watch, ain't that right? At least, that's the way it seems on TV. Do you watch *CSI*? I love *CSI*. I never miss an episode.'

'What's your name?'

'Mary-Kate Franklin. And what's up with the white hair? Did you see a ghost or something?'

'If by "something", you mean a faulty bit of DNA, then I'd have to go with the something.'

She gave him the look. At least she tried to. The sun was behind him and making her squint.

'What was your impression of Mr Gifford?' he asked.

'Well, he was always polite enough, but they say that as well, don't they? It's always the quiet, polite ones. Am I wrong?'

'No, Mrs Franklin, you're not wrong.'

'You know something, I like you, young man. You're very polite.'

'I'm quiet, too.'

She let loose with another burst of witchy laughter, then said, 'You think he killed her, don't you?'

'Nobody's saying that anyone is dead, Mrs Franklin.'

'Oh, she's dead all right. You know, I always wondered what happened. One day she was there, the next she wasn't. It was suspicious, that's for sure. Mr Gifford said that they'd split up and she'd moved out, but I always had my doubts.'

Winter took out the photograph that he'd stolen from the attic and unfolded it. He held it in front of Mrs Franklin. She squinted, then started making impatient grabbing motions with her fingers. Winter handed it over.

'Do you recognise this woman?'

'Of course I do. That's Mrs Gifford.'

There was no hesitation. No doubt whatsoever. She handed back the photograph and Winter folded it into his jeans pocket.

'What was her first name?'

'Cathy.'

'And what was she like?'

'Quiet as a church mouse.'

'Scared quiet?' he suggested.

'No, more shy quiet. I always had to ask her to speak up. My hearing's not as good as it once was.'

'Did you see her much?'

'Most days. She always asked about my garden. I got the impression she was lonely.'

'How come?'

'Because I never saw any of her friends or family visit. She didn't work, either.'

'You know for a fact that she didn't have a job?'

'Of course I know that for a fact. I wouldn't be telling you otherwise. I once asked her what she did for a living. This was back when she first moved in. She told me that she did the accounts and bookings for her husband. He's a photographer, you know. He does weddings.'

'You mentioned that Mr Gifford was quiet too. What sort of quiet was he?'

Mrs Franklin leant forward and picked up her glass. She wedged the straw between her lips and took a long, slurping sip. 'Heavens, where are my manners? Can I get you gentleman a drink?'

'We're good, thanks.'

'Are you sure? It wouldn't be any trouble. And I make a pretty mean ice tea, even if I do say so myself.'

'I'm sure, but thanks for the offer.'

Mrs Franklin took another sip and put the glass back down. 'You were asking about Mr Gifford.'

Winter nodded. 'I wanted to know what sort of quiet he was.'

'Actually, he wasn't that quiet. I'm not saying that he was the life and soul of the party, but he was no shrinking violet, either. Not like Mrs Gifford. He was really quite charming, and not in a sleazy way. He could be funny, too. He was good at putting you at ease. Which makes sense, given his job. He'd need to put people at ease there.'

Mrs Franklin went quiet. A troubled expression flitted briefly across her face and then she was smiling again.

'You just thought of something,' Winter said gently. 'What was it?'

'I was just thinking about this one time when I was talking to Mrs Gifford, and Mr Gifford was there, too. This must have been about four years ago. I was upset because one of my friends had died. What I remember is the way that Mr Gifford was looking at me. He was just staring like he'd never seen a woman cry before. It was only for a second or two, but it made me feel uncomfortable. And then he was back to normal, trying to cheer me up. You know, I haven't thought about that in ages.'

'Did anything like that ever happen again?'

'No, it was just that once.'

'How long did the Giffords live here?'

'It's got to be six or seven years. Maybe a bit longer. They moved in after they got married.'

'And when did Mrs Gifford move out?'

Mrs Franklin sucked in a sharp breath. 'Now there's a question. It wasn't the year before last. I know that for a fact because that was when my Bertie passed.' She stopped talking and smiled at a secret memory. A good one by the looks of things. 'It was the year before that. Definitely the year before. I remember because 2012 was the year we went on a cruise. It was our diamond anniversary. Sixty years, can you believe that? Anyway, that was the last vacation we took together.'

'When was your anniversary?'

'June 16.'

'Did Mrs Gifford move out before or after your cruise?'

'It was the week before. I remember because I was busy packing when the moving truck arrived.'

'And you didn't see Mrs Gifford while the movers were there?'

'Or Mr Gifford. The movers did everything. We thought that they must have sold their house, which was strange because we hadn't seen any For Sale signs. Of course, the reason we didn't see any signs was because the house hadn't been sold. But we only realised that when we saw that Mr Gifford was still living there.'

'If you thought that he'd murdered his wife, why didn't you go to the police?'

'I wanted to, but Bertie talked me out of it. He was always telling me to mind my own business. He used to say that I had too much imagination for my own good, and he was probably right. Anyway, a couple of months pass and the police haven't turned up to arrest Mr Gifford, so I start to think that maybe Mrs Gifford has just moved out. And then Bertie's cancer came back and I was too busy dealing with that to worry about what was happening further along the street.'

'When did you last see Mr Gifford?'

She sucked another sharp breath through her teeth. 'Some time yesterday, but I'm not sure when. Maybe the evening.'

'You haven't seen him today?'

Mrs Franklin answered with a definite shake of the head. 'No, I haven't. His car was gone when I woke up. I figured he must have had an early appointment somewhere. Of course, I'm thinking different now.'

'What sort of car does he drive?'

'A Ford. I'm not sure of the model but it's an SUV.'

Winter smiled. 'Thanks for your help, Mrs Franklin.'

'My pleasure. Are you sure I can't tempt you to a glass of iced tea? It's another hot one today.'

'Much as I'm tempted, I'm going to have to pass. But thanks for the offer.'

Winter walked back across the lawn to the path. Jefferies was beside him, matching his pace stride for stride. Neither spoke until they reached the sidewalk. A little further on up the street, Anderton was still talking to Freeman. Judging by the body language, things were winding up.

'I've got to ask,' Jefferies said. 'Where did you get that photograph from?'

'Which photograph?'

Jefferies smiled. 'You know what I'm talking about. The one that's in the back pocket of your jeans.'

'Oh, that one. I found it.'

'Just like you found Kirchner's laptop.'

'Like I already told you, I don't know anything about that.'

'Of course you don't. And I don't suppose you know how it managed to turn up at headquarters this morning. It was sent special delivery, by the way. And it was wrapped in bubble wrap. Whoever sent it wanted to make sure that it got to us in one piece.'

Winter smiled. 'I've got no idea how that might have happened.'

'According to our computer people, whoever looked at it didn't do any lasting damage.'

'That's good to hear.'

'You know, maybe it would be best if you gave me the photograph.'

Winter took it out and handed it over. 'On the bright side, we now know that Gifford was married. And we know what his wife looks like. That sounds like two for two, if you ask me.'

'Maybe so.' He paused. 'Look, I don't mind bending the rules for Anderton, but there are limits. Stealing evidence is a step too far.'

'I'm hearing you, Jefferies. I promise to be good in future.'

'See that you are.'

'If Gifford murdered his wife, then her stuff needed to go somewhere,' Winter said. 'A storage unit is one possibility. I'd offer to look into it, but that would take me and Anderton all day. You guys have the resources to do it in a fraction of that time.'

'No problem.'

'You also need to be on the lookout for his car.'

Jefferies smiled. 'We're way ahead of you. The BOLO has already been issued. So what do you think? Did he kill her?'

Winter shrugged. 'He's definitely capable of killing her. As for whether he did or not, that would depend on whether there was a good enough reason to. He's not going to kill her for kicks. He's not wired that way.'

'So, what would constitute a good reason?'

'Maybe she'd become surplus to requirements, or maybe she was somehow getting in his way. If either one had happened, then he wouldn't have thought twice about doing it.'

'Jesus, that's cold. You make it sound like he's swatting a fly.'

Winter thought this over, then said, 'Yeah, that's exactly what it's like.'

53

Winter lit a cigarette, then settled down on the kerb beside Anderton's Mercedes to wait. Ten yards further on was the police cordon. The two police cruisers that had been used to create it were parked nose to nose at an obtuse angle. The cars blocked his view of Gifford's house. Not that it mattered. He'd seen everything he needed to see for now.

Global BC's news truck turned into the street and parked behind the Mercedes. The timing was interesting. To get here so quickly, either they'd been listening in on a police scanner or they'd been tipped off. A Pontiac Firebird came screeching into the street. Charlotte Delaney was behind the wheel. It skidded to a stop behind the truck. By the sound of it, she'd left ten feet of tyre marks on the tarmac.

Winter did a slow count from twenty and had just got to five when he heard footsteps. He couldn't see who it was because the truck was in the way, but it had to be Delaney. The two technicians that had come with the truck were both male, and these footsteps were definitely female. 'Three, two, one,' he whispered to himself, and then she was standing right in front of him. Her shoes had a two-inch heel and were the exact same shade of red as the Firebird. Coincidence or a conscious decision? Winter was veering toward the latter. Her pant suit was black and tight fitting. She smiled down at him.

'Mr Winter, it is so good to see you again.'

'And you, Ms Delaney. Always a pleasure. Nice car, by the way.'

'Yes, it is. So, what happened to that exclusive you promised?'

Winter took a long drag on his cigarette and shook his head. 'It didn't pan out. You know how it is. Some stories fizzle and die before they have a chance to really get going.'

She held his gaze for a second longer than was comfortable. 'How long have you been here?'

'We arrived twenty minutes before Freeman's people.'

Her perfectly plucked eyebrows went up in surprise. 'You got here before the police?'

'We did. Anderton is filling in Freeman as we speak. Incidentally, she was instrumental in identifying the killer. You might want to mention that in your next report.'

'Have any arrests been made?'

Winter smiled. 'I couldn't possibly comment on something like that, Ms Delaney. This is an ongoing police investigation that's now moving into its most sensitive phase.'

'Sensitive how?'

Winter's smile widened. 'Like I said, I couldn't possibly comment. Ah, here's Anderton now.'

Delaney turned around in time to see Anderton squeezing between the police cruisers. She didn't look any worse for wear as a result of her confrontation with Freeman. In fact, there was a bounce in her step, as though the whole experience had somehow energised her. The bounce faded a little when she spotted Delaney. She came over and stopped in front of the reporter. They stared at each other for a moment. Delaney broke the silence.

'Good to see you again, Laura.'

'I wish I could say that the feeling was mutual.'

Anderton looked down and waited for Winter to meet her eye. 'We need to go.'

'And where are you going?' Delaney asked. 'If you don't mind me asking.'

'Actually, I do mind.' She looked down again. 'Let's go.'

Without another word, she walked over to the Mercedes and *blip-blipped* the doors open. Winter took one last drag on his cigarette, crushed it out, pushed the butt back into the pack, then stood up.

'You still owe me an exclusive,' Delaney said.

'I've got your number on speed dial. As soon as I've got anything, I'll be in touch.'

Delaney flashed him an I'll-believe-it-when-I-see-it look. 'Have a nice day.'

Winter watched her walk back to the news truck before climbing into the passenger seat of the Mercedes.

'The woman's a pussycat,' he said.

'No, Winter, she's a viper.'

'And snakes are perfectly harmless so long as they're handled properly. Incidentally, Jefferies says that he's already sent Gifford's passport picture.'

Anderton took out her cell and checked it. She tapped an attachment onto the screen then held the phone toward Winter. Like every passport picture he'd ever seen, this one was bleached out and made Gifford look guilty. Maybe not guilty of murder, but certainly guilty of something.

'We need to talk to Sobek,' Anderton said. 'Maybe we can jog his memory by showing him this. Kerrisdale is only five minutes away. I'll call to let him know we're on our way.'

54

Anderton stepped into the porch and pressed her eye against the top scanner, and her thumb against the bottom. Ten seconds passed, then the door clicked open and a disembodied voice said, 'I'm on the firing range.' They followed the sound of gunshots through the house, the noise getting louder the deeper they went. Each shot was followed by twenty seconds of silence. Enough time for Sobek to readjust his aim and take a couple of deep breaths. They descended the stairs into the basement, turned right and walked past the closed door to Sobek's office. They stopped outside the door at the far end of the corridor and waited for the next gunshot. Even with their hands pressed over their ears, it was still loud. Anderton opened the door and they went in.

Sobek was stood in a combat stance at the end of the range. Legs apart so his weight was distributed evenly, left hand supporting the right to steady the gun. Ear defenders to protect his hearing and shooting eyeglasses to protect his sight. He looked over and saw them standing in the doorway. The gun went down, the ear defenders ended up around his neck. He hit a button and a small motor burst to life. The target started floating toward him like a ghost. Winter estimated that the length of the range was about twenty-five yards, which was consistent with a full-length bowling alley. The flooring hadn't been changed since the previous owner lived here. It was slick and glossy and the markings were still visible. Sobek was a yard back from the foul line. Another five yards on from that, the arrows tapered to a point.

Winter and Anderton walked over. Sobek didn't acknowledge them. His attention was fixed on the target. Winter counted twelve holes. The gun was a Glock 19, which meant there were still another three bullets, which was worth bearing in mind. All the bullets had hit the target. Nine in the chest, three in the head. The head was covered with a copy of the photo composite. Sobek studied the target for a moment then turned to Anderton.

'Any progress?' he asked.

'We've identified the killer.'

For a long couple of seconds Sobek just stood there, absorbing the news. The brief smile that fluttered across his face was there and gone before it had a chance to take root.

'Does the name Billy Gifford mean anything to you?' she asked.

He shook his head. 'Never heard of him.'

Anderton took out her cell phone and switched it on. Gifford's passport picture was already cued up. She handed the phone to Sobek. He stood looking at it for the best part of thirty seconds. 'I've never met this person,' he said eventually.

'Take another look.'

Sobek took another look, this one longer than the last. He was concentrating hard, trying to place the face. He handed the phone back and shook his head. 'I'm sure I've never met him.'

'Yes you have.'

'You sound pretty certain of that.'

'We are.'

Anderton pressed her phone screen twice and Sobek's picture appeared. She passed the cell to him. He glanced at the screen, then looked back at Anderton for an explanation.

'Billy Gifford is a professional photographer. He did some promotional pictures for your company.'

Sobek didn't say anything for a while. He'd slipped back in time, digging deep into a memory that would have been vague to non-existent. He got hold of something he could hook on to and nodded to himself. 'Yeah, I remember now. It was shortly before Isabella's murder.'

'Can you remember when, exactly?'

'I can't, but it would be easy enough to find out. It'll be in my diary.' Sobek looked at Gifford's picture again. He was staring hard, still trying to place the face and not quite managing to. He shook his head. 'I still don't recognise him.'

'What exactly can you remember about the photoshoot?' Winter asked.

Sobek turned to him and let loose a long sigh. 'Not much. It was organised by Alison Farnsdale, my PA at the time. She was responsible for looking after our website. That's what the pictures were for. I remember that the photographs were taken in the conference room, and I remember that I was up first so I wouldn't have to hang around waiting. And therein lies the problem. The whole thing was over in less than a minute. I went in, sat down, had my picture taken, then left and went back to work. I don't remember anything that passed between us, although I dare say something must have been said.'

'There's a good chance that Gifford was at Isabella's funeral,' Winter said. 'Before you say anything, just think that over. It might help if you close your eyes and picture the scene. He would have been hanging around on the periphery, and he would have had a camera. He was probably posing as a press photographer.'

Sobek closed his eyes. For almost a minute he just stood with his eyes shut. The faint emotions flickering across his face were there and gone in a heartbeat. Mostly his face was a complete blank. He opened his eyes and shook his head.

'To be honest, I'd struggle to tell you who was there and who wasn't. But that's not really surprising. I attended the funeral on autopilot. All I wanted was to get home and lock the doors.'

He handed the cell phone back. Anderton put it away.

'What else can you tell me about Gifford?'

'We can tell you that he's not at home.'

'You've been there?'

'That's where we've just come from. The police are there now. We were able to take a look around before they got there.'

'Did you find anything?'

Anderton and Winter shared a look. 'Yeah, I guess you could say that,' she said.

While Anderton filled Sobek in, Winter walked over to the gun cabinet and checked it out. There were a couple of rifles and half a dozen handguns. He seemed to have a thing for Glocks. There were two 17s and another 19. Boxes of ammunition were stacked up neatly next to the safe, all different calibres. Sobek could have started his own small war. How many of the weapons were actually licensed? How many were legal? How many had had their serial numbers filed off?

Winter replayed the day's events, searching for relevance, searching for significance. The trip to the records office, the trip to the newspaper offices, their search of Gifford's house and the interview with Mrs Franklin. Things were still moving fast, and he wouldn't have it any other way. They had to tread carefully, though. Gifford was clever and resourceful, and he was still out there. They couldn't let him slip through the net because their enthusiasm had got the better of them. There were two questions he kept returning to.

Was Cathy Gifford alive?

And where was William Gifford?

The first question was down to the police to answer. It was like he'd told Jefferies, they had the resources. They'd be able to access the records that needed to be accessed. Maybe she was working, in which case her Social Insurance Number would point them in the right direction. Or maybe she had family who knew where she was. Mrs Franklin had said that Cathy Gifford's family never visited but that didn't mean they were all dead. Estrangements happened. Winter could count on one hand the number of times he'd seen his mother in her final years. That didn't mean he didn't know where to find her.

When he opened his eyes, Anderton and Sobek were staring at him. He had no memory of closing his eyes, but he must have done. It was a habit he'd had since he was a kid. With his eyes open it was too easy to get distracted. There was just too much sensory input. Too many visual stimuli. When his eyes were shut it was so much easier to think and focus. Sobek was studying him intently, like he was trying to crawl inside his head. Winter just stared back, unimpressed. Anderton had her phone in her hand. She gave the impression that she'd just taken a call and had something to share.

'What is it?' Winter asked.

'Good news and bad. The good news is that Cathy Gifford is still alive. The bad news is that she won't talk to the police. She doesn't want anything to do with Gifford. Says it's a part of her life that she'd rather forget about.'

'So we turn up at her house with the thumbscrews. She'll be talking in no time.'

'And that would probably work. The thing is, she doesn't live in Vancouver any more. Hell, she doesn't even live in Canada.'

'Where is she?'

'Idaho. A small town called Nordman.'

'Then what are we waiting for?'

'Winter, it's got to be five or six hundred miles to Idaho.'

'We need to talk to her, Anderton. She moved out just before Isabella Sobek was murdered. That isn't a coincidence. Also, she's going to know Gifford better than anyone. Her insights will be invaluable.'

'And you're not hearing me. We're not talking a quick trip to the store to pick up some groceries here. It would take us the rest of the day to drive there. Then, after we've talked to her, we'll have to turn around and drive all the way back again. We'll be driving through the night.'

Winter smiled. 'Who said anything about driving?'

55

Boundary Bay Airport had two runways and a scattering of buildings. Hangars and maintenance sheds, for the most part. The southern boundary pushed right up to the water's edge. They walked into the terminal building side by side. For once Winter didn't have to wait in line to get his passport checked. That didn't mean security was lax, it just meant that they were the only ones there. The woman doing the checking was as serious as any border guard he'd come across. Once upon a time the US–Canadian border had been billed as the longest unprotected border in the world. That all changed after 9/11. These days there were eyes in the sky and satellite surveillance and thermal imaging in the more high-risk areas.

Sobek's little Cessna was fuelled up and ready to roll. It was sitting on the tarmac, glinting and sparkling in the bright August sunlight. It looked brand new, like it had just rolled out of the factory. They climbed aboard, buckled up and put on their headsets. The pilot turned and they shook hands across the seat back. He introduced himself as Dan. He was in his fifties, his hair turning to grey. He gave off a been-there-done-it vibe. Dan went through his final checks then taxied to the end of the runway. He hit the throttle and they buzzed along the runway, picking up speed. They were in the air in a fraction of the distance of a passenger jet, climbing steeply over the water, the plane bouncing and bucking as it went higher. The Cessna levelled out when the altimeter hit nine and a half thousand feet. They were heading east, passing over an immense forest. There were trees as far as the eye could see, spreading out from horizon to horizon in every direction.

'I've been thinking,' Winter said.

Anderton turned to face him. 'About what?' Her voice was infected with static, all mid and top end and very little bass.

'Billy Gifford. Right now, we don't know a huge amount about him, but we can speculate. What income bracket would you place him in?'

'Middle to upper. His house is a good size and it's in a nice part of the city.'

'And that's interesting straight away. No matter how good he is at his job, I doubt that he could afford a place like that on the money he earns as a wedding photographer.'

Anderton thought this over. 'He must have inherited money when his parents died.'

'That's what I'm thinking. His social status isn't a new thing. He's always been in the middle to upper income bracket. His father was a surgeon and he owned a light aircraft. That's a long way from collecting food stamps.'

'So how does that help?' Anderton went quiet again, then said, 'The house is his safe place. That's where he feels most comfortable. Inside those four walls he can be the person he wants to be. But that's been taken away from him. He can't go home, because if he does he's going to be arrested. That's got to throw him. The more unsettled he is, the more unpredictable his behaviour is going to be, which isn't necessarily good.'

'Granted, but on balance I'd prefer things like this rather

322

than how they were. Yesterday he was still calling the shots. That's not the case any more. We've got him on the run, and that's always going to be good. The upside of him acting unpredictably is that he's going to be making mistakes.'

Anderton sighed a staticky sigh. 'Sure, but how much collateral damage is there going to be in the meantime?'

'That's the downside. In any war there's always going to be collateral damage. All we can do is try to keep it to a minimum.'

'Amen to that.'

Winter looked out of the window again. There was nothing but trees below. This really was the wilderness. Most of that forest had probably never been touched by human feet. They hit a patch of turbulence and the plane suddenly dropped.

'We should be out of this soon,' Dan said. There was a smile in his voice, reassurance in every syllable.

The plane bounced one last time, then the air settled and they were flying level and true again. Winter looked over at Anderton.

'I've been thinking about what it must have been like for Gifford when his mother was in a coma,' he said.

'Me too. It must have been grim. He would have buried his father then watched his mom die, and he would have gone through it all on his own. It's a complete tragedy. And he was just a kid. It's heartbreaking.'

'Heartbreaking isn't the right word. Let me ask you something. Do you think that killers are born or made?'

Anderton mulled this over. 'Based on what I've seen, I'd say it's a bit of both. Some people are born bad, no doubt about it. Then there are others who gravitate toward the dark side. For the most part, though, it's not a black and white situation. There's a huge grey area, and that's where most killers seem to originate from.'

Winter nodded. 'That's more or less how I see it. Now, if we apply this idea to Gifford then the one assumption we can make is that he's always had psychopathic tendencies. And I'm talking all the way back to when he was kid. We don't like to think of children being psychopaths, but just because we don't like to think about something it doesn't mean that it doesn't happen. You said his parents' death must have been heartbreaking. I'd argue that it was more of an inconvenience.'

Winter stopped talking and looked at Anderton. She nodded for him to continue.

'Look at it from the point of view of the ten-year-old version of Gifford. For his whole life there had been someone there to make sure that all his basic needs were met. His parents fed him and clothed him and put a roof over his head. The fact that they did this meant that he didn't have to worry about doing those things for himself. Then one day he wakes up and both his parents are dead and all of those things he'd taken for granted aren't being done for him any more. That's going to be a huge inconvenience.'

Anderton's eyes narrowed. 'You were about the same age when your father was arrested.'

'So?'

'So, it sounds like you're talking from personal experience.'

'Maybe,' he admitted. 'Okay, let's fast forward. Gifford meets Cathy and they get married. What does he get out of the transaction?

'Sex. Companionship.'

'Sex would have been a part of it. The companionship wouldn't really mean anything to him. He's a psychopath. He just doesn't need that sort of social interaction.'

'So, what do you think he gets out of the deal?'

'A support system. Remember, Gifford is pathologically pragmatic. If Cathy hadn't enhanced his life in some way then he wouldn't have married her. She dealt with his books and appointments. Right there you have evidence of one of the ways that she made herself useful to him. Judging by the food in his kitchen, it's a safe bet that she did the cooking, so that's another way. I'd also bet that she did the housekeeping and the laundry. That would have been the deal they had. He earns the money. She looks after the house.'

'It sounds like something from the 1950s,' Anderton said.

'Doesn't it? Okay, so fast forward a little further. Cathy wakes up one day and decides to leave. At this stage we don't know exactly what happened, but what we do know is that Gifford was furious about it.'

'We do?'

'We do. You saw the house. After Cathy left, Gifford erased every last trace of her. It was like he sanitised the place. He didn't want anything left behind that might remind him of her. All the pictures were taken down and he arranged for a moving company to come in and take away her belongings.'

'Maybe Cathy arranged that.'

Winter shook his head. 'No way. Gifford's neighbour said that Cathy was nowhere to be seen when the movers came in. But usually if you're moving out you arrange for your ex to make themselves scarce while you retrieve your belongings.

These are your prized possessions. You're going to want to make sure they're safe.'

'Why do you think he was so angry? I mean, it's not like he loved her.'

'Again, you need to look at this from Gifford's perspective. Cathy's dealing with all his basic needs. When she left that must have been a massive inconvenience for him.'

'Like when he was a kid and his parents died.'

'Exactly. And that's the second reason. All of a sudden he's ten years old again. He's basically being forced to live through his parents' death for a second time. That's where this whole series of events started. That's Ground Zero. Revisiting it is not a place he wants to go. He was unstable before this happened, but this pushes him over the edge.'

'And he starts killing.'

'And he starts killing,' Winter agreed.

'I keep thinking about those pairs of photographs in the attic. He's clearly fascinated by emotions. Where does that fit into things?'

'I think that goes back to when his parents died, too. Ten is the no-man's land of childhood. You're not quite a child any more, but you're still a few years away from being a teenager. It's an age where adulthood has never seemed further away. Imagine how much worse it was for Gifford. His father's dead and his mom's in a coma. Day after day, he's sat by her bed with well-meaning people continually asking if he's all right. He knows that they expect him to feel sad, but he just doesn't get it. And he's in a hospital. Wherever he looks there's grief and despair and this confuses him even more. He knows that the nursing staff are talking about him behind his back. He knows that his lack of emotion makes him stand out. This would frustrate him but there's nothing he can do. He can fake the happier emotions, but these new darker emotions leave him puzzled.'

'And when Cathy walks out all of this comes back to haunt him. Only this time he's older and that puts him in a position where he can go and find answers.'

'That's the theory I'm working on.'

They both went quiet. For a time the only sound was the low, continuous thrum of the Cessna's engine. Winter looked out the window at the blue sky stretching all the way to the horizon. His thoughts were chasing each other and getting nowhere. In a situation like this, it was best to stop chasing. He turned to Anderton.

'What?' she asked.

'I'm going to take a nap. Wake me when we get there.'

56

A sharp finger poked into Winter's arm and his eyes sprang open. For a brief moment he couldn't work out where he was. Then he got it. He was in Sobek's Cessna, heading to Idaho. He peered out the window. There were still plenty of trees down there, but there were also signs of civilisation. Houses were grouped together to form small towns and villages. Roads cut through the landscape like long grey scars. From nine and a half thousand feet Idaho looked vast and uninviting. He put his headset back on and repositioned the microphone.

'We'll be landing soon,' Anderton said.

Winter glanced at his watch. 'An hour and fifty minutes. We're ahead of schedule.'

They started the final descent. Ahead and to the east, a large lake shimmered in the sunlight. The further the Cessna descended, the bigger the lake got until they were flying right over the top of it. They banked to starboard, kept turning and turning until they were back over land. The runway was straight ahead. A large, long area of trees had been cleared away and the ground flattened out to create a crude landing strip.

The plane dropped lower and the landing strip grew until it seemed to fill the whole windshield. And then the wheels hit the ground and the plane was bumping and jostling and bouncing. Winter gripped the edge of the seat to steady himself. Anderton gripped his arm. The plane slowed some more then came almost to a standstill. Dan taxied over to where a row of planes were parked up and cut the engines. Winter took off his headset. His ears were still buzzing, his bones still vibrating.

'We'll be about an hour,' Anderton said to Dan.

'No problem. I'll be here waiting.'

They climbed down from the Cessna and walked over to the admin building. The border agent who'd been called in to process their paperwork was as serious and efficient as the woman who'd checked their passports at Boundary Bay. He looked at everything twice, then welcomed them to the United States and wished them a good day.

Anderton had phoned ahead and there was a car waiting when they got back outside. The car had come in from Coolin, a small town down on the bottom tip of the lake. They drove out of the lot onto Highway 57, a two-lane road that ran south to north, following the shoreline. Coolin was to the south. Nordman was north. It only took five minutes to drive there. During that time they saw only two vehicles. A car and a truck, both going south.

They turned off the highway and were back in civilisation again. Or as close to civilisation as they were going to get. There was a small general store and a scattering of homes. Two centuries earlier a group of settlers had decided to call this home. The place was picturesque enough but Winter had to wonder what they were thinking.

Cathy lived near the edge of the lake. Her house was half the size of the one she'd shared with Gifford. There was more land, though, maybe twice as much, the boundary marked with trees. Like Gifford's house, this one was made from wood that was so dark the building was almost invisible. There was a Dodge Ram parked out front. The side panels of the truck were streaked with mud and dirt and the tyres had deep treads. It was the sort of vehicle you'd want if you were living this far into the middle of nowhere. The weather was pleasant enough today, but three or four months from now it would be a different story. When the snow started falling you'd want a vehicle like this.

Anderton turned to the driver. 'Can you wait here, please?'

'Sure.'

By the time they'd got out and closed the back doors, the driver already had his cell phone out and was checking for a signal. He'd kept the engine running so he could take advantage of the air conditioning. Winter followed Anderton up to the front door. She knocked and stepped back. No one answered. There was no answer the second time. Or the third. She frowned. Winter glanced over his shoulder at the Dodge.

'The car's here, which means that someone's got to be in.'

'What if she's got a second car? What if after she got the call from the Vancouver police she decided that she had pressing business that need to be tended to in Texas? Or Rio? Or somewhere else that's a thousand miles away from here?'

Winter shook his head. 'Look at the house. The wood needs retreating and the paint on the window frames is peeling. This isn't a two-car household.'

'So where is she?'

'Maybe she heard us arrive and she's hiding in the cellar.'

'In that case, you'd best get to work with your picks.'

'Before I do that, maybe we should take a look out back. You don't live out here in the boonies because you want to spend your life stuck indoors. A day as beautiful as this, it would be a crime to stay inside.'

There was a well-trodden dirt path that led all the way around the perimeter of the house. The land at the back of the property dropped away gently toward the lake. A line of tall Douglas firs partially blocked the view, and beyond that there were glimpses of the water sparkling in the sunlight.

One part of the yard had been cultivated to create a large vegetable garden. The vegetables were grouped according to type. There were beans on long sticks, lettuces, potatoes, cauliflowers. The chicken run was made from offcuts of wood. The wire was bent and misshapen. There were seven well-fed chickens scrabbling around in the dirt and pecking for corn. Another area had been cordoned off to create a sty. Two piglets were lounging in the cool mud.

The dirt path carried on down to a gap in the treeline. A golden retriever suddenly bounced out from between the trees. It spotted Winter and Anderton and came skidding to a halt. Every muscle was taut as though it was getting ready to attack or retreat. Cathy appeared on the path a second later. She saw them and stopped dead. She looked ready to run as well. She was dressed in worn, ripped jeans and a red plaid shirt. Her hair was tied back in a single braid that reached just below her shoulders. She was slim, fit and tanned.

'Who are you and what do you want?' she called out.

'We just want to talk to you' Anderton called back. 'We're investigating the murders in Vancouver.'

'I already spoke to the police there. I told them I couldn't help.'

'Couldn't or wouldn't?' Winter called out.

She looked at him. Her eyes were suspicious and a little fearful. 'I want you to get off my property.'

Winter walked over to the dog and told her to sit. She glanced uncertainly at Cathy, confused about what was happening. Winter ordered her to sit again. This time she obeyed. He crouched down and gave her a scratch behind the ears. To start with she wasn't sure, but it didn't take long to win her over.

'What's her name?' he asked.

Cathy hesitated. 'Roxy.'

'She's beautiful.'

Cathy said nothing.

'She looks young,' he said. 'What is she? Three? Four?'

'She's almost four.'

'So you got her just after you moved here. It was part of your new start, right? How long had you been planning on leaving your husband?'

Cathy stiffened and all the suspicion left her eyes. There was just fear there now. Winter stayed crouched down to make himself as small and unthreatening as possible.

'Cathy, we just want to talk. That's all.'

'I don't want to do this. I can't do this.'

'I understand how hard this must be, but if it wasn't important we wouldn't be here.'

'I can't,' she whispered.

'Billy has already murdered four women,' Winter said. 'If we don't stop him then he's going to kill again and again and again. Now I realise how upsetting this must be, us just turning up like this. All you want to do is forget and move on, and here we are dragging you back into the past. But here's the thing, no matter how bad you're feeling right now, it's nothing to how you'll feel when Billy kills again. Because when that happens you're going to have the guilt to deal with as well. It doesn't matter what you tell yourself, a part of you will always be wondering if they died because you refused to help us.'

Cathy still hadn't moved. She was staring at Winter like she wanted him to disappear. She'd be going over everything he'd just said, projecting into the future and not liking what she saw. He reckoned it would take thirty seconds to come to a decision. In the end it took twenty. Without a word she started walking toward the house. Halfway along the path she gave a whistle. Roxy gave him a quick I-gotta-go look, then stood up and bounded after her. Cathy didn't say anything as she walked past Anderton. She wouldn't even glance at her. Head down, she marched toward the house, Roxy trailing at her heel. Winter walked over to Anderton.

'Well, she hasn't told us to leave,' she said. 'On that basis, I'm figuring she's going to talk.'

'And I'm figuring that we should go after her before she changes her mind.'

57

They caught up with Cathy on the back porch. The table she was sitting at was made from weatherworn wood. There were four chairs around it, all made from the same wood. Winter sat down opposite Cathy and Anderton took the seat on the left. Roxy was curled up in a tight ball in a shady spot beneath the table. There were two pairs of rubber boots standing by the back door, one large, one small. The small ones looked to be Cathy's size, which got Winter wondering about who owned the larger pair.

Cathy was gazing at the trees at the far end of the yard, and the glimpses of water beyond. The air here was so much cleaner than in the city, the light sharper, the colours brighter. The whole scene was tinged with golden sunlight. If those long-ago settlers had passed through here at this time of the year, then their decision to stay suddenly made a whole lot more sense. There was no offer of a drink. No nod toward hospitality of any sort. Cathy just wanted them to say what they needed to say, and for them to get the hell out of her life.

'How certain are you that Billy killed those women?' she asked.

'There's no doubt whatsoever,' Winter replied. 'He did it.'

She didn't say anything for a while, just stared at the trees while she tried to process this. 'You're probably wondering why I stayed with him so long? I mean, how could I? He's a monster.'

'Except he wasn't a monster, was he?'

'Not really. And definitely not at the start. This might surprise you, but Billy has a great sense of humour. That was one of the things that attracted me to him. He seemed to know exactly what to say to make me laugh. And it wasn't just me. I saw him do this with other people, too. It helped with his work. He could put anyone at ease.'

'But you suspected that something wasn't right about him?'

'Again, not at first, but later on, yes, there was something. That's why I left him.' She paused. 'I still can't imagine him killing anyone, though. He's just not capable of doing that.'

'Isn't he?'

'No, he isn't.' There wasn't much conviction in her voice. It was as if by saying it aloud, she would be able to convince herself of something that she knew was a lie.

'How did you meet him?' Anderton asked.

Cathy smiled sadly. 'This is going to sound pathetic but I met him on a dating site.'

Anderton returned the smile. 'That doesn't sound pathetic at all. A lot of people use dating sites nowadays. I mean, it's tough meeting a decent man, right?'

'Except there are no guarantees that you are going to meet a decent man. There are just as many assholes on the internet as there are in bars and clubs. More, probably.'

'You thought that Billy was one of the good ones, didn't you?'

Cathy nodded. 'I was convinced of it. On our first date we

went out for coffee. There was an instant connection. We had so much in common. He had a great smile, too. I remember getting home and convincing myself that he wouldn't call. I had his number and I decided that I'd give it three days. If he hadn't called by then, I'd call him. He phoned the next day and asked me out to dinner. Four months later we were living together. Six months after that we were married.'

'Tell me about the wedding.'

'There's not much to tell. We got married at City Hall. It was just the two of us. Well, us and some random guy we pulled off of the street to act as a witness. No family because neither of us really had any. You probably know what happened to Billy's parents, and his foster parents had retired to Florida. He doesn't have anything to do with them these days. There was some sort of falling out, but he wouldn't talk about it. As for me, my dad walked out before I was born and my mom died of ovarian cancer when I was twelve.'

'And after you were married you went to live in Argyle Street?'

'That's right. The first six months were great. The house needed decorating so I was focussed on that. And I was in love with Billy so I chose to ignore the danger signs.'

'What signs?' Winter asked.

'He started getting clingy. Little things to start with, but after a year or so it started getting worse. He'd want to know what I was up to and where I was going. If I went out he'd want to come with me. There would be times when I'd be watching TV or reading a magazine, and I'd turn around and catch him staring. At the start of our relationship I liked it when he paid me attention, but this was getting weird. I felt like I was being suffocated.'

'He took photographs of you, didn't he?'

Cathy grimaced and rolled her eyes. 'Like I already said, the attention was nice to start with. And he was a photographer. It's what he did for a living. To be honest, I would have been more upset if he *hadn't* taken my picture. I mean, why would he take pictures of everyone else and not me? But it got to the point where there was always a camera pointing in my face. Obviously it wasn't all the time, but that's what it felt like.'

'He hung the pictures up in the house,' Winter said. 'Lots of them.'

Cathy's eyes widened. 'How did you know that?'

'We were there earlier. There were marks where the picture hooks had been.'

'The first time he put up one of my pictures I was flattered. It was the best photograph anyone had ever taken of me. And then another one appeared, and another. It eventually got to the point where they were in every room of the house. Do you have any idea how creepy it is to have your own eyes following you wherever you go?'

'You clearly weren't happy in the relationship,' Anderton said. 'Why didn't you just leave?'

Cathy laughed but there was no humour there. 'Believe me, I tried.'

'What happened?'

'One night we had a big argument. I can't even remember what it was about. Something stupid and unimportant, no doubt. Anyway, we were in the kitchen and I suddenly had this moment of clarity. What the hell was I doing here? I wasn't happy. So I told Billy I was leaving. His response was to tell me he was going to kill himself. And then he grabbed a knife. Before I could stop him, he ran it up his arm. There was so much blood. It seemed to be everywhere. I couldn't believe what he'd done. I mean, how crazy is that? I grabbed some towels and used them to stem the bleeding. By the time the paramedics arrived Billy was unconscious. I really thought I'd lost him. When he came back around, he told me that he loved me and couldn't live without me. He didn't come out and say that he'd do it again if I left, but the implication was there.'

'But you did manage to leave him.' Winter nodded to the boots lined up neatly beside the porch door. 'Does that have anything to do with the second pair of boots?'

Cathy smiled the first genuine smile that they'd seen. 'It has everything to do with them. They belong to Brett. He doesn't take photographs, and he doesn't hang them up in every room of the house. He works for the Forestry Service. He is one of the good guys.'

'Did you meet him online too?'

She nodded. 'I was looking at dating sites one day and something about his profile picture made me want to know more, so I sent him a message. He messaged me back and we started chatting. He's so laid-back and open, the complete opposite of Billy.'

'So how did you manage to get away from Billy?' Winter asked.

Cathy didn't answer for a while. She was staring at the top of the Douglas firs that ran along the edge of the lake, watching them wave gently back and forth in the breeze. There was sadness in her eyes, a wish that things had turned out differently.

'Billy bought me a kitten for my birthday, a cute little silver-grey tabby. I called her Sprinkles. Weird name, I know, but it suited her. Anyway, one day I woke up and found her lying dead at the back door. It turned out that she'd been poisoned. The most likely explanation was that a neighbour had put down some rat poison and she'd eaten it. That's what Billy thought had happened.'

'But you were never convinced.'

Cathy shook her head. 'I couldn't shake the feeling that Billy killed her. I didn't have any proof, just a feeling. He was actually really nice about the whole thing. He couldn't do enough for me. Those doubts still nagged away at me, though.'

'How long had you had Sprinkles for?'

'About three months.'

'Long enough to get attached, then?'

Cathy smiled another genuine smile, this one tinged with sadness. 'I was attached from the word go. I've always been a sucker for animals.' She pointed to the sty. 'Take those piglets, for example. Brett thinks we're going to eat them. That is so not going to happen. They're way too cute.'

'Was Billy still taking photographs of you around this time?'

'Actually, he stopped for a while.'

'Do you think he might have been photographing you secretly?'

Cathy sat up straighter in her chair. Even though the temperature was in the mid-seventies, she had her arms around herself like she was suddenly cold. 'It's possible, I guess.' She shook her head in disbelief. 'Jesus, what a freak. I can't believe I stayed with him so long.'

'So how did you get away?' Anderton asked.

'Brett drove up to Vancouver to rescue me. This was a couple of weeks after Sprinkles died. All I took was some clothes and a few personal belongings.'

'And Billy didn't kill himself.'

'Clearly not.'

'Did he try to find you?'

'I guess so, but I can't say for sure. The only thing I can be certain of was that he never found me. Not that I expected him to. Idaho might as well be a million miles from Vancouver. And Nordman is pretty much off the grid. Then there's the fact that we're in a different country. Those were the main reasons I moved here. Well, that and Brett, of course. I was confident that Billy would never find me. And even if he had, there's no way that I was going back.'

'Were you ever allowed in his office?' Winter asked.

'No, that was his space. If the door was shut I was supposed to leave him alone. I didn't mind at first. I was struggling to get work, so we were living off of the money that he was earning. And it made sense. He needed peace and quiet to do his work. But as time went on, I began to wonder what he got up to in there.'

'Were you ever tempted to sneak in and take a look?'

'Of course I was tempted, but the door was always locked when he wasn't at home.'

'What about the attic?'

Cathy gave him a confused look. 'What about it?'

'That's where Billy was building his bombs.'

'Not while I was living there. And I know that for a fact. I needed to get something out of there just before I left. There were no bombs in there, just junk.'

Winter hesitated. 'I'm really parched. It's all this talking. Would you mind getting me some coffee, please?'

58

Cathy got up and went inside, her footsteps tapping across the old wood. Anderton waited until the porch door had swung shut before turning to face him.

'*I'm really parched.* Nobody says that any more, not unless they're taking part in a remake of *Gone With the Wind.* And if you're dehydrated, water is better than coffee. But it takes time to make coffee, so I start wondering why you want Cathy out of the way. What's on your mind?'

Winter smiled. 'I want to take Cathy back to Vancouver. We can use her to draw Gifford out. He was clearly obsessed with her, and this was an obsession that ran deep. It isn't going to disappear overnight.'

'You think he's still in love with her?'

Winter shook his head. 'Anderton, he was never in love with her. Gifford's a psychopath. A narcissist. He is incapable of loving another person. You need empathy to do that and he doesn't have any.'

'But he tried to kill himself. Surely that proves he had some feelings for her.'

'He tried to kill himself because he didn't want her to leave. She fulfilled a useful function in his life. If she'd left, it would have inconvenienced him. Pathologically pragmatic, remember?'

'But to attempt suicide?' Anderton shook her head. 'I just

don't see it. It's too extreme. He didn't go across the wrist, Winter, he went up the vein. That proves he was serious. I'm sorry, I'm not buying the "pathologically pragmatic" line. Not this time.'

'That's because you're thinking like a normal person. Try thinking like a psychopath.'

Anderton was still shaking her head.

'Okay,' he went on. 'So Cathy tells Gifford she's leaving. The first thing he's going to do is establish if this is an idle threat. It's not, so he starts running scenarios. He needs to do something that will stop Cathy in her tracks, and he needs her to think twice about doing anything like this again. Slashing his vein is the perfect solution. Cathy is immediately invested in the situation. If he threatens to do this again, she's going to spin back in time and see herself covered in blood trying to save him.'

'But he could have died.'

Winter shook his head. 'Cathy wasn't going to let that happen. Yes, they'd just had a big fight, but as soon as he cut himself she would have been straight on the phone calling an ambulance. It's what anyone would have done, and Gifford knows that. He would have been thinking about ambulance response times while he was cutting his vein open. And that's another thing. He only cut one vein open. If he'd been really serious he would have cut open both arms.'

'It's still a huge risk. He's gambling with his life.'

'You're still thinking like a normal person. Psychopaths are risk takers. The bottom line is that he wanted to stop Cathy leaving him. This was the solution he came up with. What's more, it worked, at least in the short term.'

343

Anderton thought this over for a second. 'Okay, I can see what you're saying, but I'm still not a hundred per cent convinced.'

'But you're in the high nineties.'

'Try the low nineties. Okay, let's say we somehow manage to persuade Cathy to come back to Vancouver. What then?'

'We get Charlotte Delaney to interview her. If Cathy goes on TV acting all tearful then that could be enough to persuade Gifford to give himself up. At the very least he might try and make contact with her.'

'Okay, the first thing that's wrong with that scenario is that it involves Charlotte Delaney, and anything involving Charlotte Delaney is never going to be a good idea. As for persuading Gifford to give himself up, that's bullshit and we both know it.'

Winter smiled.

'You want to put her on TV so Gifford goes after her. He's obsessed and he's angry. Seeing her again after all these years is going to tip him over the edge. As for what that looks like, or how much danger Cathy will be in, well, that's another matter. I've got to hand it to you Winter. It's a pragmatic solution to a tricky problem. It's also a psychopath's solution.'

'We can keep Cathy safe. Play it right and she'll never be in any real danger.'

'But she'll still be in some danger.'

'Have you got any better ideas?'

Anderton shrugged and sighed. 'At this stage, no. So how the hell do we persuade her to get on a plane and come to Vancouver? I mean, she didn't even want to talk to us.'

'Leave that to me.'

Thirty seconds later the porch door creaked open and Cathy came out carrying two mugs. She handed one to Winter, put the other on the table, then sat down. Winter looked over and waited for her to meet his eye.

'We'd like you to come back to Vancouver with us.'

She shook her head. Her face was set and determined. 'No. My life is here now. I'll never go back there.'

Winter took out his cell phone and pulled up a picture of Isabella Sobek's mutilated body. He held up the phone so Cathy could see the screen. Then he explained to her exactly what she was looking at, right down to the last detail.

Then he explained why it would be her fault if Gifford killed again.

Right down to the last detail.

59

It was almost six when they landed back at Boundary Bay. A headwind had pushed against them all the way, adding fifteen minutes to the return journey. This leg had taken a little over two hours. Winter was up front next to Dan. Anderton and Cathy were in the seat behind. Cathy hadn't said a word since they'd left Nordman. She was locked into her own little bubble of misery, staring out the side window of the Cessna. In the end it had taken three photographs to break her. She eventually cracked when she saw an autopsy picture of Alicia Kirchner with her ribcage wide open.

The drive from Boundary Bay to the Shangri La took forty minutes. Nobody said a word for the entire journey. Nobody had said a word in the Cessna either, but the engine noise had made that an acceptable silence. This was anything but. The Mercedes was a quiet ride and you could barely hear the engine at all. Anderton had switched on the radio, but this just seemed to highlight how strained the silence was.

They parked in the hotel basement and took the elevator to the third floor. Freeman and Jefferies were waiting in the conference room. Charlotte Delaney was up on the stage with her crew, getting organised. The two large padded chairs that had been set up in the middle of it were angled so they weren't quite facing each other. A camera on a tripod had been positioned to catch both chairs. The lights that the TV technicians had brought in were dazzlingly bright.

Winter gave a whistle and Delaney's head jerked up. She looked over and he waved her to come and join them. Cathy had winced when he whistled. She gave the impression that she would prefer to be anywhere but here. And who could blame her? This morning she'd woken up in paradise, and now she was in hell. There was a round of introductions. Cathy didn't shake hands. She was hugging herself as if she was cold. Everything about her body language screamed, 'Go away and leave me alone.'

'We're almost set up,' Delaney said. 'The plan is to prerecord the interview. That way we can edit before broadcasting. We'll air directly after the seven o'clock round-up.'

Winter turned through three hundred and sixty degrees, starting at the chairs on the stage and finishing back there. The conference room was painted in brown, beige and white. The carpet was brown, the upholstery on the chairs was brown. They could have been in any conference room, in any hotel, anywhere in the world.

'This isn't going to work,' he said. 'It's too anonymous. We want Gifford to assume that Cathy is staying here. There's nothing for him to latch on to.'

'We were going to mention the hotel in the link,' Delaney said.

'That's too brief, and if he does catch it then it could come across as being too obvious. The last thing we want is for him to think this is a trap. On the flipside, if he doesn't catch it, then how is he going to know that this is the Shangri La?'

'So what do you suggest?'

Winter took out his phone and ran an image search for

the 'Shangri La lobby'. The first picture that came up showed a comfortable seating area that had a polished floor, a high ceiling and tall windows. The Asian-inspired art on the walls would help Gifford to narrow things down further. He held up the phone and moved it in an arc so everyone could see.

'This is where we do the interview. When Gifford sees Cathy his first reaction will be shock. He hasn't seen her for over three years and there she is on his TV. Once the initial shock wears off, he'll start to wonder where she's staying. He knows that she doesn't live in the city. If she did he would have found her by now. That means she's staying in a hotel. Chances are he'll recognise the lobby because he's photographed weddings here, but even if he doesn't it's not a problem. He'll just search the internet until he's joined the dots. Just make sure the artwork is visible, but keep it at the edge of the shot. The key here is to lead him in the direction we want without making him suspicious.'

'Okay,' Delaney said. 'That makes sense.'

She turned to her crew and started barking out orders. Ten seconds later they were hustling toward the stage to get their equipment moved downstairs. Delaney was leading the way, striding out in front like she was going to war.

'A quick word, please,' Freeman said to Anderton.

They went off into a huddle at the side of the room. Jefferies tagged along with them, leaving Winter and Cathy standing all alone in an awkward silence.

'How are you holding up?' he asked her.

Cathy just stared at the empty stage.

'Look,' he went on, 'I know you probably hate me and I can live with that. I'm not looking for a new best friend here,

I'm just trying to find a way to make this as painless as possible.'

She turned slowly to face him. 'I don't know you well enough to hate you.'

'That's good to hear. So back to my question. How are you holding up?'

'How do you think?'

'I think that right now you'd rather be sat on your porch with Brett, drinking cocktails and watching the sun go down.'

Cathy almost smiled. 'Brett prefers beer and the porch faces east, so it's better for watching the sun rise, but aside from that I'd say that pretty much covers it.'

'This is a very brave thing you're doing.'

'It doesn't feel like it.'

'That's how you know you're being brave. Anyone who claims to be brave should be locked away. For everyone else's safety, not just their own.'

'Do you think this is going to work?'

The question sparked off a whole load of different scenarios inside Winter's head. In some the plan worked, in others it didn't. In some they were victorious. In others all he saw was disaster.

'If I didn't think it would work I wouldn't have brought you here.' He smiled reassuringly. 'Do you know what you've got to do?'

'I read the statement, then answer some questions.'

'Put like that, it's not so scary, is it?'

'Aside from the fact that there's going to be a TV camera pointing at me, and my crazy ex is going to be watching, no, I guess not.'

'Billy needs to think you're on his side, so bear that in mind. We want him to view you as an ally. That's key here. His obsession with you is currently dormant, but it's still going to be there. We want to tap into that. Seeing you on TV will send him tumbling back in time to when you were together. If that happens then there's a good chance he'll try to reach out to you.'

'How do you know he'll be watching?'

'Because he won't be able to help himself. Serial killers follow the news religiously. Two reasons. They get a buzz out of hearing about their exploits, and it enables them to keep tabs on what the police are doing. The interview will get repeated throughout the evening. At some point he's going to see it.'

'Is that what he is? A serial killer?'

Winter nodded. 'Without a doubt.'

'Jesus, how could I not have known? I was living in the same house as him. We were sharing a bed.'

'Don't be too hard on yourself. He wasn't active when you were together. Those urges would have been well hidden.'

'Even so.'

Winter hesitated. 'My father was a serial killer and neither myself nor my mother suspected a thing. And he was active while we were living with him.'

'You're bullshitting me, right? You're just saying that to make me feel better.'

'No, I'm not. Cross my heart.'

'You must have suspected something.'

'In hindsight, the signs were there, but at the time it never occurred to me that he might be a monster. And why should it? Look at your situation and you'll see that it's not much different. Because that's the really scary thing here. Serial killers like Billy and my father are experts at hiding in plain sight.'

'When he comes for me, the police will be waiting to arrest him. That's the plan, right?'

'They'll get him long before he gets anywhere near you. The interview will flush him out. As soon as he breaks cover he'll get taken down. And remember, you'll be staying at a different hotel. You won't be in any danger whatsoever. I can guarantee that. Any questions?'

'Just one. When can I go home?'

60

Winter was sitting arm-to-arm with Anderton on one of the lobby's sofas. On the other side of the walkway, a sound man was clipping a microphone to Cathy's top while Delaney sat there quietly, psyching herself up. The cameraman had set up a small monitor so they could see what was being recorded. Cathy and Delaney were in the middle of the screen. At the right-hand edge of the shot was a glimpse of a painting that evoked the Far East. On the left was part of a window that held the reflection of another painting. This one was distorted but the Asian influence was still evident. Jefferies and Freeman were sitting on the next sofa along. Both of them had their eyes glued to the monitor. The sound man did a quick sound check then gave the thumbs up and moved out of shot. Delaney sat back in her chair and got comfortable. Then she faced the camera.

'We are joined this evening by Cathy Gifford. Her husband is suspected of being involved in the August 5 bombings. Mrs Gifford is now going to read a short statement.'

So far, so good. Delaney was sticking to the script. She hadn't come right out and accused Gifford of being the killer. And she had used Cathy's married name, which would help to establish a bond with Gifford. Cathy unfolded a sheet of paper and cleared her throat. When she spoke her voice was two tones higher than usual and there was a slight waver.

'Billy, if you're watching this, please get in touch with me.

People are saying the craziest things about you, things that I just can't believe are true. The man that I married isn't capable of doing the things they're claiming. You are a good person. A loving person.' Cathy paused to compose herself. She cleared her throat again. 'I know things haven't been good between us, but whatever problems we've had can be solved. Nobody knows you as well as I do, and that's how I know you're innocent. Together we can clear your name, so please contact me.'

Cathy folded the sheet of paper and curled it into her hand. Her knuckles were white from holding it so tightly. The strain was showing and she looked on the verge of tears.

'Are you okay to answer some questions?' Delaney asked.

Cathy nodded.

'You clearly think that your husband is innocent. How can you be so sure of that?'

'Because I know my husband. He's got a great sense of humour. He's one of the funniest people I've ever met. He works as a photographer. People warm to him immediately. They like him. How can someone like that be guilty of the sorts of things he's being accused of?'

'If your husband was sitting opposite you right now, what would you say to him?'

'I'd tell him that whatever's happened doesn't matter, we can work this out. There's nothing that can't be fixed.'

'Is there anything else you'd want to say?'

'Only that if people knew Billy the way that I know him, they'd realise he couldn't possibly be guilty of these crimes.'

This was where the interview was supposed to wind up. All the points that needed to be covered had been covered. Short and sweet was the name of the game. Winter caught the way Delaney looked at Cathy and realised that wasn't going to happen. Her next question was off script, but not unexpected. Delaney softened her voice, aiming for a tone that was confidential and trustworthy. It's just the two of us, that voice promised, you can tell me anything.

'If Cody Hooper was sitting opposite you, what would you say to him? In case you don't know, Cody was Myra Hooper's son. Myra was murdered yesterday morning by the August 5 Bomber.'

The camera zoomed in on Cathy. This move had clearly been planned in advance. Again, this wasn't completely unexpected. Anderton went to stand up and Winter touched her arm. Her head snapped toward him.

'Can't you see what's going on here,' she whispered. 'This is an assassination. We've got to get Cathy out of there.'

'Just give it a little longer.'

'No, this isn't fair on Cathy.'

'It's not fair, but you need to trust me on this one, okay?'

Anderton stared for a second longer then sat back down. Cathy's face filled the whole screen. The monitor might have been small but Winter could still make out every line and wrinkle. Her eyes were haunted. She wasn't crying, but the tears weren't far off.

'Cody was ten,' Delaney prompted. 'And now he's going to grow up without his mother.'

'I don't know what I would say to him,' Cathy stammered. 'All I know is that Billy is innocent.'

'And what would you say to Lian Hammond's husband. Lian was murdered on August 5 last year.'

Now the tears came. They were streaming down Cathy's

face. She wiped them away, but as soon as she did there were more to take their place. 'Billy didn't do it,' she said quietly.

'What about Alicia Kirchner's husband, and Isabella Sobek's? What would you say to them?'

Winter walked over and positioned himself between Cathy and the camera. 'This interview is over.'

Delaney smiled. 'No problem. We've got everything we need.'

'You stepped over the line.'

'I disagree. It's important that our viewers see Cathy as human. Tears are one of the best ways to achieve that.'

There was no response to that. At least there wasn't one that he could be bothered to give. Winter held out his hand and helped Cathy to her feet. She laid the microphone on the seat and he led the way back toward reception. Behind them, Delaney was conferring with her camera operator, no doubt checking to make sure he'd got everything. Anderton had gone into a huddle with Jefferies and Freeman. They were talking in whispers, autopsying the interview.

Winter carried on walking until he found a quiet corner. He guided Cathy toward a sofa and sat down beside her. She wiped the tears away and looked at him.

'I totally screwed that up. I'm sorry.'

'You're kidding, right? You were awesome.'

'No I wasn't. By the end I could hardly string a sentence together.'

Winter shook his head. 'You did good. Really good.'

Cathy wiped her eyes again. 'The person I was describing back there wasn't Billy.'

'I know.'

355

'And everyone watching is going to know that, too. Billy included. This was a complete waste of time.'

'It was not a waste of time. I promise you. Billy might suspect that you're not being truthful, but there will be a part of him that wants to believe. It doesn't matter about anyone else who's watching, all that matters is that Billy thinks you might be telling the truth.'

Winter heard footsteps and looked up. Anderton and Jefferies were walking toward them. Jefferies was looking as cool as ever. He stopped in front of Cathy and waited for her to look at him.

'Thank you for doing that,' he said. 'I realise how tough it must have been.'

'When can I go home?'

'We've booked a flight for you for tomorrow morning. You'll need to change in Seattle, but you'll be back in Idaho by lunchtime. Tonight you're going to stay in one of our safe houses. There will be armed police guarding you at all times. Your ex won't be able to get within a hundred miles of you and that's a promise.'

'So what happens now?'

'Now you're going to come with me. There's a car waiting outside.'

Cathy stood up. There was a quick round of thank yous and goodbyes. Cathy was anxious to get away, which was totally understandable. Today had been like a bad dream. The sooner she could wake up to a newer, brighter day the better. Winter watched Cathy and Jefferies walk away, then turned to Anderton. She wasn't smiling and she didn't look happy.

'Outside, now. We need to talk.'

61

'You haven't been entirely truthful,' Anderton said.

Winter lit a cigarette. Behind them, the skyscraper that housed the Shangri La stretched way above their heads. The glass glinted and shimmered and flashed in the evening sunlight, reflecting buildings and sky. It was six hundred and fifty-nine feet tall. Sixty-two storeys. Floors one through fifteen were occupied by the hotel, the rest was residential. The view from the penthouses must have been stunning. Look north and there were the mountains. Turn west and there was the water. To the south and east the city stretched way into the distance.

'I said, you haven't been truthful.'

'I heard you.'

'That isn't a denial, or an apology.'

'No, it's not.'

'Cathy isn't the bait, is she?'

Winter kept quiet.

'Come on, Winter, I know what's going on here. I'm not stupid. This is why you wouldn't let me step in and stop the interview. You wanted Delaney to make Cathy cry.'

He took another drag and blew out some smoke. 'Look around, what do you see?'

'It doesn't matter what I see. What do you see?'

'I see a disaster just waiting to happen. You know how this

one's going to play out as well as I do. Freeman is going to have shooters on rooftops and people watching all the ways in and out of the hotel. It'll be total overkill, but that's the way it's got to be done because that's what it says in the rule-book. The problem is that the rulebook doesn't work in this situation. If Gifford gets even a hint of a trap he's going to disappear. This is strictly a one-shot affair. We don't get a second chance.'

'You knew that Delaney wasn't going to stick to the script. You knew that she was going to attack Cathy.'

'Not for certain.'

'But you strongly suspected that it might happen.'

'I'll admit to that much.'

'At what point are you going to tell Delaney that you've pointed a psychopath in her direction?'

Winter took a long pull on his cigarette. 'Do you know how many views "FBI Guy Loses His Shit" has had on YouTube? Almost quarter of a million. That means that two hundred and fifty thousand people have seen Delaney dissing Gifford. And you can bet that a fair few of those views were actually made by Gifford himself. Then there's the fact that the interview was on heavy TV rotation. Delaney might be saying what everyone else was thinking, but that's not how Gifford will perceive it. Every time he watches the interview it reinforces the idea that Delaney has a vendetta against him.'

'And the interview with Cathy is going to reinforce that idea even further,' Anderton said.

Winter nodded. 'His obsession with Cathy has just been awoken after a long slumber. Despite everything that happened, I'm betting that he'd welcome her back into his life with open arms. He's probably itching to get all those pictures out of storage so he can hang them up around the house.'

'He'll be looking for a big gesture to win her back,' Anderton said. 'Let's face it, a bunch of roses and a box of chocolates isn't going to cut it in this instance. How do you think it'll go down?'

'His MO has worked up until now, so he'll probably stick to that.' Winter took another drag. 'This is the point where you're going to try to convince me that we need to involve Freeman. Before you do, I've got a question. What did Freeman say to you when he pulled you aside in the conference room?'

Anderton hesitated, her face suddenly hardening. 'He thanked us for bringing Cathy in and asked if we could hang around to babysit her through the interview.'

'And what else?'

'He said that after the interview we should make ourselves scarce.'

'Okay, here's another question. If you take this to Freeman, what will he do with it?'

Anderton sighed. 'He'll bring in the shooters and the watchers, and it'll be a complete circus.'

'The other thing to bear in mind is that there's no guarantee that Gifford will go after Delaney. You wouldn't want to get charged with wasting police time.'

'Right now, that's the least of my concerns.'

'So what are your concerns?'

'Where do you want to start? Okay, firstly, there are only

two of us. That's nowhere near enough manpower to carry out an operation like this.'

'Agreed. So what's the minimum amount of people you'd want on an operation like this?'

'That would depend on the size of Delaney's house.'

'Judging by what I saw on Google Maps, I'd say it's about half as big as Sobek's.'

'In which case I'd want at least four people. Two to watch the front, two to watch the rear. That would be the absolute minimum.'

'That's what I figured, and that's why I've asked Sobek to arrange for a couple of PIs to join us. They're already at Delaney's house, keeping an eye out for Gifford. Me and you make four. Okay, what's your next concern?'

'As much as I hate the woman, we can't just put Delaney in danger like this.'

'She won't be in any danger. If Gifford sticks to his MO then he'll want to be in place before she gets home.'

'And what if Delaney gets home before him? He altered his MO with the latest murder, remember? He waited until the Hoopers were asleep before breaking in.'

'I remember, and if he tries that here we'll be ready for him. He's not going to get anywhere near Delaney. A guy acting suspiciously in the dead of night is going to be easy to spot.'

'A guy who might have a bomb,' Anderton put in.

'A small bomb. Worst-case scenario, he blows himself up in the middle of the street and wakes the neighbourhood. Nobody's going to get hurt, and nobody's going to cry at his funeral. Okay, next concern?'

Before Anderton had a chance to say anything else her cell phone rang.

'That's probably Jefferies,' Winter said. 'He'll be calling to tell you that Gifford has hacked into the Shangri La's computer system and gained access to the guest register.'

Anderton took out her phone, glanced at the display, then connected the call. The conversation lasted less than twenty seconds. She hung up and put the phone away.

'That was Jefferies. Gifford has hacked into the Shangri La's computer system. He now knows that Cathy checked into room 325 at lunchtime.' She paused. 'Or should that be he believes she checked in, since she isn't actually staying here?'

'Gifford is comfortable with computers but I'd venture that hacking into a hotel system goes beyond his capabilities.' Winter paused. 'On the other hand, Sobek's computer guy would be more than capable of pulling off something like that.'

'The one who found the RAT on Eric Kirchner's laptop?'

'One and the same. Anyway, that's who hacked into the Shangri La's system.'

'And the reason you got him to do that is because you want the police to think that Gifford is coming here.'

'I just want to make sure that Freeman stays out of our way.' Winter took a last drag on his cigarette and crushed it out in the smokers' trash can. 'You brought me to Vancouver because you wanted my input. From what I know about Gifford, softly-softly is the way to go. That said, this is your call. If you think the way forward is to take this to Freeman, then go for it. It would be a mistake, but that's just my opinion.'

'Do you really think we can pull this off?'

'I'm sure of it.'

'How sure? And be honest.'

'About ninety-nine per cent. Which is as good as it gets.'

'How likely is it that Gifford will go after Delaney?'

'I'd say about fifty-fifty. We've presented the bait in a way that's tempting. Whether Gifford takes it or not is down to him. But even if he doesn't, I'd say there's a good chance that he'll try to reach out to Cathy. To do that he needs to break cover, and when he does, he'll get taken down.'

Anderton frowned as she weighed up the pros and cons.

'Okay, your turn,' Winter said. 'Do you think Freeman could do a better job than us? And be honest.'

Anderton's head went slowly from side to side. 'No, I don't.'

62

Anderton parked one street away from Delaney's house. The car was filled with the smell of hot coffee and there was a box of doughnuts on the back seat. Stake-out supplies. Winter found his cell and called the number Sobek had given him. The man who answered sounded confident and in control. He was economical with his words and precise with their delivery. Winter told him where they were parked and he said he'd be there in two minutes. One minute and five seconds later a figure emerged from Delaney's street. Fifty-five seconds after that he was sliding onto the back seat of the Mercedes. He was older than Anderton and thin to the point of malnutrition. His skin was deeply tanned, like he'd spent most of his life outdoors. Anderton turned in her seat and smiled at him.

'Hey there, Pascoe. Long time, no see.'

'You two know each other,' Winter said.

'Are you kidding? We go way back. Pascoe retired from the force about five years before I did. We worked some cases together back in the day.' She turned to Pascoe. 'How are things looking over there?'

'All quiet. No sign of Gifford or Delaney. Culver is watching the house at the moment. He's just a kid but he's got good instincts and good eyes. There are only two ways to get into Delaney's house. Either a rear approach via the yard of the house that backs on to hers, or a direct approach straight up her driveway.

'In that case, you guys can cover the rear and we'll cover the front. We'll touch base every thirty minutes.'

'Of course.'

Winter gave it a second to make sure they were finished. 'Sobek said you'd have something for me.'

Pascoe reached into his jacket and brought out a small string-tied cloth bag. There was a clunk of metal colliding with metal as he handed it over. Winter untied the string and tipped out the contents. Two Glock 19s landed in his lap. He held one out to Anderton. She looked at it for a second then took it. Winter ejected the clip from his, checked to make sure it was full, then banged it back in. Locked and loaded. Anderton was going through the same checks with hers.

'I'll text you when I get back to the car,' Pascoe said. 'No point us all being in the street if Gifford turns up. We don't want to scare him off.'

He got out of the car and walked back the way he'd come. The text arrived two minutes later. Anderton started the car and pulled away from the kerb. She hit the turn lights and cruised gently into the street where Delaney lived. There was no sign of Pascoe's car. Presumably he'd exited via the other end of the street.

Delaney's house was two-thirds of the way along. It looked deserted. There were no lights on, and no bright red Pontiac Firebird parked on the driveway. It was compact and tidy, and not quite what Winter had expected. He thought that she'd go for something more showy. Something that made a statement, like the Firebird. Maybe she didn't spend much time here, or maybe TV journalists didn't get paid as much as he thought. They were only a five-minute drive from the Global studios, which might explain it. Maybe this was just a handy place for her to hang her hat. Nothing more, nothing less.

Anderton drove past the house and kept going for another hundred yards. She swung in to the kerb and killed the engine. The sightline was good. If anyone approached the house they'd see them. At the same time, they were far enough away not to be noticed. The sun was still up, which wasn't ideal. This sort of work was best done in the dark, slumped down in your seat and hiding in the shadows.

The sun dropped from the sky at eight forty-five. Bang on schedule. Blue turned to purple and orange, and then there was the inevitable fade to black. The streetlamps winked on at nine. The Mercedes was parked in a dark spot halfway between the two nearest lights. The night sky was clear but there was too much light pollution in this part of Burnaby to see the stars. The moon hung in the north. White, bright and ominous.

Stakeouts drove Winter nuts. They always had done. There was too much hanging around, too much inactivity. The neighbourhood was a quiet one. The whole time they'd been parked here they had seen only two cars. The first had turned into a driveway further on up the street. They'd had to duck down when its headlights washed through the SUV's interior, but it hadn't come close enough to cause a problem. The second car had come in from behind them and parked at the kerb near Delaney's house. For a moment they'd got excited, but it hadn't been Gifford. They'd watched the driver get out. Watched him walk up to the front door of the house next door to Delaney's. Watched him let himself in. Watched the house lights go on. Anderton had let out a long sigh. Then they'd gone back to waiting.

Ten o'clock came and went.

Eleven o'clock.

Winter's phone vibrated at eleven-thirty on the dot. Just like it had done at eleven and ten-thirty, and every thirty minutes before that. Pascoe's text was one word long and identical to all the others that he'd sent. *Clear*. Winter's reply was one word long and identical to all the other replies that he'd sent. *Clear*.

'Still thinking fifty-fifty?' Anderton asked him.

'He might be aiming to get here in the early hours so he can catch Delaney when she's sleeping. That's what he did with Myra Hooper.'

'And what if Delaney isn't coming home tonight? What if she's got a boyfriend and has decided to stay at his place?'

'If that's the case then it actually works to our advantage. You were worried about Delaney being put in danger, right? Well, if she's staying at her boyfriend's then she's not going to be in any. And what's even better is that this won't affect Gifford's plans. If he turns up in the early hours and sees all the lights off he'll assume that she's in bed, and carry on regardless.'

Anderton took out her cell and searched for a number.

'Jefferies?'

She nodded then raised a hand for quiet. The call lasted all of ten seconds. She hung up and put the phone away.

'There's no sign of Gifford over at the Shangri La,' she said.

Winter turned and looked toward Delaney's house.

Everything was dark and still. A couple more minutes passed then the rear mirror suddenly filled with light. Winter glanced in the side mirror and saw the silhouette of a Firebird. The car passed into the wash of a streetlamp and he saw that it was red. He could hear the engine, throaty and low-pitched, not quite a roar but not far off it. There were two people in the car. The dark made it impossible to see faces. The shadow-person in the driver's seat was presumably Delaney. You didn't own a car like that and let other people drive it. The shadow-person in the passenger seat might have been male, but it was impossible to tell for sure. Her boyfriend, perhaps. Or maybe a girlfriend, if that's how the wind blew.

The car pulled on to the driveway, the engine died, the headlights went off. The person in the passenger seat got out first. It was still impossible to see a face, but judging by the size and build and the way they moved, this was a male. He was carrying a small overnight bag, so presumably he was planning on staying. The car doors closed with a bang. Delaney got out and led the way. She unlocked the front door and they went inside. A second later the door closed and the street fell quiet again.

'She's got her boyfriend with her,' Anderton said. 'That could complicate things.'

Winter thought about everything he'd seen in the last thirty seconds and shook his head.

'That's not her boyfriend, Anderton. Did you notice how slowly she was driving?'

'It's a residential area and it's getting late. Of course she's going to be driving slowly.'

'You've clearly never driven a muscle car. Get behind the

wheel and it's like you're possessed. It's like slipping into a Stephen King story. You just want to put your foot down and drive everywhere at a hundred miles an hour. That's exactly what Delaney was doing the first time I saw her driving that car. She braked so hard she left ten-foot tyre marks on the tarmac.'

Anderton thought this over. 'If that was Gifford, he wasn't using a gun to coerce her. It's dark, but I could make out that much.'

'Guns aren't his weapon of choice. Bombs are.'

She frowned. 'This doesn't fit with his MO. Up until now he's always gone after his victims in their homes.'

'He's devolving. When that happens their behaviour becomes increasingly unpredictable. All bets are off. Think about the way his MO changed with Myra's murder. Breaking into the house when she was asleep. Approaching Cody in the park. He's unravelling. That was just the start of it.'

'I'm going to call this in. We need back-up.'

Winter nodded. 'No arguments here. We still need to get in there, though. And fast. We have the element of surprise, but if we wait for the cavalry we'll lose that advantage. At the moment Gifford will be familiarising himself with his surroundings. We don't want him getting too comfortable. That would be bad for Delaney.'

'Agreed.'

Anderton took out her cell phone and called Freeman. While she did that, Winter texted Pascoe to let him know what was going down. Anderton kept things brief. By the time she was hanging up, Winter was hitting send.

'You ready to do this?' he asked.

'Ready as I'll ever be.'

63

They got out of the Mercedes and crossed the street. The hedges, trees and fences hid their progress along the sidewalk. The shadows hid their progress up the driveway. There were no lights on in the front of the house. The window panes in the door were dark and empty. Winter took out his lock picks and went to work. Slowly, slowly. Feeling. Teasing. The final pin succumbed and he pushed the door open an inch so it wouldn't lock again.

He put his picks away and drew his gun. Anderton already had hers out. He pushed the door open a little further. No squeaks, no creaks, just the gentle movement of a door opening on well-lubricated hinges. It took a moment for his eyes to adjust. The details of the hallway slowly made themselves known. The angles of the bannister, the shadows of the pictures, the shape of a table. Sounds came to them out of the silence. Voices. Winter listened more closely. Not voices plural, a single voice. Gifford's. He caught Anderton's eye and motioned for her to follow.

The voice led them away from the stairs and down a corridor. Light snuck out from around the closed door straight ahead, a dim glow that went all the way around the frame. They edged nearer and stopped in front of it. Winter could hear Gifford on the other side. He was talking in a professional voice, the one he no doubt used to put his clients at ease.

It projected confidence and suggested that everything would be okay. It was also a liar's voice. Based on what Winter was hearing, things were not going to be okay. At least, not for Delaney.

'You know,' Gifford was saying, 'you really shouldn't have made her cry.' He paused as though he was waiting for a reply. 'Cathy and me, we might have had our problems, but that happens in relationships. You're not always going to see eye to eye. That doesn't mean I don't care what happens to her, though. When you love someone, you love them forever. That's the way it works.'

Anderton put her hand on the handle and counted down from three on her fingers. She hit zero and pushed the door open. Winter burst past her, his gun leading the way, eyes taking in everything. Anderton was a step behind, covering him. Delaney was bound to a chair with silver duct tape, eyes wide and terrified. The strip of tape across her mouth stopped her screams getting out. She saw them and started struggling to break free, the chair rocking back and forward, legs banging out an uneven rhythm.

Gifford was four feet away, next to the kitchen table. His face was completely expressionless. No joy, no sorrow, and nothing in between. Winter was struck by how normal and unthreatening he looked. This wasn't some big tough guy. Not even close. Under ordinary circumstances you wouldn't give him a second glance. He was wearing a white button-down shirt and tan chinos. His jacket was laid neatly on the table next to his bag. The girdle wrapped around his midriff had two bombs sewn into it, one on each side of his stomach. This time he'd used a full pipe. Instead of the blast being directed inwards it would go out in all directions, spreading white hot shrapnel throughout the kill zone.

'Drop your guns,' Gifford said.

The professional reassurance was still there in his voice. He locked eyes with Winter. His face was serious but there was the hint of something that might have been a smile. Winter didn't move. Nor did Anderton. They were standing there with their Glocks aimed at Gifford's head. Gifford was standing with his feet slightly apart, looking relaxed. His right hand was curled around the bomb trigger on his belt.

'I will detonate this bomb,' he said. 'Don't think for a second that I won't.'

'Nobody needs to do anything rash,' Anderton said quietly. 'We can find a way to work through this.'

'Okay, let me tell you how this works. The only way it works. You're going to lower your weapons and you're going to do that right now.'

'Nobody needs to die.'

Anderton was still speaking quietly, but Winter barely heard her. All his attention was fixed on Gifford and the bomb. That was all that mattered. Everything else was secondary. Gifford was acting like this sort of thing happened every day, like he was completely in control of the situation. The fact that there were two guns aimed at his head didn't seem to faze him. Winter had seen this before. The absolute self-possession that some psychopaths displayed was disconcerting. Their backs could be all the way against the wall and they'd still think they were in charge.

'You have three seconds to comply,' Gifford said calmly.

Winter looked at the bomb vest, just for a fraction of a

second, but it was long enough to see everything he needed to. The wires trailing from the bombs met in the centre of Gifford's stomach and travelled down to his waist. His hand was wrapped around the trigger attached to his belt. Winter's brain was working fast, going through the possibilities.

Was he using a dead man's trigger?

No. That wouldn't be practical. It wouldn't be the pragmatic solution. He used the bomb vest to coerce his victims. 'Do what I say or I'll push the trigger.' It was all bluster and hot air. He didn't actually want to use it. He wasn't suicidal, he just wanted his victims to think he was. Like he'd done with Cathy when he cut his arm open.

Could the threat be neutralised without shooting Gifford in the head?

Yes.

Gifford had already got to 'two'. His voice sounded as distant as Anderton's. Winter shifted his aim and fired. The first bullet hit the top of Gifford's right arm. His hand flew away from the trigger and he let out a howl of pain. The second bullet blew out his left kneecap. It had to be the left. If he collapsed to the right he might accidentally trigger the bomb. It was like felling a tree. Gifford crashed to the floor, falling to the left, away from the trigger. His face was white. He was huffing and puffing and trying to bite back the pain.

'Don't move,' Winter yelled.

Gifford froze, and then something in his expression changed. This was the face of someone who'd opted for suicide by cop. Winter had seen this before. He thought about all the people who'd been murdered, all those lives that had been ruined, and it was so tempting. Gifford's left hand started moving toward the trigger, but Winter was faster. He covered the distance between them in two strides and stamped on Gifford's wrist. Then he shot him in the hand. This time there was a scream. It was loud and harrowing and seemed to go on forever. Winter raised the Glock and aimed at Gifford's head.

'Stop!' Anderton yelled. 'Don't kill him!'

The gunshots were still ringing inside Winter's head, affecting his hearing. Her voice sounded muffled. He stood there for a second longer, staring along the barrel, the adrenaline making him itchy. Gifford was making little mewling noises and squirming in agony. He was desperate to get away from the pain, but there was nowhere to go. His breathing was shallow, his face pale. His blood was staining the floor tiles. The bullets had missed his arteries and internal organs. The bones in his hand had been shattered, and he'd be walking with a limp for the rest of his days, but he'd live.

Winter lowered his gun and tucked it into his waistband. Then he hunkered down next to Gifford to get a closer look at the bomb. As far as he could tell the only way to detonate it was by pressing the trigger. No booby traps, no surprises. He started to remove the trigger from Gifford's belt and Anderton took a sharp intake of breath.

'It's okay,' he said. 'It's not going to go off.'

'And you're sure of that?'

'Ninety-nine per cent sure. Gifford isn't suicidal.' Winter glanced at Gifford. His eyelids were fluttering as he struggled to stay conscious. He was totally out of it. 'He's designed this bomb to be reused. It's more robust than it looks. He doesn't want it going off accidentally. This is what he would have used to coerce Myra. He probably used it on the other victims too. Remember, he's pathologically pragmatic. If something's working, why fix it?'

'Even so.'

'Okay, what do you suggest? We just leave the crazy guy with a live bomb attached to him?'

Before Anderton could say anything else, Winter finished removing the trigger and stood up. There was a nine-volt battery fitted into the back of it. It was a brand-name item that had cost no more than a couple of dollars. In a different context it would be no big deal. It could be used to power a toy or a clock or a smoke detector. In this context it was the difference between life and death. He unclipped it carefully. For a brief moment all he saw was a bright white flash of light, but it was only his imagination.

'All done,' he said.

'So, I can breathe again?'

'Yeah, you can breathe.'

A sudden clattering sound made them both turn. Delaney was glaring at them from the kitchen chair, issuing demands with her eyes. She rattled the chair legs against the floor again. The message was clear: free me now.

'We could leave her like that until the police get here,' Winter suggested.

'Don't tempt me.'

Anderton went to find some scissors and Winter took another look at Gifford. He had stopped squirming and was drifting in and out of consciousness. The blood from his wounds was spreading slowly across the floor. The girdle had a row of hooks and eyes down the front. Winter unfastened them one at a time, working from top to bottom. Then he rolled Gifford off the girdle, each jerky movement eliciting sharp gasps and groans. Winter carried the girdle to the table and laid it down gently. Even though it was disarmed it still gave off a bad vibe. Send nine volts of electricity into the detonators and it would be capable of killing every person in the room.

The first thing he saw when he unzipped Gifford's bag was a second bomb. It was just lying there, inert but potentially deadly. The device was encased in a plastic sleeve, and only half a metal tube had been used. Myra Hooper had been killed by a similar bomb. And Lian Hammond. And Alicia Kirchner. And Isabella Sobek. There was a spool of wire in the bag and a reed switch. There were more batteries, too, all the same make as the one he'd removed from the trigger. The bag contained everything Gifford needed to ensure Delaney met the same fate as Isabella and the others. The difference was that Delaney was a minor celebrity. Unpleasant though she was, her death would have sparked a wave of public sympathy. Gifford would have had more grief than he'd have known what to do with.

Winter looked over at the chair. Anderton had managed to free Delaney. She'd also removed the tape from her mouth. Delaney was weeping freely and acting like Anderton was her new best friend. Her words were coming out in a torrent, one long endless rush of relief. Tomorrow she would no doubt start to wonder about how they'd managed to get here so quickly, but for now all she cared about was the fact that she was still alive.

Winter suddenly became aware of someone else in the room. He hadn't heard them come in because his ears were still ringing. He turned around expecting to see Pascoe and his buddy. They would have heard the gunshots. Hell, the whole neighbourhood would have heard them. It wasn't Pascoe, though.

Sobek was standing in the doorway, his eyes fixed on Gifford. There was a Glock 17 in his hand and he was wearing a Kevlar vest. He looked every bit as relaxed as Gifford had done earlier, every bit as in control. There was even the ghost of a smile playing at the edges of his lips. This was the moment that he'd been waiting for, the one he'd been dreaming about all these years. Sobek strode across the room and pointed the gun at Gifford's head. His left hand was curled around the right to support and steady it. Not that he needed to. There was no way he'd miss from this range. And if by some miracle he did, there were another sixteen bullets in the clip. Winter drew his gun and aimed at Sobek's head.

'Put the gun down.'

Sobek's full attention was still on Gifford. His gun hand was steady, his finger on the trigger. A little more pressure and Gifford would be a dead man. Anderton came up alongside Winter. Her gun was trained on Sobek, too.

'The police are on their way,' she said. 'If you kill him, you'll be the one who ends up in prison. He's not worth it, Sobek.'

'Who said anything about killing him? All I want to do is talk.'

Winter didn't trust a word he was hearing. Sobek's voice was too quiet and too even. He had means and motive, and now he had the opportunity. 'Put the gun down and step back.'

'Or what? You're going to shoot me?' Sobek shook his head. 'I don't think so.'

He knelt down and ran the tip of the Glock along Gifford's upper arm. He stopped when he got to the bullet wound, paused for a second, then dug the end of the gun into it. Gifford screamed and his eyes sprang open. Both Winter and Anderton started moving. Winter was aiming his gun at the back of Sobek's head, just above his ponytail.

'Take another step and I will kill him,' Sobek said quietly.

They stopped moving.

'All I want is to talk,' he added. 'After everything he's done, I don't think that's too much to ask.'

'In which case, drop the gun,' Winter said. 'You don't need a gun to talk.'

Sobek ignored him and pushed the barrel of his gun into Gifford's wounded arm again, harder this time. Gifford let out another scream.

'Have I got your attention?' Sobek asked pleasantly.

Gifford nodded.

'And you know who I am?'

Another weak nod.

'Do you believe that I'm capable of killing you?'

Another nod.

'Do you know why I'm letting you live?'

Gifford shook his head.

'Because I want you to remember this face. I want it to be the last thing you see before you go to sleep, and the first thing you see when you wake up. I want you to understand that the reason you're wasting your life away in a prison cell is because I let you live. I want you to suffer through each and every one of your remaining days. When you take your final breath, I want you to remember me.'

Sobek dug the gun barrel into Gifford's arm once more. This time he didn't stop when the screaming started. He just kept going, piling on the pain. Winter covered the distance between them in five strides and pushed his Glock into the back of Sobek's head.

'Drop the gun! Now!'

Sobek ignored him and carried on digging with the gun barrel. Gifford was thrashing weakly, trying to get away. His screams had turned into sobs that were getting quieter with each passing second. Winter flipped the Glock over then smashed the butt into the side of Sobek's head. There was a dull thud as it connected and Sobek dropped to the ground. Anderton walked over and looked down at the two bodies.

'Did you have to hit him so hard?' she asked.

'I had to make sure he was going to stay down.' He nodded toward Gifford's unconscious body. 'So was it all worth it?'

Anderton's smile lit up her whole face. 'Totally worth it.'

Epilogue

Atlanta has the busiest airport in the world. More than a quarter of a million people use it every single day, catching a thousand flights to all points of the globe. Today Winter was just passing through, waiting for a connecting flight. Three hours from now he'd be in the air and on his way to Madrid. Another day, another killer to hunt down. The bar he was sitting in was loud, everyone talking at once. One wall was made entirely from glass and looked out over the runways.

The TV screen was tuned to a news channel, the sound muted. Even so, it was a fairly straightforward process to work out what was going on. The script was pretty much the same as it had been yesterday, the same as it would be tomorrow. Winter had one eye on the TV screen, and one eye on the planes taking off and landing on the other side of the window. Killing time, because that's what you did in airports. The whisky was overpriced, but it was going down easily enough. Too easily. One more and he'd call it quits. His plan was to anaesthetise himself to the point where he slept the whole way to Spain.

The story onscreen changed to a new one that made him immediately sit up and take notice. More than five months had passed since he'd been in Vancouver, long enough for the whole episode to get buried in his memory. He'd been halfway around the world since then, worked another half a dozen cases. The face on the screen sent him tumbling back in time. They were using Gifford's police mugshot. The board he was holding up gave his number as 325-676-21. The top of his head was level with the line for five foot four. His face was completely expressionless. No joy, no sorrow, and nothing in between. He still managed to look guilty of all the sins of mankind, though. According to the ticker at the bottom of the screen he'd just been murdered.

Winter grabbed his carryon bag and pushed his way to the bar, ignoring the protests and shouts. One guy went to grab his arm and he shook him away. The guy must have seen something in his expression because he backed off immediately, hands held high to pacify. On screen, Gifford's photograph had been swapped for Nicholas Sobek's. This picture dated back to the days when he'd been a mover and a shaker. They'd had to use this one because they didn't have anything more recent. His hair had been short and tidy back then. No beard. He looked a totally different person. Until you saw the eyes. Then there was no doubt that this was the same person.

'Turn up the TV,' Winter called out.

The barman ignored him and carried on serving a customer.

'Hey!' he hollered.

The barman stopped and turned. Some of the other travellers had turned as well, everyone staring like he was a dozen different kinds of crazy. An empty space had suddenly opened up all around him.

'I said, turn up the volume!'

'You need to calm down, sir, or I'm going to call security.'

'No, what I need is for you to turn the volume up on the TV.'

The barman kept on staring, working through his options. Winter took a twenty from his billfold and slapped it down on the bar. Which added a new option into the mix, one that was hopefully more appealing than calling security.

'I'll give you twenty bucks to turn up the volume. So long as you do it now.'

The barman looked at him for a second longer, then picked up the twenty and went to find the remote. By the time he got the sound going, the story had finished. It took a couple of minutes for Winter to find somewhere quiet enough to make a call. He was in some sort of service corridor, away from the noise and bustle. He scrolled through the contacts list on his phone, looking for Anderton's number. She might be retired, but he was betting that her winged monkeys were as efficient as ever. She answered on the seventh ring. There was no preamble, she just jumped straight in with, 'You've heard the news then?'

'It was Sobek, wasn't it? He killed Gifford.'

'Sobek has an alibi,' she replied. 'Gifford was in prison at the time of the murder. Sobek wasn't.'

'He was involved, though. He's got to be. We're back to those quacking ducks again, Anderton.'

'Of course he was involved. The police know that, too. That's why they're so keen to talk to him.'

'Which shouldn't be too difficult. All they've got to do is rock up to his house and knock on the basement door.'

'That was the first place they looked. The house was

deserted. Jefferies reckons that he hasn't been there in the last forty-eight hours.'

'You better run me through what happened,' Winter said.

'Okay, Gifford was enjoying a nice relaxing shower when someone slashed his femoral artery. Despite the fact that there were six other people in the shower at the time, nobody saw a thing. Jack Datt says that the wound was consistent with an improvised shiv, possibly a toothbrush. It wouldn't have taken Gifford long to bleed out. The warm water would have sped things up even further.'

'It should be easy enough to work out who did it. All you've got to do is talk to the wives and relatives of the guys who were in the shower with him. If any of them are driving brand-new cars or booking exotic holidays then you've found your man. Sobek had the means and motive. The only thing missing was opportunity, and it sounds like he solved that particular problem. So where is he if he's not at home?'

'Right now that's the million-dollar question.'

'The Cessna?' Winter suggested.

'Still at Boundary Bay. And both cars are still in his garage. That's one of the things that make this so weird. It's like one second he was there, the next he'd disappeared.

'And like that, he's gone.'

'Yeah, I saw that movie, too.'

'Not that the cars would have been a whole lot of use,' he continued. 'If he'd driven up to a border checkpoint in an Aston Martin or a top-of-the-range Mercedes, people would look twice. Right now, he's going to want to exist below the radar.'

'Way below,' Anderton agreed.

'Heading to the US makes sense, though. Sea-Tac is only a couple of hours from Vancouver. From there he could fly anywhere in the world. If he's worried about Seattle being too close he could keep going south to Portland. There's an international airport there. Or maybe he'll do the tourist thing and drive down the Pacific Highway and catch a plane from LAX. Whatever he decides to do, he's got plenty of options.'

'That's the theory the police are currently working on. They've been talking to the car rental agencies, but no joy so far.'

'It's unlikely he'd go down that route. He wouldn't want to risk the car being fitted with a tracking device. It's more likely that he picked up something cheap and anonymous from a dealership, somewhere happy to deal in cash and not too concerned about paperwork.'

Anderton sighed. 'And that's the theory I'm working on.'

The line went quiet. The only sound was the gentle static wash created by the signal travelling up to space and back again.

'What is it?' Anderton asked. 'I can hear you thinking.'

'Sobek's not going to be happy.'

'Why not? The person who murdered Isabella is dead. That's got to be a cause for celebration.'

'Yes, but he wasn't the one who did the actual killing.'

'You think that matters?'

'I think he would have liked to have done it,' Winter said. 'However, I also think that he values his freedom too much to do anything stupid. He proved that much back in Delaney's kitchen. He could easily have killed Gifford. Believe me, he was tempted. I could see it in his face. It took every ounce of willpower he possessed to stop himself from pulling the trigger.'

'But if he had done that, it would have been him who ended up in prison.'

'Exactly. What matters is that Gifford is dead. The fact that he didn't kill him is something he'll learn to live with.'

'Pathologically pragmatic,' Anderton said.

'Got it in one.'

They fell into another brief silence. The static being beamed down from outer space sounded louder than before. This time it was Winter who broke it.

'Sobek's gone for good. You realise that, don't you? The only way he's going to get caught is if he breaks cover, and why would he do that?'

Anderton sighed. 'Yeah, I know. Killing Gifford was always his end goal, wasn't it? He used me, Winter.'

'Only as much as you used him. You'd made it your mission to catch Gifford, and he enabled you to do it. Don't forget that.'

'But my intention wasn't that he should die. That's the difference. I wanted to see him brought to justice.'

'And therein lies the problem. Justice means different things to different people. If you ask Sobek, he'll tell you that justice has now been served.'

'No, Winter, what Sobek got was revenge, pure and simple.'

'Is there any real difference?'

There was a long sigh on the other end of the line. 'Look, I've got to go. Take care of yourself.'

'You too. And keep me in the loop. If you hear anything from Sobek, I want to know.'

'Sure. Same goes for you.'

Winter killed the call and scrolled through his contact list. Sobek's cell number went straight through to a recorded voice informing him that it hadn't been possible to connect the call. Maybe he was out of range. More likely he'd dumped the phone. Not that Winter had expected anything different. There was a good chance that he would never hear from him again. There was every chance that nobody would ever hear from him again.

On the way back to the bar, he kept seeing Sobek in the faces of the people he passed. Heading through Atlanta made sense, though. A quarter of a million passengers a day, and a thousand flights to all four corners of the globe. If you were looking to disappear, it was as good a launch pad as any.

A loved-up couple was sitting at his table. The overpriced whisky was long gone. He ordered another, found a new table and spent the next couple of hours watching the planes. His gate was finally called and thirty minutes later he was getting settled into his seat in business class. Within five minutes of the meal plates being cleared away he had his eyes closed, his seat fully reclined, and the whisky was working its magic. His sleep was as deep and dreamless as the ocean crashing darkly thirty-five thousand feet below.

Acknowledgements

As always, family comes first. Karen, Niamh and Finn, you guys are the best. I couldn't do this without you.

Camilla Wray is both an agent and a friend. Her support and gentle encouragement through the years has been unwavering, and for that I am truly grateful.

Nick Tubby . . . a good friend is one who stands by you when things get tough, but the best friends are the ones who help you to keep standing. Thanks for everything, buddy. I appreciate it.

Huge thanks to Dan Bailey for answering all my questions regarding Vancouver and flying. Your help and insights were invaluable.

Kate O'Hearn once again helped me to keep my Americanisms straight. If you've got kids, check out her books – they're awesome.

Winter's theory about the Lindbergh kidnapping was adapted from John Douglas's book *The Cases That Haunt Us*. If you want to know how the real-life profilers do it, his books have got to be your start point.

HAVE YOU
READ
THEM ALL YET?

Also by James Carol

Broken Dolls

It takes a genius to catch a psychopath

Jefferson Winter is no ordinary investigator.

The son of one of America's most notorious serial killers, Winter has spent his life trying to distance himself from his father's legacy. Once a rising star at the FBI, he is now a free-lance consultant, jetting around the globe helping local law enforcement agencies with difficult cases. He hasn't got Da Vinci's IQ, but he's pretty close.

When he accepts a particularly disturbing case in London, Winter finds a city in the grip of a cold snap, with a psychopath on the loose who abducts and lobotomises young women. Winter must use all his preternatural brain power to find the perpetrator before another young woman gets hurt.

As Winter knows all too well, however, not everyone who's broken can be fixed.

'Strikingly well researched
and written with a real swagger.' *Daily Mail*

ff

Watch Me

Everybody's got something to hide . . .

Ex-FBI profiler Jefferson Winter has taken a new case in sunny Louisiana, where the only thing more intense than the heat is a killer on the loose in the small town of Eagle Creek.

Sam Galloway, a prominent lawyer from one of Eagle Creek's most respected families, has been murdered. All the sheriff's department has to go on, however, is a film of Galloway that shows him being burned alive.

Enter Jefferson Winter, whose expertise is serial criminals. But in a town where secrets are rife and history has a way of repeating itself, can Winter solve the case before someone else dies?

'Toe-clenching, nail-biting, peep-from-behind-your-fingers suspense.' S. J. Bolton ff

Prey

Has Jefferson Winter finally met his match?

Six years ago a young married couple were found brutally stabbed to death in their home in upstate New York. Local police arrested a suspect who later committed suicide. But what if the police got it wrong?

Ex-FBI profiler Jefferson Winter is drawn into a deadly cat-and-mouse game with a mysterious female psychopath as she sets him a challenge: find out what really happened six years ago.

The clock is ticking and, as Winter is about to find out, the endgame is everything . . .

'I read this in one compulsive sitting . . . A must-read for fans of Chris Carter, M. J. Alridge and great crime fiction.' *Crime Warp*

ff

A JEFFERSON WINTER NOVELLA

Presumed Guilty

Five Victims. One Killer. An open-and-shut case?

Special Agent Yoko Tanaka is one of the best profilers in the FBI. She's observant, smart and professional, but doesn't really play well with others. She's been called in to consult on the case of 'Valentino', a killer who steals his victims' hearts. Literally.

With five women already dead, time is running out for the police to catch the killer before he strikes again. Within twenty-four hours of Yoko's arrival they have a suspect in custody: a precocious nineteen-year-old kid called Jefferson Winter whose IQ is off the charts. He's also a textbook psychopath and the son of one of America's most notorious serial killers. Not only does he confess to the murders, he knows details of the crimes that only the killer could know. It's an open-and-shut case, or is it?

'A brilliant, conflicted profiler.' Stephen Fry

ff

A JEFFERSON WINTER NOVELLA

Hush Little Baby

Don't say a word . . .

FBI profiler Yoko Tanaka is in Tampa, Florida, helping the local PD with their 'Sandman' case. Three mothers and their daughters have been found murdered in their homes. The mothers have been brutally stabbed while the little girls have been smothered in their beds and posed to look like they're sleeping.

Defying FBI protocol, Yoko makes a detour to Sarasota to entice Jefferson Winter to join the case. Winter has now graduated from college and is playing piano in a tourist bar. At first he's reluctant to get involved but that's the thing with Winter, what he says and what he means are usually two different things. All Yoko knows is that he's the only person who can help her before the Sandman claims another two victims . . . but what Winter doesn't know is that Yoko might also be able to help him.

'Leaves you desperate for more.' *Daily Mail*

ff

Open Your Eyes

Before it's too late . . .

Jefferson Winter is at the beginning of his FBI career. He's young and unpredictable, but he has a gift – he can understand the mind of a murderer like no one else.

Winter is in Las Vegas with Yoko Tanaka, a tough agent with the unenviable task of showing him the ropes. The bodies of three young women have been found and each of them is missing a limb.

If the case is to be solved, Winter must be free to act – yet Tanaka's superiors are watching closely, and it soon becomes clear that this killer doesn't make mistakes.

> 'Jefferson Winter is a welcome new genius, and I
> can't wait to meet him again.' Neil White